VINES AND FIRE

Goddess of the Trees: Book One

Vines and Fire

Goddess of the Trees: Book One

Sorrel D. Richmond

Tulip Poplar Publishing, LLC

ISBN: 979-8-9909834-1-0(Paperback)
ISBN: 979-8-9909834-0-3(Hardcover)
ISBN: 979-8-9909834-2-7(e-book)

Library of Congress Control Number: 2024913640

Any references to historical events, real people, or real places are used fictitiously. Names, characters, and places are products of the author's imagination.

Front cover image by My Lan Khuc.

First printing edition 2024.

Tulip Poplar Publishing, LLC
P.O. Box 392
1612 Jordan Dr.
Saxapahaw, NC, 27340

www.writersdrichmond.com

Dedicated to my wife, children, and the West Virginia wandmaker whose name I wish I knew.

We are the children of the woods. Born on a slab of lime-stone under the full, brilliant face of the moon. We are set high on a hill over looking the world. We are the pine, the oak and the pawpaw. Our roots grow deep.

This novel contains references to rape, assault, and suicide.

THE TREES

First Mother
Black Cherry

Imogene
Oak

Ida
Papaw

Martha
Red Maple

Thelma
Cedar

Edith
Sweetgum

Ola
White Ash

Beulah
Birch

CHAPTER 1

Beatrice

The voices of her ancestors swarmed Beatrice's mind as she tried to cook dinner for herself and her son. Encouraging. Pleading. Reprimanding.

Get control of Forest, Beatrice.

He's a threat to our way of life.

Bring him to the Trees. We can change his mind.

We can make him stay on the mountain where he belongs.

He's playing with fire!

"Please." Beatrice closed her eyes and raised her right hand with the plea. "You've given me enough to think about. I need to figure this out on my own."

Open windows allowed sunlight to infuse the space, and channeled fresh air throughout the room. Beatrice scooped up heavy quartered onions in her hands and dropped them into the pot sitting atop the wood-burning stove. She stirred them in, her grandmother's wooden spoon in hand. The onions melded into the rich stew of deer meat, potatoes, celery, and carrots, with thyme and bay leaf to season.

She shook her head and continued to work. What could

they possibly understand about her predicament? The Goddess hadn't given Beatrice a girl to raise. She had given her a son, and Forest had his own ideas for his life. His own dreams.

Her grandmothers had much to say about her son, his practices, and his ambition, and gave unsolicited advice about how to continue their lineage with a son instead of a daughter. Though the voices scattered her mind from time to time, she still found gratitude for the Goddess-given gift of communing with them.

Bring him to First Mother! they whispered. *Ask her to intercede with the Goddess. She can change him into a woman.*

Beatrice could not fathom asking the Goddess to change Forest, not even from his first cries when she held him up for Grandmother to see, and the tree had gasped and whispered: *It's a boy.* She felt no regret, though occasionally her brain fed her stories that the disruption in the lineage was her fault. When the summer's thick, hot air made it hard for her to sleep, Beatrice worried that this new thing had happened because of the man who had stolen her innocence.

Forest wasn't a baby anymore. He was now a man discontent with life in the quiet woods, though he'd never admit it to his mother, and each of his ventures off the mountain threatened to change everything.

A final voice stood out above the rest: *Please, Beatrice, come to me.*

Beatrice stopped cutting the onions, inhaled deeply, and listened.

Let's talk.

Beatrice nodded to the voice and put the last of the onions into the pot, checking the fire underneath it one last time, then she rinsed her hands in the bowl of water she'd used to wash the vegetables, and dried them on her apron. Removing the apron, she sighed, and left her home

and her stew for a moment to go speak with her grandmother in the woods.

The forest floor was soft under Beatrice's feet, which
were accustomed to the sticks and branches, bits of acorn,
rocks, and the occasional bone that jutted from the earth.
She moved toward the Rock, half eager to see Grandmother's face, half trembling with the trepidation that
filled her each time she visited the flat, gray slab of lime-
stone, the place of birth and death.

She stopped for a moment and leaned against a tree as
a cascade of nausea flowed through her. She swallowed
hard and closed her eyes, then she shook her head, willing the wave to pass, and continued on. None of the trees
knew Beatrice was ill, not even Grandmother. She often
thanked the Goddess that she had learned to both quiet
the voices in her head and block the trees from reading
her private thoughts.

When Beatrice found the Rock, expansive and tilted
slightly downhill, she moved across it tenderly, savoring
the warmth on her feet. She kneeled at the large birch tree
that stood at the Rock's edge and pulled from her pocket a
small chunk of chocolate from the piece the baker in town
had given Forest for his birthday. Beatrice folded her body
all the way forward until her forehead touched the tree's
roots and laid the chocolate down.

"Good afternoon, Grandmother."

The tree creaked slightly, and small popping noises
alerted Beatrice that bark was shifting into a face. She
didn't move until she heard her grandmother, Beulah,
speak.

"Hi, Beatrice." The voice was soft, and slowly, a few roots
rose from the ground and lifted Beatrice's chin. Blue eyes
shone within the curves and angles of the face-shaped
bark. The tree whispered, "I haven't seen you since the
spring equinox. Why?"

Beatrice lifted her torso and reached out to touch the smooth gray bark, then sighed and hung her head. "It takes a lot to stay alive, Grandmother."

"You avoid this place," Grandmother said, and Beatrice felt the tendrils of her grandmother's roots take her shoulders. "You avoid your gifts. You don't have to work so hard."

That wasn't entirely true. She used her gifts when her body would allow it, but the more the sickness took her, the less power she could wield, and the less energy she had to visit the Rock.

"I know this place scares you, but you don't need to be afraid of me, Bea."

Beatrice fidgeted with a twig, her eyes drifting to the Rock. Summers prior, Grandmother had told her the truth about the night she was born. Just as the women who came before her, Grandmother had tended to her daughter while she labored, and when it was time, led her to the Rock where she gave birth to Beatrice.

When Beatrice latched onto her mother's breast, Grandmother did not willingly give her body to the ground as her ancestors had done. She looked instead to the sky and begged to stay. But the ravenous earth pulled her into its hungry mouth while her eyes wept, and her throat screamed, and her daughter looked on with terror. The earth scrambled Beulah's cells into a different construction and thrust her up through the ground as a birch tree.

"I don't understand what's happening with Forest. He's so restless," Beatrice confessed. "I don't know how far to let him roam. And if he goes ..."

"Forest loves you. He would never leave you on this mountain forever."

Beatrice lowered her face, which grew hot at the words "leave" and "forever."

Mother did. The words formed in Beatrice's brain but didn't leave her lips.

"He's spending so much time in town. What if they're right, Grandmother? What if I should have asked the Goddess for help with him a long time ago?"

"What help do you think She would have given, Beatrice? Where do you think Forest came from?"

Grandmother was right. When Beatrice had been at her lowest, the Goddess chose to give her a son.

"I can't imagine what it's like to hear our voices all the time, Beatrice."

"I can quiet them when I really need to."

"Do you ever hear her voice?" Grandmother inquired.

Beatrice understood her grandmother's question. Voices of the dead spoke to her. Not only her grandmothers atop the mountain, but also those in the small town at the foot of the mountain. If she heard her mother's voice, that would mean ...

"No," Beatrice whispered. "I haven't heard her."

"I can't hear the voices of the dead, and neither of us can predict the future. Maybe you should ask Forest for help. He's told me he has friends who read fortunes—"

"I prefer to take things as they come," Beatrice interrupted. Immediately, guilt rose within her both for the way she spoke to Grandmother and the implications of her words.

"I think—well, I hope—the Goddess is doing a new thing with us, Beatrice. It all started with me. With my resistance and my tears and my wailing, and other things I can't bear to share with you."

Beatrice looked up into her grandmother's face. "You can share anything with me, Grandmother."

"Oh, Beatrice, I haven't protected you from so many things. Let me protect you from my sadder stories."

Beatrice lowered her face again. "So, what do I do?"

"Stop trying to figure out what to do. Just be, Beatrice. Just breathe. Be open to the journey that is coming. To the roads that lie ahead. Forest is bringing the world closer to us, but this time you don't need to fear. You're older. Wiser. Stronger."

Grandmother wrapped thick roots around her back and drew her in. Beatrice succumbed and pressed her face into the bark.

"And you have me," Grandmother said. "You always have me."

The tree released her.

"Please don't be a stranger. I'm lonely out here."

Beatrice surveyed the trees surrounding the Rock.

"Grandmother, they would talk to you if you opened up to them."

We've tried for years, Beatrice.

Don't waste your breath.

She hates it here.

Beatrice looked around at the bark-veneered, once-human bodies as they whispered. Her gaze stopped at Ola. Ola, her great grandmother, never spoke. Beatrice once asked Grandmother what Ola was like, but the tree had only tutted and grumbled that she didn't care to talk about her mother.

"I am not like them, Beatrice. I don't have a gift."

Beatrice put her hand up to her grandmother's face. "I'll come more often," she said. "You mean so much to me."

"I love you, Beatrice."

"I love you, too."

Beatrice lifted herself from the tree and made her way back into the forest.

***

On her way back, Beatrice pulled arm-length leather gloves from her pockets. High-pitched piping sounded overhead, and she gazed up at the great wings stretched out in the sky. When she came to a clearing, she lengthened out her right arm, and a golden eagle swooped down and anchored herself, the weight of the landing jostling her briefly.

"Hey, Gertie." Beatrice smiled and stroked the eagle's head. "How are you today?"

The eagle released a small whistle in response.

"There's something wrong, Gertrude," Beatrice spoke tenderly. "So many things feel wrong."

Gertrude drew her beak across Beatrice's face, which turned up Beatrice's lips. Gertrude was aging, as was she, but Beatrice begged her to stay as long as she could. She needed her, and, somewhere deep inside, she thought that one day Mother would be home and all three would reconcile. Emotions flared within Beatrice each time she thought of her mother—cascading like a violent rainstorm, jumping like the flames of a bonfire, or gnawing like a mouse on the edges of an old book.

Gertrude's spirit had left her human body when she was a toddler. The chubby little baby her mother birthed loathed human flesh, and more than that, she resented her dependence on others. She hated how short she was and how impossible it seemed to gain any forward movement. Gertrude wanted to fly, so she abandoned her body in a silver string and Beatrice, only fourteen, had watched as the thin, glittering ribbon floated to the sky. The very next day, she found a tiny abandoned eagle tweeting at the bottom of a tree, and she knew it was Gertrude. She took the bird to her mother and tried desperately to explain, but her mother was too desperate to pay attention.

"Get that bird out of here!" her mother had shouted, pacing the floor with a screaming baby.

"Mother, can't you see? It's Gertrude! Mother, she didn't like being a baby, so she—"

At that, her mother came closer and towered over Beatrice. She appeared to grow in all directions as her eyes turned red; a heat emanated from her body as she pulled back a hand.

"Stop!"

Papa's voice halted her mother's arm, and she shrank, her eyes wide at her own behavior.

"Beatrice ..." Her mother reached out her hand, but Beatrice fled from the homestead and hid in her garden until Papa finally came for her.

The rest of the evening involved panicked packing. When Beatrice refused to pack a bag, Papa pleaded, but Mother stormed into her room and packed it for her. Beatrice left in the middle of the night and hid. Her mother and her stepfather went to town the next day without her, to save the dying little body, never to return.

Upon occasion, Beatrice would remind Gertie how boldly selfish her actions had been, and Gertie would confess her greatest regret was making her mother cry.

"Come on, Gertrude. I have stew on the stove."

***

Beatrice found Forest rocking on the front porch, a whittling knife and a pine branch in his hands. His companion, Arcas, a black bear who was once the smallest of his litter, slumbered at his feet. Beatrice had Gertrude. Forest had Arcas.

Though his eyes were green and hers brown, Forest resembled Beatrice so much it was like looking in the mirror. He glanced up at her through the curls of dark brown hair that dangled around those green eyes and olive skin, his mouth curled in a mischievous grin. He knew she didn't like the wand making, and he did it anyway.

That morning, they had spent hours in the forest gathering ginseng, unconcerned that they were a week ahead of the official harvest season. No forest ranger patrolled their part of the mountain, for which she was grateful. Forest always hastened through the woods while Beatrice took

8

her time, and gave more of her attention to the veins on the leaves, the twists of the roots, and the smell of the soil. While Beatrice was busy digging, Forest traveled from tree to tree, and when he thought his mother wasn't looking, he held a branch, whispered words, and pressed his knife into the wood. She watched as he peeked around to make sure she wasn't on to him.

"So," Beatrice said, sitting down in the rocking chair beside him, "how was your afternoon?"

Forest nodded his head, eyes twinkling. "It was good."

He held the wand out toward Beatrice, and she inspected it with reluctance.

"Tell me about these, again." She took the wand in her hand, stroking its smoothness.

"People use them for all sorts of things, Mother."

"Spells?"

Forest nodded with a chuckle. "Yes, spells."

Beatrice handed Forest the wand back and reached down to scratch Arcas behind the ear. She didn't abide the ideas of spells, nor the fact that Forest felt so drawn to the group of people (witches, they called themselves) who lived downtown and brought the Christians to the verge of seething rabidity. But they offered him something that she could not: magic.

Forest, like Beatrice's grandmother, never showed signs of a gift, so they had never made the sojourn to First Mother to celebrate, nor to figure out how Forest fit into the line. The trees added this to their long list of concerns about him, but they never uttered an unkind word to his face.

"What spells, Forest?"

Beatrice toed the line between showing interest and patronizing him. Forest's sigh let her know he felt her question was the latter.

"Wands help focus energy. Energy, intention, words ...

you use words, Mother, don't you? Imogene used words—words were her magic." Forest became defensively breathless with each word.

Imogene, First Mother's daughter, was the family weaver. She wove thread into clothing and words into stories and poems. She organized the books that her mother had brought with her up the mountain, kept records, and had created a false deed for the property.

"Forest." Beatrice placed her hand on Forest's arm. "Slow down. I really want to know."

Forest swallowed, and his shoulders released. He told her more about the wands and how his coven used them. She listened, asked questions, and let him talk for as long as he wanted.

"You aren't telling them details about our family, are you, Forest?"

"No." Forest shook his head and focused his eyes on the floor. "Mother, I know the rules."

"And you are leaving through the same opening in the Hedge each time you go, right?"

Beatrice had grown the strong boundary from her very palms as protection from the outside world. But Forest wanted to come and go as he pleased, and she had made a discreet opening just for him.

"Of course I do. Thank you for opening it for me."

"You're welcome." Beatrice bent down, gave her son a kiss on the forehead, and made her way back to her stew.

Close the Hedge, Beatrice, before it's too late!

With a heavy sigh, Beatrice closed her eyes and shut off the voices for the rest of the night.

CHAPTER 2

Stella

The bright August sun brought a shimmer to the river rapids. Stella drove over the bridge that led into the old West Virginia town and glanced toward the water spilling over the dam of the hydroelectric plant. Some houses where the bridge met the town stood firm and well kept, with fresh coats of paint; others decayed and threatened to fall into the river. Here and there, businesses filled storefronts: a crafting store, a florist, an outdoor outfitter. But mostly, all was quiet. The town held the quality of being haunted by itself. Perhaps no spirits nor souls loomed in the unlit houses, but the town seemed to mourn for what it once was.

Stella parked on the side of the street and drew her briefcase onto her lap. She had used her time on the plane to read through notes and compose questions for the woman she was about to interview. Now, she thumbed through the information she had curated on the Wiccan school and church that somehow found itself in this small mountain town. The church offered online classes, workshops, and tools to practice the craft.

With a deep inhale and exhale, Stella placed the sheets back in her briefcase and closed her eyes. She did not want to be here. But Stella was new to the magazine, and her editor gave her no choice. Witches were in, and the witches at odds with Christians in a tiny mountain town in West Virginia promised a good story, so her editor assured her.

Just breathe, Stella.

Two large blue planters of bright yellow mums flanked the sides of four steps that led to the front door of a white two-story home. The main door was wide open, with a screen door closed to keep insects and other creatures from entering. Stella noticed the smell of dampness, and the house, just like the town, felt haunted by its own ghost. She glanced around for a doorbell and, not seeing one, knocked on the metal door. The lack of any stirring encouraged Stella to knock again, and when this proved futile, she called, "Hello?"

"Come in!" a light voice sounded from the kitchen.

Stella opened the screen door and stepped into the home, which offered fresh smells: wood smoke and baked bread. The bottom landing of a staircase greeted Stella to her right. She noted cozy living room on the left, and the kitchen straight ahead.

"Hi there." A petite, gray-haired woman with large glasses set atop a round face made her way into the entrance and reached out to shake Stella's hand.

The woman looked nothing like a witch. Her body was upright and clothed in loose-fitting blue jeans and a red sweater, layered over a cream-colored turtleneck, with a heavily floured apron tied atop.

"Nice to meet you." Stella shook the woman's hand and found it warm. "I'm Stella."

"And I'm Wanda. Please, come in. Make yourself at

home." The woman ushered Stella into the living room and gestured for her to sit down in a leather recliner that faced a fireplace. "I'm so sorry for the delay. I'll be right back, dear. Would you like tea or coffee?"

"Do you have anything without caffeine?"

"Oh sure. I'll bring you some tea."

The woman left briefly and returned with a tray holding biscuits, small jars of jam, and a stick of butter.

"One last trip," she assured Stella and went back for the tea.

"Lemon balm and chamomile, soothing to the nervous system and the soul. Please, grab a biscuit."

Do I look that anxious? I don't believe in witches.

Stella fought rolling her eyes at herself. What was there to be afraid of?

It's a different state, Stella. Not a different planet.

Wanda took a biscuit for herself and slathered it with butter and a scoop of deep purple jam.

"Blackberry," she specified, took a bite, closed her eyes, and expressed an "mmm."

The voice in Stella's head told her she would gain ten pounds just from looking at the piping hot bread. Still, she reached for a biscuit, plopped it on a small saucer, and went for the blackberry jam. She found it luscious and made sure Wanda knew it was the best biscuit she had ever tasted, though there hadn't been many predecessors.

Wanda gave Stella permission to record, and the reporter launched into the list of questions she had about the Wiccan religion itself, how Wanda started the church, and how the school operated.

"Do you feel welcome here?"

"Well, we've certainly had our run-ins with a few of the Christians in town. Not all of them, mind you. Some of them even include us in interfaith functions. Others claim we sacrifice children and drink their blood."

"Do you?" Stella asked, hoping her smile showed the facetious nature of her question.

Wanda did not return Stella's smile, instead answered with a quick, "No. We do not. Those rumors have roots in antisemitism—they're harmful not just to our community, but others as well. Do some research on blood libel. You'll find what you need to know."

"I'm sorry," Stella apologized, and anxiety waved over her, tightening the muscles between her ribs and shallowing her breath.

She cleared her throat and stared down once more at her list of questions, but they blurred before her eyes. The simplest things sent her to this place these days. The attacks weren't new to Stella, but these were different—sweaty palms, nauseated stomach. Stella swallowed and closed her eyes tightly.

"Are you alright?" Wanda asked.

"Yes," Stella lied. "I'm sorry that I asked you that. I was joking, I don't believe ..."

"That's alright, that's alright. Take a sip."

Stella did, and after a few deep breaths, she got back to work.

"What first drew you to the Wiccan Church?"

"Well, my mother was a witch. She'd never in a million years call herself that, but she was always working magic with herbs and prayers. We went to church, but we also celebrated the turning of the seasons."

Wanda took a bite of biscuit and a sip of tea.

"I went off to college in St. Louis and met my husband there. He had strong convictions that the world needed the lessons of Wicca. I kept studying after he died. There are the dark sides, you know, as with anything. More and more comes out about the founder, and as I learn about decolonization and cultural appropriation, I ..."

Wanda continued talking, but Stella fought to keep

14

herself present in the room. After Wanda finished answering the question, Stella asked to use the restroom, dizzy as she walked down the hall. She sat on the toilet and cupped her head in her hands.

The visions came.

Not here, not now, Stella pleaded. But the images flashed before her eyes despite her protestations.

Golden hair framed a woman's face, with bright blue eyes that stared into her own. The woman placed her hands on Stella's cheeks and whispered, "I love you." The warm sight was replaced by the image of blood pouring down the glowing face. It coated Stella's hands and dripped down her arms.

This. This is what I'm afraid of.

Everything tightened in Stella's body, and she squeezed her eyes together until the action brought pain. All breathing ceased, but the flow of blood continued as Stella's vision panned out from the woman's face and her whole body came into view, naked and slick with velvety, crimson fluid. Still, she smiled and breathed, *"I love you."*

Stella felt her body roll onto the bathroom floor, and she hugged her knees into her chest, until her consciousness gave into the lack of oxygen.

***

A tender hand jostled Stella's shoulder, and a pungent smell under her nose brought her back.

"Are you alright?" Wanda asked, taking it upon herself to place a cold palm against Stella's forehead.

"I'm so sorry," Stella stammered. "I'm not feeling very well."

"We can do this another time," Wanda said, helping her up.

"No, no." Stella stammered. *I need to get this over with. I need to go home.* "I just need a moment, and maybe a glass of water."

Wanda kept her hand on Stella's elbow as they made their way through the kitchen and back into the living room where Wanda urged Stella to sit, but she declined, choosing instead to stand.

"What happened?" Wanda inquired.

What indeed? Stella herself wasn't sure what caused the wild, haunting hallucinations that had started six months prior. Stress? A brain tumor? Only one person knew of the secret visions: Marin, the psychic who had read her future.

Roger, Stella's partner, had surprised her with a visit to a fortune teller, something she'd never do on her own. Her mind had conjured stereotypical images of multicolored tapestries, smoking incense, and a crystal ball. What she'd found instead surprised her. The psychic, her long white hair pulled into a long braid that draped over her shoulder, sat at table holding only a stack of cards, an unlit candle, and a cup of steaming tea. The woman used every tool in her arsenal but never saw the woman with the blue eyes who brought Stella unease, only dirty feet, the woods, and a faceless woman and a faceless man with dark hair that hung in curls.

When the visions started, Stella had wondered if the golden-haired, blue-eyed woman was Marin in her younger years, but the woman in her dreams had a softer, rounder face than the psychic, and her eyes were a more brilliant blue.

"I haven't eaten much today," Stella said, deciding to sit and finish the biscuit if for no other reason than to convince Wanda to continue. "This will certainly help."

Stella finished the biscuit and sipped more of the tea, and much to her relief, found that the combination revived her some. Stella picked up her pad, pressed the recording button on her phone, and resumed. Wanda answered generously, and Stella found her easy to interview once she learned to refrain from sarcasm.

"Tell me about the tools you use," Stella asked, and Wanda encouraged her to stand and turn toward a corner of the living room that she had not noticed before. Ashes, remnants of dried herbs, and stalagmites of hardened candle wax littered the semicircular table that served as an altar.

"Magic's messy," Wanda apologized.

The first item Stella noticed was a well-worn, leather Holy Bible. "A Bible?" she inquired.

"Oh yes!" Wanda whispered. "Do you know how many spells are in the Bible? Abundance. Courage. Protection. We do need that last one."

"Why?"

"Oh, we've had a few run-ins with the police. They find every possible code violation they can and slap us with a fine. We had to get rid of our chickens! Take a ride around and see how many townsfolk have chickens!"

Wanda walked through the items on the altar and associated them with their corresponding elements: a pentacle, a sharp knife, a chalice, a candle, and a wand.

"This," Wanda whispered as she lifted the wand with two reverent hands, "this piece fills me with joy." She glanced up from the wand and into Stella's face, and Stella could see the wonder in the older woman's eyes.

"Why is it so special to you?"

"Well …" Wanda reverently placed the wand back on the altar. "I rarely spend money on my tools, but this wand showed up in a store about a half an hour from here in Virginia. Turns out, the wandmaker lives right here, right up atop the mountain on the other side of the bridge. His name is Forest. Lives with his mother, Beatrice. Off the grid." Wanda waved her hands to emphasize her point. "Very, very private people. They come down from the mountain once a week and set up a booth at the farmers' market. She has a greenhouse up there and grows amazing vegetables all throughout the winter."

Midde of winter? On top of a mountain. How?

Excitement built in Wanda as she talked about the wandmaker and his mysterious mother.

"She also makes jams and jellies, although I find mine a bit tastier, if I do say so myself," Wanda chuckled. "But oh, her soaps and shampoos!" She put up a pointer finger. "I'll be right back."

Once Wanda was out of the room, Stella picked the wand, gave it a flippant flick, then surveyed it more carefully.

Feels as much like a toy as one you could buy at a theme park.

The witch returned holding a crudely cut bar of soap and a corked glass bottle. "Please put that down."

"I'm sorry," Stella said. "I couldn't help myself."

"I understand." Wanda smiled. "Smell these," she said, handing Stella the bar and bottle.

The soap and lotion had a lemony, floral scent Stella instantly loved.

Now these feel magical.

"But the best part is the way they make you feel," Wanda said. "She has to infuse them with magic. I just know she does. Here ..." Wanda shoved the items into Stella's hands. "Please take them!"

"Oh! Thank you," Stella replied. "Do you think there is a chance I could meet this woman and her son?"

"Oh, I don't know. Forest comes down for Sabbats and fellowships with us, but Beatrice hasn't stepped foot in this home, nor any others in town."

"I'm assuming you've never visited them on the mountaintop."

Wanda's lips puckered as she blew out an almost-whistle of a breath. "No," she responded.

"Could you get an interview with the wandmaker for me? What was his name, Forest?"

"The market is tomorrow. You should come and meet them yourself."

"Do you think they'd talk to me?"

"Forest definitely will. He loves to talk." Wanda chuckled. "I make no promises about Beatrice."

Stella and Wanda continued on until Stella had the information she needed, and she left feeling that the story perhaps wasn't in the Wiccan church, but in the wandmaker.

***

Stella returned to the small motel attached to a Dairy Queen next to the river and turned the key to her room. She hated everything about it—the cramped space, the outdated decor. She grimaced at the faded gray carpet, stained brown in many places, and an equally stained bedspread.

She completed her travel routine of examining every layer of the bedding. Lifting the comforter. Shaking the sheets. A dampness clung to the cloth itself, and a mustiness within the walls of the room invaded Stella's nose. But the sheets were white and clean, and she found no evidence of bedbugs or spiders, so she moved to the bathroom. Square chartreuse tiles lined the small shower and mildew grew in the corners. Stella ran her fingernails through her hair.

What to do?

Stella's teeth clenched, and her chest tightened. Her palms grew sweaty, and she felt another attack coming on. She had to get out of the room. She rushed to her car, grabbed her toiletries bag, and rummaged through with no grace until she found her anti-anxiety meds. She let the strawberry-flavored pill dissolve and rested in the driver's seat until the meds did their job. Then she made her way back to her room.

With a sigh, she sat down at the small table in the corner of the room and pulled out her laptop. She thought of Roger and considered checking in with him as promised, but the day's interactions, both on the physical and spiritual planes, had gutted her desire to connect with anyone, especially him. She tried to explain it to him once, but he'd shrugged it off as part of her panic disorder.

Stella scanned through her notes and organized them in a bulleted document. As she typed, her body began buzzing with excitement at meeting the wandmaker and his mother. The phone rang just as Stella had developed a rhythm and determined an approach to her writing.

Roger.

"Hi." She smiled as she spoke, hoping the gesture made her sound pleased to hear from him.

"Hey. How are you? I hadn't heard from you today, so I thought I'd check in."

"I'm ..." Stella paused. "I'm alright."

"Good! How was your interview?"

"I had a panic attack in the middle of it," she confessed with a sigh.

"Oh. I'm sorry, Stella. Was it the—"

"Yes, Roger. It was the visions."

"Did you ever take a moment to call—"

"No." Stella stood and paced the floor. *I haven't called my therapist. I haven't called a psychiatrist.* "Roger, I told you. These ... whatever they are ... are not hallucinations."

"Okay, okay, Stella. Calm down."

Stella rolled her eyes.

"It's been a long day, and I need to get these notes organized. I'm going to the farmers' market tomorrow to secure a couple more interviews."

"Okay. I love you, Stella. I didn't mean to upset you."

"It's okay." Stella sat down on the bed and rubbed her forehead.

"Will you check in with me tomorrow?"

"Of course I will."

"I love you, Stella."

"Goodnight, Roger," Stella replied.

She ended the call, took a hot shower, and turned down the bed. Instead of grabbing her laptop and phone, Stella turned her steno pad to a new page and began writing her visions down in as much detail as she could. In the form of ink on paper, the images made even less sense, so she jotted down all the things the psychic saw. Her gaze moved to the corner of the room where a cobweb dangled from the ceiling.

Wanda!

Risking interrupting Wanda's dinnertime, Stella called.

"Hi, Wanda. I hope I'm not interrupting dinner."

"No, no. Have more questions?"

"Just one. Could you tell me what Forest and Beatrice look like?"

"I'm not sure what that's got to do with anything. You're going to see them tomorrow."

"Please."

Wanda huffed. "Well, they both have thick, dark brown hair. Forest has beautiful green eyes and Beatrice has brown. They're both tall, but Beatrice is just a tad taller than—"

"That's all I needed, Wanda. Thank you so much. I'll see you in the morning."

Beatrice and Forest. Brown hair. Dirty feet.

"How am I supposed to sleep now?" Stella asked the ceiling. Then she went back to writing, hypothesizing what these two people had to do with her future.

Surely Marin didn't just see a series of interviews. And what about the other woman?

21

Heart pounding, Stella scribbled all the thoughts that came to mind when she thought about blood, and in the end, the pencil traced one word over and over: mine.

CHAPTER 3

Madeline

Madeline shuttered her eyes and rubbed her temples with her fingertips. No matter how hard she tried, she couldn't shake the visions that had started plaguing her brain after her appointment with Stella Thomas six months ago. And as if these hostile intrusions weren't enough, Madeline had spent the night fighting demons. She rarely had nightmares, but last night, memories of the day she had left her oldest daughter alone on a mountaintop ripped her out of sleep.

The three people who had witnessed Madeline's greatest mistake made their appearance: a dying infant, a teenage girl with fists balled at her sides, and her husband, who insisted there had to be another way. When she woke, she ran to the urn that held his ashes along with those of her youngest daughter and wept, releasing endless forgive-mes into the night air.

She considered canceling her date but chose instead an extra coffee, a cold shower, and makeup, which she now had to fix given her mascara had imprinted black smudges under her eyes. Tonight, she hoped the stuff would make her seem more fun and confident instead of the distracted mess she felt inside.

I'm too old for this.

Normally she could turn down the volume of the messages that invaded her headspace, but these were meant for her, she was certain. For the first time, Madeline was seeing glimpses of her own future, and what a terrifying future it was. She was determined to keep them under control and hadn't shared them with Gwen, the woman she'd been dating for several weeks now.

After tidying up her eyes and sliding on lip gloss, Madeline moved to her bedroom and pulled the heavy, smooth urn into her chest.

"Eric," she whispered. "I met someone. We were friends for a bit, but we're more than that, now. Will you give me your blessing?"

Madeline stroked the cool surface, wishing for the first time that she had her oldest daughter's gift of speaking with the dead. With a sigh, she placed the urn back down and returned to her living room where a semicircular table held her version of an altar. Kneeling, she touched the feet of the felt Goddess. Her Goddess, with wild red hair and green eyes. After she'd spent a week sitting at her youngest daughter, Gertrude's, bedside, Eric had encouraged her to get out of the hospital room and take a walk downtown. She'd found a craft store on the corner that sold wool and felting needles. Her mother had taught her how to work the needle, stabbing it over and over again, until the threads bound together to form a shape. The ornaments she made with her mother were full of late-night giggles, but the Goddess in her hands was infused with blood and tears. She had formed the doll sculpture from memory of the one time she had met the Goddess face to face, the night she'd disobeyed her mother and gone to the Rock.

"I know I don't talk to you very much." Her throat dried. "I'm still angry."

Madeline shook her mother's cries from her head.

"I would like some clarity about this woman. Gwen. I don't want to ..."

She wasn't sure how to finish the statement. When Madeline first met Eric, it never occurred to her to involve the Goddess, to ask for help, blessings, or permission. Perhaps this time around, if dating bloomed into something greater, having the Goddess on her side would help.

"I don't even know how to talk to you," Madeline said, stroking the red hair with her thumbs. "How to worship you, if that's even what you want. Anyway. Should I do this?"

Madeline slumped, annoyed with herself for expecting an answer, then propped the felt Goddess against the wall and left her apartment.

Clothed in blue jeans, a Mets t-shirt, and a matching baseball cap, Gwen exuded youthful energy and Madeline could feel the excitement vibrating from her. She gazed at Gwen, whose hopeful hazel eyes searched her own. She allowed this vision, the one standing flesh and blood in front of her, to take over.

"You look so beautiful, Gwen." Madeline took both of Gwen's hands in her own, kissing the top of each. Her date seemed to relax as they walked hand in hand to the subway.

Six dates had passed between them, and she grew fonder of Gwen with each moment they spent together. She accommodated Madeline's idiosyncrasies, so it felt only fair for Gwen to choose tonight's date destination despite any discomfort it brought Madeline. In addition to being her first live sporting event, the baseball game served as an opportunity to meet Gwen's brother, Ben. Meeting family brought a seriousness to the relationship Madeline wasn't sure she was ready for. Eric had never spoken of his family nor asked her to visit with them, so the mere idea brought trepidation to her heart and belly.

Gwen chose tacos for dinner, and Madeline accompanied hers with tequila, prompting an eyebrow raise from Gwen.

"I've never seen you drink before."

"I don't," Madeline replied. She took a sip, relishing the burn as it slipped down to her belly. "Usually."

"Are you nervous about the game? We don't have to go. We can—"

"It's not your job to keep me comfortable," Madeline interrupted. "I'm looking forward to the game."

"Ben is going to love you," Gwen said as she opened each of her tacos and topped them with a layer of salsa.

"It's not Ben." Madeline took a bite of a taco. She had become more adventurous with her food choices, sometimes wondering what her mother would think of all she had access to in the city. Of course, if her mother were here, she'd see right through Madeline's lie. "Well, I am a little nervous about that."

Gwen stopped arranging her tacos and locked eyes with Madeline. "Talk to me, Maddie."

"It's work," Madeline said with a sigh. "I usually keep strong boundaries with my clients. I'm able to turn the messages on and off. But that's no longer the case." Madeline considered how to explain when and how the images started. *Stella.* "Remember the night I went over on an appointment and you came to my office? Well, I didn't tell you this at the time, but, I couldn't see the client's future well. Her name was Stella."

"Does that happen often?" Gwen furrowed her brows and took a bite of her taco.

"No. It's never happened." Madeline's readings had always been clear and thorough.

"Was she satisfied with the reading, though?"

"I don't know. Her boyfriend scheduled it for her." Madeline rolled her eyes. "He had been drinking. When I read for her, all I saw were impressions, like a Monet painting. Leaves. Dirty feet. A man with dark brown hair. But now, there's more."

Madeline hesitated to dampen the evening, but Gwen's face was expectant, and they had grown close.

Isn't this what people do with the ones they love? Open up? Share?

"I keep seeing her with a woman. Older than us, but not by much. Maybe early sixties. She's short, with big, round glasses, and she's holding a wand. Something seems so familiar about her. And there's blood. So much blood. The man with brown hair—I still can't see his face ..." Madeline shook her head and looked down at her food, her stomach churning. " ...he's lying on the snow, bleeding, and he has a wand on his chest."

Gwen's eyes were attentive and sympathetic, and Madeline felt tears come.

"I can't describe the way it hurts." Madeline pressed a palm to her chest and rubbed as if she could soothe away the ache that haunted her since the day she left the mountain. "I haven't felt pain like that since I lost Gertrude."

"Oh, Maddie." Gwen placed her hand on Madeline's cheek, and she allowed the touch for just one breath, then swigged the rest of her tequila.

"These visions aren't just pieces of her future." Madeline wiped her face with her fingertips. "They're a part of mine." Madeline's eyes moved past Gwen to a little girl spinning around and around in between bites of taco. Dark curly hair. Brown eyes. "I'm sorry," Madeline apologized, reorganizing herself. "I can let this pass." She closed her eyes and breathed in and out. "But thank you for listening."

"You can come to me, Madeline. We're in a relationship. You're my person, and I hope I'm yours, too."

27

Madeline reached out and squeezed Gwen's hand. "You are my person, Gwen."

"Don't mention the visions in front of Ben. Not yet. He doesn't believe in such things."

"Does he know I'm a psychic?" Madeline smirked, cocking an eyebrow at her date.

"Yes, and he thinks it's silly." Gwen tucked her chin, her eyes sheepish. "There's actually a secret I've been keeping from you."

Madeline searched Gwen's eyes, grateful that the woman had secrets of her own to share.

"I see spirits. Ghosts, I guess. Not all the time, thank goodness. I can't hear them, but I can see them. I don't think I'm a psychic, exactly, or a medium, but, well ..."

Madeline listened to Gwen's story of a little girl named Nancy who played marbles with her and laughed at Gwen's bad jokes. Her own thoughts drifted to Beatrice, who heard the voices of her grandmothers, and she wondered if Beatrice had ever heard Gertrude's voice.

"Well," Madeline said as Gwen finished her story, "I certainly believe you, Gwen."

***

The size of the arena, the number of human bodies, and the myriad smells overwhelmed Madeline. Laughter and whooping invaded her ears. New York itself was a loud place, but the arena pushed her to the point of discomfort. But then she locked eyes with Gwen, whose smile took over her whole face, and couldn't resist her own happiness.

They made their way to their seats, where a man with a neatly kept goatee stood, a polite smile stretched upon his face. He was taller than Gwen but shorter than Madeline.

"Maddie ..." Gwen gestured between Madeline and Ben. "This is Ben. Ben, Maddie."

Madeline reached in front of Gwen to shake Ben's hand and found his grip on the verge of being too tight,

28

and though he smiled, his face held an undercurrent of protectiveness.

"Nice to meet you, Maddie. I've heard a lot about you."

"All good, I hope." It was a line Madeline heard in a movie once and now had a chance to use.

"Of course." Ben withdrew his arm and sat down in his seat, then leaned across Gwen to talk to Madeline. "Watch much baseball?"

Gwen recommended the two switch places so they could chat, which made Madeline's heart beat a little faster. She doubted she could keep the look of apprehension off her face, but wanting nothing more than a perfect evening, she switched seats and answered Ben's question.

"I know nothing about baseball." She tried a charming smile, but it felt awkward on her lips. "There's a ball and a bat, that's about it." Would she ever learn this dance that they played out here in the wild? This constant and continual need to impress, this display of peacock feathers.

"We'll talk you through it," Ben reassured.

And they did. Both of them. Simultaneously, they pointed at players and explained the rules, none of which Madeline cared about. She laughed aloud each time the team scored, and Gwen jumped up and down in her seat. Once, when Gwen left for the restroom, Ben turned to her, his face grim.

"Gwen has had it rough in love, Madeline," he said.

Madeline nodded. "I know, Ben, I'm a widow, too."

"It's taken years for her to consider a relationship. Don't hurt her."

Hurting Gwen was both the last thing Madeline wanted to do and her greatest fear. She understood the tension between being willing to be vulnerable and the primal, animalistic need to protect oneself.

"I don't want to hurt her."

"Then don't." With the last word, Ben went back to watching the game.

Gwen returned and they watched the Mets beat the Braves seven to five. Gwen once again jumped up and down and wrapped Madeline in a tight hug. It was the longest they had ever held one another; Gwen hadn't pressured, and Madeline hadn't offered. Equally exhilarating and terrifying, Madeline felt heat bloom from the center of her chest. The very top of her crown tingled, and her toes were on fire. She could feel her date's reluctance when she let her go.

"Wanna go for hot chocolate?" Gwen asked.

Madeline agreed and asked if Ben cared to join.

"I have an early meeting tomorrow, I'm afraid." He reached out his hand. "It was nice meeting you, Madeline."

"Likewise," she replied, and offered a smile.

Gwen continued to explain the ins and outs of baseball as they walked hand-in-hand toward the chocolate shop that, according to Gwen, sold the best hot chocolate in the city. The store was small but offered a beautiful display of assorted chocolates Madeline found too magnificent to eat. Gwen recommended cardamom hot chocolate with square homemade marshmallows. Steaming cups in hand, they walked down the sidewalk, eventually settling down on a bench.

"That hug felt nice, Gwen," Madeline confessed, her face warming. "I really needed it."

She watched as Gwen took a sip of her hot chocolate then licked her upper lip.

"Anytime you need affection, Maddie, you know where to find it." Gwen squared her body with Madeline's. "Will you share a kiss with me?"

Madeline's heartbeat thundered against her ribcage.

"There's so much you don't know about me, Gwen. Skeletons in my closet."

Eric. Gertrude. Beatrice.

Gwen seemed to ponder this for a moment as she surveyed the foot traffic.

"We all have skeletons in our closets, Madeline."

"Not like this," she whispered as she watched the marshmallows dissolve into her chocolate, melting in a froth around the top. "You have no idea what I've done."

Gwen jerked her head back.

"Maddie, I know you're a psychic and a bit on the witchy side." Gwen paused. "I'm assuming no animal sacrifices."

"No." Madeline shook her head.

"Human?" Gwen smiled.

"No!"

"Okay." Gwen grew quiet and swirled the contents of her cup. "These skeletons ... could they hurt me, or do you think I'll judge you?"

"You would definitely judge me."

"Then you don't know *me* very well. I don't judge people." Madeline felt Gwen squeeze her hand then let go.

"We all judge people," Madeline replied. Goddess knew she judged herself.

"Look ..." Gwen smiled. "I'm asking for you to share a kiss with me, Madeline." She used her hands to frame the words. "Not the night or the rest of your life."

Madeline searched Gwen's face, knowing that, eventually, the woman would want the night and perhaps the rest of her life. She also knew she could promise nothing. Gwen took Madeline's hand again in her own and brought it to her lips. After confessing to herself how much she wanted the woman, Madeline brought her body closer and bent down to place her lips against Gwen's.

When Madeline pulled away, Gwen asked, "What's the hardest part, Maddie?"

"About what?"

"Letting me in."

Madeline thought back to the day she'd first met Gwen when she sat at her feet and took her first yoga class. All the postures and stretches had felt wonderful until one. Ustrasana. Camel pose. Gwen had cautioned the practitioners to be wary of their low backs, but for Madeline, it was the emotion of opening her heart and her throat that hurt the most. She ran to the bathroom, tucked herself into child's pose, and did her absolute best to close herself off again.

"I'm terrified," Madeline answered.

"Me too, but there's nothing I can do about it now. I'm too far gone."

"What do you mean?" Madeline questioned.

"I love you, Madeline."

Madeline hadn't heard those three words from anyone in two decades, and they were bombs that detonated from inside her and stole her hearing and her breath. She closed her eyes and rummaged through the memories. Eric breathed the words into her hair one night just before Gertrude passed. Beatrice, a bundle of carved flowers in her hand, whispered them to her as she comforted a sick Gertrude. Perspiration popped from Madeline's skin.

Goddess, don't let me cry.

"I know it might seem fast, Maddie. But I haven't felt this way in ten years."

Madeline opened her eyes. "I love you, Gwen."

"You look like you don't feel well."

"I haven't heard those words in a very long time."

Gwen kissed her again, then they sat for a while, hands entwined, watching the people as they passed.

Gwen interrupted the silence. "So, you don't mean literal skeletons."

Madeline chuckled and shook her head, but her smile faded, and she thought of Beatrice and the dead young man with the wand upon his chest.

"I'm not ready for the night to end," Gwen said with a sigh. "We could walk the city or catch a late movie."

"I'm overstimulated, Gwen."

Gwen's eyes roamed the city streets, then flashed back up to meet Madeline's.

"Maybe I do want the night," she whispered. "Come home with me."

Madeline pulled away. "I am not ready for that."

"Can I at least walk you home?"

"Yes, please."

They peered into storefronts and swapped stories about their childhoods as they walked. When they made it to Madeline's apartment, they stood outside the front door and kissed again, longer, harder.

"Maybe you can come in for a little while," Madeline breathed. They tumbled into her home, and onto her couch, where Madeline gave Gwen the time and affection she could, but nothing more.

CHAPTER 4

Gwen

Gwen watched Madeline's hands tremble as she scooped a spoonful of lemon balm tea into the silver mesh infuser. During one of her morning readings, Madeline had briefly lost consciousness and, after thoroughly terrifying her client, made the decision to clear the rest of her schedule. She'd called Gwen, and Gwen came. Vulnerability was a tenuous, frayed offering in Madeline's hand, but she offered it nonetheless, and Gwen accepted.

"Here, let me take over," she suggested with a tender voice.

Madeline made her way to the couch and sat, head in hands. Gwen brought over a tray holding the steeping tea, two cups, and honey.

"Maddie," she said, rubbing her hand up and down Madeline's arm, "maybe you should clear your schedule for another day or two. Just rest. Can you do that?"

Madeline closed her eyes and nodded. "I think you're right," she said. "It's getting worse. I have to figure this out. I'm all over the place."

Gwen allowed silence to wrap around them for a moment as she gathered the courage to ask her next question.

"Madeline, have you ever considered talking to someone? A therapist, maybe. You lost your daughter and your husband." Gwen's mind briefly flashed to Abbie, her wife who had died ten years ago in a car accident. She knew loss, and if Madeline would allow her, she knew she could help bear the burden. "That's a lot."

Madeline's eyes locked with her. "No," she responded flatly. "I don't ..." She didn't finish her sentence.

"What about another psychic?" Gwen suggested, energetically crossing her fingers that she wouldn't hurt Madeline's feelings. "Maybe they could help you see things more clearly."

Madeline's eyes moved to the teacups in front of them, but she said nothing.

Gwen poured tea and a spoonful of honey into each. "Did I offend you?"

"No." Madeline paused and shook her head. "Things are just different with me. A therapist would have me committed and I don't know that a psychic could see ..."

Madeline stood and paced back and forth, using her hands to explain herself.

"I don't know that I want to see more of my future than I already have. The images and sounds I've seen ... they're terrifying." Madeline sat back down beside Gwen, cupped her tea in her hands, and grumbled, "I'm not sure why anyone wants to see their future."

Gwen considered Madeline's point. For so long, she had maintained presence, rarely allowing her mind to reflect too long on the past nor fleet ahead to the future. Madeline made mindfulness difficult. Gwen imagined the future with her. Making love to her, dancing with her, marrying her, growing old with her.

What if she read my future?

"I have an idea," she whispered. "What if you did a reading for me?"

"That's not a good idea." Madeline's voice held a solemnity Gwen wasn't used to from her. "I'm not like others who sugarcoat things. And once I see, I can't unsee."

Gwen took Madeline's hand. "I'm not afraid."

"Maybe I am," Madeline replied. She rested her back against the couch and continued to sip on her tea, and Gwen moved her body closer.

"I'm going away next weekend," Madeline said. "I was going to lie to you and tell you I was going to a conference, but I'm not. I'm going home."

Gwen felt tension grip her core. "For how long?"

"I don't know for sure," Madeline said. "I go once a month. Sometimes I'm there for two days, others three or four."

"So, those weekends you weren't up to seeing me … I'm assuming you lied to me then, too."

A nauseous disappointment gnawed at Gwen's ribs as she considered the long days Madeline allowed to pass without any communication.

"I'm sorry I lied." Madeline squeezed Gwen's hand, the warm gesture reassuring. "That's not something I do. It's complicated. I can't quite … I haven't been able to find …" Madeline's voice lowered. "I can't explain."

"It's okay. You don't have to," Gwen said, keeping her voice calm though she fidgeted with her earlobe the way she always did when she was nervous.

Why lie about this?

"But if I knew how the trip was going to end …" Madeline mumbled. The two held a long silence before Madeline tilted her head. "Maybe I should read for you. But you have to be sure."

"As long as you promise not to lie to me."

"I promise, Gwen."

Madeline reached for Gwen's hands and traced the lines

on the right with her fingers, then did the same on the left. She closed her eyes. Silence stretched for a moment, then Madeline, eyes still closed, asked, "You're definitely sure?"

Am I sure?

She swallowed. "Yes, Maddie. I'm sure."

Gwen watched as Madeline's relaxed face morphed into a frown, eyebrows scrunched together.

"I see you at a funeral. You're going to lose your mother. Soon."

Gwen's eyes misted over, her jaw clenched and released, then she nodded and exhaled.

"Okay," she said, her voice cracking.

"She'll make it clear she's ready to go." Madeline's head tilted again. "Someone will offer her help, but she'll reject it."

"Do you see yourself yet?" Gwen asked, desperate to get the image of her mother lying in a casket out of her mind.

"Maybe," Madeline breathed. "I think I'm the one offering help, but I'm not completely sure." She shook her head, then opened her eyes. "Maybe I should stop."

"I'm okay," Gwen stammered before taking a gulp of tea. "Is this helping?"

"Not yet."

"Keep going," Gwen said, and she held tightly to Madeline's hands as she watched her eyes close again. "Something good is bound to happen."

Madeline gave a cautious half-smile, then closed her eyes. After a few breaths, her lips spread into a grin.

"You're in love, Gwen, and you are going to have a blast. I see your feet walking in the sand and sea foam. You're laughing. I hear the ocean and birds. I smell the salt air." There was a catch in Madeline's voice when she opened her eyes and said, "I feel your hand in mine. I've never actually been to the ocean, Gwen. Will you take me?"

"I would love that, Maddie. But if you haven't been, how do you know what it smells and sounds like?"

"I'm existing through you right now."

When Madeline closed her eyes, Gwen shifted uneasily. Her mother would die soon, but she would at least have more time with Madeline. *Who lied to me.* Confidence and comfort seemed to settle within Madeline's body now as her shoulders relaxed and eyebrows released.

"I see a Christmas tree here, in this apartment. You're decorating it with pictures."

"Pictures?" Gwen questioned.

"Some are mine," Madeline whispered excitedly. "I smell hot chocolate and something sweet baking. The fireplace is going. You're singing Christmas carols. Your voice is beautiful."

Madeline opened her eyes for a moment, framed Gwen's face with her hands, and kissed her. A giggle escaped.

"I'm feeling better," she whispered.

But Gwen still felt uneasy about Madeline's trip, and she told her so.

"Well, I know I make it to and from West Virginia and that we're still in one piece at the end of it."

"Please keep going," Gwen urged. "This isn't just for you. I want to know more now."

"Okay," Madeline offered a small smile, resettled into her body, and closed her eyes. The smile fell hard and fast, and her eyebrows gathered. "You're leaving me. Pulling a suitcase behind you."

Gwen watched a tear drift down Madeline's face.

"When?" Gwen whispered. "Why?" But Madeline didn't respond. "Madeline ..."

Madeline began to rock forward and backward, tears falling steadily, then she clutched her chest, doubled over, and wailed in agony. Gwen gave the woman's shoulders a shake.

"Maddie, what's wrong?"

"It hurts." Madeline opened her panicked eyes and placed her hands on Gwen's cheeks, searching her face. "Someone is going to hurt you." Madeline unbuttoned Gwen's shirt from the bottom and placed her hands on Gwen's ribcage then closed her eyes again. Those warm fingers brought a shiver down Gwen's back. "Snapped bones. Swollen face. You can't breathe."

"Maddie." Gwen kept her voice gentle as she tried to coax Madeline back into the room, back into the present. "Madeline." She raised her hand to touch Madeline's face, and the woman collapsed into her. Gwen allowed her body to be moved as Madeline sobbed into her chest. "It's okay. I'm here, and I'm safe."

Madeline continued sinking into Gwen's embrace but kept her hands under the blouse. The feeling of Madeline's skin on her own melted her.

Now is not the time, Gwen.

"You don't know what's going on inside of me with your hands on my body."

"I'm sorry." Madeline pulled away and stood to retrieve a glass of water from the kitchen. "I felt everything. Excruciating." Madeline swallowed hard, then her eyes darted at Gwen. "And that wasn't a romantic touch."

"It felt good anyway," Gwen whispered with a disappointed smile and buttoned her shirt.

"I'm scared now," Madeline said.

Gwen scanned Madeline's face, as well as her own heart. The woman before her wasn't the same one she had met the first day in the yoga studio. As the visions increased, Madeline grew more irritable, frustrated, and perhaps more paranoid. Worst of all, she pulled away from Gwen with each episode. Gwen patted the space beside her on the couch, then placed her hand on Madeline's chest just above her heart, feeling the rapid beat.

"What kind of help would you be able to give my mother?" she asked.

Madeline's eyes aligned with her own again, but her countenance remained firm.

"I'm a healer."

Gwen canted her head. "A healer?"

Madeline nodded.

"There really are things you aren't telling me, aren't there?" Gwen reached up with her fingers and massaged her thumbs around Madeline's ears. "You're trying to protect me from secrets, and it's making you crazy."

Madeline's voice turned quill sharp. "You think I'm crazy?"

"No," Gwen responded. "But you will be. This is why you haven't formed deep relationships with people, isn't it? Especially romantic."

Madeline's face was flushed and pleading, but she offered no words.

"What would happen if you were truly honest with me?" Gwen asked. "No more lies."

Madeline just shook her head and turned her gaze downward. "You'll think I'm crazy." Exasperation filled her voice. "And I don't know that I feel safe enough."

Gwen winced at the suggestion that Madeline took no comfort in her love, but she pivoted and continued to focus.

"You know, when I lost Abbie, I was in therapy twice a week for eighteen months. You've experienced intense trauma. You need to see a therapist. And I think you need more skin-to-skin contact."

Gwen took hold of Madeline's hands and slid them under her shirt so that they were once again pressed against her flesh. She inhaled deeply; Madeline's arms kept their tension.

"Trust me, Madeline. Trust us. Let me take you to the ocean."

Madeline tucked herself into Gwen's arms. "I don't want you to feel responsible for me, Gwen. I wouldn't blame you if you left."

"Left? I don't think you get it," Gwen said, squeezing Madeline tighter. "I really, really love you, Madeline."

The rational part of Gwen's prefrontal cortex nudged her with the question: *Is love enough? Perhaps she is too broken.*

"Can I show you?" Madeline asked as she pulled out of Gwen's arms.

"Show me what?" Gwen asked.

"What I can do." Madeline swallowed a gulp of water. "Some of it, anyway."

"Yes. I want to know all of you."

And what I'm getting myself into.

Madeline drew in a breath, then lifted her hand. A blanket draped on a chair began to move. It slithered down the seat then creeped in a wave across the air, coming closer and closer until it wrapped around Gwen's shoulders. She felt excitement and warmth travel through her as the blanket cocooned her.

"Do you want to see the healing, too?"

The sound of scraping metal came from the kitchen, and a knife traveled toward them. All sense of comfort left Gwen's body as Madeline took the knife into her left hand and pressed the blade into her palm. Blood leaped to the surface of Madeline's skin and Gwen felt her chest tighten. Madeline placed the knife on the table and traced a circle of gold around the wound with her left middle finger. Skin knitted itself together until no blood nor scar remained. A new feeling: an adoration almost to the edge of worship filled Gwen. Mouth parted, she placed her hands on Madeline's face and kissed her.

Gwen allowed silence to stretch between them before

asking her next question. "Were you not able to heal Gertrude?"

Madeline's body stiffened and her breath stilled. "I tried so hard, but the illness was stronger than my gift."

"What is it you can't find back home?"

Madeline said nothing.

"If you ever want me to come with you—home, I mean—I would be happy to join you."

Madeline's eyes grew wide, and she pulled her hands back.

It was Gwen's turn to be paranoid. "Please tell me there's no one else."

"Gwen, I barely have the courage to love you, much less another person."

Gwen softened and rebuked her own words. "One thing at a time."

***

The smell of coffee and the gentle clinking of plates and mugs comforted Gwen as she waited at the coffee shop for Ben to arrive. She sipped her tea and people-watched with observant curiosity, settling into her familiar station in the city: alone in a crowd. Ben surprised her with a squeeze to the shoulder, and she stood, pressing her brother toward her, left side to left side, heart to heart. She felt like she could cry, so she held her brother for an extra breath or two.

"I ordered for you," she said, gesturing to the steaming cup on the table.

"How did you know I'd be on time?" her brother asked, a small smirk on his lips.

"You are never late."

"How's it going?" Ben asked, taking his coffee in his hands and sipping with an "mmm, thank you."

Gwen sighed, picking her own hot cup up in her hands. "Things are interesting."

"Okay ..." Ben said, leaning toward her.

"Madeline did a reading for me." Gwen kept her eyes on her cup as she dunked her tea bag up and down.

"Really? She didn't make you pay for it, did she?" Ben chuckled.

"Of course not." Gwen tutted and gave her brother a gentle flick on his ear. "But she saw some concerning things."

"Before you keep going," Ben said, raising his palm, "isn't there a conflict of interest here? She could say anything to get whatever she wants out of you, and—"

"Ben," Gwen interrupted. "The things she saw weren't reassuring, okay?" She sipped her tea and considered how much to tell him, since she hadn't asked Madeline for permission to share. "It's Mom."

"Mom is doing well, sis. She had a great checkup last week."

"I know you take good care of her." Gwen reached across the table to place her hands on top of her brother's. "She saw us at her funeral."

Ben said nothing, but his narrowing eyes questioned her. Gwen closed her own momentarily then glanced up at the ceiling, unable to meet Ben's gaze.

"Well, you know how I feel about psychics or seeing the dead," Ben said. Gwen looked back at her brother to see him wiggling his fingers. "Nothing against Madeline, of course."

"Or me?"

Though she tried to keep her voice playful, underneath the words bubbled a silent resentment; Ben didn't believe one very important truth about Gwen—she *did* see dead people. She had told him once, about the girl with the long French braid and tattered pink dress who lived in their apartment and played marbles with her. Ben refused to believe the apparition was real, so she twisted the story of the girl from a ghost into an imaginary friend. The girl, whom she'd named Nancy, cried on the day Gwen left college.

Ben's face grew remorseful. "What did Madeline see specifically?"

"Madeline was with us in the hospital visiting Mom. She ..." Gwen drew in a deep breath, held it at the top, and released it through puffed cheeks. "She offered to heal her, but Mom said no."

"Heal her?" Ben's eyes narrowed.

Gwen could feel the shallowing of her breath.

I've said too much.

"Like I said, things are interesting." Gwen closed her eyes. "I can't say more. I haven't processed it enough to share right now."

"But the two of you are doing well?"

"We are," she said with a smile. "Do you ever miss Laura?"

Ben leaned back in his chair and stretched his back. "When I think about my time with her, it wasn't all bad. We traveled and saw the world together. Granted," Ben's face soured. "I lost my chance at having children."

"You don't know that," Gwen suggested, and immediately regretted it as her brother's eyes cut into her.

"We are forty-nine years old. How many forty-nine-year-old women do you know who want to start a family?"

"I'm sorry, that wasn't ..." Gwen hesitated. "There are younger women out there." She covered her mouth with her hand, appalled at her own words.

Ben rolled his eyes and shook his head. "We were talking about *you*, remember?"

"I'm sorry." Gwen looked out the window and watched all the people walking down the sidewalk, eyes forward, mindless to those around them. "Ben, I think it's time for you to start believing in magic."

"I take it Mom didn't accept Madeline's offering. In the reading, I mean."

Gwen pressed her lips together and shook her head.

"Come have dinner with us tonight, please. Bring Madeline. I'm sure mom would like her nails painted."

"Will do."

***

The call from Ben came the next morning. A heart attack had put their mother on life support, where she stayed until Gwen could say goodbye. Madeline went with her to the hospital, and as the three of them stood at her mother's bedside, Gwen watched the woman whisper, "I can heal you" to her mother, rubbing her hands together, bringing forth a golden glow. With Madeline's words, Gwen's mother's eyes opened, clearer and brighter than ever.

"No." Her eyes darted between Gwen and Ben. "I'm ready to go on now." She reached out and held each one of her children's hands. "I love you."

Then she lay her head down, closed her eyes, and rattled her last breaths.

After spending half an hour with their mother, Gwen and Ben processed all the paperwork that goes with death. Once home, they reminisced about their parents.

"Is it ridiculous to say I feel like an orphan?" Gwen asked.

"Ridiculous or not, I feel that way, too." Ben took a sip of brandy and straightened himself on the edge of the couch. "We need to talk about the elephant in the room."

Gwen watched her twin turn his attention to Madeline.

"Your hands were glowing."

Madeline turned to Gwen and shrugged, her face asking, "What do you want me to do?"

Gwen smiled, took a sip from her hot tea, and gave Madeline a nod. Madeline demonstrated her telekinetic and healing powers in the same way she showed Gwen

46

the day before, and a wide-eyed, pale-faced Ben became a believer.

"Do you believe me now when I tell you I see spirits?"

Ben's nod was short and quick. "Yes."

That night, Gwen asked Madeline to stay, content just to be held.

"You never talk about your mother or father, Maddie. Are they still living?"

"No. I suppose you could say I'm an orphan, too."

"Did you have a good mother?"

"The best."

Gwen fell asleep listening to stories about hand-felted Christmas ornaments, a pet rabbit, and burned biscuits.

CHAPTER 5

Beatrice

Beatrice questioned her decision to return to the market every week. Vegetables, apples, and cherries needed to be picked. Soaps wrapped and nestled into a basket along with glass bottles of her home-blended shampoo. And, of course, Forest brought his own boxes full of carvings. He whittled otter, beaver, bear, fish—all the creatures that lived in the West Virginia woods and along the river. He was wise enough to leave his wands at home.

Forest's smile each time he met a new patron, however, encouraged Beatrice to keep loading products into crates and towing them down the mountain, despite her growing fatigue. People loved Forest and his creations. And Forest loved them back. The soaps and shampoos attracted customers who claimed Beatrice could sell the concoctions for a higher price. She didn't think she and Forest needed money, though Forest disagreed. He worried about her illness and urged her to see a doctor in town, which Beatrice refused.

The bright August sun had warmed the morning,

promising a busy market. Beatrice closed her eyes and encouraged the vines to come, drawing them from somewhere deep inside of her. The rope—thick, green, and alive—gathered and snaked from her palms. She turned to Forest, whose eyes always displayed awe at the sight of her gift.

"Ready?" she asked, a slight smile on her lips.

Forest nodded, his throat bobbing. With a backpack full of wooden creatures, Forest grabbed the vines and eased himself down the mountain side. Beatrice followed, then urged the creeping plants to cradle the boxes and carry them down. She offered them thanks as they receded back into her hands. She and Forest pulled a cart from the hiding spot she had created behind the thick foliage of rhododendron, whose blossoms had already come and gone. After filling it, Forest took charge of the cart, and the two walked to town.

Artisans of all kinds filled the tents. Sam, a baker with round cheeks and curly hair that lay close to his scalp, offered samples of bread, and typically sold out within the first hour of the morning. Sam was the one outsider whose company Beatrice enjoyed. He kept her and Forest well supplied with bread. He kept his word and, on the occasion that Forest needed help tending to something when Beatrice was unwell, Sam was there. Beatrice gave the man a nod and noted the blush that formed on his cheeks as he returned the gesture.

As always, Wanda, a member of Forest's coven, arrived at their table first, carrying an assortment of jellies and jams, each a different color. Beatrice's eyes cut to Forest, whose face turned pink.

"Forest! Good morning," Wanda said. "I brought these for you. Hello, Beatrice." Wanda glanced at Beatrice as she laid the jams down.

"Wanda." Beatrice bowed her head in greeting.

"Forest put in an order last week. The barter system!" Wanda turned, and Beatrice watched as Forest handed the woman a bag of whittled animals to sell online.

Beatrice spread a tablecloth across the table, sat out baskets of produce and arranged the soaps, shampoos, and lotions. She repositioned them this way and that until finally content, then stepped behind the booth, prepared for customers. Single-mindedly focused on the display of containers and produce, she hadn't noticed a new figure join Forest and Wanda. A woman of medium stature, with light brown hair, a round face, and green eyes, stood with her hand stretched out to Forest. Beatrice's gut clenched. People often showed attraction to her son, but this woman exuded something different. A probing invasiveness swirled in the way the woman eyed him, prodding Beatrice from behind the table and toward her son.

"Beatrice, meet Stella," Wanda said.

Stella reached out her hand and smiled politely. Beatrice glanced at the hand, then locked eyes with the woman before gripping the hand in her own.

"Stella's from New York. She's here to work on a magazine article."

"Ahh." Beatrice smiled and let Stella's hand go. With a forced gentleness she asked, "What's interesting to write about in these parts?"

"She's writing about us," Wanda said. "About the church and school."

"Well, I'm sure Wanda will share everything with you." Beatrice glared at Wanda as she spoke. *You will tell her nothing about us*, she thought, and Wanda, using her own intuition, gave a solemn, discreet nod.

"I was actually hoping to interview you, Forest."

Beatrice watched Stella turn toward her son.

"Why would you want to interview me?" he asked, his

eyes darting between Beatrice and this well-manicured stranger.

"Your wands. They're beautiful."

Beatrice inhaled deeply and returned to her booth once more, staying within eavesdropping distance.

"I want to know your part of the story, and I think other people will, too."

Beatrice's grandmothers spoke to her, their words beating drums through her brain.

Don't let him do it, Beatrice!

Just look at her!

But Forest beamed, and the sight of his smile turned the edges of Beatrice's own mouth up.

"I would love to give an interview," Forest said, and he glanced at his mother, who managed a smile and a nod.

"Could we meet after the market?" Stella asked.

"Well, I need to help my mother back up the mountain, and—"

"No, no." Beatrice waved her hand. Fear pulled at every seam and what ifs clawed at her heart. She swallowed. "It's alright, Forest. I've got it."

Forest's face softened, and he settled plans with Stella. The two moved closer to the booth and a new wave of anxiety prompted Beatrice to rearrange the items on the table once more.

"Wanda gave me a couple of soaps and a shampoo. They're delicious."

Beatrice cocked an eyebrow, and unable to control her sarcasm said, "Well, you aren't supposed to eat them."

Stella chuckled awkwardly. "I mean the smell is delicious."

Beatrice responded with methodical slowness, "I know what you meant."

"You don't want me to interview Forest."

Beatrice eyed Forest over the woman's shoulder. He and Wanda had gone to another vendor for coffee.

"Forest is a grown man." Beatrice kept her voice low. "He can do what he wants."

"But it bothers you."

Beatrice leveled her eyes and squared her body with Stella's.

"Yes. It bothers me."

"Well, I don't bite." The woman tried to smile.

I do.

Beatrice kept the threat to herself. "I'm not afraid of you," she lied, shaking her head.

"Good. There's nothing to be afraid of."

Stella turned to peruse the other vendors, but Beatrice kept her eyes on the woman. The skirt suit, the scarf tied loosely around the woman's neck, the high heels, the makeup. These things separated her from the rest of the people milling around. Something unsettling moved in waves up and down Beatrice's spine, something chilling yet familiar. Something so foreign, wrapped around feelings of home.

Customers arrived, gobbling up the produce and the carvings and the soaps, but choosing Wanda's jams again and again. Beatrice clicked her tongue.

Why do I even try?

In between sales, Beatrice watched Stella, who stayed until noon when the market wound down. Beatrice began to box up the jams no one bought, reprimanding herself once more for bringing them in the first place, when the woman appeared in front of her.

"Can I help?" Stella gestured to the table.

"No," Beatrice said. "There's only one box. I don't need help."

Before letting Forest out of her sight, Beatrice pulled

him aside. "If you tell her about our family, she'll think we're crazy. They may come for us."

"I'll be careful, Mother. I'm a good judge of character. Wanda's great, right?"

Beatrice glanced at the short woman, then back at her son. "I suppose."

"Mother." Forest took her hands in his, a comforting gesture. "You need to get over the fact that her jam is better than yours."

Beatrice tutted, and Forest grinned. "Go on."

She watched as Forest got into Stella's car and the two drove off, before making quick strides to Wanda.

"I need to speak with you. Privately," Beatrice insisted.

"Well, I'm famished," the woman said, bending over her own boxes of unpurchased items. "Come have lunch at my house."

Absolutely not.

"That would be lovely."

***

Wanda led Beatrice to her car where three men holding Bibles and a woman in a long denim skirt waited. Beatrice and Wanda exchanged glances. Wanda offered the men a nod and a "Good afternoon. How ya doin'?"

"Doin' alright, doin' alright. Reckon you have a minute to hear the Word?"

"'Fraid not." Wanda tilted her chin and took another step towards her car.

"You're in danger of hellfire, Wanda, you know that? That church you got—devil worship. Nothing but devil worship."

"That's what you keep tellin' me." Wanda unlocked the car, placed boxes in the trunk, and slid into the driver's seat.

Beatrice stared the group down. She wasn't afraid of them. In fact, she'd tried to help them once. She had come upon women from the group complaining about menstrual cramps. When she'd offered them a tincture for the pain, the women refused. Wanda had encouraged Beatrice to keep her remedies to herself.

"Don't cast your pearls before swine," Wanda had said, a quote from their own holy book.

Still, this sect wasn't hostile toward Beatrice like they were toward Wanda. Instead of Bible verses and threats of damnation, they gave her a cold but healthy distance. Beatrice eased into the car and followed Wanda's instructions to buckle her seatbelt. She'd never been in a car before. The buttons and steering wheel and levers stole her attention for a moment until the woman in the denim skirt shouted a string of Bible verses.

"Have you gone to the police? Forest tells me it's getting worse."

Wanda snorted. "The preacher and the police chief are brothers. They won't help."

"Well, don't you have spells to protect you?" Beatrice asked, peering out the back window at the wagging fingers.

"There is one thing I like about them." Wanda pressed down on a lever, causing a clicking noise before turning left.

"Oh?"

"They know that we're real."

***

Wanda's home smelled of morning biscuits and age, not unlike her own. Beatrice took in the upholstered fluffy furniture, the fireplace, the carpet stretched from one end of the living room to the other, the lights and their switches, lamps on side tables, pictures hanging on the wall, and finally, Wanda's altar. Beatrice moved toward it, and, before she realized what she was doing, picked up Forest's wand.

"I have chicken salad and sourdough bread. Sliced green apple on the side. Sweet tea."

Beatrice nodded and placed the wand back down with reverence.

"Need help?" she asked Wanda.

"Sure. You can slice the apples."

The kitchen offered many interesting things for Beatrice to scoff at, admire, and even envy: a dishwasher, a refrigerator, smooth countertops, a toaster, and an electric stove. Wanda pulled two apples from a bowl and handed Beatrice a knife. The women worked in silence, honoring an unspoken agreement to wait until seated before talking.

Before long, they sat at a small round table nestled in the corner of the kitchen. Through the window, Beatrice surveyed a large screened-in porch and garden beds full of vegetables: ripening tomatoes, green peppers, climbing green beans, winter squash, and root vegetables. An herb garden stood separate, full of sage, rosemary, thyme, oregano, bee balm, lemon balm, mint, chamomile, and many others.

Beatrice turned back to the table and focused her eyes on her lunch. Wanda generously salted her green apple, and when she offered the shaker to Beatrice, she did the same.

"They're good with salt," Beatrice said, taking a bite.

"So is watermelon."

"Most things are better with salt." Beatrice smiled.

Wanda chuckled.

"What has my son told you about us, Wanda? And what did you tell this woman?"

Wanda finished a bite of her sandwich and said, "Mm, it's good. Take a bite."

Beatrice picked up the sandwich, breathed in the soft sour scent of the bread, and took a mouthful. Her eyebrows jerked upward at the texture and flavor of pulled chicken, sliced grapes, and pecans. "It is good. Now tell me. And don't lie. I will know if you're lying."

Another untruth. Beatrice could grow any vegetable or tree or flower or vine she wanted, but she couldn't read minds.

"Forest doesn't talk about you much, Beatrice."

The statement brought a strange combination of relief and sadness to Beatrice's chest.

"He's told me and the others not to ask questions about you." Wanda ate a few more bites, wiped her mouth, and continued. "He told us you live on top of the mountain. No plumbing. No electricity. You hunt and eat from your garden. He said he doesn't have a father."

Beatrice's chest grew tight, and she made eye contact with Wanda. "All of that is true," she responded. "Is that all he's told you?"

Wanda tilted her head to one side then the other as if weighing whether to say more.

"Tell me, Wanda." Beatrice's voice bordered on aggressive.

"He told me you're sick."

The tightness turned to a heat that flushed Beatrice's face. "That is also true." No longer hungry, she took a sip of Wanda's sweet tea. It was perfect. She had bought glasses of the iced drink a few times at the market, but they were always too sweet. "This is good," she whispered.

"He said you're sick to your stomach a lot, and your energy is gone. We've noticed the change, too."

"I don't know what it is," Beatrice said, feeling herself soften and hating herself for it. "None of my tinctures or teas or salves work."

"Do you have any other symptoms?"

"I'd rather not talk about it, please."

"Would you be willing to see a—"

"No." Beatrice shook her head. "No."

"Forest has a community down here who will do anything in the world for him. And you're his mother, so we're here to support you, too."

Beatrice forced herself to eat another bite of sandwich and a slice of apple. "So, what did you tell the journalist?"

"Stella. Her name's Stella. She wanted to see my altar and asked about the wand. It's my favorite tool, you know. I told her you two lived on the mountain, off the grid. You're very private people. I told her Forest is a talker, but you're not."

When Wanda stopped, Beatrice asked, "Is that it?"

"Yes. That's it ... he wants to talk to you, Beatrice. About our practices. Has he asked if he could build an altar yet?"

"Ask me?" Beatrice retorted. "Forest doesn't have to ask me to do anything, Wanda. Listen, we're different, and not just in the ways you know. We are not witches, and—"

"Forest is a witch, Beatrice."

Beatrice's nostrils flared.

"We don't invite people, because it's not safe. I've had awful experiences with—"

"Oh, believe me, we've had awful experiences with people down here as well. Anyway, I don't ask Forest questions."

"*She's* going to. And Forest will answer despite himself."

"Forest will do whatever he needs to keep you safe."

Beatrice took a deep inhale. "I'm sorry, this is truly good, but I can't eat anymore. I don't feel well."

"That's alright." Wanda took Beatrice's plate and her own to the sink, rinsed them, and placed them in the dishwasher. "Can I show you my garden? It doesn't compare to yours, I'm sure, but it serves me well. Course, if you're not feeling well ..."

Beatrice stood, her stomach sour, her palms sweaty. "I'd like to see it."

As they walked amongst the herbs and vegetables Wanda planted, Beatrice continued her own interview.

"How often do they bother you?"

"Oh, they keep on with it," Wanda said. "Shouting at me from across the road. Telling me that if it was legal, they'd burn me like they did in the old days. Here." Wanda pinched off a sprig of spearmint and handed it to Beatrice.

"Thank you," Beatrice said, rubbing the leaves between her thumb and forefinger before bringing the scent to her nose. "Forest hates that you're alone in this house." She turned her eyes toward Wanda.

"I'm alright, Beatrice. I do have strong protections."

Beatrice turned her attention back to the garden, and when she had seen it all, she asked Wanda to take her back. When she crossed the road and stood at the foot of the mountain, she reflected on the many times she and Forest made the trek back up. This time, he did not join her. With waves of her fingers, she coaxed tendrils from the ground, which grew into vines, took hold of the box, and guided it up the mountain as Beatrice climbed.

Her eyes stung. She squinted at the sky and saw Gertrude circling overhead. Beatrice didn't want to talk. She closed her eyes tightly to squeeze out any voices from her grandmothers, and she continued to climb. Alone.

CHAPTER 6

Stella

The diner smelled of reused grease and sugar, not unlike the Coney Island funnel cakes Stella used to share with her father on their summer excursions.

God, I miss him.

Stella often wondered what he would think of her. Unlike her mother, he had always praised the best things about her. She glanced at Forest, wondering what Beatrice was like as a mother. The fluorescent lights, one of which flickered incessantly, and the red painted walls overwhelmed Stella. She considered asking Forest to go elsewhere, but the tension was a spring pulled tight between them, and she worried that switching plans could affect what little trust had developed.

A woman in black pants and a pink polo embroidered with the letters DQ moved them down a narrow pathway past the kitchen and into a large dining area. Windows lined the entire rear wall of the restaurant, allowing an expansive view of the river and the mountains it grew.

Stella and Forest sat down at a table near the windows and watched as ducks paddled by.

She drew in a deep breath and tilted her head from side to side. This morning at the market, she'd played the role of professional New York City journalist impeccably. But the mask was heavy and exhausting.

Get it together, Stella.

Still annoyed with herself from the clumsy interactions with Wanda, Stella vowed to get this one right, hoping that if things went well, Beatrice would talk to her.

"Are you staying in town?" Forest asked.

"Yes. Next door. River's Edge," Stella replied as she pulled a notepad, pen, and her phone out of her bag. "Have you ever given an interview before?" She studied the mix of eagerness and trepidation on Forest's face. He shook his head, jostling his deep brown curls.

"Well, you'll answer a series of questions, and I'll take those answers and write the story around them. Paint a picture for the readers. The restaurant, the river, the ducks."

"Why me? Wanda is much more involved in the church—"

"Well ..." Stella interrupted Forest, though she struggled to find the words. "The church and school are interesting, but your story feels ... unique. How many people live off the grid on top of a mountain and carve wands?"

Stella watched Forest shift in his seat as the server walked to the table.

"Do you have hot tea?" Stella asked before the server could place the menus down.

"No, ma'am. We have Coke products, sweet and unsweet tea, milk, and coffee."

"I'll have hot water with lemon, then."

Stella glanced at Forest, whose thick eyebrows furrowed over the menu as the server hovered over the two of them. Silence drew into awkwardness as the server held up her pointer finger to another table with a quick "be right with you" followed by a sigh.

"He needs a minute," Stella said, but Forest interjected.

"No, I know what I want. This looks good." Forest pointed to something on the menu, and the server nodded. "Make it two," Forest said and handed back the menus.

"Actually, I don't—" The server turned away before Stella could resist, reining in the frustration that threatened to cloud her face.

"Thank you," she said.

Remember the goal. Make it to the top of the mountain.

"Sharing a meal with others brings me joy. So ..." Forest fidgeted with the napkin-wrapped utensils that lay on the table. "What questions do you have?"

Stella took a deep breath and placed her phone in front of her. "Do you mind if I record you?" she asked.

"What do you mean?"

"I push this button here." Forest watched intently as Stella turned the phone and pointed to a red spot on the glossy surface. "And the microphone will copy our conversation so I can listen to it later."

Forest wrinkled his brow.

"Here," she said. "Let me show you."

Stella recorded herself saying hello, then played back the sound.

"How does it do that?" Forest asked, taking the phone into his own hands, which made Stella's stomach flip. He seemed to notice her discomfort and handed the phone back with an apology. "It feels like magic to me," he added. "Don't get me wrong. I've used a phone before, but how? And who thought of it? Who—"

"I don't know how it works," Stella said. "But do you mind if I use it?"

"I guess not." Forest shrugged.

Stella asked about Wicca and learned that Forest was

relatively new to the practice. His magical tool of choice was the wand he made from a branch of a sacred tree. His countenance changed as he talked about the tree. He avoided eye contact, and Stella felt she could almost see the filter that caught the words he wasn't supposed to say.

A vision came. A new one. A tree falling, roots ripping from the ground. Blood oozing. After a few deep breaths and sips of hot water, Stella returned to the conversation.

"I'm sorry." Stella shook her head. "Long day. You were talking about a sacred tree."

"I've said all I'm going to say about her ... it."

Stella was grateful. The last thing she wanted was more visions today.

Forest detailed a few of the rituals the coven enjoyed on each of the eight sabbats, confessing that the winter solstice was his favorite.

"I guess you shouldn't have favorites," he said. "But it's my mother's favorite. The days lengthen. It's a move toward life and light."

"Tell me more about your mother," Stella said as the server sat down tall paper cups full of ice cream and crushed cookies. She sighed. It wasn't his fault; there was no way Forest could have known how diligent Stella was with her diet. Only yesterday morning, Stella had fussed at Roger for bringing home bagels for breakfast. She'd ripped out the insides, smeared on a minimal amount of cream cheese, and choked it down with frustration.

"My mother?" Forest responded before taking a spoonful of the ice cream. He nodded with approval at the taste, his eyes focused on his spoon.

"Does she practice Wicca, too?" Stella prodded.

Forest took a deep breath and met Stella's eyes before speaking. "I won't say much about her." His reply was solemn, and Stella's shoulders slumped. "She also observes the changes in the seasons with ritual and prayers, but they are family practices, not Wiccan practices."

"What does she believe in?"

"Believe in?" Forest's eyes narrowed. "I don't understand what you mean."

"I'm talking about faith. Faith is believing in things we cannot see."

"I know what faith is." Forest chuckled uncomfortably. "It doesn't make sense to me when talking about the Goddess. We don't believe in anything we can't see."

"How do you see the Goddess? How do you see magic?"

"How do you not see magic?" Forest rebutted.

Stella's eyes widened, then softened. Moments passed; breath, the only sound between them. She paused the recording, inhaled, and eyed the ice cream like a warrior preparing for battle.

I might as well try to enjoy it.

Stella noticed Forest's eyes on her as she carefully moved around a tiny piece of cookie before bringing it to her lips. It was good, and she rolled her eyes with pleasure.

"Have you never had ice cream before?" Forest asked.

"I'm strict about what I put in my body."

Forest gave a slow nod, his eyes piercing.

Stella allowed herself to taste the ice cream, feeling the texture of the cookies against the cool, sweet soft serve. Ducks allowed the river's current to carry them, and she watched them be carried, admiring how they moved so gently down the stream. Her eyes climbed up the looming mountains towering over the river's bank, and she smiled.

"It really is beautiful here," she said.

Stella took one last spoonful of ice cream, knowing well she wouldn't eat the entire dessert, and picked up her phone once more.

"I think I'd like to go in a different direction," she said.

"What can you tell me about your life? What was your first memory?"

"My mother," Forest said without pause. "I remember rocking on our front porch, nursing, and her singing to me. She told me the stories about her mother and grandmother—the entire line of our family."

Stella wrote feverishly as Forest talked.

"Do you have a father?" Stella pushed away feelings of guilt for intruding; she was a journalist, after all.

"No," Forest said.

Stella thought of her own father. He brought such balance to the family. Her mother brought home the bread, and her father toasted it. Stella had been nineteen when he died. While she grieved, her mother had morphed into someone unrecognizable. Bitter. Selfish. The loss crystallized all her proclivities toward a controlling nature.

Stella studied Forest's face. His brow knit together in hesitation, but he inhaled a large breath and continued. "Stop recording. If you want to hear the rest of it, stop recording and promise you won't use this in your story."

The hairs on Stella's arms stood, and a shiver ran down her back. She stopped recording, pulled a napkin from the dispenser, and scribbled an informal contract. She signed it, passed it to Forest, who read it and signed it as well.

"I don't know much, but I'm not sure how viable a contract on a napkin will be." He cleared his throat. "I'm the son of my mother and the Goddess. No father."

Stella couldn't speak. The words Forest poured out so courageously were impossible to believe. Forest, as though feeling her thoughts, added, "I'm a child of the woods. The women of my family don't lie with men to have children. They know the Goddess. The Creator."

"How does it work?" Stella asked after a few silent moments.

Forest paused. Stella watched his chest expand with each breath.

"My mother told me that when she was fifteen, the Goddess called her to the Rock—it's a large, flat piece of limestone in the middle of the woods—where my grandmothers have birthed their babies and transitioned for generations. She lay down on the Rock and the Goddess opened her womb and gave her me."

Stella's brows scrunched together as questions layered themselves atop one another. She took a deep inhale and an exhale and prepared herself to explain the birds and the bees to this twenty-year-old man, but her gut, delayed as it was, reacted to the piece of the story that troubled her the most.

"Fifteen?" She grimaced.

"Well, the women before her went when they were eighteen. I'm not sure why she was so young."

Stella pressed her eyelids closed and swallowed. Warring thoughts sparred within her brain. Pragmatic intellect told her that Forest's words could not be trusted, but something deeper in Stella's gut whispered that the magic was true. She fluttered her eyes open.

"What about your grandmother? Is she still living?"

Forest's eyes searched the ceiling as if he'd find the words there, then he scanned the room, even searching behind him for eavesdroppers.

"Normally, when a woman is ready to give birth, her mother stays until the baby is born and latched onto the breast. Then, she lies down on the Rock and all the energy and fats and minerals of her body break into the tiniest of pieces and mate once more, this time with the earth. A tree shoots up from the ground, carrying the soul of the woman inside. But—"

"Wait." Stella held up her palms. "So, when you said

transition, you mean your family members turn from human to tree?"

Forest swallowed. "I should not have—"

"It's okay, Forest." Stella gestured around the table. "No phone. No notes."

No one would believe me anyway. Hell, I don't know if I believe it myself.

Forest's eyes darted around again, avoiding all eye contact.

"My grandmother's story is different."

"What happened to your grandmother?"

"That's my mother's story to tell."

Forest changed the topic and described his home on the hill, painting a vivid description for Stella of the house, smokehouse, the dairy shed, outhouse and bathhouse, which were separate, and the enormous greenhouse Beatrice maintained. He explained the charms that brought water to the kitchen sink and kept the bathwater hot and clean.

"Listen, I have to get home." Forest stood up from the table and took his empty milkshake cup in his hands. "It was nice meeting you. I hope you have what you need."

Panic washed over Stella. She wanted more, so much more. The desire—no, the need—had nothing to do with writing a magazine article.

"I need more time with you," Stella said. "Could we meet again? Maybe tomorrow."

"It's harvest time. There's a lot to do, and my mother isn't well."

Stella's thoughts drifted to Beatrice. The woman certainly didn't look unwell.

"Forest, do you think your mother would talk to me?"

Forest chuckled softly and shook his head. "No."

"You haven't even given me an hour."

Stella watched as Forest ran his fingers through his

hair, a darkness shadowing his face. "I didn't have to give you that."

"You're right. I apologize."

"I didn't realize things would be this ..." Forest stuffed his hands in his pockets and paced. "My mother will hate that I've told you these things. And she needs me. It's harvest time."

"I'd really like to see what harvest time is like, Forest."

"She won't like it." Forest tapped his foot in a quick, aggressive manner. "She really, really won't like it."

"Meet me here early in the morning," Stella said. "Before you start your day. I'll follow you."

"I can't meet you here. You'll have to get up the face of the mountain on your own. I'll send Arcas to meet you at the top."

"Whose Arcas?"

"Arcas is my bear, my companion."

Stella's mouth gaped.

"He's safe." Forest lowered his chin and looked up into Stella's eyes. "His mother left him for dead. We raised him. He won't hurt you. I promise."

"You want me to follow a bear to your house?" Stella asked incredulously.

"Listen, if you want more than what I've given, I have to trust you. And perhaps the greatest way for us to test this out is for you ..." Forest jutted his finger at Stella. " ...to come up the mountain and follow my bear."

Stella was silent, sure that Forest expected her to pack up her phone and her notebook and leave. But she closed her eyes and whispered, "Okay."

"Okay. Plan on being to the top by six."

Stella wondered how Forest kept time as she eyeballed the mountain through the window.

"It's steep."

"Do you have good shoes?"

"I do."

"Wear those and dress in layers. It will be chilly in the morning." With that, Forest pulled out a wad of cash from his pocket and laid it on the table. "There's a huge wall of holly. Arcas will lead you to a spot you can slip through. I gotta go."

"Bye," Stella murmured.

When the server came, Stella covered the cost of the ice cream and tucked Forest's money in her pocket to return it the next morning. She glanced once more at the face of the mountain. Her chest tightened, and her eyesight blurred, but she clenched her fist and told the visions not to come.

I will meet you at the top of the mountain.

Clarity returned, and Stella finished her ice cream, watching the sun dip behind the mountains and the moon create sparkling diamonds on the river. She stayed until the server told her it was closing time, then she walked to the River's Edge, took a long shower, and covered herself in bed. Stella dreamed of a flat rock nestled deep in the forest. She lay upon its coolness, gazing into the branches of a leafy birch tree.

CHAPTER 7

Stella

A crumbling of barriers had occurred within Stella the moment Forest asked *How do you not see magic?* Before those words, she'd thought she had it all together. Everything in its place. Her daily meal plan and exercise regimen. Her professional trajectory. The course of her relationship. All the boxes in place like the five main points of plot on a story arc.

Her alarm startled her awake at four thirty. Unlike most mornings, she rose without hitting snooze, desperate to be on time. Stella felt her heart move in a random rhythm that deep breathing failed to slow. Her heart stalled. It hastened. Her hands trembled.

Why am I this nervous?

Stella moved to the bathroom and washed her face. She considered makeup but suspected Beatrice might think more of her if she didn't wear it. Shuffling around the room, she settled on a light gray sweater, a pair of hiking boots, and a leather jacket. She arranged her hair in a bun, loaded a backpack, and locked the door behind her.

Stella jogged across the road to the graveled shoulder and glared upward at the sheer, rocky face of the looming mountain. As she searched for a solid foothold, Stella found herself grateful for the time she and Roger had spent rock climbing in the Berkshires. Halfway to the top, a hold below Stella's right foot gave way. Her arms tensed and prepared for the weight they had to catch with little warning.

A bead of sweat trickled down Stella's forehead as she scraped the surrounding rock with her feet, searching for a new hold. A car sped by and honked its horn, but Stella kept focused. After spending all the muscle-power her right leg offered, she swung her left leg around, and when it seemed her arms couldn't hold anymore, her foot made purchase and she pushed herself upward to the place where the rock ended and the forest floor began. Scents of the woods swirled around her, and the coolness urged her to zip up her jacket, which was now torn from the climb.

The forest floor glistened with sunlight that glinted through the branches, and Stella reached down to touch dew-glossed leaves. The visions came, and this time, she did not resist. She closed her eyes. A beating inside her, rich as the soil underneath, offered a different cadence to her own heartbeat. The two rhythms collided and twisted until Stella's heart found a new pace, and she exhaled in surprise. The clacking and clicking of teeth interrupted the silence.

Stella's eyes sprang open, and she found herself nose-to-nose with a black bear. Arcas.

Holy shit!

The bear opened its mouth, bellowed, then turned and walked away from Stella. The adrenaline of the climb had made her forget about Arcas. Stella's heart thudded in her chest and wetness coated her palms. She'd seen a bear, once, in the zoo, behind panes of glass. Her legs failed her, and the bear moved farther away until he realized Stella was not with him, then he turned, lumbered back to Stella, and clicked his teeth aggressively. Arcas opened his jaws and took hold of Stella's right jacket sleeve, urging her to come. She stumbled forward, and the bear let go, continuing to walk with expectation.

"Okay," Stella said, raising her hands in surrender. "I'm coming."

The bear grunted and Stella followed, paying careful attention to avoid tripping on a root. Once in a while, the bear turned around, moved behind Stella, and nudged her forward.

"I'm going as quickly as I can!"

After half an hour of hiking, Stella smelled something new: breakfast. The scents of bacon and coffee wafted on the breeze, reminding her that she hadn't eaten yet. She came to a thick wall of holly writhing with vines and searched for the spot Forest said to go through. Once on the other side, she saw a plume of smoke in the brilliant almost-fall air.When she reached the pinnacle, she glanced down toward the other side of the mountain to see the five log structures Forest had described. Arcas bounded down the hill and to the front of the largest cabin, and Stella followed. Forest's voice pierced the air.

"There you are."

His curly, damp hair hung around his face, and he wore the same button-up flannel from yesterday. He seemed exhausted and sad.

"Good morning," Stella said.

"What happened?" Forest pointed toward the rips in Stella's jacket.

"The rocks and your bear." Stella nodded toward Arcas.

Forest grimaced. "I'm sorry."

Stella shrugged and followed Forest toward the house.

"I've never seen her so angry," he said. "Never raised her voice at me until last night."

"I can go back, Forest," Stella offered, but she was relieved when he shook his head.

"She's making breakfast," Forest explained as Stella took the two steps leading to the front porch. He gestured toward two home-hewn rocking chairs, and they both sat down. A large black bucket of green fruit soaked at Forest's feet.

"What are those?"

"Walnuts," Forest answered. "Black walnuts. We're going to remove the hulls so that we can dry and cure them for the winter."

Arcas lumbered up onto the porch as well, and Stella watched him nuzzle Forest's ribs until the man reached down and scratched his head.

"Tell me about him."

Forest, his voice full of affection, told Arcas stories, starting with the moment he and Beatrice first found him as a cub. Stella listened without taking notes, content to be the tale's only audience.

"Time for breakfast," Beatrice's voice rang into the mountain air, and both Stella and Forest turned.

Stella placed her palms against her cheeks, unsure of where the flushed sheepishness came from. Writing stories put bread on her table, yet she felt so intrusive with this family. The door led straight to the kitchen where a small table sat with two chairs on opposite sides. To the left, Stella noticed a wood-burning stove, a sink, and an island for food preparation. Above the island, a rack held various pots and pans.

The smells of bacon, cooked eggs, and baked bread filled the space, along with a pungent, spicy aroma Stella could not place. Forest retrieved a rocking chair from the living room so that Stella had a seat at the table. Beatrice stood,

74

regal, with her olive skin, dark eyes, and curly locks of deep brown tinseled with silver.

"Stella," Beatrice said with a nod. "Welcome."

Stella read reluctance and frustration on Beatrice's face, but it was evident the woman had made an earnest effort at hospitality in the copious amounts of food on the table.

"Thank you," Stella replied.

Beatrice blessed the meal, offered thanks to the Goddess, and asked for blessings. She thanked each woman who came before her for their gifts. Her eyes remained closed for a moment, but then she opened them and nodded for Stella and Forest to sit.

The plates on the table were circles of well-sanded and shellacked wood.

"Please." Beatrice urged Stella to fill her plate first, and as Stella did, she considered how much cholesterol was in each slice of crispy bacon.

"I'm sure Forest told you I'm not fond of guests." Beatrice's voice was interrogative, guarded, but also somehow warm.

Stella finished filling her plate before responding. "He told me this upset you." She remained still as she waited for Beatrice's response.

Beatrice filled her own plate and grabbed a big, hot biscuit, pulling it open with her fingers. Forest did the same.

"We interact with customers at the market and Forest enjoys his time with the Wiccans downtown. But we keep to ourselves otherwise."

Sitting across from Beatrice, Stella felt microscopic. She thought about Reina, the senior editor at her magazine, with her power suits, high heels, and war paint.

She doesn't hold a candle.

Stella examined the food on her plate and pulled off a bite of biscuit. Heaven. Salty, buttery, tender, crunchy heaven.

"I understand why you want to keep this place to your-selves," Stella said.

"He told you everything about us." Stella watched Beatrice lock eyes with Forest.

"I didn't record much of it," Stella stammered.

"Do you know what people would do if they knew?"

A silly newspaper headline flashed into Stella's mind: *A Real-life Poison Ivy Lives in the Mountains Of West Virginia.*

"They'd make a spectacle out of you if they actually believed it."

Beatrice narrowed her eyes. "No. They would kill us."

Stella narrowed her eyes and tilted her head. She found this possibility highly unlikely, so, since she couldn't respond appropriately, she kept her mouth shut.

"Do *you* believe it, Stella?"

The visions flashed in no particular order. Tree roots. Blood. Blonde hair. Stella swallowed and confessed, "I don't know."

"Don't you think it's time to go home?" Beatrice asked.

"Mother!" Forest admonished, and Beatrice glared at him.

Stella was slow to respond. Only forty-eight hours ago, she'd felt desperate to leave West Virginia. Now, she bristled at the idea of returning to the metal and glass and noise.

"It's busy out there. And dirty, and—"

"It's busy here on this mountain as well. And there's certainly plenty of dirt," Beatrice snapped.

"It's a different kind of dirt," Stella continued. "Scummy. Chemical. And people. There are so many people."

"New York is much bigger than the town down there," Beatrice commented, and Stella realized Beatrice and For-est knew more about the outside world than she realized.

"Eight and a half million people," Stella said.

Forest choked a little on his biscuit. "Million?"

"Million. People walk the streets without paying attention to those around them."

The room went silent for a moment.

"What kinds of shoes do people in New York wear?" Beatrice asked as she took another bite of biscuit.

"There are as many types of shoes as there are people," Stella said with a smile. "I don't wear these around the city."

She held out a foot for Beatrice to inspect. To Stella's surprise, the woman grabbed it and pointed to the thick rubber sole of the boot.

"Disconnection," she said, and unlaced Stella's footwear, removing it along with her sock. Stella sat still, her gaze finding Forest, who simply shrugged and half-smiled. If she were in the city among her peers, this action would have appalled her, and she would jerk her foot away. But threads of trust were fragile, and Stella wanted to gain Beatrice's, so she remained still even as the woman took her fingernails and ran them along the sole of her foot.

"Our feet on the earth keep us grounded." Beatrice cradled Stella's foot in her hands. "Take the other one off and place your feet on the floor. You'll feel different."

Stella did as Beatrice asked and placed her feet against the floorboards, which only made them cold. She wanted to explain that it was more than shoes that disconnected people in her world from nature. Concrete. Light. Noise. She couldn't find the words, so she picked off another piece of biscuit. Only then did she look down at Beatrice's feet, which were bare and dirty.

Dirty feet.

Stella closed her eyes and drew in a deep breath.

Not fucking again ...

"Are you alright?" Forest asked, and she nodded.

Though her stomach swirled and her palms sweated, the

visions did not come, and Stella took a sip of cool water to wash down the heat that was rising within her. She met Beatrice's eyes.

"There are protections all around this property to keep out anyone who may try to harm us."

Stella winced at the suggestion that she meant harm. The visions continued to knock against her brain, so she allowed them to come as she had when she first entered the forest. She closed her eyes and her heartbeat searched and found the rhythm of the woods.

Dirty feet.

Blood.

Blue eyes.

The creaking sound of a falling tree.

Laughter.

Running through the forest.

A rattling.

The sights and sounds warmed her body from the crown of her head to her toes. She opened her eyes to find Beatrice and Forest staring at her with narrowed eyes.

"I'm not used to such a heavy breakfast."

"If you mean us harm ..." Beatrice growled.

Stella didn't respond immediately. She couldn't. She couldn't make promises without knowing what her visions meant. Without knowing her place on this mountain.

When the silence lasted too long, Stella finally said, "I have no desire to hurt you." That she could assure the woman.

Beatrice nodded. Stella ate more for breakfast than she had in over five years, and when the meal seemed finished, she offered to help Beatrice clean up.

"No," Beatrice responded firmly. "Thank you."

A pang of unexpected disappointment moved through Stella.

"Breakfast was delicious. Thank you."

"You're welcome, Stella."

Stella watched as Forest gave his mother a hug and a kiss on the forehead.

What am I supposed to make of them?

"Let me show you around before we get to work," Forest said.

Stella forgot for a moment that she had no shoes on. When she reached for them, Beatrice snatched them from the ground.

"Keep your shoes off. Tell me how you feel when you get back."

Stella nodded and followed Forest. The grass was cool and damp under her feet, and she felt leaves crumble under her weight. She couldn't name the feeling stirring within her. A small hum of anxiety, like the buzzing of bees around a playground trash can, threatened to inflame her, but something else moved through the air, whispering "all is well."

Forest led her to the bathing cabin where a huge soaking tub sat full of steaming water. Forest dipped in his hand and encouraged Stella to do the same.

"It's a charm," he said, smiling. "Two of my grand-mothers work together. It's always hot and clean."

Stella smelled the bars of soap Beatrice had made and lathered up her hands with homemade shampoo. "Do you make a lot of money from selling these?" she asked as she rinsed her hands then returned the items back to the shelves.

"We don't want for much. But my mother may need a doctor soon."

"She doesn't look sick," Stella replied, following Forest out of the cabin.

"It comes and goes. Some days are better than others."

"Oh, speaking of money ..." Stella reached into her pocket and pulled out Forest's cash. "You overpaid by a lot."

"Thank you." Forest folded the bills into his pocket.

"Is there anything that you can't grow or hunt that you buy from town?"

"Chocolate and coffee." Forest ushered Stella to another building. "This here is where we use the bathroom."

The space was much more pleasant than Stella expected. A smooth wooden bench with a hole in the center stretched the width of the building. The room smelled of cedar, and a large window in the ceiling allowed ample light to infuse the space. Toilet paper and wood chips sat in separate baskets within arm's reach of the hole.

Stella followed Forest to a cabin with a smoking chimney. The smokehouse. On the table lay two large slabs of meat and hams hung in the corners. Across the room, two wheels of cheese and an assortment of nuts littered the table.

"Where do you get milk for the cheese?"

"From the baker. He keeps a few cows on his property."

"Which one of your grandmothers built the smokehouse?"

Forest paused, and his face clouded over. He placed his hand on the door frame and eyed the space. "My grandmother's husband built it. He taught my mother and grandmother how to keep meat."

"So, your mother did have a father?"

Forest shook his head. "Stepfather. It's not my story to tell."

Forest moved past Stella, leaving her curious. The more she moved around the property, the more it enchanted her. The moss skirting roots and covering the rocks. Stories of mothers and talking trees. Her eyes traveled up the trunks and moved among the branches to the leaves that swayed in the wind.

A frigid dampness pervaded the next building, and the only light came from the opened door. Through the middle of the building ran a small stream of water, and within the stream sat large glass jars of milk.

"Feel the water," Forest said, so she bent down and dipped her fingertips in.

"Brr."

"Well, that's it, really."

Forest walked her back to the front porch. He pulled a pair of gloves, two pairs of pliers, and a couple of knives from a wooden box. Stella assumed the gloves Forest handed her were his mother's. She felt like she was hijacking them as she slipped them on her hands. Forest pulled one of the green fruits from a bucket sitting at the feet of a rocking chair, and Stella sat down to watch him.

"You make a small cut, then you smash them, like this." Forest pressed the hull with his hands firmly and tossed it into a black device that sat on a small table. He then cranked the attached handle and the green hull was decimated, allowing a loose black walnut to fall from the other side.

"We'll prepare them first." Forest sat and continued making slight cuts and giving the hulls a smash. Stella did the same. "What else would you like to know?"

Stella considered grabbing her backpack from the house and asking Forest the questions she had prepared, but those wouldn't provide the answers she was searching for. The curiosity developing inside of her centered around neither the witches of West Virginia nor the wandmaker.

"I want to know more about your mother."

The sound of twigs crunching at the edge of the wood drew Stella's attention. Beatrice moved toward them, and as she grew closer, Stella noticed perspiration on her forehead and a paleness in her skin. Her eyes were wide at the fear that Beatrice may have heard her.

"Are you feeling okay?" Forest asked.

A hesitant, weary smile formed on Beatrice's face. "No,

I'm not. I gathered as much ginseng as I could before I lost my breakfast in the woods."

Stella followed as Forest stood and directed his mother into the house to a chair that faced the fireplace. Stella surveyed the room, her eyes landing on thick volumes that lined a bookcase.

"We have to stop. I'll take you back to the road," Forest said, regaining Stella's attention.

"One minute." Beatrice made eye contact with Stella. "Give us a moment alone, if you don't mind."

Forest's lips were tight as he gave a nod and left.

"How is your research coming?" Beatrice asked, her voice weak.

"We don't need to talk about that right now," Stella said as she sat down on the adjacent chair.

"Oh, please," Beatrice pleaded. "Don't do that. Don't feel sorry for me. I want to know about this article."

"I haven't worked on the article yet."

Beatrice nodded.

"You can read it when I'm finished." It was an offer Stella had never given an interviewee before. They rocked for a moment in silence.

"I want more time with you, Stella. I need to know why you're here." Beatrice stopped rocking. Her countenance changed and her eyes closed. "And ... I think I need your help. How long do you plan on staying?"

"I don't know."

"Come with me on an outing," Beatrice said, opening her eyes. "You already know our secrets, so you might as well see it all."

Warmth flooded Stella's body.

Dirty feet. A falling tree. Blue eyes. I love you, Stella.

She kept her eyes open and locked on Beatrice's, growing more confident that she could allow the visions to come without letting them take over.

"I want you to meet the trees."

What?

"This morning, you barely wanted me in your home. Now you want me to meet your family."

"Like I said, I need your help."

"I grew up in the city. I won't be much help in the woods."

Beatrice offered a grin and whispered, "I don't need your help in the woods, Stella. I'll explain."

"When?"

"Tomorrow, before the sun comes up. Bring a change of clothes. I don't know how long we will be gone."

"Beatrice ..." Stella's belly trembled at the sound of the woman's name on her lips. "Are you up for it?" Stella asked, and a flash of anger passed across Beatrice's face.

"I will be fine," she reassured. "I'll see you in the morning?"

"Yes," Stella breathed. "Yes."

CHAPTER 8

Beatrice

Beatrice and Forest never argued, but Stella's appearance seemed to make them both hypervigilant.

"I wish you had been kinder to her." Forest took a bite of his breakfast and swallowed it with a swig of coffee. "And now you're taking her to the Rock *and* the Peak?"

Beatrice had sojourned to the Peak to visit First Mother once before. Fifteen and heartbroken, she'd pleaded for the great tree to ask the Goddess to let her have a child early. The Goddess had answered her prayer.

"There's something about her, Forest. I can … smell it on her. She's here for a reason. And she may be able to help me with my illness." Beatrice choked down one more bite and regarded her son. "I'm sorry I got angry. You don't know all that's happened here on this mountain."

All that's happened to me.

"Then tell me." Forest laid his open palms on the table.

"Maybe someday," Beatrice said, though she knew she'd never share her darkest secrets with him. "You'll be alright while I'm gone?"

"Of course."

"Forest." Beatrice hesitated. She wiped her hands on the cloth napkin on her nap and took a sip of coffee before continuing. "Do you find Stella attractive? I wonder if she—"

"No, Mother." Forest stood and reached for Beatrice's plate to take to the sink, adding a final "no," as he turned away.

Beatrice's eyes fell to the floor, and she wondered if every mother worried about their sons the way she did Forest. She pressed up from the table, grabbed a walking stick, and moved closer to him.

"Be careful, Mother," Forest said, and Beatrice suspected he meant more than drinking enough water and taking things slow.

"I will," she said and gave him a hug.

When Beatrice stepped out the front door onto the porch, she found Stella scratching Arcas behind the ears and thanking him for accompanying her up the mountain.

"I think I can make it by myself next time," the woman said.

Beatrice stepped forward with a "good morning" and smiled. Stella did not reciprocate.

"Ready?" Beatrice asked.

"No," Stella admitted, and Beatrice watched the muscles in her jaw tense and release.

"Coming anyway?"

A nod. Good enough for Beatrice. She knew the trip would be longer than Stella expected; she also knew the woman would climb all the way. Beatrice hadn't a clue what the ramifications of bringing an outsider into the sacred circle might be, but she chose to follow her gut.

"I packed a few extra things," Beatrice said. "I'm taking you to the Peak."

"The Peak? How long will that take?"

"At least two days."

Stella's eyes widened.

"Come on." Beatrice jerked her head. She could hear Stella's footsteps behind her, clumsy and twisting around the branches as they made their way behind her home. The summer's ripeness was ending, but the forest's lushness still held warmth and humidity.

"We'll start at the Rock."

A silent Stella made no effort to catch up with Beatrice, who wasn't moving quickly herself. Her body wouldn't allow it. Beatrice wanted the woman to walk beside her. To talk with her. Stella showed humility and reverence as Beatrice challenged her to the climb, both qualities she appreciated.

A sound from above cued Beatrice's glance upward.

"Ahh. Joining us, Gertrude?"

Beatrice bent over, opened her pack, and pulled out her leather gloves. The great golden eagle drifted overhead, swooping down in elegant circles until she landed heavily on Beatrice's arm. Beatrice observed an open-mouthed, wide-eyed Stella, appreciating the awe that filled the woman's face.

"Gertrude, this is Stella. Stella, meet Gertrude. Can she touch you, Gertie?" Beatrice asked the bird.

The eagle gave a gentle coo.

"Come on." She gestured to Stella with an outstretched arm. Stella didn't move, so Beatrice took the woman's hand and guided it up to the eagle's wing with a humble stroke. She could hear Stella's breathing, short, shallow bursts.

"Tell her thank you," Beatrice whispered, and she found Stella's eyes spilling tears.

"Thank you," Stella said.

"I'll tell you about her when I know I can trust you."

Gertrude lifted off from Beatrice's arm and pumped her wings until she was high in the air. Beatrice made eye contact with Stella, who wiped her tears with her sleeve.

"Do you usually cry this easily?"

Tears frustrated Beatrice, unless they were Forest's. Stella frowned and didn't reply. Beatrice took her walking stick to the earth once more. As they continued hiking, each voice chimed in.

Edith. *She's a threat.*

Martha. *Tell her to leave.*

Imogene. *She'll weave lies about you.*

Thelma. *We don't want to see her.*

Even Ida, the only other plant worker in the family. *Don't bring her here.*

Beatrice paused and closed her eyes for a moment, isolating the voice she trusted the most.

I want to meet her, Beatrice. Grandmother. *Be kind. She's afraid.*

I'm trying. Beatrice pushed the thought into the air.

Don't listen to her! Edith insisted.

Beatrice clicked her tongue and started walking again.

First Mother's voice brought her to a halt. She steadied herself against a tree, closing her eyes.

Try not to fear, Beatrice. You are right. She is here for a reason.

"Are *you* alright?" Stella asked, interrupting the voices.

"Yes. They talk to me all the time." Beatrice opened her eyes but continued leaning on the tree. "My ancestors. My grandmother. My great-great grandmother. They all have different things to say about you."

"Do they want me here?"

"Most of them don't. But my grandmother wants to meet you."

Beatrice tried to make meaning of the woman's arrival as they continued walking, Stella following more closely now. Forest was clear he didn't want Stella as a partner, but could she be a new vessel and continue the line?

The ground beneath the women's feet sloped upward

as they came closer and closer to the Rock, and within a few moments, they arrived at the place of first and final breaths.

"Which one is your mother?"

Of course, she would ask.

Beatrice, her grandmother whispered, *open up to her.*

"She's not here," Beatrice said as she locked eyes with Stella. "My mother left when I was fourteen."

"She left you here? In the forest?" Stella's voice was steeped in judgment.

Beatrice nodded.

"Two years before she left, a man came. He was hunting in the woods and hurt himself. A broken leg. His name is Eric." Beatrice considered her use of the present tense and shifted. "He was wonderful. My mother fell in love with him ..." Beatrice firmed her voice. " ...and they had a child together." Beatrice focused her attention on her feet and curled her toes in her shoes. "My sister grew ill, and Mother insisted on taking her to the hospital. So, they left, and I haven't seen them since."

"Beatrice ..." Stella whispered. "I'm sorry."

Beatrice stared into oblivion for a moment, reliving those last moments when she heard her mother and Papa in the woods searching for her, pleading, finally deciding they couldn't search any longer. Their youngest daughter needed them more.

Tell her.

"My mother wouldn't listen to me." Beatrice's tight, dry throat made her voice crack; she reprimanded herself for getting emotional. "Gertrude, my sister, didn't like being human. She hated the feel of the body. The bones and the clunkiness of it. So, she abandoned it. Her spirit left before her body died. I watched a silver ribbon rise from her sick little body into the sky and right into an eagle's nest."

Stella's eyes narrowed and her brow furrowed. "Gertrude is your sister?"

Beatrice looked up into her grandmother's branches. Gertrude, perched high, watched carefully over their movements, listening intently to her words.

"Her spirit in a different body. She's ..." Beatrice looked back at Stella. " ...more than the rest of us, somehow."

"Demigoddess," Stella whispered.

"What?" Beatrice questioned.

"When a god, or goddess, mates with a mortal, the offspring is called a demigod in many mythologies."

"I know different mythologies." Beatrice reflected on the volumes of books Imogene stored in bookshelves around the home and the stacks Forest brought from the library. "Is that what *you* think we are?"

"I still don't know what I believe." Trepidation spread over the young woman's face and silence took over.

"Come." Beatrice broke the tense silence. "Meet my grandmother."

She turned, walked softly over to the Rock, shifted to her knees, and bowed until her forehead touched the roots of a birch tree.

"Good morning, Grandmother. I told you I'd come back soon," she breathed to the roots. "Come closer, Stella," Beatrice encouraged without looking. "Kneel." She felt movement beside her as Stella bowed in her peripheral vision.

Movements created bulges and ripples in the tree's bark until the face of Beatrice's grandmother appeared. Through the gray, white bark, blue eyes pierced. Beatrice felt Stella's body stiffen beside her and the woman released a gasp before suspending the function entirely.

"Breathe, dear," Grandmother said. "Don't be afraid. You can touch my face."

Stella didn't move and, once again, Beatrice had to guide

the woman's hand for her. Beatrice could feel the tension in Stella's body and encouraged her to relax.

"I never thought I'd see the day when *you* told someone else to relax, Beatrice." After the quip, Grandmother turned her attention to Stella. "My name is Beulah. I'm glad my granddaughter brought you."

Stella's mouth moved but no words came. Beatrice smirked at the speechlessness.

"I'm taking her to the Peak to meet First Mother."

"No chocolate today?" Grandmother asked without acknowledging Beatrice's comment.

"We're out. I'll bring you some soon," Beatrice replied.

"You like chocolate?" Stella asked with a trembling voice, and Beatrice smiled.

"Mmmm. It's delicious."

"How do you—"

"Through my roots. It dissolves and decomposes. I'm sure it tastes better with a tongue, but it's still wonderful to me."

"Did you have a chance to try it before you ..." Beatrice watched Stella's face redden and knew the woman wished she could eat her words.

"No, Stella," Grandmother responded.

Stella's face grew more serious as she studied the tree, from her roots to the highest branch.

"Did it hurt?" Stella asked as she fingered the bark along Grandmother's eyes.

Beatrice's eyes widened at the question and she looked from Stella to the tree, whose countenance darkened. Beatrice had pondered this question many times, but fear of hurting her grandmothers—or perhaps fear of their truth—prevented her from asking.

"Not physically," the tree responded, her voice tender.

Beatrice's eyes continued to dart back and forth between the stranger and her grandmother.

"My entire body tingled, and for a moment I was nothing

more than energy. Then I felt my toes grow long and my spine stretch, and my arms grow into the sky. I wasn't a tall woman. Now, I can see for miles. I suppose that part isn't so bad. But I will never forget my daughter's terrified face."

Beatrice's stomach roiled at the mention of her mother, and her face came to mind despite her resistance. Blue eyes full of tears. Hair wild and unkempt. The indignation Beatrice had felt the moment her mother left rose within her again, a flame from her bowels to her throat.

A wind rippled through the forest, reminding Beatrice to breathe.

"It would have terrified me," Stella replied.

"We need to keep going." Beatrice felt a catch in her throat again and cleared it away. She stood and nodded to Stella. "There's a cave that makes a good camping spot. I'd like to reach it before nightfall."

Stella stayed at the base of the tree and raised her hand once more to Grandmother's face. "Can I come again?" she asked.

"Please do."

"Thank you for showing me your face."

Beatrice felt a hard constriction in her throat and embers of tears behind her eyes. She had not predicted that her own heart would break again. She closed her eyes tightly for a moment, trying to blink away images of her mother. Her long blonde hair and high cheekbones. When she wasn't successful, Beatrice clicked her tongue and glanced back at Stella, who moved reluctantly toward her, brushing dirt and bits of leaves from her clothes toward her. "Come on," Beatrice urged, and they continued walking.

"I don't want to talk anymore about my mother," Beatrice said as she led Stella toward her great-grandmother, Ola.

"Okay," Stella whispered and placed her hand on Beatrice's back.

CHAPTER 9

Madeline

Madeline zipped Gwen's hiking pack after reviewing its contents. Sleepless nights haunted by visions of Gwen packing her suitcase persuaded Madeline to ask the woman she loved to come with her up the mountain. She promised Gwen that as they climbed, she would tell her everything.

Gwen eyed her expectantly. "Do I have what I need?"

Madeline nodded and bent down for a kiss. The two had spent the evening in separate beds in a tiny, dank hotel room overlooking the river. Gwen worked hard to pull Madeline out of anxious melancholy by leading her through a short yoga practice and finding a comedy for the two of them to watch. When the movie was over, Gwen straddled Madeline's body and kissed her mouth and her neck and her throat and her ears. But fear kept a secure hold on Madeline, and she swallowed down thoughts of giving in fully to the physical sensations that coursed through her. Eventually, Gwen kissed Madeline on the forehead and moved back to her own bed.

Madeline strapped her own pack to her back and gathered up her phone and the room key. "Ready?" she asked Gwen, who nodded in reply.

As the two walked across the road, Madeline glanced up at the face of the rock, then back at Gwen.

"I've got this," Gwen assured as she moved to find secure hand and footholds.

They ascended with ease. Gwen gave Madeline a high five when they reached the top, then looked back, her eyes roaming over the mountains. Madeline tugged on her hand. Impatient. Anxious. "Come on."

"It's beautiful. Can't we slow down so that I can take it all in?"

Madeline laced her fingers through Gwen's, joining her in admiring the view. Orange and yellow leaves peppered those still green, and through a break in the trees, she could see the river.

"That's the New River?" Gwen asked.

"Yes," Madeline said.

"What's the town like?"

"I haven't been since Gertrude died." Madeline did her best to keep the impatience from her voice. "But it's small and tired. The city may overwhelm me, but at least I can hide there. In a small town like that one, everyone knows everyone."

Madeline turned, pulled Gwen's hand, and they walked without speaking for several minutes.

"Madeline." Gwen interrupted the quiet. "I can't imagine there is anything you could tell me that would make me leave you. Well, if you're a serial killer ..."

"What I'm going to tell you is more unbelievable than that," Madeline insisted.

"Are you a CIA operative?"

"I'm not even sure what that is."

94

Gwen's eyes flicked upward, and Madeline took a deep breath.

"I was raised on this mountain. We didn't have electricity or a modern toilet. We ate what we hunted and the vegetables and fruit that we grew or foraged."

Madeline closed her eyes and felt Gwen squeeze her hand.

"I had a mother, but not a father ..."

Madeline told the tale of First Mother and how the world thought she was nonsensical, so they institutionalized and overmedicated her. She spoke of the Goddess who lifted First Mother out of despair and created a family with her. Generations of women born to serve as vessels for daughters to live and breathe the life of the forest. She shared stories of her mother, whose hair was golden like her own, but so long it touched the backs of her knees. Stories of roasted rabbit and chestnuts, the art of baking biscuits, and an orphaned coyote pup, Pepper, whom she nursed from infancy and became a protective companion. Occasionally, Madeline's eyes welled with tears that spilled down her cheeks, and Gwen would stop walking and wipe them with the sleeve of her shirt.

"Do you understand so far?" Madeline asked.

Gwen's eyes were wide as she said, "As much as I can."

"But do you believe me?"

"Of course I do, Maddie."

They stayed still for a moment, taking in the sounds of the forest, the birds, and the breeze.

"Do you know the names of all the trees and birds?" Gwen asked, her eyes scanning the branches.

"Not all of them," Madeline said, her eyes upward toward a red cardinal that perched on a branch of an oak. "I'm sure Beatrice does by now."

"Beatrice?" Gwen's voice was curious. "You have another daughter."

"Yes." Madeline's mind flicked to her mother instead of to Beatrice. Perhaps she just wasn't ready to share about her eldest daughter. "My mother didn't want to go." Madeline felt lightheaded and moved toward a fallen log to sit for just a moment. "She held onto me." Her cries turned into sobs, and she covered her face in her hands and brought her head between her knees.

"Hey. Slow down. It's okay." Gwen placed a hand on Madeline's shoulder.

"The thing is," Madeline continued, "I knew it would be that way for her. She never wanted it. She never wanted me to go to the Rock in the first place, but ..."

"The Rock?"

How in the world do I explain it?

Madeline prepared herself for Gwen's inevitable departure from her life. There was no way the woman would stay once she heard what Madeline had done.

"The Goddess came to me," she whispered. Gwen's lips parted, but she kept her hand on Madeline's shoulder. "Our Goddess. She has wild red hair and gray eyes. Anyway, she showed Beatrice to me ... this tiny, brown-haired toddler with a big giggle."

Madeline painted the picture of the moment her daughter took her first drink from her breast, and her mother sank deep into the ground, weeping with reluctance, then sprang up again with branches and leaves.

"A tree?" Gwen pulled her hand from Madeline's shoulder, tucked her chin, and looked up through furrowed brows. "Your mother changed into a tree?"

"And every woman before her." Madeline started walking again, choosing silence for a long time.

"My daughter was such a beautiful child. She looked so different from me. Thick, curly dark hair, with these intense, dark eyes. We had different gifts. Beatrice was a plant worker. She knew all the plants in the woods and

96

how they could heal. She was forever blending concoctions to try on me. But she was also so human. She could feel when I was sad. And she never let me use magic to do the dishes. She always did them with her hands. My grandmother was a healer. My great grandmother wielded fire. I can do both."

Gwen raised a palm. "Wait. You never mentioned fire."

Madeline felt her face flush. "It only comes when I'm angry. You must think I'm crazy."

"No, Maddie. I don't." Gwen took her hand and squeezed it. "I've seen you heal and predict the future and move things with just your thoughts. Why wouldn't I believe you?"

"Thank you," Madeline said, then continued the story. "When Beatrice was twelve, a hunter came through. Eric. She found him in the woods. He had broken his leg. He was lost and cold and hungry. And very handsome. I let him in, nursed him back to health, and he went away. Then in the springtime, he came back and asked me to marry him, and I said yes. I loved him," Madeline sighed, "and so did Beatrice. They were so similar. They liked to create things and whittle together. Eric taught her how to use his camera and hunt and different ways to smoke and cure meat."

Madeline smiled as she talked about her wedding day. Beatrice had woven a flower crown for her and arranged a beautiful bouquet with a floral combination Madeline never would have thought to put together.

"The next year, I had Gertrude. She looked like Eric, and Beatrice adored her, or at least I thought. She was a fussy baby."

Madeline called to mind the sleepless nights walking the floor with Gertrude. It didn't matter if she was well-fed and dry, she wailed.

"She got sick when she was eighteen months old.

Coughing. Raging fever, all of it. Eric and I agreed to take her to the hospital in town. Beatrice refused to go with us. She said she needed to stay and keep after the house. Home meant so much to her. 'I'll be fine!' she insisted, but I packed a bag for her, anyway."

Madeline's eyes felt irritated and exhausted from the crying.

"Anyway, she hid. We searched and searched, but we couldn't find her. Gertrude's body was giving up." Madeline stopped walking again and squared her body with Gwen's. "I chose one child over the other. I left my fourteen-year-old daughter in the middle of the woods on a mountaintop." Her hushed voice pleaded. "What kind of mother does that?"

A long pause invaded the space between them.

"The hospital in town told us we needed to take her to a bigger city in Virginia. Gertrude was in such poor shape we didn't have time to find Beatrice and tell her we were going farther. We were there for two months before she died in my arms. I couldn't let go of her little body, and Eric couldn't stand being near her. He went back to the house, and I held her until they forced me to let her go. He was hanging by his belt from the closet shelf when I got back."

"Oh, Maddie. Come here." Gwen wrapped Madeline in a tight embrace. Clouds gathered and grayed the sky above them, and misting drizzle began to fall. Madeline pulled away from Gwen and felt panic zip up her body.

"I had no way to give them a proper funeral. I only had enough money for one urn and the fee to collect their ashes."

They walked farther into the forest, and eventually they came to their destination: the Hedge. Madeline examined it. It was taller than ever and wrapped with tangles of thorns. She pulled the pack from her back and withdrew the letter she had written for Beatrice. She did this every time she came to the Hedge, praying that one day her words would make through the green wall even if she couldn't.

Tucking them into the roots, Madeline whispered, "Please, get this to her. I mean her no harm." She understood the possibility that the words had slipped through, and Beatrice remained unforgiving. Glancing back at Gwen she insisted, "Do not follow me," and began to climb.

She ascended around seven feet without incident, but without warning the Hedge began to writhe. The green, snaking vines pulled Madeline from her hold on the branches and held her in the air before lifting her higher and hurling to the ground, where she landed. Sickening cracks and excruciating pain stabbed through Madeline as various bones in her body snapped, bringing a wave of nausea over her. But before she could be sick, daylight faded to darkness.

A vision. A message. A warning. Something formed in her mind as she lay unconscious.

For the first time in twenty years, Madeline saw her daughter. Her face was tilted downward, but she recognized the deep chestnut curls, now highlighted with silver. Beatrice kneeled over a body and vines flowed from her hands around the limbs and deep into the mouth. Madeline ran toward the scene and realized it was Gwen! Her Gwen, laying before her daughter, who was killing her. Fire and the sizzle of heat and vines flooded Madeline's vision, and the fire was losing.

"Madeline." Gwen's voice sounded so distant. "Madeline!"

Madeline's body throbbed as she felt her breath return to her. She moaned and rolled to her side, her vision blurred. The deep, quiet unconscious beckoned her, and she closed her eyes again. Golden shimmers moved within and around Madeline, mending muscles, knitting bones, and relieving bruises. When she opened her eyes again, her vision was clear.

"We have to go!" she cried as she bolted upright. "Now."

Standing brought a brief lightheadedness, but after a breath, Madeline had her hand on Gwen's elbow urging her to move.

"You can't be here, Gwen," Madeline panted.

The women ran over rocks and tree roots as fast as their feet would carry them. They scaled down the rock at the edge of the mountain, and at the bottom, Gwen's eyes probed Madeline's.

"We need to keep going."

Madeline led Gwen across the road, and her hands shook as she withdrew the keys to the rental car from her pocket and threw them to Gwen.

"You drive," she instructed as she removed her pack, threw it in the back seat, and jumped into the passenger side.

"Some of our things are still in the hotel, Madeline."

"They don't matter," Madeline said.

"Maddie—" Gwen started.

"Go!" she insisted.

"Madeline ..." Gwen tried again, her voice calm but firm. "I want to get my things from the room."

"Of course." Madeline shook her head as if it would stop the panic. "I'll stand watch out here. Will you get my things as well?"

Gwen nodded. Within five minutes, she spun the car out of the driveway of the hotel.

Half an hour passed in silence, then Gwen started to cry.

"I thought you were dead, Madeline. Your life is terrifying." Madeline watched Gwen's throat bob. "What did you see when you fell?"

"She's going to kill you. If she ever gets the opportunity to be around you, she's going to kill you."

"Who?"

"Beatrice."

***

Madeline resisted Gwen's affections on the way home. This woman she'd only known a few months had become so dear to her heart, and now she had to pull back. No, not just pull back—sever. Sever any attachment or hope. The trip home took eight hours, and though Madeline wanted to part ways at the airport, Gwen insisted on making sure she was home safe.

"Let me tuck you in," she said at the door, looking up into Madeline's face.

"Gwen, I think we need to take some time apart."

Gwen shifted her weight from foot to foot and crossed her arms tightly across her chest. "How long are you thinking, Maddie?" she asked.

"I don't know, Gwen. You would be crazy to stay with me after what I saw."

"Let me come in."

Madeline closed her eyes and opened the door. Gwen followed close behind her as she entered her apartment.

"Listen," Gwen started, "I'm okay with space and time. I need to process everything myself, but don't give up on us." She lifted her warm hands to Madeline's face, then pulled them back with a simple ask. "Call me, okay?" she said as she turned to leave Madeline's apartment without offering a kiss.

***

A day passed, then a night. Then another day and night. Two weeks, and Madeline continued to curl into herself. She cleared her schedule and set up a greeting on her phone, claiming she was booked for six months. Sleep took her in the day, and anxiety made her pace the floor at night. Now that she had seen Beatrice's face, that was all Madeline could see.

101

CHAPTER 10

Stella

Stella couldn't stop thinking about Beulah's blue eyes.
Is it possible? Could Beulah be the woman I keep seeing?

They were the precise shape and shade of blue, and the voice, oh the voice! The words, 'I love you, Stella,' replayed in Stella's mind, and she could almost feel the touch of warm palms on her face.

"Stella." Beatrice's voice drew Stella out of her reverie. "Next one."

Stella stopped behind Beatrice, in front of a tree at least ten feet taller than Beulah with a thicker girth. The tree's bark wasn't smooth like the birch tree's. Rough and brownish gray, the corky bark peaked in ridges that formed irregular diamond shapes. Stella reached out to feel the difference between Beulah's bark and her mother's, but before her fingertips could make contact, Beatrice stopped her.

"No!" Beatrice pulled Stella's arm back and gave her a disapproving glare. "This is Ola. My great-grandmother.

She doesn't speak to me. She doesn't speak to anyone. Grandmother says it's because Ola feels guilty about the way she treated her."

"What did she do to Beulah?" The intense protectiveness Stella felt over the tree startled her.

She watched as Beatrice's gaze swooped from the top of the tree and back down to its roots. "It's not my story to tell."

Seems to be a theme.

Beatrice turned to Stella, arched one eyebrow, and added, "I learned what little I know about Ola from her mother, Edith. Her gifts included healing and insurmountable strength."

Beatrice stopped talking for a moment and glanced back at Beulah, whose face had receded into the bark. She brought her voice down to a whisper and leaned closer to Stella. "Her favorite treat was spiced orange tea. I bring her some each year on her birthday. I bring them all something they loved on their birthdays." Beatrice tilted her head and refocused her eyes on the tree. "It would be wrong to leave her out."

"What kind of tree is she?"

"White ash." Beatrice walked toward the next tree, but Stella didn't follow.

"And this is Edith, Ola's—"

"Beatrice," Stella said, taking off her pack and laying on the ground. Beatrice watched her with frowning eyes. "Can I please take notes? Just for me." Stella pressed her hand against her heart to emphasize the point.

Beatrice responded with crossed arms and narrowed eyes.

"Listen, I can fill a notebook with a list of enchanted trees, take it to my editor, tell her about seeing a face in bark—a talking face, no less—and she'll look at me like I'm crazy. And then she'll fire me." Stella bent down, unzipped her pack, pulled out a notepad and a pen. "There's no story here for the readers of my magazine."

"Then who would you be writing for?"

"For me," Stella repeated.

Beatrice agreed to Stella's request, then turned back to the tree. "As I was saying, this is Edith."

"The bark is different." Stella walked to Beatrice's side. "It doesn't make diamond shapes like Ola's does."

As Stella took a step closer to the tree, her foot rolled on a round object underfoot. Beatrice caught her from falling.

"Edith is a sweet gum tree, and what you just stepped on is a seed capsule."

Stella bent down and picked up the spiky, round ball. "We have these in New York. Sheesh, Beatrice. You had me out here with no shoes on." She playfully threw the seed pod at Beatrice, who released a small laugh. "We have all kinds of trees in New York. I've just never really slowed down enough to notice the differences."

"Their leaves are different, too."

Stella bent down once more to pick up a star-shaped leaf.

"There was a time I could tell you the difference between an oak and a maple leaf, but ..." *That was when my father was alive.* Stella lifted herself up to stand again and sighed. "Edith. What's she like?"

"Edith worked with fire. Her charms keep a fire in the stove and the bathtub water hot. Her companion was a salamander."

Stella couldn't keep the smile off her face if she tried. "How does one keep a salamander as a pet?"

"Oh, no, no, no." Beatrice shook her head. "Companions are not our pets. They come to us on their own terms and stick around whether we like it or not. I'm sure Edith and the salamander took good care of each other."

Beatrice introduced each grandmother along the way. Stella's hand complained at the rapid scribbling. Edith's mother, Martha, a red maple, worked with water. She channeled it from a spring and into a pool. Her charms ensure clean water in the sinks and in the bathtub.

"Okay, but who built the sinks and the bathtubs?" Stella interrupted.

"We're getting there, Stella. One grandmother at a time."

"Wait!" Stella grasped Beatrice's arm before she could move to the next tree. "What was Martha's companion animal?"

"A great egret."

They moved on to a large conifer, with berries nestled against scale-like green leaves, its brown bark peeling away in shaggy strings. This time, Stella couldn't help but touch bark, leaves, and berries, but once Beatrice began to speak, Stella recorded notes in her notebook.

Thelma. Juniper. Dog companion. Metal worker. Crafted pots, pans, and utensils. Worked with Martha to bring water into the house. Stella wanted to ask about the bathtub again, but one look at Beatrice's pale and clammy face made her refrain.

"You okay?" she asked.

"Are you hungry?" Beatrice asked back, avoiding the question.

"Yes," Stella affirmed. "I was just about to ask you the same."

"My appetite has been off. Forgive me." Beatrice caught Stella's gaze. "These days I eat only because I know I'm supposed to. Nothing seems appealing." Beatrice motioned with her finger to an outcropping of rocks. "Here is a good spot."

They walked toward the gray, moss-covered stones and settled down on them. Stella moved things around in her bag until she came to her metal water bottle. She watched with curiosity as Beatrice pulled out biscuits, wrapped and tied in thin fabric, extracting one for Stella and one for herself, followed by dried deer meat, apples, and nuts.

"I can cook something more substantial for dinner," Beatrice said.

"Cook? With what?"

"I brought things to cook with." Beatrice's voice was a little lighter than it had been and offered playfulness at Stella's question.

"How heavy is your pack?" Stella asked.

Beatrice seemed to breathe in the frustrating question and then sigh it out, then she handed Stella the pack.

Jesus.

"Let's switch for a bit after we eat," Stella suggested.

"You got quiet on me," Beatrice said then bit into her biscuit.

"So did you," Stella responded, before tugging a piece of spicy, chewy jerky into her mouth.

"My grandmother likes you."

Stella closed her eyes, and the visions bubbled up again.

"What do you see?" Beatrice asked. "You've been having visions. I've noticed your face. My mother's face changed in the same way when she saw things."

"I had someone tell me my future," Stella offered, then she opened her eyes and took a bite of her biscuit. The texture of the cold bread differed from the biscuits right out of the oven, but she enjoyed it anyway.

"Oh. And what did she say?" Beatrice asked with a face full of skepticism.

"You won't believe me."

"Tell me anyway."

"Well, I wasn't the one to set up the appointment. The man I'm with, Roger, he scheduled it. She wouldn't read for him because he'd had alcohol beforehand."

Beatrice nodded. "And apparently, he wasn't taking it seriously. He would have asked you if he had."

"I know. Anyway, she still offered to read for me."

"And what did she use?" Beatrice asked, palming a handful of nuts.

"Tarot. Tea leaves. My hands."

"Mother didn't need anything like that," Beatrice said, her gaze moving to somewhere past the forest. Stella noticed Beatrice's mention of her mother, but feared bringing attention to it.

"She saw me leaving New York. She saw woods and a woman's dirty feet and a man's curly dark hair. She couldn't see faces, though. That really frustrated her."

"What was her name?"

"Marin."

Stella watched as Beatrice stopped eating her biscuit and wrapped the second half back up. "I don't trust most people who say they can read futures."

"You never told me what Beulah's ..." Stella searched for the right word "gift is."

Beatrice turned her face toward Stella's. "She doesn't have one."

"Oh."

Stella finished her lunch in silence, taking her time even though Beatrice had satisfied her own diminished appetite with a few nibbles. As she ate, a frustration built inside of her at the dismissal of her experience.

"Will you meet me halfway, Beatrice?"

"What do you mean?" Beatrice looked at Stella a little more softly.

"You are offering me something here, something empowering and humbling. And it could change my life, but remember, I had a life before I came here. I don't have the same connection to the earth." Stella watched as Beatrice's eyebrows furrowed. "But I have experiences."

Catching Stella off guard, Beatrice reached out, grabbed her hand, and flipped it over to review her palm. "Divining is not my skill. I work with plants and speak with animals and my ancestors." She leveled her eyes with Stella's. "My mother could snap her fingers and make things move. Spark fires. Heal. I can't see the future, but I trust my gut. You're here for a reason, I'm just not sure what."

Neither am I.

Stella breathed more freely as the wall between them eased.

"We only have two more trees to visit before we get to First Mother. The cave is just a bit further."

"Let me do the cleaning up," Stella said. "You rest a bit."

Defeated resignation darkened Beatrice's face. The woman nodded and sat on the rock. Once Stella finished packing up, they climbed until they found the cave where Beatrice wanted to camp. Stella never went camping as a child. Never slept outside with her shoulder blades pressed into the earth as she lay wrapped in a blanket of thick, inky darkness pierced by stars. Beatrice went to sleep at once, and Stella listened to her heavy breathing.

Are those dirty feet yours, Beatrice?

***

The sound of retching woke Stella, and she leaped up to find Beatrice emptying her stomach behind a tree.

She placed a hand on Beatrice's back as she continued to cough, the smell of vomit wafting between them. "Are you alright?"

"No." Beatrice leaned her head against the tree as she spoke. "But we only have a little farther."

"Would eating something help?"

"Sometimes it does. Other times, everything just comes right back up."

"Maybe you should see a doctor," Stella said.

"No," Beatrice said with finality, then she began gathering wood, only to tire with little effort. Stella took over, and Beatrice sat down on a rock and placed her head in her hands.

"What about your great-grandmother?" Stella asked. "You said she was a healer."

"She won't help me. I'm sure of it." Beatrice raised her head and faced the sun with closed eyes.

"Beatrice, I think you're really sick."

"I think I'm dying," Beatrice replied unsentimentally as she opened her eyes to Stella.

"And you'd rather die than go to a doctor?"

Beatrice drew in a deep breath. "Next year, I'll be the same age my grandmothers were when they transitioned." The woman swallowed and cleared her throat. "I want to be with them in these woods. And I'm in Forest's way."

"Forest would be heartbroken if something happened to you."

"He has no future with me. He has no future in the woods." Beatrice's eyes flicked down briefly, then back up to search Stella's face. She smiled a whimsical smile and moved once again around the cave. Beatrice started a fire and withdrew the small cast-iron skillet from her pack. Stella offered to help, but Beatrice refused. Instead, she scooped butter and cracked eggs into the skillet and held them over the fire. The eggs sizzled for a few moments, then Beatrice expertly flipped them to the other side without breaking the yolks.

Stella noted her traveling companion's food intake: the half biscuit she didn't eat during yesterday's lunch, nothing for dinner, and half of an egg for breakfast. When Beatrice finished, she sat with her back against the rock, crossed her legs, and closed her eyes.

"What are your other symptoms?"

"I'll show you, but not now. We need to finish."

After only a few minutes of walking, Beatrice paused at a smaller tree clothed in dense layers of clustered, oblong leaves. Beatrice peeled back the foliage and whispered, "Hi, Ida." Then she tilted her head as if listening. "Please, Ida ..." Beatrice's lips formed a small smile, and Stella wondered what the woman was asking of the tree. "Well, can I at least share a pawpaw with her?" The small smile turned to a grin as Beatrice said, "Thank you."

Beatrice pulled out from under the leaves, holding a green fruit that covered the size of her hand. "Ida had one of the same gifts I have. She worked with plants. This ..." Beatrice held the fruit out for Stella to investigate. " ...is a pawpaw."

Beatrice unzipped her pack, withdrew a knife, and sliced it in two, revealing a creamy yellow meat and a few seeds. She removed the seeds and handed half to Stella.

"Like this," she said, then pressed against the skin, smashing the contents upward. Stella watched Beatrice take a bite, then sigh contentedly.

Stella followed directions. The flavor, a cross between a banana and a mango, shocked her. "Mmm. Delicious."

"Ida and I get along. She's not happy with me right now, though." Beatrice finished eating the fruit, then tossed the skin to the ground. "Imogene is next."

Beatrice explained that Imogene, First Mother's daughter, was the keeper of stories who organized the books that her mother brought with her up the mountain. A Christian bible. A book of fairy tales. Frankenstein. Leaves of Grass. The Legend of Sleepy Hollow. Political texts from the time of the Revolution, things most men thought First Mother had no business reading.

"She was a writer, like you. She's the one who wrote the first journal. Every woman after her kept her own and added it to the collection. Except my mother." Beatrice sighed. "My mother put doors on the bookshelf and locked the books up. I broke into it after she left. Imogene was also a weaver. She brought forth thread the way I can bring forth vines, spun it, and made clothes of all sizes, thinking ahead." She came to a stop in front of a tall oak tree. "Imogene, weaver of thread and stories."

"Wait! Will you show me your vines?"

"Not yet."

Oak bark shifted, and Beatrice's eyes widened. Stella took a step back as eyelids lifted, revealing bright disks of amber.

"Hello, Stella."

"Hi," Stella whispered in return.

"Beatrice tells me you want to write our story, and I give you permission to write it."

"What?" Beatrice glanced toward Stella, then back at Imogene.

"Make it a work of fiction."

Stella squirmed under the tree's gaze. "I'm not trained in fiction, but I can try."

The tree smirked. "You don't need to be trained to be a good storyteller. Write it. It would please me for our story to be out in the world."

A tingling tickled Stella's skin, gooseflesh popping to the surface.

"That won't please the rest of us!" Beatrice rebuked.

"Don't let my mother scare you, Stella." Imogene ignored Beatrice's argument. "She's kind."

With that, the tree closed her eyes. Beatrice released a sigh and rolled her eyes. "Let's go."

The next moments passed in silence.

"Alright," Beatrice said softly. "Be very humble, Stella. She's the Goddess's companion."

"Companion?" Stella asked.

Beatrice glared at Stella and drew closer. "Lover," she released in a tense, low whisper.

"Oh ..."

After several minutes of climbing, they came to a large

pine that stretched to the sky. Beatrice kneeled and bowed her head, and Stella did the same.

"Beatrice." A voice, powerful and steady, vibrated from the tree.

"Hello, First Mother."

The shifting of bark revealed a round face and dark brown eyes.

"I've brought you an offering." Beatrice's own voice didn't falter, but Stella noticed a formality in her movements as she sliced oranges into small wedges and arranged them around the root of the tree.

"Thank you, Beatrice. My favorite. They remind me of Christmas. Now, who is this?"

"Stella. She's a writer from a city far from here. She wants to write about us."

"Well, I ..." Stella wanted to clarify Beatrice's statement.

"Why have you brought her to me?" First Mother interjected.

Stella glanced at Beatrice and noticed silent breaths rising and falling from her chest. Her own body grew tense, and she nibbled on her thumbnail as she waited for Beatrice to respond.

"Because I don't know why she's here, First Mother."

"I suspect you hope she will be a new vessel; a new daughter of the woods. Yes?"

Beatrice kept her head down. Stella's heart pounded. She wanted to be part of the conversation as her brain propelled her to the worst-case scenario. Beatrice could force her to stay. Tie her up with those vines. Make her lay with the Goddess, whatever that looked like.

Beatrice lifted her head once more. "I don't understand why things are the way they are for me. I'm the only one who had a son." Beatrice's voice grew quieter with each word.

113

"I don't know why the Goddess gave you Forest, Beatrice," First Mother said. "She doesn't tell me everything."

"If Forest has children, will they—?"

"They will belong to him and his partner."

"Why?" Beatrice whispered in a shaky voice. "Why wasn't he given ..."

"I don't know. Forest's future is up to him. The Goddess does not dictate—"

"What have we done to make Her so angry?" Beatrice cried. Her face fell, and a flush came upon it. Stella stopped biting her nail and placed a hand on the woman's back.

"I know our Goddess," First Mother said, her voice soothing. "She will continue building a family for Herself. She could create planets, but aways chooses family."

A wind rustled leaves around the forest floor, swirling them up in gentle spirals.

"And Stella does not want this," First Mother explained, and Beatrice turned her eyes to Stella. "And the Goddess will force no one to join Her against Her will."

"I was hopeful." Beatrice slumped as she confessed.

Stella noticed how much her face had changed. The sun both shadowed and highlighted the woman's exhaustion and emotions.

"Go home now and do not worry."

The conversation between First Mother and Beatrice might have finished, but Stella still had questions.

"Wait," Stella said. Both gray and brown eyes found hers. "Do you know anything about Beatrice's mother? Do you see her?"

"That is a bold question," the tree spoke. "No. Occasionally, the trees strike up a conversation about Madeline, but no one knows what has become of her."

"Don't you want to know where she is?"

"Madeline separated herself from this family the moment she watched Beulah transition. She made it clear by

114

avoiding us that she wants nothing to do with this family." A root pulled from the ground and wrapped around Beatrice's shoulder. "The Goddess tells me she does still pray, occasionally."

"She's alive." Beatrice's voice was small.

"Indeed. You are not the oldest human in our line."

Stella watched as Beatrice drew close and whispered something to the tree.

"Only you can decide that," the tree whispered back.

"Thank you," Beatrice responded.

Beatrice stood, extended her hand, placed it on the tree, and closed her eyes. "Let's go."

"Are you okay?" Stella asked as they began to descend.

"I'm …" Beatrice seemed to search the forest floor for the words as she walked forward. " …sad."

"I'm sorry," Stella replied.

"Never mind." Beatrice waved her disappointment away with her hand. "So, this man, Roger—"

"I'm going to end it," Stella interrupted.

The reality hit Stella like a bucket of cold water dumped on her head, and evidently it had the same impact on Beatrice, who halted and gleamed at Stella with a renewed hopefulness.

"What about Forest?"

"I'm not …" Stella shook her head. "He's young."

"Well, how old are you?"

"Thirty-one," Stella said.

Beatrice's eyes narrowed. "I thought you were younger."

"Thank you," Stella replied.

"It wasn't a compliment."

CHAPTER 11

Beatrice

Exhaustion weighed Beatrice down, and her eyes threatened to flutter closed even as she walked. She and Stella stopped at the cave to set up camp and sleep. The evening had been a lovely one; the warm night air folded around the frog's croak and the cicada's whir. All night long, Beatrice dry-heaved until her abdominal muscles twisted into a cramped knot. When they woke, Stella insisted she carry the pack, and Beatrice acquiesced.

"We're not going back the same way," Stella said, keeping a close distance behind Beatrice.

"It's hot today," Beatrice explained. The more they walked, the more she relied on the walking stick to support some of her weight. "I'm taking us past a swimming hole to cool off. It's quite a ways from the Rock. We won't pass the trees again."

Beatrice glanced back briefly at Stella in time to catch flashes of disappointment and consternation flit across the woman's face.

"Can you swim?" she asked.

"Yes, I just wasn't expecting ..."

The humid forest air clung to Beatrice's skin, and droplets of sweat popped out on her brow. Dizziness swept over her, and she stopped for a moment to lean against a tree.

"We're almost to the cliff. Are you afraid of heights?"

"You didn't mention a cliff," Stella responded.

"Well, are you?" Beatrice asked, both aware of and frustrated by the irritation in her own voice.

"I *am* afraid of heights. But I think until this trip, I would have been afraid of talking trees."

Beatrice made eye contact with Stella, then closed her eyes and took a deep inhale and exhale through her nose.

"We can sit and rest if you'd like," Stella encouraged.

Beatrice shook her head, opened her eyes, and continued walking. "It's just around the corner."

She led Stella close to the edge of the rocky cliff and peered into the blue-green pool fed constantly by a tumbling waterfall.

"How far down is it?" Stella asked.

"Twenty feet, maybe?"

"I don't think I want to do that." Stella's voice revealed resistance.

"I'll go first," Beatrice promised.

She hoped the cold water would revive her; if it didn't, she wasn't sure she would make it home alive. For the past several months, she had felt apathy toward living; somehow, First Mother's words, the mere suggestion that the Goddess would keep the family going, stirred in her a desire to stick around.

Beatrice stripped her clothes off with her back to Stella, not quite ready to reveal her disfigured flesh. The cool rock under her feet invigorated her body and spirit, thank the Goddess, and briefly, she felt well and young and able once more. Standing on the edge brought memories of her mother. Every summer, they'd climb midway up the mountain to swim. Her mother's laugh resounded around the pool as they jumped together, over and over again, until they exhausted themselves. They'd splash each other and see which one of them could hold their breath the longest. Then, they'd lay down a blanket and nap on the sunlit forest floor. Her mother had been so careful not to bring her near the trees, though Beatrice didn't know it at the time.

Shaking the memory away, Beatrice dove in headfirst, arms over her head. The jolt of the brisk water elevated the sensations of being human. Her flesh and muscles and bones felt relief, if only for a moment. Her head breached the surface, and she drew in a deep intake of breath. Then she turned back toward Stella, who stood feet away from the edge of the cliff.

"I promise you, it's deep enough that you won't hurt yourself." She drew her hand out of the water and motioned. "Come on."

"I was on the swim team in high school. Other kids made fun of me all the time because I was afraid of heights." Stella moved tentatively toward the edge. "That, and I was bigger than everyone else. The coach never stopped them."

A tenderness swirled in Beatrice while fear emanated from Stella in a lavender aura.

"I won't laugh at you, Stella. If it's too much, you can walk down that way." Beatrice pointed toward a series of rocks that made rugged steps down the edge. "The water feels amazing, though. I'm going to turn around now."

Beatrice turned her back to Stella and swam across the pool. A splash alerted her that the woman had joined her in the water. She turned in time to see Stella's head bob out of the water, a smile on her face.

"That was fun." Stella laughed, and Beatrice laughed with her.

"I know. I love this spot." Beatrice treaded in the water. "Tell me more about the swim team," she urged. Instead of an outsider or a potential partner for Forest, Stella became more and more of an individual to Beatrice with each secret she shared.

"My stroke was the dolphin stroke. I was the fastest on my team and competed at the state level. So many of the girls hated me because I could beat them in the dolphin race. Every time. Even at my size."

"Show me the dolphin stroke."

Stella's face flashed red, but she turned, and Beatrice marveled as the woman's arms rotated and her legs propelled her across the pond. Stella flipped in the water and made her way back to Beatrice.

"Impressive," Beatrice responded.

"I love swimming."

"Me too," Beatrice responded. "Have you ever seen a dolphin? Is that how they swim?"

Stella chuckled. Instead of growing irritated at Stella's chuckle, Beatrice let it go.

"I have seen a dolphin, but they don't swim quite that way. Dolphins don't have arms."

Knitting her eyebrows together, Beatrice tutted, "I know dolphins don't have arms, Stella."

Beatrice swam toward a rock outcropping; she could feel the heat on her face and skin. The simple act of pulling herself onto the rock drained her. All the exuberance and exhilaration the cool water brought her evaporated, and heaviness took over. Beatrice crossed her arms over her chest while Stella swam toward her slowly.

"Come up," she encouraged, patting the rock.

"I don't like being naked in front of other people."

"I won't look at you. I need you to look at me."

Stella pressed her palms against the rock and hoisted herself up with ease. Beatrice turned to reveal her bare breasts. The right one was swollen, redness formed flamelike streaks up the sides of it, and the nipple drew in toward Beatrice's ribs.

"I don't know exactly, but ..." Stella paused. "When my grandmother developed breast cancer, one of hers looked like this."

Beatrice drew in an inhale, held it for a moment, and then released. "I've heard of it." A couple of her regular visitors at the market had died from the disease; their names ran through Beatrice's head.

"How long has it been this way?" Stella asked. "May I?" Stella lifted her hand and moved it toward her. Beatrice allowed it, but winced in pain as Stella pressed her hand against the inflamed breast. "Sorry," Stella apologized and withdrew.

"I noticed changes around six months ago. I had something like this before, when Forest was a baby. My milk became all strange. Lumpy. I ran a high fever."

"How did you get better?"

"I used herbs. Cabbage leaves. Rosemary."

"This isn't the same thing, Beatrice. I don't think you can get rid of this with herbs. I'm sorry."

"I know. I've tried."

"You need a doctor."

"No." Beatrice shook her head with finality. "The women at the market never got better, even after they cut the cancer out and gave them medicine that made them so sick."

"First Mother just told us that your mother is still alive. I could—"

Beatrice's eyes watered at the thought, but she shook her head. "I don't think I have time for you to find her."

"Your great-grandmother, then. Ask her."

"I can't imagine she would help me." Beatrice turned toward Stella. "I've never seen her face. I've never heard her voice. The stories Grandmother tells ..."

Grandmother's blue eyes weeping tree sap came to

Beatrice's mind. Tales of not being allowed to come to the Rock because she had no gift, tales of being tied down to a chair or the bed as punishment. Beatrice stood and paced, feeling the warmth of the rock underneath her feet. How golden her own mother had been.

"Maybe this is the way it's supposed to be. Maybe I'm supposed to die like any other human. Maybe I'm much more human and much less Goddess. The thing is," Beatrice sighed, "unlike my mother and my grandmother, I don't think living as a tree would be so bad."

Beatrice's eyes moved to the waterfall as it rushed fresh breath into the pool below. "I suppose I can try," she said, leaning into the suggestion that Ola might help her. "She will want an offering. We will go back to the house."

"You can do that after."

Beatrice nodded and sat back down on the rock, allowing the sun to dry her skin. She couldn't talk to Stella anymore. Fatigue had fully taken each of her cells, and she knew Stella was right. She couldn't make it home to prepare an offering for Ola.

I don't think Grandmother is going to like it.

***

Beatrice and Stella rested for over half an hour, and then Stella stood, dressed herself, and hoisted the pack of food and clothes onto her back. Beatrice fought back the urge to share the load. She thanked the Goddess that the rest of the journey was downhill, though she still paused repeatedly to rest her forehead on a tree when dizziness came. Twice, she stopped to dry-heave pure acidic water onto the leaves at her feet.

Finally, they made it to the Rock.

Hesitation grew in vines around Beatrice's chest, but she walked forward toward her great-grandmother. She kneeled and pressed her head against the bark, which felt hard and cold.

"Great-grandmother Ola, I'm so sick. I'm dying. I don't have an offering, but I will bring one. Can you …" Beatrice paused. She knew her grandmother could heal her, but was she willing? " …will you heal me?" She kept her eyes downcast. No creaks in the bark. No movement. No voice in Beatrice's head. "Please." She hated to beg, and until this moment, she'd had no need. Not since she was fourteen. She raised her voice. "Please!"

"Beatrice." Soft and gentle, Grandmother called her name. "She will not help you."

"I don't want to go to a doctor. I don't want to do that." Beatrice walloped her fist against the tree upon which she leaned. Beatrice hated crying even more than she hated begging, but she was too tired to tense up her body enough to fight the tears that slipped down her face.

"Who do you think healed you all those years ago?"

Beatrice lifted her body away from her great grandmother, stood, and walked toward the talking tree. "I don't know."

"I healed you. I think I can do it again. Stella, run back to the house and get Forest. Lie down, Beatrice."

Beatrice obeyed. The earth creaked and groaned underneath Grandmother, underneath the Rock itself. Roots slid up around Beatrice and formed webs around both of her breasts and under her arms and down into her groin, beneath her jaw, and around the sides of her throat. Buzzing air moved around them, and Beatrice's heart shook within her chest as a faint green glow emanated from the roots spreading over the surface of her skin.

"I think it will be best if you sleep, Beatrice."

Beatrice resisted, trying to wriggle free from the vines running around her. As her eyes closed, she thought of her mother.

CHAPTER 12

Stella

Beulah's roots still cradled Beatrice when Stella returned to the Rock with Forest. Green light radiated from the tree until it encircled Forest and Stella as well. Black, oily ooze wept from Beatrice's pores, and Beulah used roots to push it from her skin. She formed balls with the sticky poison, and when she was finished, lumps of darkness lay to the side of the Rock. Slowly, Beulah retracted her roots back into herself. Beatrice remained still, but breath stirred in her chest, and Stella sighed in relief.

Forest ran to his mother and kneeled by her side, his hands cupping her face, then his eyes moved to the black, glistening sludge. "What is that?"

"Your mother had cancer, Forest," Stella said.

"It's alright, Grandson," Beulah said. "It's all gone. Take her home and tuck her in bed."

Stella watched as Forest gathered Beatrice up in his arms. The way her head lolled from side to side propelled her to Beatrice's side. She touched the woman's cheek.

Though it was clammy and pale, her skin was warm and her breathing even.

"Do you think she's alright?" Forest asked.

"I do," Stella said. "Let's get her home."

"Wait, Stella," Beulah said, and Stella jogged back to the tree.

"Come closer," Beulah asked, and Stella obeyed. "Stay for a little while."

"Thank you for healing her," Stella spoke.

"She's my family, Stella. She's a child of the woods." As the tree spoke, her roots moved from the ground and up to Stella's face. The velvet touch surprised Stella, and a chill ran through her.

Those eyes.

"I need your help," Beulah whispered.

"How so?"

"Let me tell you a story ..."

Beulah's story stirred empathy and sadness and hope and wonderment within Stella's chest. The tree asked so much of her, but the spark in the blue eyes turned Stella's insides liquid until she knew she would do anything for the woman. And at the end of Beulah explaining the plan, Stella agreed to tell no one.

***

Stella stayed to help Forest for two days after the healing. On the second day, she asked Forest if he could sit with a soundly-sleeping Beatrice so she could visit Beulah.

"She wants to tell me stories," she explained.

"Don't include the trees in your interview, Stella," Forest said, his eyes focused on the floor.

"No." Stella rebuked the thought. "No, this is not for the interview. Forest ..."

I don't want to leave.

"Can I stay a little longer?" she asked.

126

Forest smiled. "You can't keep sleeping in front of our fireplace."

Why not?

"I can at least help until she wakes up." Stella stood with her hands clasped in front of her.

"I wish she'd wake up," Forest admitted, and Stella nodded. "After that, I think you should go."

Stella watched Forest's jaw clench and release, surprised at the change in his attitude toward her.

"I'm not going to write the article, Forest." she said.

Forest shifted his weight in his chair. "Why not?"

"This place ... your life ... it's too special. Delicate. Sacred ... I can't ..." Stella tried to wiggle the tightness out of her jaw. If she wanted to help Beulah, she had to have Forest's trust. "Look, your mother shared a lot with me, and now I want to know everything that your family will allow me to know. And I will keep it to myself. I will go when you and your mother tell me to," Stella promised, though after the trip to the Peak, she wasn't convinced Beatrice would ask her to leave.

I have to help Beulah.

The thought tugged at Stella's mind and heart, more of a command than a stirring of altruistic motivation.

The two finished eating breakfast, and the conversation turned to lighter subjects: grinding acorns for flour, an upcoming trip to the market for olive oil, chocolate, and coffee. Stella moved to clear the table, but Forest stopped her with a hand to her arm.

"Go," he said. "You have stories to hear. Arcas can take you."

Forest didn't know the promise that Stella had made to Beulah; the promise was vague even to her, but Beulah's eyes had conveyed a conviction that Stella could help her.

She stepped down from the front porch and searched for Arcas, whom she found behind the smokehouse, working a walnut around in his mouth. The bear had not quite warmed to her, nor she to him, but there was trust and a mutual respect growing between them.

"Arcas," Stella said lowly, and the bear moved his brown eyes up toward hers without stopping his assault on the nut. "Could you help me?"

The bear let out a grunt, dropped the walnut, and hoisted his great body up onto his feet.

"Can you take me to the Rock?"

A snort, and Arcas walked in the direction Stella remembered. She scurried across the forest floor to walk beside him, to talk to him as though he could answer back.

"Thank you for taking me. I hope I'm not causing too much trouble."

Stella stared at the bear as if he would say to her, "No, no. No trouble at all."

Arcas merely glanced at her briefly and lumbered on. Stella decided it would be in her best interest to avoid annoying her guide, so she walked quietly and watched the ground for rocks and exposed tree roots that threatened to ground her. She blocked out little twinges of apprehension that stirred at the base of her spine. She chose to believe that Beulah would keep her safe.

***

When they reached the Rock, Stella relieved Arcas of his duty, then tread lightly upon the stone surface, thinking of the women who had birthed and died here. She reconsidered the word. Not died. Changed. She focused on Beulah as she walked forward, trying to work out the science of it all. How did the women change? How would this thing Beulah was asking of her work?

Stella dropped to her knees when she reached the tree and placed her hand on the smooth, gray bark. Under her hand a face formed, and the eyes, slow to open, shone bright blue. Stella considered telling Beulah about the things she had seen, but decided against it.

"Hi," Stella said, smiling. She reached into her back pocket and brought out a chocolate bar. She had gone back to town once for new clothes and to buy Beulah a treat. "I brought you this."

She flashed it in front of Beulah, then broke it into tiny shards, which she placed around the roots. Stella's eyes roamed over the tree's face. Was there a blush on the bark? Surely not, but there was a warmth there Stella hadn't noticed before.

"Thank you for your help," Beulah said. "You don't have to bring me anything else but you. How is Beatrice?"

"Still sleeping. Her pulse and breathing are strong."

"I wasn't sure I could heal her by myself. The tumors had taken over."

"I know." Stella thought back to the black goo.

"How is Forest treating you?" Beulah asked.

She contemplated telling the whole truth—that Forest, it seemed, had traded places with his mother and no longer felt safe around her.

"He's been very kind," she said instead. That part wasn't untrue.

"Where are you sleeping?"

"On the floor in front of the fireplace."

Beulah made a clicking noise. "Like Cinderella! I don't like that."

"It's been fine, honestly. I told Forest this morning that I'm not ready to leave, but I didn't ask to stay."

"Well, don't ask them. Tell them!" Beulah insisted, her voice rising.

"It's their home, Beulah."

"It's mine, too! Or it will be again."

Stella brought her hand again to the bark-fleshed cheek. "Are you ready to do this?" she inquired.

"I don't know," Beulah confessed. "But I guess there is only one way to find out."

Stella unbuttoned the cuff of the flannel shirt Forest let her borrow and rolled it up past her forearm, exposing the tender inside of her elbow and the blue veins within.

"I hate needles," she explained to Beulah. "I tried to donate blood once—people can donate it and it's banked for those who need it. Anyway, I passed out."

The thought of it brought a clamminess to Stella's hands, which she rubbed on her jeans.

"I don't think you'll feel anything," the tree assured her. "Why don't you lie down?"

Stella positioned herself so she could still see Beulah's face. The roots moved underneath her until they cradled her, and she smiled and gave a nod. One of Beulah's roots lifted out of the earth, and she laid it down gently across Stella's lap. The root elongated into slender, thin tendrils until they were smaller than a capillary, the bark becoming invisible to Stella. She felt a moment of pressure, then nothing. Unhurriedly, cranberry red blood crept down the tiny, imperceptible tube and Stella drew in a sharp intake of breath. At least this part was working.

This was what Beulah asked her for: blood, freely given every day until the tree had all she needed to become human again. Perhaps one day, someone would ask what was in it for Stella. For that, there was only one answer: magic. She would be part of the story. But more than that, Stella had no choice but to help Beulah, a fact she hadn't quite admitted to herself.

"Would you like to sleep?" Beulah offered.

"No. Tell me stories."

"I suspect you have more stories to tell me than I have to tell you."

"We can take turns," Stella insisted.

"Do I have to tell the sad ones?" Beulah asked.

"You don't have to tell me any. I'm sorry. I don't mean to pry. I'm a journalist. I like a good story."

"Mmm," Beulah hummed.

"Everything okay?" Stella's body tensed and she sat up.

"Your blood is so warm." Beulah smiled and moved on. "Most of my good stories are around my daughter, Madeline."

"I love that name," Stella said, and let her body relax.

"Oh? Are there many Madelines in the city?"

"Yes. It's one of those names that was rare until it wasn't." Stella turned her attention to the thin string of blood that now seemed to flow more rapidly. "How does it feel now?"

"It burns like fire," Beulah replied.

Stella's stomach clenched. "Maybe we should stop."

"No. I'm fine, Stella."

The memory of finding her barely breathing father on the floor of his office flashed into Stella's brain. She had known who to call for help in that situation, even though the help didn't get there quick enough.

"If something goes wrong, what do I tell them?" Stella's heart rate quickened at the thought of bringing harm to Beatrice and Forest.

"I will tell you if I think I need their help. This is going to be messy."

"And no one has ever done this before? How did you know—"

"Oh, Stella, I don't know, exactly." Beulah's voice had released its patience. "I don't want to be at this rock any longer. I cannot live for eternity as a tree. I hate it. I hate it the same way Gertrude hated her human skin."

"I'm sorry," Stella apologized. "I just don't like keeping secrets."

"I don't want to give her hope. Beatrice won't understand. If any of us actually wanted to be a tree, it would be her."

Stella smiled. *How true.*

"And she'd try to stop me."

Stella's eyes moved from Beulah to Ola. "Does your mother ever show her face?"

"Once in a while. She doesn't speak anymore, though. Our relationship was complicated."

Stella considered asking for details but thought back to Forest's words.

It's not my story to tell.

"My relationship with my mother is complicated, too. I was too fat until I was too thin. My skin too dry or too oily. My clothes too frumpy or too skimpy."

"Hmm. Well, our differences show up in our magic. The women before me had discernible powers, and my daughter ..." Beulah tried a whistle, and it brought a giggle from Stella. "She could do it all. Move things with her mind. Start fires with the snap of a finger. Heal. See the future. If Mother knew my Madeline, she would tremble."

"I had a psychic tell me I could see the future if I wanted to," Stella said.

"Have you ever?" Beulah asked.

"I think so," Stella whispered. "I've had ... visions. I'd rather not ..." Dizziness swept over Stella, and she closed her eyes. "I'm choosing hope." She wasn't one for saying such things, but Forest's question—*how can you not see magic?*—had reworked her somehow. "I'm beginning to believe that there is always hope."

"Perhaps," Beulah responded, and the two settled into a gentle, comfortable silence. Stella fell asleep in Beulah's soft cradle while the tree continued siphoning her blood.

***

"Stella." The voice came like a mother and a sister and a best friend. "We're done for the day. Take your time."

Stella readjusted to sitting on her knees. Lightheaded,

132

she leaned her head against Beulah. She had little sense of where she was or how she got there.

"You're in the forest with me, Stella."

Stella extended her hand and fingered the wooden eyelids. For a moment, bark became flesh, but when Stella blinked, the vision was again a tree.

"Oh. It's you." Stella smiled. "I'm a little dizzy." She felt her stomach rumble. "And hungry," she added.

"It's lunchtime. I'm sure Forest will have food ready for you. There's no sign of Arcas. Do you think you can make your way back?"

"I think so. Did you have an animal friend?"

"Yes. We all did. My mother's was a bobcat. My daughter's, a coyote she named Pepper."

"A coyote!" Stella responded.

"And mine was a rabbit. Willa."

Stella chuckled.

"I'll see you tomorrow, Stella."

Stella didn't question her direction, nor did her footing falter. She walked among the roots and rocks and slippery leaves as though she had walked the trail from the Rock to home thousands of times.

CHAPTER 13

Beatrice

Beatrice slept lightly most nights. Deep sleep was dangerous. That was when her eyes moved too quickly in their sockets and the man came back for her. Fifteen years ago, she had created a tea that kept the nightmares away, but on the second night after her grandmother pulled out the disease, her body craved healing and wholeness, and the depths of sleep took her.

The man with the rifle slung over his shoulder came up the mountain to the place where Beatrice and her deer companion, Willow, rested in front of a bonfire. Beatrice watched him raise his rifle and end Willow's life. She screamed in horror and ran to the deer, whose blood seeped into a pool around her. The man grabbed Beatrice, lifted her slight, fourteen-year-old body over his shoulder, and slammed her to the ground. Arms and legs flailed as she landed blows on his body. To his head. To his jaw. But one crashing punch to her face knocked the wind out of her. She couldn't fight as he ripped at her clothes. She screamed, and when he finished taking what he wanted, he unsheathed his knife and thrust it into Beatrice's abdomen just below her left rib.

Beatrice, both the girl in the nightmare and the woman lying safe in her bed, bellowed.

"Beatrice!" A shaking of her shoulders woke her into the present with a gasp.

Stella stood over her with knitted eyebrows, pieces of her dark, thick hair falling into her green eyes.

"I'm sorry." Beatrice raised herself up.

"Don't apologize," Stella replied. "Are you alright?"

"I really need to use the bathroom." Beatrice moved as swiftly as her body would allow, but her bladder released itself onto the floor. "Oh no," she croaked. Heat rose to her face.

"It's alright. You were asleep for two days. Of course you needed to use the bathroom." Stella's words were encouraging. "Let's get you in a hot bath."

"A bath sounds lovely." Beatrice sighed, then her eyes met Stella's. "You stayed."

"Well ..." Stella paused. "I couldn't leave Forest alone."

Beatrice allowed Stella to hold her arm as they moved through the house and outside to the bathhouse. A brilliant, cloudless sky caused her to squint.

"We've taken turns. I've stayed with you, mostly. I don't really know what I'm doing around here yet."

Beatrice stopped walking.

Yet?

When they reached the bathhouse door, Beatrice said, "I can take it from here, Stella. Thank you."

Stella placed a hand on Beatrice's back and rubbed it. It felt nice. "Your screams were ... horrific."

Beatrice nodded. "I'm sorry."

"Are you sure you're okay?"

Beatrice shook her head. "No. Not really. But my body feels much better. Now, let me go get cleaned up."

"Beatrice ..." Stella stopped her from walking into the bathhouse once more.

Beatrice found herself bothered, wanting to be alone and warm and safe, but she turned back to the woman. "Yes, Stella?"

"May I stay with you?" Stella's eyes were full of both courage and fear.

"Stay?" Beatrice felt the urge to cry as an aching loneliness she'd resisted permeated her entire being. What would it be like to have a friend? "How long?"

Stella shrugged. "I know I'm another mouth to feed and I'm not much help, but this feels like home."

Beatrice felt a relaxation in her body. Her shoulders slid away from her ears and her jaw softened. "I wasn't expecting this." Silence stretched out before them in miles of spoken and unspoken words. "Why do you want to stay? What about this feels like home?"

Stella squirmed and her face blushed. "I came for the story, but ..." The woman nibbled at the skin on the edge of her thumb. Beatrice narrowed her eyes. "I spent time with your grandmother and got to know Forest more while you were sleeping. I'm just not ready to leave this magical world yet. And, I have a piece of fiction to write." Stella's furrowed frown eased into a smile and she straightened a bit.

Beatrice gave a slow nod. "I can't let you sleep on the floor."

"I'd be happy to sleep right there."

Beatrice clicked her tongue and shook her head at the thought. "I'll need to ask Forest."

"Of course."

Beatrice turned once more, determined to make her way to her bath. Stella didn't stop her, and once in the bathhouse, she slipped out of her wet clothes, disgusted with herself. She eased into the large bath full of steaming water and gave thanks to Martha and Edith, who responded, "You're so welcome, daughter."

Beatrice dunked her head into the water and grabbed a washcloth and bar of soap she had crafted with lemon balm and rosemary. She scrubbed her face with the cloth, glanced up at the sun beaming through the skylight, and tried to release it all into the water. The nightmare left quivers in her core. She wrapped the washcloth around the soap again, worked up a lather, and raked the memories off her body. She'd never told Forest about the man who was the real reason she put up the Hedge.

For so long it had provided protection. Beatrice had allowed Forest to bring Stella through the opening and hoped it was the right choice for Forest. She knew it was the right choice for her. She was healed now and, assuming Forest was in favor, she would share space with another woman in a way she hadn't since she was fourteen, navigating the small kitchen with her mother.

Beatrice closed her eyes.

Mother.

After her mother had left with the shell of Gertrude's soul, she'd wondered what became of her, and for a while, Beatrice wanted to find her again. The desire to find her faded as she lost herself, intentionally, to Forest's needs of diapering, feeding, and teaching.

Once more, Beatrice dunked herself into the water, drowning out the memories. The man. Mama. Papa.

Something about Stella was driving Beatrice back into herself, into stories of her family, into the magic, and this movement back home into her own soul brought so many emotions. The divinity within her created an unstoppable, unrelenting pull that exhilarated her. If she allowed herself to realize all the power she possessed, the strength of her own skill ... if she was even half as powerful as her mother and as resourceful as her grandmother, could she finally let down the Hedge completely?

Beatrice fluttered her eyes open, stood and eased out of the bathtub, then she wrapped herself in a towel and sat on a small chair nestled in the corner. She didn't feel better. Her words to Stella had been lies. Even after the bath, her bones, muscles, and joints ached without apology, and nausea and fatigue still weighed her down. Standing once more, she slipped on clean clothes and opened the door to the fresh air that was turning cool and autumnal.

Beatrice tried to enjoy all seasons equally, knowing there was nothing to cling to but the cadence of change. Leaves fell. Plants died. Arcas slept. But the transitions continued. Dinner and sleep would come a little earlier as the days shortened. Chores would change, and there would be longer stays by the fire, humming and whistling and mending clothes. Thick soups made of pumpkin and winter squash, spicy pies, and stews would replace salads. Beatrice and Forest would talk more and peruse the books their grandmothers kept over the course of their lifetimes. But if she were honest, the shutting down of the growing season and the dimming of the light always made her a little sad.

Beatrice walked into her home and found Stella at the kitchen table, huddled over a cup of tea and a book. Grandmother's book. Stella's eyes scanned the page with soft respect.

"Forest and Beulah said it was okay," Stella said, glancing up at Beatrice. "Do you mind me reading it?"

"No." Beatrice sat down with a sigh. "Are you alright? You look pale."

Stella palmed a few walnuts and tossed them into her mouth. "Just hungry. How are *you* feeling?"

"I'm still so tired," Beatrice confessed.

"Rest." Stella stood. "Let me get you something to eat."

Beatrice was too tired for words but gave a nod and rested her elbows on the table and her head in her hands. She was ravenous. Empty. She closed her eyes and listened to Stella move around the kitchen, who placed before her a steaming cup of hot tea, vegetable soup, a few cheese slices, and a crudely made biscuit.

"I made the biscuit," Stella said apologetically. "It tastes better than it looks."

Beatrice picked up the biscuit and found it dry in her hands, but not wanting to hurt Stella's feelings, she took a bite and smiled. "We will figure out how to make space for you, Stella."

"Thank you. I'm very grateful for that."

Stella sat down and opened Grandmother's book up again.

"There are many more where that came from," Beatrice responded. She thought of Mother's journals that she never had the opportunity to read. She didn't know if Mother had read the other women's books, nor why she'd locked them up, and it made her wonder what she wrote about. "Stella, you offered to help me find a doctor. If I needed your help to find someone else ..."

Stella glanced up at Beatrice. "I'm a journalist. Finding people is part of what I do."

Beatrice's belly contracted and her mouth grew dry. She took a sip of tea, then ate, bite by bite, until all the food Stella supplied was gone.

"I think I need to lie down again." Beatrice stood and took her dishes to the sink.

"I'll clean up," Stella said.

"Thanks. Do you know where Forest is?"

"He went to town. He said his coven is preparing for the fall equinox gathering they're having in a few weeks."

"Ahh," Beatrice said. For the longest time, Beatrice and Forest had observed the transition of seasons together, alone. She forced a smile as she turned to leave the kitchen. Before she could leave the room, conviction gripped her.

"Write it," she said. "Like Imogene said."

Stella looked up, eyebrows knitted together, eyes searching for Beatrice's meaning.

Beatrice waved her hand as if to sketch out her specific meaning. "Like a story. A piece of fiction. I'd like to read your writing."

Stella's eyebrows lifted. "I'd love that, Beatrice."

"And the next time you go to town, buy your own book." Beatrice gestured to the book in Stella's hand, and the woman nodded, smiling.

***

Beatrice made her way to her bedroom and sat on the edge of the bed. She stared down at the old trunk in the corner, the trunk that First Mother had carried with her up the mountain on her journey away from town. She sank off the bed and kneeled before it. She had never opened it. The trunk was a sacred space for the woman of the house to keep her things and opening it would solidify her role as matriarch. Also, she was not prepared to see her mother reduced to the items in this time capsule. But the trunk held her favorite quilt Grandmother had made, and the dress Mother wore on her wedding day, and a stack of love letters—conversations between Mama and Papa.

Her face flushed; the letters were not for her, but she reached for them, anyway. The papers were folded neatly, dated, and in order. Beatrice flipped to the last one and read.

Dear Eric,

Thank you for the love you've shown Beatrice. She truly adores you. You have awakened something in her, something she wouldn't have found on her own. I told her this morning that we will be married and that you'll move in.

141

She smiled a great big smile and squealed. I told her she could call you Papa.

Every time you make love to me, Eric, I go somewhere else. I feel sorrow for all my mothers who came before me who never felt a touch like that ...

Beatrice stopped reading, her chest aflame. She didn't want to read about a man's touch, even if it was the gentle touch of her Papa.

"Where are you?" she whispered, and for the first time in two decades, Beatrice cried for her mother.

***

A gentle knock on the door prompted Beatrice to wipe her eyes and stand.

"Come in." Her voice came out scratchy and weak.

Forest came in, his green eyes full of relief. "Stella said you were awake. How do you feel?"

"Still tired. Not sure how that's possible."

Forest eased down beside her, and his eyes moved to the trunk. "You've been crying."

Beatrice motioned toward the letters and dress and quilt. "I went through her things. I figured it was time."

A puzzled look flashed over Forest's face, so Beatrice explained the rites of passage that each woman practiced once their mother transitioned to a tree; she'd empty the trunk of her mother's things, burn the items, and fill the trunk again with her own possessions.

"That would be such a hard task. I don't think I could do it." Forest looked down and shook his head. "You don't have to burn them, you know. We can find a place to put your mother's things."

Beatrice swallowed. "I'll decide later. There's something we need to talk about. It's Stella. She wants to stay with us."

"For how long?" Forest's eyes narrowed. The suspicion in them surprised her.

"Until we all tire of each other, I guess."

"Do you want that?"

"Forest, I don't want you to feel you have to take care of me anymore. Or keep me company. And I'd like a friend."

Forest stood, turned away from her and crossed his arms. "Where will she sleep?"

"I'm too tired to think through everything now. We can figure it out. I know we can."

Forest turned back to Beatrice, a rueful smile on his face. "You sure changed your mind about her."

"I did. Having her here on the mountain feels right."

"The daughter you never had?"

The sadness in Forest's voice broke Beatrice. She stood, took one long stride toward him, and placed her hands on his arms. "For starters, Forest, she's only four years younger than me, and I've never wanted you to be any different from what you are."

Forest averted his eyes briefly, then enveloped her in a giant hug. "So, she'll be more like an aunt than a sister?" he asked, his arms still around her.

"If that's how you want to think about it, yes."

When Beatrice pulled away from Forest, she found his countenance returned to its typical form, calm and content.

"Let me tuck you in."

Forest pulled back the covers and Beatrice snuggled in, drifting into a peaceful nap.

Chapter 14

Stella

The afternoon before she rented a car, drove to Charleston, and boarded a plane to New York, Stella had walked through the woods with Forest. When she asked him for a wand, she could see apprehension in the furrow between his brows and the way he combed his fingers through his hair.

"I want to gift it to someone; the psychic who predicted you and your mother and …" Stella couldn't bring herself to say Beulah. As much as she tried, she couldn't deny her affection for the tree, which moved into her chest and flushed her face. "I won't tell her anything about you, Forest. I promise."

Forest led Stella into his bedroom and pulled the basket of wands onto his bed, closing his eyes. "Great-grandmother allowed me to make four wands from her branches. I gave one to Mother, though she'll probably never use it. I gave one to Wanda. Something is telling me to send one with you to this psychic and to give one to you."

Stella had whispered a thank you, commented on their

145

beauty, and marveled at the weight of them in her hands. Holding them, knowing they were once pieces of Beulah, brought a shiver to her spine. Now, the wand rested in her bookbag as she lumbered through the city ready to make her goodbyes.

Roger. Stella wanted to talk to Roger first, because it would be the easiest goodbye. The longer she'd been away, the more she'd realized she didn't love him. Perhaps she never had. She called him as the plane touched down in LaGuardia and arranged for the two of them to have coffee. He was wearing a navy sweater over a red and blue button-up shirt, and he smiled at her and stood, opening his arms to embrace her. Stella allowed the hug.

"Hey," he said. "How was your trip?"

"Good," she said, and smiled genuinely as her thoughts touched on Beatrice and Forest and Beulah.

"Yeah?" Roger smiled back. He had already ordered her a black coffee and scooted it across the table closer to her. "I've missed you. Is your article written and ready to go?"

Stella shook her head. "No. I'm not going to write it," she said as she tucked a piece of hair behind her ear.

Roger's eyebrows crinkled, and his lips turned upward in a smirk. "Why not?"

"I'm just not." She sipped her coffee, grimacing as the hot liquid scalded the roof of her mouth.

"Reina is not going to like that," Roger admonished.

Stella kept her eyes on Roger's, trying to channel that honest part of herself she'd excavated in the woods. "I'm leaving New York."

The crinkle in Roger's eyebrows deepened into a furrow, and he repositioned himself in his seat. "What do you mean?"

"I came back to New York to settle a few things. I reached out to a real estate agent, and he already has an interested buyer. I wanted to say goodbye to you and my mother."

"What are you going to do, Stella?" Roger snorted, twisting his coffee mug around on the table. "Move to West Virginia?"

Stella thought about her new home, the rugged, dusty comfort of it, then she focused again on Roger, who gave her an incredulous stare.

"Yes." She fidgeted with her coffee mug. "This isn't my home. This isn't what I want for myself anymore."

He narrowed his eyes at her and a muscle in his jaw jumped. "Stella, this makes no sense. Editor in chief is exactly what you've always wanted. Look, over the past two years, I begged you to slow down and take a deep breath, but now you're just quitting. Is there even a newspaper there that will hire you?"

More worried about my job than our relationship. Telling.

"I don't plan on working for a while. Well ..." Stella tried to cool her tongue with a sip of water before her next statement. "I've considered writing fiction instead." She closed her eyes and inhaled deeply. "Anyway, I guess you could say I'm moving off the grid."

"Off the grid?" Roger chuckled, but then his face changed. Now mottled within the incredulity on his face were sprinkles of concern. She thought he glanced at her chewed thumbnail. "Where, exactly, are you going to live?"

Stella felt her hackles rise. "I can't tell you that." Roger could manipulate people into sharing more than what was best for them; the trait made him a damn good salesperson.

"How are we going to communicate?" He shifted again in his seat as realization filled his face. "That's what you want to tell me. We are no longer."

Stella nodded and allowed the hot ball of anger she felt for herself to nestle into her chest. Anger at how much of herself she had given and how much she had withheld.

"I'm sorry, Roger."

"Stella." Roger picked up his cup and examined it again.

"I've loved you more than you've loved me for a long time." The tense muscles in his jaw and cheeks released with the sadness. "The breakup with me isn't completely surprising, but I am shocked you're leaving New York for West Virginia. What has you so smitten?"

Stella could barely breathe.

"Oh. Is it a warlock?"

Stella shook her head and looked down at the table. Staring into the dark liquid steaming in her cup, she lost herself, her mind floating to the conversation she'd had with Beulah before she left. Face pink, she had pressed her head against the tree's bark, gathered her courage in a bouquet of flowers to lay at her feet, and whispered "I love you" to the tree.

Beulah hadn't responded with words, but her roots lifted and wrapped tenderly around Stella, who accepted both the oddness of the feeling as well as the likelihood Beulah would never reciprocate. Neither of these truths changed her heart. In fact, the unrequited nature of her love pressed her head even further underwater. Stella basked in the holy selflessness of it, the reverence, worship, and generosity. Giving to Beulah filled her up.

Roger's finger tapping on the table redirected Stella's attention. "This isn't like you. Are you in a cult? Have you become one of the witches?"

"It's not a cult," Stella said and took a few sips of her coffee as she mulled over the word witch. "And I don't think I'm a witch."

"You're not sure whether or not you're a witch?" he asked, draining the remnants of his coffee.

She pinched the bridge of her nose. "It depends on your definition of the word."

The two continued talking and finished their coffee. Stella explained as much as she could to Roger about the life she was choosing, reassuring him she was safe. They finished their conversation and walked to Stella's apartment so Roger could gather his things. When she opened the door, the clinical whiteness of the walls struck her. Before the mountaintop, the decor felt modern and minimalist, but now, the starkness chilled her. She moved to her bedroom and retrieved a pair of pajamas, a novel, and a toothbrush Roger had left behind.

"I think this is it," she said as she laid Roger's things on the couch.

"Give Helen my best," Roger said, and Stella raised an eyebrow. "She's going to flip, Stella."

"I know."

"Hug?" Roger opened his arms to her, and Stella pressed herself into him. He squeezed her, sniffled, and pulled away.

"Will you please let me know that you're safe once in a while?"

"I'll try. Take care, Roger." Then she handed Roger his things and shut the door behind him.

***

Stella took the next hour to pack things she felt could be of use to her in the forest. Warm clothes and duck boots. Her grandfather's pocketknife from a hundred years ago that her father left her when he died. It had been twelve years since he passed away, leaving Stella only with her mother's fear, guilt, and shame.

On her bedside table, she found her favorite picture of him. They were at a birthday party, Stella just a baby. He lifted her over his head, and she stared down with wide, eager, happy eyes. Hints of trust and mischief played in the look she gave him. A willingness to take risks. A fire that burned for more than just A's on a report card, or perfect dives, or stacks of published magazine articles. When had those feelings gone away? Stella allowed tears to flow as she traced the outline of his face.

"I miss you, Dad. I think you'd love the mountain. I hope you would, at least."

Stella swallowed hard, wiped her eyes with the back of her hand, and slid the photo into her backpack. The realtor would be there soon. Movers were coming to pack her things and put them in storage. Then she would meet with Reina to put in her resignation and have lunch with her mother. Her last visit would be to the psychic.

She sat on her white couch and wrapped herself in a white throw. Questions circulated in bubbles that popped without answer.

Will the house stay this warm?

Will I miss my things, my space, my job?

She thought of Beulah.

Stella felt a panic rise in her chest at the remembrance of blood leaving her body, but before it could fully manifest, the doorbell sounded. She refolded the blanket and draped it over the couch, then opened the door to find a gentleman in a black suit with a red nametag, and a woman with glossy black hair and even glossier lips. She let them in, grabbed her keys and purse, and left. On the way to her office, she passed the coffee shop where she had met with Roger, then took the stairs to the subway.

I can certainly live without being a human sandwich.

Stella searched for the divine in the humanity surrounding her. A mother rocked a toddler and peered into the child's face with joy. An old man sat in the opposite corner, nodding off, then snorting himself awake.

How do you not see magic?

The question repeated itself as she stepped out of the subway and into the bright sunlight.

Quitting her job wasn't as difficult as Stella imagined. She entered her boss's office without an appointment, prompting much frustration and impatience. When Stella turned in her resignation, the editor offered her more money, a vacation, and a chance to choose her assignments. Reina told Stella she was one of the best writers on the team, a remark that both stunned Stella and filled her with pride. She thanked her former boss for the compliment and gave her a smile.

Stella glanced at her watch. She wasn't quite ready to think about her mother, but she had little time to make it to the French restaurant the woman loved so much. Stella's father had hated the place and always ordered a hamburger, which her mother would roll her eyes at. Stella walked down the broad sidewalks of New York, breathing deeply, feeling the concrete under her feet. Her feet. They felt so different, so restricted and separated from the earth as she walked upon it. She missed the softness of the forest floor. The coolness of her bare skin against the earth.

Helen was early and already seated at the busy restaurant. She stood when Stella walked in, and Stella took in her stylish red bob and pale blue dress that hit just above her knee. The familiar physical sensations that accompanied a visit with her mother filled her: shoulders tightened, palms released sweat, and breath shallowed.

"Stella!" A broad smile spread across Helen's face, raising her cheekbones even higher. "It's so good to see you. It's been much too long. You work too hard." Her mother embraced her tightly. "You look good. Have you lost weight?"

Stella thought back to the milkshake and hot biscuits. Doubtful.

"A little," she replied and smiled. Anything to please her mother, for at least a moment.

"So," Helen started, "you wanted to meet. You said it was important. Is it about you and Roger?"

"Let's order first, Mom."

This was going to be Stella's last go of French food, she felt certain, and she wanted to enjoy it. When the server came and poured ice water into their glasses, she ordered porcini mushroom tartlets and poached artichokes.

"And we will both take rosé," Helen added. "Gee, Stella. That's enough for lunch itself."

Stella put her fingertips to her brows for a moment and breathed deeply. "Well, I'm going to be busy at dinnertime," she lied. "So, this is my chance to fill up."

A memory bubbled up, unsolicited, of Stella telling her mother she wanted to join the swim team. "You'll need to lose at least ten pounds before then," her mother had responded.

"You seemed pensive on the phone." Helen took a sip of her water. "What's going on?"

"I'm leaving New York." Stella closed her eyes and brought their faces to mind, their beautiful, untamed faces.

"Come again?"

"I'm moving out of state, Mom," Stella said.

"Did you get a job somewhere else?"

"No," Stella said, and her thumbnail, as though it had a will of its own, made its way to her teeth.

Helen sat back in her chair, and Stella knew she was fighting an eye roll, which she had always said was very unladylike, even though she succumbed to the habit herself.

"I'm here to say goodbye."

"Stella, you're scaring me." Helen pressed her torso toward the table and lowered her voice. "You act like you mean forever."

"Don't be scared, Mom." Stella willed her heart to usher in compassion. "I fell in love with West Virginia."

Helen's eyebrows jerked upward, and her mouth dropped.

"I know. It shocked me, too. I'm moving in with a family I met. They live off the land and sell produce at the farmers' market and—"

"Stella, you have your entire life ahead of you. You have

a man who loves you. I've seen the way Roger looks at you. You could have a home and a family with him."

"I don't love him." The words tumbled out of Stella's mouth, her skin itching at the thought that she could have committed to such a life of conformity. "Would you want me to marry someone I don't love?"

"There's more to marriage than love."

The server placed two plates and the hors d'oeuvres on the table. Though Stella had arrived with an appetite, her mother's words made her stomach roil.

"Didn't you love Dad?" she whispered.

For a moment, Helen was soft as a tuft of cotton. All the hard edges blurred.

"Of course I did." Helen reached out and touched Stella's hand. "And I love you, too." Her eyes watered as she begged, "Don't do this to Roger. Don't do this to me. You are really making something of yourself in this world."

The nugget of compassion fled from Stella as she watched her mother recenter herself in the narrative.

"I have no interest in making it in *this* world. The 'success' that I have here doesn't appeal to me anymore." Stella filled her plate and began eating. What calmness she'd invited flamed into anger. "At least there, productivity isn't the only value."

I'm just another human resource in New York.

Helen was silent, providing an unfortunate moment for Stella to think.

Human resource. Am I just a resource to Beulah?

"West Virginia?" Helen enunciated the words and brought Stella's thoughts back into focus.

"Yes."

"Will you promise me to be careful, Stella? I know what can happen."

I know what can happen. Stella hadn't understood why her mother repeated the phrase so often until she was an adult and learned about her brother. When Stella was three, her mother had a baby boy, Daniel. At nine months, he tried to climb out of his crib, fell, and broke his neck. Her father told her once, when it was just the two of them enjoying life over bowls of cold cereal, that it took hours—and force—to remove the baby from her mother's arms.

"Yes, Mom. I'll be careful."

As she had with Roger, Stella shared what she could about her new home, and by the time the two finished eating, Stella's stomach was stuffed. She promised Helen she'd call and write, then gave her a longer hug than usual when she left.

***

At least this last task brought Stella joy. Getting back to New York, quitting her job, and saying her goodbyes had prevented her from making an appointment with Marin, and as she approached the storefront, she realized the psychic was not in her shop. A secure lockbox, just large enough for the wand, hung to the right of the glass door. Stella withdrew the wand Forest had given her from her backpack and nestled it inside. She pulled a pen and a notepad from her pack and wrote:

> *Marin,*
> *I found them. This wand is for you.*
> *Take care,*
> *Stella*

CHAPTER 15

Gwen

Gwen's legs and her own selfishness propelled her through the rain that pelted the city. An umbrella would have been wise, but she wanted to feel the raw discomfort of the water. Enough was enough. Two weeks had passed since the journey up the mountain had brought Madeline visions of Gwen's body entwined in Beatrice's vines. Two weeks since Madeline had used the words "space" and "time," insisting that the only way to protect Gwen was to separate from her.

By the time she reached Madeline's apartment, Gwen was soaked, her hair saturated with rain and her wet jeans clinging to her legs. The initial coolness of the water had turned to a cold chill. It was early autumn, those days when morning and evening offered different seasons.

She rang Madeline's apartment and, to her surprise, Madeline buzzed her in without question. In the halls of the apartment building, the air conditioning blew, and the chill turned into a frigid iciness that brought Gwen's arms across her chest and a quiver to her chin. When she made it to Madeline's doorstep, her love was already waiting.

"Gwen, what are you doing? It's pouring. Get in here, you'll catch a cold."

With a hand on Gwen's elbow, Madeline directed her to her bedroom. The room surprised Gwen: a four-post bed draped in an old quilt rested against the wall and a rocking chair sat in the corner, another quilt neatly folded and placed across the back. Madeline opened a drawer in a large chest and pulled out a pajama set, then from another a pair of pink, polka-dotted underwear. Gwen felt her face flush.

"Let me get you a towel," Madeline said, and she brought a hand to Gwen's cheek. "You're freezing." She opened the door to her bathroom and returned with an oversized white towel that could swallow Gwen whole.

Gwen knew her face was pleading, and she hated it. She was a successful woman with a successful business and a line of people desperately wanting to spend just one class under her guidance. But Madeline brought her down to a disciple.

"Change, and we'll talk," Madeline whispered.

Gwen nodded, speechless. With great difficulty, she pulled off her wet clothing, then rubbed the terrycloth towel against her skin and roughly through her hair, which she detangled with her fingers. She held up Madeline's panties and felt her eyes burn. She slipped them on, dragged the soft pajama shirt over her head, and pulled on the too-long pants, which she rolled up so she wouldn't trip. She turned to open the door, but the presence of a tall, thin man with a sharp-featured face shadowed by a leather cowboy hat startled her. She started to call Madeline's name, but the man shook his head slowly and placed a finger to his lips.

Gwen swallowed.

"Who are you?" Her voice came out as a hoarse whisper.

The man pointed to the gold ring circling his finger on his left hand, then to another corner of the room where a small corner table sat. On top of it, a blue orb.

"Eric."

The spirit nodded, smirked, then moved into the corner next to the urn. Gooseflesh erupted on Gwen's skin. She'd been lucky enough to only cross paths with kind ghosts and prayed Eric wouldn't be the exception.

"Does she know you're here?" Gwen swallowed.

Eric gave a slow head shake in response, then he jutted his finger to the urn and toward the bedroom door.

"You want out of this room?"

The man moved his mouth, but Gwen couldn't read the words. She never could hear them. Only see them. She thought of how hard Nancy tried to speak, frustrated until her fists balled by her sides and tears streaked down her face, while Gwen would sit, helpless.

"I can't understand you." Her voice, a breathy whisper, trembled as she spoke.

Eric pointed to himself, then back to the door, then back to the urn and to the door again.

A knock disrupted the conversation between Gwen and the ghost.

"Gwen. Are you alright?"

"Just one minute," Gwen responded, then pleaded with the apparition in front of her, "Can I tell her?"

A slow smile formed, then a nod of the head. She drew in a breath, then opened the door and made her way to the living room.

"I made us some tea," Madeline said, setting two cups of steaming amber liquid on the oval wooden table.

"Gwen," Madeline said, and the mere sound of her name out of Madeline's mouth brought tears to her eyes.

"Listen, you asked for space and time," Gwen started,

forgetting about Eric for a moment, "but I didn't realize we wouldn't speak at all."

"Gwen, your life is in danger."

"I'm not sure how a phone call or a text message could bring about the vision you saw."

"It's safest for me to keep my distance."

"But Maddie," Gwen said, "I haven't shown you the ocean." Her voice trembled as she spoke, and she made no efforts to control it. "We haven't had Christmas together. There are so many things that we haven't done." She ran her hand along Madeline's arm. "If you think your daughter is that angry and that violent, you shouldn't go back, either."

"The visions are getting more ..." Madeline's voice faded briefly. "Intense."

Madeline paused and circled her teacup with her finger, then stood abruptly, left the room, and returned with a wooden wand in her hand. "Stella left this in my lockbox."

"Stella?" Gwen didn't recognize the name.

"She's the woman I couldn't get a clear read on, remember?"

Madeline held the wand out for Gwen to inspect, but when Gwen reached for it, she jerked it away.

"The man in the snow made this wand. This is the wand laying on his chest in my vision." Madeline sat down beside Gwen. "The energy is almost more than I can handle. I'm not sleeping. I eat enough to stay alive but not enough to have the energy to do readings during the day. I haven't worked since our trip to the mountain."

Madeline squared her body to Gwen.

"All of these things lead to Beatrice, I know it. And I know Stella is there, on top of my mountain, with my daughter and the man with the curly hair. The wandmaker. I called her so many times. She won't answer."

"Then keep going. I promise, I won't follow you. But don't give up on us."

Please, don't give up on us.

Gwen had loved her wife Abbie with every cell of her being, but this insatiable need to be with Madeline overshadowed any concern she had for these visions or her own safety.

"I have nothing to offer you, Gwen." Madeline sighed. "I'm gutted. Empty."

"You don't have to offer me anything," Gwen said, placing her hand on Madeline's cheek. "Your existence brings me joy. You don't have to be whole all the time. I love you."

Madeline said nothing in response.

"Is being alone easier?" Gwen questioned, pulling her hand away. "Holding this by yourself?"

"It's a double-edged sword. It threatens to eat me alive, but at least no one else is in danger. Gwen, I've never been wrong."

"Then is there anything you can do to stop it?" Gwen winced at her own raised voice.

"I can't just let these things happen." Panic flooded Madeline's eyes, and her voice also elevated. "I have to keep you safe, and if I can help this man—this wandmaker—I have to try."

"But this isn't sustainable," Gwen rebutted, then with a small smile added, "I'm good for you, Madeline."

Madeline placed her hands on Gwen's face and brushed her cheeks with her thumbs. "You can never follow me."

"I swear I won't." The warmth of that skin-to-skin contact brought Gwen a sense of peace she hadn't felt in two weeks.

"When can we go see the ocean?" Madeline asked.

"I'll book us a trip right away."

"Stay for dinner?" Madeline's smile still showed hesitation. "Green beans, squash casserole, and biscuits."

"Smells delicious," Gwen said, then she kissed the edge of Madeline's mouth.

"We have a little time before dinner is ready." Madeline ran her fingers through Gwen's hair. "I think I'm ready to let my own hedge down." The woman's fingers trailed down the length of Gwen's side, causing goosebumps to form on her skin again. "Do you mind if I use magic with you?"

Gwen gasped when Madeline kissed her jawbone right near her ear. She could feel herself opening. She couldn't answer Madeline's question now that her body was running the show. She had waited so long for this moment, but now that she was in it, she felt like a child who didn't know her way around the playground.

Madeline moved and pressed her lips against Gwen's more intently than ever, ravenous, and her heartbeat quickened as Madeline pressed her palms against her chest, urging her to the bedroom. Gwen lifted her arms as Madeline tugged her shirt off, shaking her head with disapproval.

"What?" Gwen asked, her face hot.

"I don't know how or why you wear this thing." Madeline pulled down the straps of Gwen's bra, reached around, and unhooked it. Gwen blushed as she realized Madeline had been walking around braless.

"That has to feel better," Madeline insisted as she discarded the garment to the ground, then she pulled her own shirt over her head to reveal her bare breasts. Moving her body so close that their breasts touched, Madeline brought her hands to Gwen's face and kissed her. The blue orb in the corner caught Gwen's attention and made her pull away.

"Maddie." Gwen glanced at Madeline, then back to the corner where Eric had materialized, hands in pockets, a smirk on his face.

A smirk? Really?

"What's wrong, Gwen?"

"Could you move the urn out of the bedroom?" Gwen pointed, and Madeline's gaze followed.

Madeline took long, solid steps, lifted the urn into her arms, and turned to face Gwen. Her face was pale.

"This may kill the mood, or maybe you already know it, but ..." Gwen glanced at Eric, who shook his head, and for the first time, mouthed something Gwen could lip read: *Not now.* Gwen sighed, but smiled. "He's here with you."

Madeline's eyebrows knitted together, and she stared at the urn in her hands.

"Hey ..." Gwen trailed her fingers down Madeline's shoulders. "He's not mad. I'm pretty sure he likes me. He just doesn't want to ... watch."

Madeline's eyes grew wide, and her face flushed. She took the urn out of the room and returned with a tear-streaked face. Gwen was certain the moment had passed, but Madeline cleared her throat, shook her hair, looked down at her, and purred, "Where were we?"

Gwen grazed her hands down Madeline's sides and pulled down her leggings and panties along with them. Finally, Madeline stood naked in front of her, her silver-white hair pulled back in a long French braid that draped over her shoulder. Gwen toyed with the end, then released the braid from the elastic band, running her fingers through until loose curls cascaded down Madeline's torso. Madeline hooked her fingers into the band of the pajama pants Gwen wore and pulled them easily to the ground. Gwen felt a warm kiss on her lips, then on her neck, and within moments, she lay upon her back, her head cradled by the pillow and her hips straddled by a hungry-eyed Madeline.

"You never answered my question, Gwen," Madeline breathed. "May I use my magic?"

Gwen gave a slow nod. Madeline brought her lips to

Gwen's neck and kissed it, her tongue caressing her skin while her hands claimed other parts of Gwen's body: her upper thighs, her hips, her rib cage, her breasts. Gwen's body quivered when Madeline's fingers found her nipples and kneaded them as her lips continued to graze around her neck, her ears, her collarbone.

Madeline finally rested her forehead against Gwen's. Her hand descended, and Gwen opened her thighs to greet it. Madeline rested one hand upon the pillow beside Gwen's head while the other found the bud between her folds and coaxed pleasure from it. Gwen rocked her hips with the rhythm of Madeline's massage.

"What do you like, Gwen?" Madeline asked.

"Move inside of me," Gwen urged, pulling her lover's face toward her, "and kiss my mouth."

Gwen felt gentle pressure as Madeline eased fingers inside of her wet and warm space, and her rocking intensified.

"I know the spot," Madeline whispered, her voice gravelly now. "I can feel it and see it." Gwen could tell by the change in Madeline's breathing that her own craving was intensifying. "It's golden, and if I put pressure there ... are you ready for that now?"

A piece of Gwen never wanted her lover to stop, but now Madeline could finally assuage the ache that had lived and grown and gnawed inside of her. That empty wound.

"Please," she moaned, and she felt Madeline's fingertips rise. Time stopped. Her body quivered, her breaths left her in gasps, and hot tears filled her eyes. Gwen's muscles quaked around Madeline's fingers until she relaxed completely and pressed a hand against Madeline's face.

"Feel better?" Madeline asked with a smirk on her lips.

"I've wanted you to touch me since the first time I laid eyes on you."

A timer sounded in the kitchen.

"Biscuits are ready," Madeline said with a kiss on Gwen's forehead.

"What about you?" Gwen asked.

"We have all night."

CHAPTER 16

Beatrice

Beatrice woke to the sounds of movement in the kitchen: the whisking of eggs in a bowl and Forest's whistling. Smells filled the house—biscuits baking, bacon frying, and layered above it all was the smoky, earthy smell of the wood-burning stove, and for the first time, Beatrice felt no nausea in response. She pulled on a pair of pants, her flannel shirt, and boots.

"Good morning, Mother," Forest said, surveying her face.

"Good morning." She could feel the frown on her face. "You didn't come home last night."

"I did. It was just late, that's all."

"You were with Wanda and your coven?"

Forest nodded and poured the eggs into a hot pan. "Your color is better."

"I feel amazing." Beatrice grinned. "I didn't realize how awful I felt before." This time, she meant the words. Her body felt incredible, alive with a light energy. "Today's the day we make Stella a space. A room of her own."

Forest let out a chuckle. "We don't have time to build a new room before Stella gets back."

Beatrice smirked in return. "If I use my gift, Forest, we might."

"How?"

"I don't know, exactly." Beatrice shrugged. "You know, when my mother left me, I began to doubt everything. I used my gifts less and less. I lost faith in my power—in the power of the trees. Perhaps they'll listen and help."

Forest looked up from his egg scrambling. "You were so sick. I thought you might die." His eyes grew watery; he cleared his throat and returned his attention toward the eggs. "I'm not ready for that."

"I'm not ready for it either," Beatrice murmured, grateful for the truth of it. "I thought I had it all figured out. I'd have a daughter who'd have a daughter, and I'd pass into the earth and pop up as a tulip poplar."

Forest lowered his eyes, and Beatrice could see the impact of her words. She took her son's arm in her hand.

"You embody the Goddess as much as the rest of us."

"Well, I'm still waiting for her to tell me what to do," he said.

"First Mother told me you can do whatever you want," Beatrice said, but Forest shook his head and dumped his eggs onto a plate. "I want you to be happy. I haven't always encouraged you with your own magic, with your wands, and I'm sorry."

"They're selling so quickly." A cautious smile formed on his face. "I've made almost $200. I sent one with Stella to give as a gift to the psychic. She told you about her, right?"

Beatrice nodded, sat down, pulled a biscuit toward her, and sandwiched the scrambled egg and a piece of bacon between it.

"It's going to be interesting having her here." She took a bite and realized how much she missed loving food.

166

Heavy silence fell like a blanket over the breakfast table, and Beatrice knew something was weighing on Forest's heart.

"Hey," she said. "What is it?"

"She could help you find your mother if you wanted."

Beatrice squirmed in her seat. "Oh Forest. Mother would have come back if she wanted to." She eyed her food, no longer hungry.

"Maybe she tried to come back." Forest placed his hand on his mother's.

"No, Forest." Beatrice popped the last bite of biscuit into her mouth. "I don't want to find her." With the lie bringing heat to her chest, Beatrice stood, wiped her mouth on a cloth napkin, and collected Forest's plate. "We have work to do."

The two moved outside, and Beatrice surveyed the woods around the homestead.

"Forest. Tell me I can do this."

"You can do this, Mother."

Beatrice nodded and inhaled three deep breaths. Then she incanted a prayer to the element of the earth, stable, secure, fertile. She blessed and honored fire, water, and air. A shudder ran through her and she opened her eyes.

"I feel them. Let's see how the trees will help."

Beatrice pressed her hand against her home and asked for the trees to sacrifice their essence. She asked for logs to come to her, safely and swiftly. A crackling in the forest, small pops, echoing explosions, and then a rumbling under-foot brought hundreds of logs of precise length and width. They rolled and stacked themselves at Beatrice's feet.

"Thank you," she whispered. "Now build a room."

Beatrice watched with awe as the rough, moss-crusted bark peeled back from the logs and found the wood within smooth and cured. They rotated and spun, laying down on top of each other in layers, creating sharp corners. Beatrice watched Forest smile. The process took a little over an hour. They kneeled and watched as the Goddess created space for new life in the woods. As the roof was stacked, Beatrice felt tears move down her cheeks.

"Are you alright?" Forest asked.

She had never cried in front of him before without trying to stop it.

"Overwhelmed." Beatrice stood, placed her hand on the new room and breathed, "thank you." Forest moved forward and did the same.

"Do you think she'll like it?"

Forest shrugged. "I don't know. You know her better than I do."

"Which still isn't well."

For a moment, the surety Beatrice felt about inviting Stella into her home wavered. She inhaled. And exhaled. Arcas came lumbering from the woods as Forest continued to survey the space.

"She'll need a bed," Forest said. "I can build a frame and a platform. Would it bother you if I asked Wanda to help me get a mattress? Gathering feathers will take forever."

"Yes. Ask her. Bring it to the edge and I'll help you get it up. I'm going to pull quilts and get them washed up."

She entered her home and made her way back to her own bedroom, back to the trunk where her mother lived in memories. She pulled out the quilt her grandmother had made and drew it to her nose with a deep inhale. Beatrice couldn't guess how after all these years the quilt still smelled like her mother, like roses and pine, but the scent made her reluctant to wash it. She opened the quilt completely, allowed it to rise and fall in waves, then spread it upon the bed. Against the light blue backing, dark blue panes of fabric framed an intricately embroidered flower, and Beatrice allowed her fingers to graze them.

"I should ask." She spoke the words aloud, gathered the quilt in her arms, and headed for the trees.

***

Grandmother's eyes opened, and Beatrice took to her knees and bowed.

"Don't kneel before me, Beatrice. I'm not the Goddess. Now, what do we have here?"

Beatrice laid the quilt out before her grandmother. "I opened the trunk yesterday," she said.

"It was the first time you opened it?"

Beatrice nodded. "We made a room for Stella. She needs a quilt. I thought I should ask you first. You made it for my mother."

"Yes, I made it for her. But she's not here, and you have someone to keep warm at night. Beatrice, that house, those buildings, the trunk—those things are all yours now. Completely yours. You don't need to ask. Give the quilt to Stella."

Beatrice felt her heart grow hollow and her mouth dry as she whispered, "How does it still smell like her?" Grandmother said nothing. "Why didn't she come back? Why didn't she listen to me in the first place?"

Grandmother sighed and made a clicking noise. "I don't know why, Beatrice. Why didn't she come visit me? We may never have answers to these questions."

"Everything is different now," Beatrice said. "Stella's here. I'm wondering if she could help me find her. Should I ..."

Grandmother was silent for several breath cycles.

"I don't know, Beatrice."

"Will you tell me stories about her?" Beatrice asked.

"Of course. Did she tell you I always burned the biscuits and we never had decent bread until she was old enough to bake it?"

Beatrice smiled. "Yes. She told me."

"And did she tell you about Willa?"

Beatrice nodded.

"About eating so many blackberries she got sick to her stomach?"

"She told me stories every day about the two of you."

"Maybe *you* should tell me stories about her."

Beatrice spoke as little as possible about her mother to anyone, especially to Grandmother, but today she wanted to feel her. She wanted Grandmother to know who her mother was, how golden and kind and gentle. Perfect, until she wasn't.

"Okay," she whispered.

Beatrice watched as Grandmother's roots shifted around her, forming a cradle, swaddling her until she felt safe. Then, she spoke for hours about her mother's biscuits and Papa and how her mother's face changed when she fell in love, about diving and swimming and diving and swimming and diving and swimming to exhaustion. Story after story poured from Beatrice until she had no more words to offer, and she wiggled out of her grandmother's embrace.

"Make the place nice for Stella," Grandmother asked of her.

"I will," Beatrice promised. "You've spent a lot of time with her. Do you trust her?"

"With all my heart."

Beatrice pressed herself up, touched the tree's bark, and turned away from the Rock.

***

Gertrude circled over Beatrice's head and piped her own thoughts about their mother, but Beatrice only half listened. When she made it home, she went into Stella's room. It was large enough for a bed, a trunk to store clothes, and a small vanity table where Stella could place a bowl and pitcher to wash her face. Beatrice folded the quilt and nestled it in the corner to wait until Forest came with the mattress. She then returned to her own room and surveyed the trunk. Each woman reached a point when she took over the trunk and took her mother's belongings to the bonfire. A ritual. A letting go of the human temple the soul once inhabited.

Beatrice emptied the trunk of its contents: her mother's clothing, photographs, love letters, and hair pins; sketches she had made of visions; rocks and bones; the dress she wore when she married Eric. She went to the corner of the room where she had stacked clothes and items that meant something to her: Gertrude's feathers, figurines her papa and Forest had whittled, Papa's comb, and his handwritten instructions on how to preserve meat. At the bottom of the stack were more letters. Letters from her mother she had asked Beatrice not to open until after she had had her own child. Leaving them unopened, she added them to the bottom of the trunk.

She stood and looked around at her mother's things scattered around the floor, then left the room, grabbed a wooden crate from the porch, and returned. Beatrice set aside the photographs and considered keeping the wedding dress, but thought better of it. After filling the crate full, Beatrice grabbed one of the oil lamps that hung beside the kitchen door, which she swung open and allowed to slam behind her.

Each brisk step brought Beatrice closer to the place of her nightmares, and her body responded with tension. The circle where the family lit bonfires with each changing of the season lay overgrown with weeds and grass. Beatrice bid the vegetation to clear with a wave of her hand, leaving a dry space for her. She called logs to come, and they set themselves up to burn.

With no ceremony or sacred reverence, Beatrice tossed the items out of the crate. The dress. The love letters. The sketches Mother drew. One sketch caught her eye, and she pulled it from the pile. It struck her that her mother not only had gifts the rest of the world would call superpowers, but she was also a talented artist. The sketch of a handsome man with a carefully manicured mustache and beard brought questions to Beatrice's mind.

Who on earth?

Perhaps her mother had seen the man in a vision. Perhaps he was a new husband. The idea of it brought a new rage within her belly, and she brought the corner of the sketch to the flame of the lamp. Once it caught, she tossed it into the pile of her mother's things.

I know that was hard.

It was time, Beatrice.

Remember, you always have us.

Beatrice let their voices come as she watched the fire devour memories, the ashes fluttering like snow in the air.

CHAPTER 17

Stella

Arcas was waiting for Stella when she reached the top of the mountain. In New York, she had reduced her load to a large camping bag replete with clothes, shoes, toothbrushes, and other items she considered essential. She reached out and scratched under the bear's snout, and he responded by pressing his head into her hand.

"Hi, Arcas. It's good to see you, too."

Following the bear's footsteps deeper into the woods, Stella smelled the forest and placed her hands on the trees here and there. And as she walked, she thought of Beulah.

Stella paused as she approached the house, taking in the sight of an extra room that now flanked the right side. Arcas urged her forward. She opened the door and found a bed clothed with a hand-embroidered quilt. A trunk sat in one corner, and in the other, a dresser with a bowl of clean water for face and hand washing. An assortment of Beatrice's soaps sat beside the bowl. Stella moved across the room, allowing her fingertips to slide across the quilt. She lifted the soap to her nose and sat down on the bed for a moment. After Stella's father died, none of the spaces she lived in felt like home.

They did this for me. This is home.

The space behind her eyes prickled as Stella drew her bag up onto the bed, unzipped it, and placed her clothes in the trunk. That was when she heard it, a sound she'd never encountered before. It made the hair on the back of her neck stand at attention with its soft persistence. With her bag clutched in her hand, she edged herself onto the bed and stood with her back against the wall. Inch by inch, it crept from underneath the dresser and curled around the leg of the bed, rattle shaking, fangs exposed. Stella's body quaked, and a cold sweat formed around her ribs. She screamed.

Beatrice ran into the room, and the rattling intensified.

"Stella." Beatrice spoke, motioning for calmness with down-turned palms. "Stay very still. Put the bag down slowly. It won't help."

"It's a rattlesnake. It could kill me."

"I know how to treat a rattlesnake bite, but let's give her a chance to tell us why she's here."

The snake continued to curl around the bed until it made a slow ascent onto the mattress.

"Beatrice! If it bites me ..."

"Be patient," Beatrice said. "I'm trying to read it. Be still. Breathe. And give me the bag."

With slow movements, Stella brought the bag down by her side, and Beatrice took it from her. The snake flicked its tongue around Stella's bare feet, a tickling, frightening sensation as it slithered up Stella's leg. All her energy went into keeping the fluids in her bladder from spilling, her breathing all but ceased, and she stared at Beatrice helplessly. Beatrice simply nodded at her.

"Give her time," she urged. "Remember, Forest's companion is a *bear*."

Not a snake.

The snake continued to coil up Stella's leg, up her hip, and underneath her shirt, and its tongue flicked against her skin as it smelled her. It moved around her torso and finally nudged itself through the neck hole of her shirt. The brown, triangular head raised, and Stella could feel the snake's strong muscles press against her and away from her so that Stella had no choice but to meet its gaze.

"Hi," Stella said, and the snake placed its face closer. Its tongue licked Stella's nose. Then it slid the side of its head against Stella's cheek and rubbed around her neck, continuing to coil until the long body draped loosely around her like a scarf.

Beatrice's eyes were wide, and her mouth opened. "A rattlesnake chose you."

"My Arcas," Stella breathed.

"I think so." Beatrice offered her hand to help her get down from the bed. Then, she brought her hand up to the snake's body, but the snake shook its rattle.

"Okay," Beatrice whispered. She then nudged Stella and added, "You need to name her."

"Name her?"

"Yes. The name Arcas comes from Greek stories. Are there stories of snakes you know of that could help you name her?"

"Not many positive ones," Stella admitted.

"Because they're dangerous?" Beatrice cocked an eyebrow.

"Yes."

"Well, she's waiting."

Stella thought of all the serpents in stories she knew. Kaa had scared her in *The Jungle Book,* but Nagaina in *Rikki Tikki Tavi* held nuance. As a seventh grader, Stella argued the snake was misunderstood; above all things, Stella contended, Nagaina wanted to protect her family and build her home. But then, did she really want to name her companion after Kipling characters?

Then the snake rattled its tail, and the sound itself created the name.

"Sasha," she whispered. "Do you like that?"

The snake pressed her head more firmly into the back of Stella's neck. A sense of belonging welled up inside her.

"You're very impressive," Beatrice said as she sat down on the bed, and this time the snake allowed a stroke of her fingers.

"You made a room for me," Stella whispered and surveyed Beatrice's face.

"Yes. Are you hungry?"

"I feel like I'm always hungry," Stella confessed, and it was true. She was beyond hungry. She was ravenous, craving nourishment. Nourishment from the earth. Nourishment from the Goddess. Nourishment from this family. Nourishment from hard work and dirty hands and dirty feet.

"How did you do all of this in such a short amount of time?" Stella asked as Sasha draped herself around her neck like a string of pearls.

Beatrice smirked. "My gift, Stella."

"Magic."

Beatrice balked. "Not magic. Let me show you. What's your favorite flower?"

"Hydrangea."

"Ahh. I like them, too."

Beatrice pulled up her sleeves and rotated her right wrist, her gaze focused entirely on her hand. She stopped the movement. Stella watched as stems pierced upward through Beatrice's skin, grew leaves, and blossomed at the ends into blue, purple, green, and white puffs. One final vine creeped around and bound the bouquet together. Beatrice handed it over to Stella.

"Thank you."

"I think a bush would grow nicely just outside your door." Beatrice pointed outside. "Well, I can make anything grow wherever I want it to."

They moved out of Stella's room, through the living room and into the kitchen where, outside the window, Stella could see Forest rocking on the front porch with a steaming cup in his hands.

"Stella!" Forest set down his mug and stood, but started at the sight of the snake around her neck, taking one large step back. Sasha responded respectfully, sliding down Stella's leg and wrapping herself around her ankle.

"Whoa," Forest whispered, breathless.

"Her companion," Beatrice said warmly, as she stepped up on the porch.

"She scared me half to death," Stella admitted.

"I'm sure. She's fantastic." Forest's wide eyes roamed over the snake. "And terrifying."

A small panic rose in Stella, and she looked at Beatrice. "You're sure she won't hurt me?"

Beatrice placed a hand on Stella's shoulder and gave a nod.

"What do you think of your room?" Forest's smile appeared genuine, and Stella felt relief that her presence was no longer an intrusion.

"I love it."

The three moved inside. Beatrice stoked the fire in the stove and placed a teapot on the surface. The three ate salad and bread with spiced peaches for dessert while Stella talked about her trip to New York. She explained to a disappointed Forest that the psychic hadn't been there, but she'd left the wand. When they were finished, Stella returned to her room and pulled coffee, a new, larger coffee press, and chocolate from her pack, then she prepared a cup for Beulah.

"I'm going to go visit Beulah," she said, and left the home with Sasha draped around her.

***

The stabilizer muscles in Stella's ankles seemed stronger as she walked the twists and turns of the forest floor. She was happy. Happy to be an accomplice in Beulah's magic—no, an ingredient. Seeing Beulah's roots upturned Stella's lips, and she stepped more quickly across the Rock, not thinking about birth and transition and immortality this time. Beulah's blue eyes shined open as Stella made her way to kneel at the base of the tree. Stella released the cup of coffee onto the tree's roots, and Beulah's branches trembled.

"It's so warm," the tree said. "Who is this?" Beulah's eyes widened at the sight of the snake.

"Sasha. She was waiting for me when I got home."

"She's ... fearsome."

Stella stroked the snake with her right hand. "I feel like I belong now."

"You do, Stella. How is your room? Did they make it nice for you?"

"It's lovely. I get to cover up in the quilt you made tonight."

"I'm so glad. And Beatrice is being kind to you? She can be ... reserved."

"She's opening up. Was I gone too long?"

"No, no. Everything feels good. How was your trip?"

"I did what I needed to do." Stella lay down on Beulah's roots which shifted around her body. Once again, Beulah began to sip and sip and sip. "My mother is worried about me. She thinks I'm in a cult. Roger ..." Stella's voice trailed off. "I broke things off with him."

"Ahh," Beulah responded as she took in Stella's blood. "Was that difficult?"

"Not at all, actually."

"Stella." Beulah's voice changed. "I've been thinking a lot about our talk before you left. I know you think you love me, but you need to make yourself stop."

Stella felt the blood in her body turn to ice. "Beulah," she said as she sat up, "that's not how it works. You can't just stop—"

"Try," Beulah interrupted, desperation in her voice.

"I don't want to," Stella argued. "It's both the most real and the most surreal feeling I've ever felt. I've seen you, Beulah, in my visions. I've seen your face. I cupped it in my hands. This is going to work."

"You don't know all that there is to know about me."

"Well, we all have our secrets."

"When you first came, Stella, I knew you would be the one to help me, but I didn't expect for you to ..." Beulah's eyes fluttered closed, her roots still drawing Stella's blood to her. "Before you came, I had planned to leave the mountain if it worked."

"Leave Beatrice and Forest?" The thought made no sense. Why would Beulah want to be human again if she didn't want to be with her family?

"They don't need me, Stella."

"Beulah, you saved Beatrice's life. You have a purpose in their lives."

You have a purpose in my life.

"But if I become human again, I won't have my roots. I won't have anything to offer them."

"Do you really not have any po—" Stella stopped herself. "Gifts?"

"No. I don't."

"It makes no sense." Stella settled back into Beulah's cradle. "Why would the Goddess skip you?"

"I hate the Goddess."

Stella's eyes widened at the truth Beulah shared, and

she knew without asking that the tree hadn't shared her feelings with Beatrice.

"You have these moods, Beulah," she said after several silent moments have passed. "Sometimes you're calm and wise, and others … you seem terrified."

"I'm always terrified," Beulah whispered. "The rest is all put on. I mean, if this works, then what?"

"Then you live, Beulah. And you do what you want."

"I don't know how I'll be, Stella. I transitioned at thirty-six, but my body should be seventy-two. Will you still have the same affections for me if I come back an old woman?"

"Beulah," Stella said, smiling into the tree's eyes, "right now, you're a tree."

A ripple within the brown bark turned into a smile.

CHAPTER 18

Beatrice

"A few members of the coven are coming to town to visit Wanda and me. She's invited you to join us."

Beatrice stopped rocking and narrowed her eyes at her son. The response that threatened to bubble up from her gut and out of her lips got stuck somewhere within her, and she stared at Forest for a long time without speaking.

"Never mind," he whispered, then cleared his throat. He kept his disappointed eyes focused on his feet.

"I didn't say no, Forest." Beatrice stood, stepped toward him, and tilted his face with her fingertips. "Can you give me some time to think about it?"

Forest stood and hugged his mother. She breathed in the scent of him. Now that she was healthy again, the new, strange feeling of hope stirred around inside her. Pulling out of his hug, Beatrice peered into his eyes.

"Tell me what you and your coven do on the equinox."

"Well, we start by casting a circle."

At Beatrice's confused face, Forest explained the calling in of spirits for protection and closeness.

"There's also a ton of food!" Forest launched into a description of honey cakes and apples and the celebration of the second harvest, discussions, and journaling around nature's state of balance. He used his hands as he spoke, his excitement evident on his face. By the time he was finished, Beatrice knew she had to go with him.

"What can I bring?"

Forest's eyes widened. "You'll go with me?"

"Mmmhmm."

"Let's bake an apple pie! Your apple pie is better than Wanda's."

Beatrice released a hearty laugh. "It took you two years to confess that you like her jelly better than mine. How do I know you're telling the truth?"

"I promise." Forest raised his palm.

"Apple pie it is." Beatrice smiled, then made her way back into the house.

She found Stella lying on the couch, pale-faced and clammy.

"Stella." Beatrice kept her voice low as she kneeled beside the woman whom she now considered a friend. "Are you alright?"

"Yeah." Stella's voice was thin as she spoke, but her lips curled into a small smile. "Just tired."

Beatrice pressed the back of her hand to Stella's forehead. Unsatisfied, she bent down to place her own cheek against Stella's.

"You're not feverish."

Stella sat up, pulled Beatrice closer, and whispered in her ear, "I started my period. I could use some help with it. What do you use up here to keep things clean?"

"Ahh. Come on." Beatrice led Stella to the water closet and pulled from the cabinet a basket full of pouches and shreds of fabric. "Alright. I fill one of these with strips of

182

fabric and tie it into my underwear. Do you need clean clothes?"

"No. I just wrapped up a bunch of toilet paper to get me through until you got back."

"You look so pale. Is this normal?"

"No, but I'm okay. I'll clean up and maybe take a longer nap."

Beatrice considered Stella's routines since she'd made it back from New York. She ate breakfast, lunch, and dinner with Forest and herself, and helped with various chores, then spent the rest of her time with Grandmother. Nothing could explain the waxes and wanes of Stella's energy. But Beatrice wasn't sure the two were close enough yet for her to ask any more questions.

"If you're up for it, would you like to go with Forest and I to celebrate the equinox with his coven on Friday?"

"Oh. You want to go. I didn't think you'd say yes."

Beatrice bristled, irritated that her son would talk to Stella behind her back. She crossed her arms and lifted her chin. "He's invited you already?"

"No, he hasn't. He just told me he wanted to invite you."

Beatrice's annoyance turned into a question.

Why didn't he invite Stella?

"But I'd love to come if it's alright with Forest," Stella added.

Beatrice nodded. "How about I make you a snack and some hot tea?"

"Thank you," Stella replied.

Beatrice placed cheese and apple slices on a plate for Stella, then poured hot water over a satchel of dried chamomile. Forest came in with a few new pieces of wood Beatrice assumed were for whittling.

"Have you asked Stella to come with us on Friday?" she asked.

"I told her about it," Forest said.

"But did you ask her to come?"

Forest shrugged. "I'll make sure she knows she's welcome."

"Is she?"

"Mother, I don't know how they'll feel about her. Wanda likes her well enough, but the rest of them ... she's ..."

"She's what?" Beatrice's voice as firm as the night she had almost refused to let Stella come into her home.

Forest fiddled with the wood in his hands. After a few silent moments, he nodded his head. "Wanda would like her to be there," he said quietly. "I'll invite her."

"Thank you, Forest. You know, I've never had a friend. Family, yes. But not a friend. She's important to me."

"She's been spending so much time with Great Grand-mother. Have you noticed?"

"I have. She says they talk and talk. Tell each other stories."

"It's just that sometimes she comes home looking like she does today, pale and peaked. Something just doesn't sit right."

Beatrice hadn't noticed that pattern, but trusted her son's observations.

"I'll pay more attention."

***

By the time Friday afternoon came, Stella was pink faced again and happy to join Beatrice and Forest at Wanda's home for the equinox gathering. Butterflies flurried in Beatrice's stomach and her heart flipped in her chest the closer they came to the older woman's house.

"Four other people are coming. The men who sell my wands in their store and two members of the coven who left for North Carolina."

"North Carolina is more welcoming than here?" Beatrice asked.

"Well, the particular town they moved to seems to be."

Forest listed the members' names and details he felt the two women should know before they arrived. Thomas and Jeremy, the store owners, were married and had a coven of their own. They had their own battles with a local Christian church in their town. Dani grew up in a strict Christian household and had to work hard to keep from applying the same rigid, dogmatic structures in their new spiritual life. Forest explained that Dani felt neither like a man nor woman, preferring the pronouns they and them instead of she and her. Forest paused at this last part, seemingly to give Beatrice a moment to take the information in.

"Keep going." Beatrice motioned with her hand as they crossed the bridge into town.

"That doesn't shock or bother you?" Forest asked.

Beatrice considered the question before answering. Her home and her life had been dominated by feminine energy, and her experience with the hunter had certainly soured Beatrice's opinions toward the masculine. But Papa and Forest, as well as some men who came to the market—like Sam, the baker—balanced Beatrice's feelings. The idea that someone could sway between the two energies or even exist outside of them entirely was easy enough for Beatrice to accept.

"What about it would bother me?" she asked.

"Some people won't acknowledge there are more than two genders," Stella explained.

Beatrice shrugged. "Well, until Papa, I didn't know there was more than one." She kept her voice light.

"This is a safe space for them," Forest said. "If you accidentally use 'she,' just correct yourself and move on. Don't go into a huge apology, because you'll end up centering yourself."

Beatrice canted her head. "I will do my best, Forest."

She swallowed the indignance she felt at the suggestion that she couldn't behave.

Forest went on to describe the last guest as a red-haired, ruddy-faced Henry, a young man about his age, who dabbled in dark magic.

What the hell is dark magic?

Beatrice wanted to ask, but bit her tongue, choosing a short nod instead.

"Hello there! I'm so glad you came, Bea."

The woman's habit of shortening her name burned her biscuits. The two weren't close enough for that. But Beatrice reined in the irritation. "Thank you for inviting me. I made apple pie. Where can I place it?"

Wanda ushered the three into the kitchen and gestured to the center island covered end to end with food: fruits, cheese, assorted sliced meats, nuts, a large pot full of tomato soup, and a cake Beatrice didn't recognize.

"This is the honey cake I was telling you about." Forest pointed to a square pan at a simple golden-brown cake.

"Ahhh. Looks lovely."

"Thanks," a voice said, and Beatrice turned toward the speaker, who had a shaggy bob of shiny black hair, deep dark eyes, and light tan skin. "I made it."

"Mom, this is Dani."

Beatrice's insides jerked at the word Mom. She had always been Mother. Reaching out her hand, she smiled and offered a hello, hoping that her outsides appeared more at ease than her insides felt.

"It's so good to finally meet you," Dani said. "Forest has told me so much about you."

I certainly wish I knew more about you.

"It's nice to meet you as well, Dani," Beatrice said as she fought the urge to glare at her son.

Before Forest introduced the rest of his friends, he tucked Dani in for a long hug and a kiss on the cheek.

Oh ...

Thomas and Jeremy welcomed Beatrice with hugs.

"We just love your son," Jeremy said.

"That's right," Thomas agreed with a smile.

A knock at the door sent Wanda scurrying. She returned to the kitchen with two loaves of bread and Sam, the baker. His eyes revealed discomfort as they darted from face to face.

"Please, take a plate home with you, Sam," Wanda insisted.

Sam lifted his hand. "No, no. I was just dropping off the bread. I will take my jam, though." The smile on the baker's face seemed forced, but when he glanced at Beatrice, his shoulders relaxed, the anxiety replaced by attraction.

Beatrice lifted her head, refusing to squirm under the attention. She was not inclined to fall in love with anyone. Ever. Her mother made it seem she had no choice in her own romantic undoing, but Beatrice did her best to guard her own heart. And, if Mother's belief that the heart wanted what the heart wanted was indeed true, Beatrice was certain hers did not want Sam Thompson.

Wanda handed Sam the jams with which she bartered for the bread, and he just nodded and left. As the group began casting a circle, a cold sweat broke out on Beatrice's skin, gathering in droplets that dripped under her arms. She watched her son's calm but solemn face as he used his wand to summon spirits of protection. He then blessed the meal before him, and for the first time, Beatrice acknowledged the feeling that lay under her resistance to the coven: grief. Forest chose this life, this path, and in doing so turned away from their family rituals, from the mountain, and from the Goddess herself.

And now, there's Dani.

When he finished blessing the food, Forest smiled at his

mother. She loaded her plate with a bit of everything on the island, even Wanda's jams.

"Try this one with a bit of bread and cheese," Wanda said, as she tapped the lid on a pint-sized jar filled with dark green jelly. "It's jalapeño."

Beatrice dropped a dollop on her plate, then ladled a bowl of soup for herself. Wanda had prepared her dining room for the occasion. In the center of the table, autumn décor surrounded orange, yellow, and green candles.

Stella settled in beside Beatrice. Without waiting for anyone else, Beatrice dunked a slice of bread into the soup. The sweetness of basil offset the tanginess of the dish, and a spiciness peeked through.

"Mmm." Beatrice couldn't contain the groan. "This is delicious."

"Why, thank you," Jeremy said.

Beatrice then followed Wanda's suggestion by smearing the spicy jelly on the rest of the bread and sandwiching a piece of cheese within it. Expectation danced in Wanda's eyes.

"Also delicious," Beatrice said, and she meant it. She took the time to try each one of Wanda's jams. "You win." Beatrice grinned at Wanda after her last bite of strawberry.

Wanda reached out her hand and covered Beatrice's. With a squeeze, she whispered, "It's not a competition."

Stella launched into a series of questions about the group's practices, her tone occasionally deviating back into the journalistic nature she'd originally had with Beatrice and Forest. A new fear brought ice to Beatrice's veins.

What if Stella says too much?

Beatrice swallowed the fear with a spoonful of hot soup and continued listening. Thomas and Jeremy described the particular sect of Christians who stuffed prayer cloths anointed with oil around their home, in inconspicuous places like the gutters and the mailbox.

"And what is that supposed to do?" Beatrice tried to keep the skepticism from her voice. "Don't you have your own wards and protections?" She thought about the Hedge and how strong and thick and violent it was.

"We assume the cloths are to hold our magic inside our home. To protect them from us." Thomas gestured to himself.

"They're so against witchcraft, yet they practice it," the red-haired Henry said, then snorted. "I've started using baneful magic on them."

Forest cleared his throat, and Beatrice watched him squirm in his chair.

"You've got to stop it with this love and light shit, Forest. Fuck," Henry said, then dunked a piece of bread in his soup.

"I will never hurt anyone, or impact free will." The somber conviction in Forest's eyes steeled Beatrice.

"What is baneful magic?" Beatrice asked.

"Curses. Hexes. Bindings," Henry replied as his mouth continued to work on a piece of bread.

"And what exactly do those do?"

"They cause harm," Forest said through a tight jaw.

"Don't listen to him." Henry took a swig of mead. "Baneful magic brings justice through punishment."

Beatrice shivered, despite her efforts to maintain control.

Jeremy changed the subject by pointing to Beatrice. "Spirit is strong with you."

"Is it?" Beatrice suppressed an eye roll and took a bite of the honey cake. It was dense and sweet, not something she would want often, but the quality of it matched the change in season. For a moment, Beatrice's thoughts flitted to her mother. The autumnal equinox was her favorite, the shortening of the days and cozy snuggles in front of the fire. When days went by with no sunshine, she would hold Beatrice as she cried, longing for the light.

"Beatrice." Wanda placed a hand on her elbow. "You zoned out there for a minute."

"Sorry. What were you saying?"

Jeremy explained he sensed Beatrice had a strong connection with the earth. Beatrice wasn't sure how to reply except a "thank you."

I am the child of a Goddess.

Conversations turned lighter. Members of the group teased Stella here and there about her big city ways, but Stella kept confident dignity instead of growing defensive. The night ended with a bonfire. Beatrice did her best to keep her eyes off Forest, who had his arm around Dani's waist. Flames had just started their assault on the larger logs when a voice called from the other side of Wanda's fence. She excused herself to address the voice, then returned with a sour expression on her face.

"Police," she said.

"Wanting what?" Dani asked, their voice acidic.

"Apparently there's a burn ban due to the dry weather."

Dani at once pulled out their phone and Beatrice marveled at the way their thumbs flew across the screen.

"No notice of a burn ban anywhere." They stuffed the device back in their pocket, crossed their arms, and turned to Wanda. "What do you wanna do?"

"I don't want any more trouble with them. Let's put it out."

The gathering ended as the last of the embers sizzled and steamed. Wanda insisted she didn't need help to clean up and offered Beatrice a hug.

"Thank you for coming. It means a lot to Forest."

"I enjoyed myself." Beatrice turned to Dani. "It was very nice to meet you."

"Likewise."

***

Beatrice used her vines to help Stella, Forest, and herself up the mountain's side, and when they arrived home, she pulled her son aside.

"Thank you for inviting me. I had a good time," she said.

"What did you think of them?"

"Your friends are lovely. I can see why you enjoy them so much."

"I meant Dani. They're special to me, Mother."

Beatrice closed her eyes for a moment and swallowed questions about how much Forest had told this person.

"I want you to like them," Forest said, before Beatrice had a chance to speak.

Beatrice thought about Dani and the way they moved through the group. It was obvious Forest was special to them, too.

"Forest, I know why all of this bothered me for so long."

Forest tilted his head and Beatrice could see a weary apprehension fill it.

"It feels like you're turning your back on the Goddess and on our ways. Are you angry with Her?"

"No." Forest's response was swift and firm. He shook his head and added, "No, I'm not angry. I still pray to Her, and She answers me."

Beatrice's eyes widened. "Answers you?"

"Not always directly."

"But sometimes directly? You *hear* her?"

Forest blushed. "You don't?" he asked.

"No. Never."

Forest lifted his shoulders to his ears then let them fall.

Beatrice could only respond with, "Wow."

Forest smiled and wrapped his mother in a hug. "I know this season gets long for you."

"It makes me miss my mother." The words were out of her mouth before she could stop them, and it was Beatrice's turn to blush.

"Get out there and look for her."

Not able to tolerate the pity in Forest's eyes, Beatrice mumbled goodnight, pried herself from his hug, and slipped to her room, where she cried herself to sleep.

CHAPTER 19

Gwen

The ring weighed heavily in the pocket of Gwen's down coat as she walked home, her arms full of groceries for the homemade meal she planned for Madeline, complete with her favorite apple pie. Nervousness balled in her throat, and every few moments she swallowed the fear, adding to the hard rocks in her stomach. Gwen saw no middle ground here. No Temperance card. Madeline would either say yes and open her heart to Gwen completely, or she would say no and choose her past once more. Gwen wasn't sure she could handle the latter.

Months had passed since Madeline had stepped into the studio and cracked Gwen's chest open like an egg, exposing all her runny parts, the raw nerves, heat, and emotion. The moons waxed on and on to fullness, and Madeline would leave again, packing an assortment of hiking gear, leaving Gwen alone in their apartment to ponder. To doubt.

She had taken Madeline to see dolphins and walk barefooted along the shore. Madeline's visions continued, but each time, Gwen assured her she would never follow her home. The two never discussed the passing of time, or how each second brought Gwen closer to pain and suffering.

She could feel the cased ring tap her hip as she walked, and she tucked her hair behind her ears with her free hand. Under normal circumstances, Gwen took the stairs to the apartment, but on this day, anticipation brought a quiver to her legs and her heart shook in her chest arrhythmically, so she allowed the elevator to lift her to their floor. The elevator door opened and Gwen fumbled for her keys, breathing a sigh of relief as she sat the groceries on the table.

She had planned a simple meal: pasta all'Amatriciana, substituting liquid smoke for pork cheek. On one of Madeline's trips, Gwen created the dish for Ben, who approved; tonight, she would recreate it for her lover, hoping she would soon become her wife.

Gwen drew the recipe from her pocket and smoothed it out on the countertop. She took her time peeling and chopping the onions, scattering them with smashed garlic into a saucepan in an ample amount of olive oil. Silent in her movements, the motions of her hands and wrists became meditative dedications to her love. She breathed in. She breathed out. She lengthened her exhale and prayed. Madeline had once said that all acts of creation were spells. Surely by now, Madeline trusted her enough. Surely by now, Gwen had proven her loyalty and faith in the unbelievable family stories.

Gwen diced fresh tomatoes and added them to the sauce, followed by a can of stewed. She knew Madeline's rule about tomatoes: they were best in the summer, pulled straight from the vine, ripened almost to the point of bursting. But in December, winter tomatoes would have to do. A dash of red pepper flakes. Liquid smoke.

Once the sauce was simmering, Gwen withdrew two of her mother's chartreuse wine glasses from the china cabinet. Though they were odd, she loved them. Madeline understood loving and missing your mother, so she loved them as well. She placed a bottle of red wine on the table along with settings of her mother's china, salt and pepper, and freshly grated cheese.

The phone rang. Madeline. Gwen answered, more breathless than she wanted.

"You okay?" Madeline chuckled.

"Yes!" Gwen reassured.

"I just needed to hear your voice. It's been a long day. And I'm nervous about the trip."

The moon would soon be full in the sign of Cancer, and Madeline would be gone.

"Oh, Maddie, I know." Gwen spoke softly while stirring the sauce with a wooden spoon, lifting it to her lips for a taste. More salt. "I have a good feeling about this time," Gwen said, convincing herself she meant it. Perhaps after Madeline accepted the proposal, she would put away the visions and just be with her.

On the other end of the line, Madeline sighed. "I can't keep doing this, you know."

Gwen recalled the advice she'd given Madeline in the past. *Ask around town about her. Search for a death certificate. Google the woman, for heaven's sake.* Madeline responded to each suggestion with a reminder that her family line was nothing like Gwen's own.

Returning to the call, Gwen promised, "You have me, always."

"I love you, Gwen. I'll be home soon."

Gwen ended the call, stirred the sauce, and filled a pot with water for the pasta. She took great care in chopping and tossing a salad, and placed a loaf of bread in the oven to toast. As she waited for the pasta and bread, she moved to the Christmas tree in the corner of the living room. Madeline decorated the tree with photographs instead of ornaments and encouraged Gwen to tuck her own pictures within the branches. She withdrew a picture of her mother smiling, holding her and Ben, one baby in each arm. Tears creeped into Gwen's eyes.

She returned the picture and moved her eyes to the center of the tree where a large photo of her and Madeline rested. She pressed it to her heart.

Surely.

She put it back, then found the picture that always tightened her chest and wiggled at her insides. A tall, thin man stood with one arm around a young girl. Each of them had a hand in supporting the belly of a large fish. Madeline's old life. Gwen focused her gaze on the blue orb on the mantel. She'd never asked Eric to come. She'd seen less and less of him lately, but today, she needed his advice.

"Eric?" she whispered, and he appeared before her in a form more solid than she'd seen. "I'm going to ask Madeline to marry me. Do I have your blessing?"

The spirit grinned and gave a nod.

"Think she'll say yes?"

The man shrugged with upturned palms.

"Thank you."

With that, the apparition dissolved. She couldn't bring herself to hate the man, or even be jealous, for that matter. But the little girl in the picture, she was a different matter. On the gloomiest days when Madeline was gone, Gwen hated Beatrice. She had researched her name once: bringer of joy. Gwen scoffed and placed her fingers on the photograph of the child and her Papa. She thought of the Hedge and the visions of the vines. Beatrice: bringer of fear and frustration.

Gwen moved back to the kitchen and began piecing together the meal. She brought the salad to the table, sliced the bread, and poured the wine. As she finished pouring, Madeline opened the door.

"Something smells amazing," Madeline said, making her way into the apartment and wrapping her arm around Gwen. Gwen couldn't stand another moment with sweaty palms and shaking heart. She dropped to her knees in front of Madeline and gazed into her face.

"What are you doing, Gwen?" Madeline's face wore a smile until Gwen brought forth the ring, a simple round cut diamond nestled in a thin gold band.

"Will you marry me, Madeline?"

"Gwen." The smile was gone. "Why?" Madeline asked, her eyes arched in a lack of understanding. "We're practically married as it is. We live together, sleep together, make love. Why?"

Why?

Gwen had not allowed herself to consider Madeline saying no, but she made her way to her feet and faced it.

"Because it means something to me." Gwen pressed a hand to her heart. "It's a public commitment to our relationship. It's an honoring of our love."

"Gwen, when I go away, I never know if I'll return to you. And these visions—"

"Then stop going, Madeline." Gwen's chest heaved, and every piece of her trembled, but she continued. "Don't go. Don't go ever again. Be with me here and now. She's gone. Beatrice is gone."

In the kitchen, the pasta water boiled over and the sauce began to scald. Madeline's nostrils flared, and Gwen's breath pressed forcefully in and out of her chest as she watched the woman's eyes turn from brilliant blue to fiery orange to blazing red. Madeline's palms glowed, and Gwen felt heat from her body.

"Don't you say that to me," Madeline growled. Never had Gwen seen this fury. "You do not have children. This is an ache you will never know."

Madeline seemed to grow two inches in each direction,

and though fear threatened to spark in Gwen's belly, she pulled her shoulders back, lifted her chin, and peered into those burning eyes.

"Are you the one who is going to hurt me, Madeline? Bruise my face? Shatter my bones?"

As though doused in ice, Madeline amended to herself again: blue, gentle eyes.

"I would never hurt you," Madeline said, and the quiver of her chin indicated she was close to tears.

Gwen laughed a hearty, hysterical laugh. "This hurts me."

"When I find her—"

Gwen laughed again. "If you were going to find her, you would have by now."

"I've given all of myself to you that I can."

Gwen shook her head and whispered, "Stop dinner."

Madeline twisted her hand, and the boiling pot ceased.

"I hate her." Gwen's eyes filled with tears, but she added no more.

She placed the ring on the table, then brought her body close to Madeline's, cupping her lover's wet cheeks in her hands. She pressed onto her tiptoes, drew the red face down, and kissed the trembling lips. The only sounds were city sounds and those of Madeline's sniffles. She pulled Madeline firmly by the wrists toward the bedroom, encouraged her clothes off, and pressed her down on the bed.

Gwen knew how to draw wetness from Madeline and moved with no hesitation or compassion for her nipples, her tongue lapping like a cat at the erecting nubs. Madeline gasped as Gwen pulled both of her nipples with her fingers. Then she pressed her mouth between her breasts and grazed down her torso until she found the soft lips between her thighs. She pressed them apart with her fingers and her tongue found Madeline's swollen center. Soaking in all the smells that made up her lover, Gwen considered that it could be the last time. She felt muscles clench and knew Madeline was on the edge, so she stopped her movement and stared at the tear-streaked face. Shifting on the bed, she moved her fingers inside, eliciting a whine.

Good. Whine.

Another finger, and then another. Madeline brought her head up, eyes pleading. Gwen knew how she must look. Sweat beaded down her forehead, and her hair tangled around her face. Manipulating her fingers, she buried her entire fist inside of Madeline, who cried out with the thrusts. Gwen took the index finger of her free hand and teased Madeline's most sensitive spot. The muscles within Madeline jerked and her crying broke into sobs until every inch of her trembled.

Gwen closed her eyes, summoned what compassion she had left, and eased her fist from Madeline. She stood and packed a bag with no idea how long she'd be gone, while Madeline lay curled in a fetal position on the bed, not saying a word.

***

Gwen fell into her brother's arms in the foyer of his apartment.

"Oh, Gwen. I'm sorry," Ben said into her hair.

"I know what you think about her," Gwen pressed. "You're probably relieved."

"I have nothing against Madeline." Ben took his sister's chin between his forefinger and thumb. "But these visions terrify me, and I think as long as you're with her, you're in danger."

With an exhausted sigh, Gwen grabbed her suitcase and wheeled it into Ben's home. "Thank you for letting me stay. I'll start looking for a place tomorrow."

Turning right, Gwen moved toward the guest bedroom she'd stayed in right after Abbie died. The toile bedspread hadn't changed, though the heartache wasn't quite the same. Gwen sat on the edge of the bed and rubbed her swollen, sore eyes with her fingers.

"You don't have to start looking for a place tomorrow. You can stay here as long as you like. Give it a day or two just to be sure."

Gwen closed her eyes and swallowed in efforts to muster the courage it would take to give her next confession. "Madeline scared me tonight. She ... grew and—?"

"Grew?"

Gwen opened her eyes. "I don't know how to explain it. And her eyes turned red, fiery red like the stupid cliche, but it was real, and her skin was hot like she could ... burn me."

Ben sat down beside her and for several moments, they were silent.

"She's never been wrong, Ben," Gwen whispered and laid her head on her brother's shoulder. "Once in a while, I imagine it. The vines. Beatrice. Me in the middle of some strange fantasy ... science fiction scene. It feels closer and closer every minute."

Ben locked eyes with his sister. "Whatever is coming, Gwen, I'll fight for you."

"Beatrice has every right to be mad at her mother," Gwen said, wondering if Madeline would have had a similar violent response to those words.

"But not you," Ben said.

Gwen considered the two different portraits of Beatrice Madeline painted. Beatrice, the bright, resourceful, caring soul who helped nurse her Papa to health. Beatrice, the jealous, angry daughter willing to murder for revenge.

Despite her anxiety, Gwen's hunger made her stomach rumble.

"Pizza?" he asked.

"Sounds good," Gwen said, then she curled up on the bed and cried for Madeline while she waited for the pizza to come.

***

The next night, Gwen graciously accepted the compliments practitioners gave her as they left the studio. The class had been good. Solidly themed, interesting transitions, constant reminders of mind, body, spirit. She allowed for a long savasana and during the pose she practiced loving kindness meditations, and this time, she added Beatrice to the roll.

The New York air was especially bitter, and Gwen cursed under her breath as she fumbled to lock the door in her haste to get out of the cold. Rarely did she leave the studio so late, but cleaning the space helped her take her mind off Madeline. All the practitioners had left, but when Gwen turned her back to the locked door, she realized she was not alone. Three men stood in a semicircle around her.

"May I help you?" Gwen asked, refusing to shrink.

One man moved closer. "My wife has taken your class. All of a sudden, she thinks she's a lesbian. Any idea how that happened?"

Gwen snorted through her nose and refused to allow her exterior to give away the fear that quivered inside of her. "Step back." She enunciated the words.

"No," the man said, taking a step closer toward.

Gwen reared her right arm back and swung; her fist found purchase against his cheek. She refused to give the man time to react and swung again. But when the other men grabbed her shoulders and shoved her against the glass door of the studio, she knew.

It's beginning, she thought, and though somehow acceptance stilled her soul, her body thrashed against the men until it could no longer.

CHAPTER 20

Madeline

Madeline jumped into a pair of pants and a sweater, ran into the streets of New York, and hailed a cab. It wasn't a nightmare. She had felt every rip and tear of Gwen's clothes, every kick to her ribs and punch to her face.

"Go faster," she begged the cab driver.

"Look, lady, I'm doing the best I can out here tonight, okay?"

It was the Friday before Christmas. Window shoppers lined the sidewalks, and the streets were full of vehicles of every kind. Delivery trucks. Emergency vehicles. And taxi after taxi, just like the one she was in.

Marry me, Gwen had asked, not on one knee but on both, bringing Madeline to a crossroads. Her choice: embrace the present or keep searching for Beatrice. And in that moment, Madeline chose her daughter. Then came the misery. Vitriol Madeline never expected poured from Gwen's mouth. And after, Gwen reminded her of the heat between them, packed a bag, and left.

Now, regret like cotton stuffing filled Madeline with dry nothingness and everything all at once.

When the cab finally pulled into the visitor's entrance of the hospital, she threw him too much money and told him to keep the change. Then she ran while she placed a phone call to Ben.

Madeline released a panicked shout. "What happened, Ben?"

"She was attacked as she was leaving the studio. They ransacked the place. She's in the hospital."

"I'm here."

Madeline ended the call and moved around people with no "excuse mes," following signs until she spotted Ben, still in his business suit with his briefcase at his feet.

"Who did this?" Madeline asked.

"I don't know. I haven't seen her."

"Has anyone spoken with you? A doctor? Nurse?"

"Not yet." Ben shook his head. "But it's bad enough for her to be here."

They both sat down on a small vinyl couch.

"Why are you here, Madeline?"

"Because I love her." Her heart clenched when Ben's eyebrows jumped up in disbelief. "I can help her." Madeline's voice trembled. "You know I can. I just need to get to her."

Madeline grew quiet and fingered the racoon jaw pendant that hung around her neck. A present from Gwen for her birthday. A few teeth remained, but the jeweler had replaced them with small, sculpted pieces of amethyst.

"You hurt my sister."

Madeline turned away and continued to rub her thumb against the smooth surface of the bone.

A nurse came into the room and asked, "Are you Ben?" and Ben stood with a nod. Madeline moved close as if she, too, were family.

"How is she? What happened?" Madeline asked.

"There are major contusions on her face, resulting in massive swelling. She was hit or kicked in the chest, and four of her ribs were broken."

The nurse's voice became fuzzy, and Madeline let tears fall down her cheeks silently. No sobs, but fat, lava tears.

"She'll be in the hospital for a night or two for monitoring," the nurse continued.

"Can we see her?" Madeline asked.

"Are you family?"

"I'm her brother. She's her partner." Ben gestured to Madeline, and the nurse nodded.

"When she wakes up, the police will want to speak with her and collect a statement, but you can visit until then."

"Thank you for letting me see her, Ben," Madeline said.

Ben urged her to follow the nurse with a jerk of his head. The contents of Madeline's dinner rose to her throat when she looked down at Gwen, her Gwen, lying unconscious under a thin hospital blanket, blood clumping her hair. Bruises to her jaw and neck. An eye so swollen Madeline knew it couldn't open. Her hand came to her mouth, and sobs threatened to bubble from her throat, but she refused to make a sound. The tears continued.

"Jesus Christ," Ben whispered. "Who did this to you, Gwen?"

Madeline watched as he sat down beside his sister's less injured side, took her hand, bowed his head, and bawled. She wiped the tears from her own face, cleared her throat, and sat down on Gwen's other side. She closed her eyes and rubbed her hands together until she felt it, the electric energy she could give her love. More gentle than gentle, she placed her hand on Gwen's hot cheek. There was the movement of Gwen pulling away, a rotation of her head toward her better cheek, and a low, thin groan.

"Please go, Madeline. I don't want you here right now."

Madeline felt her chin quiver, and though she bade it to stop, it wouldn't.

"Gwen, at least let me heal you. I'm sorry. I choose you, Gwen."

"You have to deal with her, Maddie." Gwen opened the eye she could and locked it on Madeline. "She's the next thing coming for me, and I don't want to face her. I don't want to go through anything else. It hurts, and I don't want to die. Please. She's coming for me."

Madeline had no argument.

"Go, please," Gwen sputtered, and her head fell back into the pillow.

Ben encouraged Madeline into the hospital hallway. Her senses were assaulted by the smells of rubbing alcohol and latex, the way the too-bright lights reflected off the too-shiny floor, and the piercing codes that alerted the nurses where to go.

"I'll never go again if that's what she wants. I'll stay right here." Madeline struggled to breathe as the sobs constricted her throat.

"Staying here will not help her."

Ben moved back into Gwen's room for a moment and whispered something to her. When he made his way back to Madeline, his face was hard.

"Let me walk you out."

Outside on the sidewalk, Ben frowned at Madeline and crossed his arms. His breath steamed in the cold. "How are you going to keep Beatrice from hurting my sister?"

"I'll find her," Madeline said, grinding her jaw. "I won't stop until I find her."

"And then what? When you find her, what will you do?"

"I don't know," Madeline confessed, shaking her head.

"What are you going to do, Madeline?" Ben stood inches away from her, his voice raised, angry, and raw from crying.

"I don't know!"

"Get away from here and leave my sister alone."

Madeline swallowed deeply, turned, and ran down the sidewalk.

***

Maybe this time, so close to the solstice, she would have a chance. She hailed another cab and once more threw more money at the driver than was due, then made her way up the stairs to her apartment.

The Solstice decorations sparkled. Toward the top, in a prominent spot on the handsome tree, sat a picture of Madeline and Gwen. Madeline kissed her on the cheek, and each of them wore a beatific smile. She reached for the picture, drew it into her heart briefly, then placed it back. She glanced at the other pictures; old photographs that Eric had taken of her and Beatrice and Gertrude. Beatrice wore a smile in all of them, while Gertrude frowned or screamed or looked away. Madeline regarded the blue orb on the mantle that housed the remains of both husband and daughter. She pulled it to her, sat down on the couch, and placed the urn on her lap.

"Maybe I shouldn't take you this time," she whispered, stroking the orb, then returned it to the mantle. In moments like this, Madeline envied Beatrice's gift of talking to the dead.

Madeline stood and walked down the short hallway to the bedroom she shared with Gwen, whose gray cardigan still hung on the back of the rocking chair. She picked it up, breathed in Gwen's scent, and missed her. She packed clothes and a small store of food. This would be her two hundred and twentieth attempt to find her daughter, and she knew what the mountain expected of her.

When she was finished, Madeline moved to her altar in the living room, drew a candle from a wooden box, and balanced it within a brass candleholder. She drew a saucer of oil and anointed the candle, drawing outward from the center.

"I release my resistance to finding her, and my resistance to letting go." She lit the candle with a match, touched the Goddess's felted feet with her fingers, and bowed her head. "Please, help me."

With her forehead pressed to the floor, Madeline thought of her own mother and wondered how painful it would be to see the tree again. When Madeline was very young, Beulah had led her to the mountain's peak weekly to speak with the tree called First Mother. She didn't understand her mother's desperation until she was seventeen and learned what was to come on her eighteenth birthday. Beulah had begged Madeline to flee the mountain with her, so they packed supplies and slept in the same room the night before they planned to leave. But in the middle of the night, Madeline's first vision came. A little girl with brown eyes and thick brown hair stole her heart. She followed the child into the woods and to the Rock, where the Goddess sparked life within her womb. Madeline remembered her mother's reaction to the indiscretion. She had stared into the fire for a long, quiet time, then promised Madeline that she'd never leave her alone, and retired to her room. Madeline had listened to her cry the rest of the night.

Madeline remained on the floor until the candle burned itself out, then she made reservations for an early morning flight, and allowed herself to sleep.

CHAPTER 21

Beatrice

Beatrice sat in a rocking chair in front of the fire, peeling potatoes for the stew she was making for supper. Months had passed since Stella's arrival. Beatrice stopped peeling to watch the woman practice crochet, her reptilian companion curled in a black and brown banded swirl around her leg with its head propped against her foot. Forest rocked and hummed and whittled at a piece of wood. Occasionally, the three would break into a conversation about the early snow, or how well-stocked their pantries were.

Stella had withdrawn money each month for them to spend on luxuries like chocolate and coffee. She would bring home other things as well, like popcorn and chewing gum, and once a book of poetry. Beatrice loved for Stella to read from the book, especially the poems about trees.

On this night, the air was cold but not so cold it could ward off snow. Arcas had tucked himself away for the winter, and Beatrice was ready to prepare for the solstice.

"There's a boar in the smokehouse for us to roast," her

voice punctuated the silence. "With vegetables and home-made bread. Forest, what is the coven doing? I'm sure they'll want time with you."

Forest scratched his beard and kept his eyes on the wood in his hands. "They'll have a meal and a bonfire, like we do. They like to pull tarot and drink mulled wine and sing."

"Ahh ..." A thread in Beatrice's heart pulled tight. Since Forest's birth, he and Beatrice had never spent a solstice apart.

"Mother, the winter solstice is your favorite. I will be with you."

Beatrice smiled at her son. "Thank you."

"It's only a week away," Stella said. "This time of year is so hectic in the city. So many social events. Parties. Exhausting."

"How did you celebrate, Stella?" Beatrice asked.

"At Christmas, we would put up a tree and decorate the house. We'd go to church on Christmas Eve."

"A Christian church?" Forest asked, and Beatrice could feel the weight of his question.

"Yes," Stella said.

"Do you believe in those things?" Forest asked, and Beatrice watched the flush grow on Stella's cheeks.

"Which things?"

"Jesus being born of a virgin," Forest said as he released his whittling from his hands and turned his full attention toward Stella. "Death and resurrection. Those things."

Stella also stopped working with her hands, but let the question linger.

"I didn't," she said. "I could never bring myself to believe those things. But, Forest, now I'm on a mountain where the trees talk, and a bathtub stays filled with hot, clean water, and the lamps are always lit unless you ask them to lower. I suppose anything is possible. Resurrection, perhaps, is especially possible."

"Why do you say *especially* possible?" Beatrice asked.

"Think about Gertrude," Stella said. "She moved her soul to where she felt it belonged. Isn't that resurrection? Aren't the trees themselves examples of it? And weren't you both born from virgins?"

The last question Stella asked brought heat to Beatrice's chest. No. Forest had not been born from a virgin.

"No," Forest argued, "the mothers on this mountain mate with the Goddess. They are partners."

Stella stopped rocking. "Forest, that's no different from what Christians believe happened with Mary and their god."

"Mary was nothing more than a child. She was not equal to their god; they were not partners."

"Your mother was fifteen!" Stella said.

Beatrice swallowed. Until she was much older, she had never considered fifteen too young to have a child.

Forest stood and stared down at Stella. "Why are you defending them? They harass Wanda in every way, they've infiltrated the police department, they bullied Thomas and Jeremy out of the state."

Beatrice had never seen Forest's face so red, his jaw so taut, or his veins protrude so from his neck. At the aggressive gesture, Sasha wrapped around Stella's leg.

"Hey, it's okay, Sasha," Stella soothed. "We're just talking."

"Forest," Beatrice whispered to her son, trying to calm him down.

"Look, all I'm saying, Forest, is that divine births and resurrections are the life-death-life cycle on this mountain, and—"

"Do you believe in their devil? Or Hell? Or Heaven? Sin?" Forest interjected.

"No, Forest. We went to church on Christmas and on

Easter. It was more about status than anything else, another expectation to fulfill."

"Not all Christians ..." Beatrice stirred the air with a finger to help her form her thought. " ...not even the ones in town—"

"No, Mother. Don't say that. All Christians. All Christians hate us."

"I'm going to make us some tea." Stella stood, walking to the kitchen with Sasha wrapped around her leg.

"Forest," Beatrice encouraged, "sit down. Remember that our path ... beliefs ... whatever you want to call them, acknowledges the presence of other gods and goddesses."

The tension in Forest's face transitioned to sadness. "But we don't attack other people, Mother."

Beatrice watched her son's chin quiver slightly as his eyes filled with tears. "Are they going after you, too?"

"Yes," Forest said, his eyes focused on the floor. "And they say things about you. They call you a witch, and they threaten you."

Beatrice shuddered at Forest's words. The group had never condemned her to her face. Stella interrupted the conversation with three mugs of steaming tea.

"Thank you, Stella," Forest said. "I'm sorry. I don't know what's gotten into me."

"It's okay," Stella said, then settled back into the rocker and picked up her crochet.

Silence weighed down the air in the room until Beatrice couldn't stand it.

"Forest, you need to cut a tree down soon," she said, sinking back into her bowl of potatoes. "We decorate a tree, too!" she said to Stella. "We put ornaments and photographs on it. And we'll have huge bonfire to celebrate the returning of the light." Beatrice smiled. "It's my favorite time of year, because it means life is returning. It's a coming home."

The conversation came to a natural silence as the three

continued working in front of the crackling fire. Then, without warning, Sasha raised her head and began rattling her tail fiercely.

"Forest ..." Beatrice kept her voice calm. "Check the front door."

Sasha raced in front of Forest, her tail still rattling.

"She wants us to follow," Stella said as she stood from her rocker.

They followed Sasha into the woods, feet crunching frozen leaves. Stella shivered. The snake pulled them deeper and deeper until they came to the Hedge, which the snake raced alongside.

"She's tracing the Hedge." Beatrice made her way to the tall wall of holly. The pointy leaves bristled at her touch, a warning not unlike Sasha's rattle. She could feel it. "Something is pressing against it, trying to get in. It's strong. And angry."

Beatrice placed her hands to the ground, closed her eyes, and began murmuring encouragements for the Hedge to thicken once more. She could hear Forest uttering his own words and Stella panting. As Beatrice continued to move along the ground, an intense heat made its way up her hands, along her arms, up and down her neck into her belly where it lodged.

"There's nothing I can do. I need to speak with Grandmother."

"Has this ever happened before?" Stella asked, trailing behind Beatrice, who hastened to a jog.

"No."

***

When they made it to the trees, Stella and Beatrice fell to their knees before Grandmother. Stella pulled out half a bar of chocolate, unwrapped it, and laid it at the tree's roots.

"Only half a bar this time?" Grandmother asked, her face appearing with a gentle smirk.

"I'll bring more soon," Stella said, and Beatrice made note of the woman's hand pressed against her grandmother's cheek.

"Grandmother," Beatrice said. "Something is trying to get through the Hedge."

"How do you know?" Beulah asked.

"Sasha brought us out to the perimeter. It's thinner, and I can't strengthen it. I don't know what to do."

One by one, pairs of eyes opened around them as the trees joined in the conversation. Beatrice couldn't remember a time when they were *all* open and ready to talk.

"I can help you with the Hedge, Beatrice," Ida vowed, and closed her eyes. "Let me see what I can do."

"We don't know that someone is trying to get in," Thelma said.

"You know that Beatrice put the Hedge there for a reason, Thelma," Beulah replied.

"Ha!" Edith exclaimed. "Look who decided to speak to us."

"Edith?" Beatrice interrogated. "Imogene ... do you have any ideas?"

"You need my mother," Imogene said.

"There's no time to make it to the Peak." Beatrice felt her throat constrict. "I need more than just First Mother. I need the Goddess Herself."

"Yes, Beatrice," First Mother's voice boomed down the mountain. "*Someone* is trying to get through the Hedge. Love, longing, and anger have been trying to break through that barrier for many years."

"Ask the Goddess for help. Please," Beatrice begged.

"She wants you to prepare for the solstice. More people will gather around the table than ever before. You must heal, Beatrice, and if you do, you will stop the burning."

"What burning?" Beatrice's voice rose to a yell as she stood, her hands balled by her sides.

"There will be blood," First Mother continued without answering Beatrice's original question.

"Whose blood?" Beatrice's heartbeat was frenetic and sweat popped along her brow. "Heal who? What?"

"I don't know. I cannot see everything. Trust yourself, Beatrice."

"How long have you known someone is trying to get in?" Beatrice's voice quaked as she spoke, and her eyes peered into the forest as if she could see the talking tree.

"I felt the presence for the first time today. I can feel desperation and weariness. Trust," First Mother's voice boomed. "The anger can be quelled. It must be quelled, or this whole forest, your home, will burn."

"Fire," Beatrice whispered. "Is it ..."

She couldn't bring herself to finish, so she thanked Grandmother and trudged back toward home. The Hedge was even thinner now and littered with ... well, Beatrice couldn't tell without moving closer.

"Forest, Stella, go on. I'll catch up."

Every cell within Beatrice's body vibrated, electrified as she walked closer and closer toward the Hedge. Folded envelopes filled the interior branches and lay in smatterings around the roots. Beatrice's heart couldn't pound any faster or harder as she kneeled on the ground. She had to instruct her body to move.

Reach out and take one.

She pulled an envelope that was still white and crisp toward her. At the sight of her name written in her mother's sweeping cursive, Beatrice brought her hand to her mouth and began to sob. Her hands quaked as she slid the envelope open.

Beatrice,

I don't know how many more times I can travel up this mountain. No matter how hard I try, this hedge won't let me through. In a way, I hope you haven't received any of my letters either. If you have, that means you want nothing to do with me.

I'm running out of words. I love you. I miss you.
Love always,
Mother

Beatrice scanned the ever-dwindling row of holly, estimating that well over one hundred envelopes were scattered within, all in different stages of decay. She couldn't sit and read them all here in the cold while Forest and Stella waited, so she used her vines to form a basket. Then she pulled out every slip of paper she could find and slipped them inside.

Forest and Stella had apparently moved slowly, waiting for Beatrice to catch up.

"What's that?" Stella asked.

"I can't talk about it now."

Beatrice walked, imagining war with a faceless enemy who could wield fire. *It can't be her.* Stella placed a hand on her upper arm, and she stopped and turned. Beatrice grew rigid as Stella wrapped her arms around her tightly. After a few breaths, she released a little, and her shoulders relaxed slightly from her ears as she embraced Stella in return.

***

While Beatrice, Forest, and Stella begged the trees for help, the house the three of them called home yawned, opened its eyes, and prepared. Walls scooted out from the floorboards and the floors themselves stretched. Kitchen countertops lengthened, and the table grew. A wooden couch settled itself in the living room. Bedrooms sprouted, beds duplicated, chests formed for the guests' clothes. The Goddess made room for the visitors without asking Beatrice's permission.

***

When the three arrived at the home, Forest was the first to pause. "It's bigger," he said after silent moments, widening his arms.

Beatrice, Stella, and Forest climbed the stairs into the kitchen, where Beatrice brushed her hand along the polished wood countertop. "The countertop and table ..." she whispered.

"The walls have moved," Stella added.

Beatrice moved through the house, noting two added bedrooms with beds and mattresses and places to store clothes.

"People are coming, and we're supposed to feed them, and apparently house them."

"Mother," Forest placed his hand on Beatrice's shoulder. "Are you alright?"

"I need a moment." Beatrice allowed her body to collapse into a chair in front of the fire.

Goddess, please protect us. Beatrice felt a tightness form around her chest, and she closed her eyes and tried to swallow it away.

"I don't know what's coming," she said to Forest and Stella, "But I will do everything to protect you both."

She paused for a moment and considered the strengths and weaknesses of the three.

"Mother," Forest said, "my coven could help us."

Beatrice looked up into Forest's pale face. His solemn eyes conveyed a desperate desire for acceptance from his mother. And besides that, she'd grown fond of Wanda. She believed that if nothing else, the woman would be safer here.

"I trust Wanda."

"Dani is in town, too," Forest added, but Beatrice bristled at the suggestion.

"Only Wanda." The hurt in Forest's face as he glanced away changed Beatrice's mind. "Alright, Forest. Dani, too."

"When do you want them here?"

"The morning of the solstice. They can each have one of the extra rooms."

"Thank you, Mother," Forest said, drawing close to Beatrice and embracing her in a hug. She held him back tightly, praying it wasn't his blood First Mother saw. "The more witches we have on top of this mountain, the better," Forest added.

Beatrice locked eyes with him.

"I am not a witch."

CHAPTER 22

Stella

Since the night First Mother spoke of blood, Stella dreamed of New York, an apartment overlooking Rockefeller Center, and the small woman she met when Marin read her fortune. The solstice grew closer, but Stella felt something tugging her back to the city. She knew better than to tell Beatrice, Forest, or even Beulah until she knew what, exactly, pulled her.

The three had followed instructions, preparing for both banquet and blood. At present, Stella decorated the tree while Beatrice worked in the kitchen. Her friend had grown quiet, refusing to answer questions about the basket she'd brought home. Stella opened a wooden box filled with handmade ornaments: miniature stuffed bears, felted stars, and perfect stacks of Queen Anne's lace Beatrice had pressed, which she gently lifted out. In the corner of the box lay a small stack of photos, and Stella, unable to resist, pulled them toward her. In the first photo, a man stood in front of the smokehouse holding up a rabbit with one hand, his free arm around the shoulders of a teenage girl with dark, shoulder-length hair, who wore a smile that showed her teeth.

"Beatrice," Stella whispered and brought her finger to the young girl's face. The next picture portrayed a sleeping Beatrice lying on a quilt next to the hearth, with a little baby curled up in a tight ball next to her. "Gertrude."

Stella flipped to the next picture. A woman with long blonde hair cradled a baby in one arm while stirring a pot on the stove. Her eyes furrowed as she studied the image.

"Marin."

Months had passed since Stella's visions had flashed through her mind, but now a wave of nausea started from the lowest part of her belly and traveled up to her throat.

Marin climbing the mountain.

Beatrice looking down on Rockefeller Center.

Marin's partner lifeless on the forest floor.

A blue orb.

Heat on her skin from a burning fire.

Blood on snow.

Screams.

The sounds of a falling tree.

Stella refused to let them continue and squeezed her eyes shut.

"Beatrice," she called into the kitchen and Beatrice came, wiping her floured hands across her apron. "Is this your mother?" Stella asked and pointed to the picture.

"Yes," Beatrice said as a flash of hesitation flickered in her eyes, then she refocused on Stella. "Why?"

"I-I've met her," Stella stammered, then she brought the edge of her thumb to her teeth and chewed on the corner. "She's the psychic who read for me in New York."

"Are you sure?" Beatrice asked and pulled the pictures from Stella's hand.

"I don't forget a face."

Beatrice flipped through the pictures as she paced

back and forth, the motions Stella had watched her make countless times when anxious or bored. Her face was pale and her breath shallow. Finally, the woman plopped on the couch, eyes filling with tears.

"She wrote to me." The words shook from Beatrice's mouth. "I found letters that night in the Hedge. They're what I've been hiding in the basket. I had no idea she'd ..."

"We have to go to New York," Stella insisted. "As soon as possible."

Even as she said the words, Stella was uncertain whether she could leave Beulah. A tightness seemed to bind them together; she wasn't sure she could tolerate a day without seeing those eyes.

"I can't leave." Beatrice stretched her palms out by her side. "People are coming."

"One of those people is your mother," Stella replied.

"No." Beatrice shook her head.

"You don't believe me?" Stella asked, sadness pricking the backs of her eyes.

"I don't know," Beatrice confessed.

Stella placed her hand on her friend's arm. "If you don't want to come, I'll go on my own."

"I don't know that I want her here." The crack in Beatrice's voice surprised Stella.

"She's coming, whether you like it or not. If you go with me, at least she will come into your home on your terms."

"Do you see the healing First Mother described?"

"I don't know." Stella shrugged at the half-truth. "Pack. I'm going to say goodbye to Beulah."

***

Adrenaline propelled Stella through the forest and to the tall birch tree whom she'd given so much of her blood. Beulah took her time in showing her face. Each day, as though tired, the face moved slower and slower to the surface.

"Hi, Stella," Beulah breathed.

221

"Are you okay?" Stella asked.

"I'm not sure," Beulah considered. "I feel ... different. You're out of breath. What did you come to tell me?"

Stella paced as she told Beulah about recognizing Madeline from a photograph, and she shared a few snippets of her vision. Madeline on the mountain. Beatrice in New York. And the blue orb. Beulah's eyes widened, but she said nothing.

"Beatrice and I are going to find her. Maybe to bring her back, I don't know, but I wanted your permission."

"My permission?"

"Can I even leave you now? In the middle?" Stella asked as the loud crack and thud of a fallen tree exploded in her mind.

"We aren't in the middle anymore, Stella. I've taken all that I need. All we can do is wait. As for my daughter ..." Beulah's voice transitioned from tender to agitated. "I don't think she'll come, but you don't need to ask my permission to find her."

Stella lifted her hand to the bark. "Are you scared?" she asked the tree.

"To hear Beatrice tell it, Gertrude made it look so easy, but I wonder if it will hurt."

Stella's voice grew firm. "I need to know, now. What do I do if things go wrong?"

Beulah closed her eyes as she spoke. "The pages of my book where I wrote about this process are hidden underneath a loose floorboard in Beatrice's room, under the dresser. I never wanted Madeline to find them. If something goes wrong, read them, and let Beatrice and Forest read them."

"And Madeline?"

"If Madeline comes, then yes. She can read them, too." Beulah opened her eyes. "What can you tell me about her?"

"I was only with her for a couple of hours, but she seemed well. Content. In love."

Beulah's eyes grew softer and peered into Stella's own. "I never met Eric. Beatrice told me about their relationship. Maybe I'll finally get to meet him."

Stella shook her head. "She's with someone new. Maybe you'll get to meet her."

"Her?"

"Yes. Madeline's with a woman. Does that bother you?"

"How could that possibly bother me?" Beulah almost chuckled. "If this works, Stella, will you kiss me?"

Stella grinned at Beulah's flirting, but a strange uneasiness coiled in the space between her belly button and her abdomen. She swallowed the feeling down.

Stella pressed her forehead against the bark to hide her concerns. "I promise."

"Take care of her in the city, Stella."

"I will." Stella kissed the bark between the brows and stood. Before she turned to walk away, she asked Beulah one last question. "There's something between us. A pull. It's tight, and to be honest, a little scary. Do you feel it?"

"Yes. But it's not scary at all to me."

"I'll miss you."

***

Stella found Beatrice, still pale faced and shaky, scurrying between rooms—the bedroom, the kitchen, the living space—finding things to tuck into a leather bag, while Forest turned in circles, bewildered, watching his mother move.

"What did you see?" Forest whispered as he took Stella by the elbow.

"I saw your mother in New York and your grandmother here." Stella felt it was best to keep most of the visions to yourself.

"I should come with you," he said.

"No, Forest. You need to stay here," Stella said, then watched as Forest's shoulders slumped.

"How long will we be gone?" Beatrice called from her bedroom.

"We'll be home the day before the solstice," Stella replied.

Beatrice clicked her tongue as she came into the living room. "I don't even know what I'm doing," she said, her arms wide and high in the air. "I want to say goodbye to my grandmother, too. I'll do that while you pack."

"Take care of my mother, Stella," Forest said, avoiding Stella's eyes.

When Stella opened her bedroom door, she found Sasha racing around the room as if she knew something was amiss. The snake made every effort to slither in as Stella zipped up her bag.

"I can't take you with me, Sasha."

For the first time, the snake lifted itself and hissed but, to Stella's surprise, the sound didn't startle her.

"I will miss you so much." She reached out her hand and Sasha nuzzled into her palm. "Listen, take care of Forest."

***

The woods were cold and quiet, and Stella could see farther into them now that the leaves had fallen, and the silence of it all, pierced only by the chirp of a winter bird and the crunch of leaves underfoot, gave the forest a heavy, lonely feel.

"Is my mother well?" Beatrice asked. "Did she seem happy? Healthy?"

"She seemed happy," Stella said, resisting the urge to gnaw at the skin on her thumb. "She's in a relationship with a woman."

"Papa must be dead, then," Beatrice said. "Mother would never leave him. And I don't think he'd leave her, either. What's this person like?"

Stella remembered the way the two looked at one

224

another and how that moment had crystallized what she knew in her heart: Roger wasn't for her. "They seemed very much in love."

Beatrice's face grew pensive, and her eyes grew sad.

"She couldn't see your face, no matter how hard she tried. You're my mentor with the dirty feet."

Beatrice's lips curled in a small smile at Stella's words. "Maybe I'm part of her future. She couldn't see her own very well."

"You know, when you're anxious, you move around like a pinball in an arcade game. Always moving back and forth. Back and forth. How does it feel to move forward?"

Beatrice didn't look at her, and the two walked in silence across the road.

"Think Wanda will drive us to a car rental place?"

"Wanda?" Beatrice cried. "I don't want her knowing my business."

"I thought you two were friends now. Besides, we don't have to tell her where we're going."

Beatrice looked away and considered, then agreed.

"Have you ever had ice cream from here?" Stella motioned toward the Dairy Queen. "We can sit and watch the river."

"It's winter, Stella."

"The sun's out." Stella squinted and pointed up at the sky.

"Fine. But I'll stay out here if you don't mind."

Stella smiled at her friend, then ordered two chocolate-dipped cones.

CHAPTER 23

Madeline

Madeline crossed the bridge into the town she hadn't set foot in since Gertrude grew ill. It was a dream that brought her here. Flashes of the future had interrupted her sleep, but this time, the vision lingered longer on the older woman's face. She woke in a sweat, finally able to place the woman in her past: a nurse in the hospital where she and Eric had first brought Gertrude.

After the dream, Madeline couldn't sleep, so she had kneeled in front of her altar with closed eyes, searching for the woman. Her mind's eye found her standing behind a booth at a holiday market, so Madeline wandered into town, trusting her gift to guide her. A group of women walking near her directed her to the basement of a red-bricked Catholic church, which sat across from a funeral home. She took narrow stairs down into a large room filled with tables angled in all different directions.

Madeline passed by tables of crocheted doilies and wash rags, handmade dolls, and art created from wood burning. She paused for a moment at a table displaying felted animals, admiring a miniature robin's nest with tiny eggs. Holding it in her hands, she thought of her mother and the ornaments the two of them made for the Solstice tree.

After placing the nest down, Madeline meandered past booth after booth, her heartbeat increasing in pace and strength as she felt herself getting closer. Finally, at the very end of the rows, she found her, the woman who had helped Gertrude. The woman standing over the dead man's body in her vision. The last few feet of the journey somehow passed quickly and slowly, time stretching and contracting like an accordion.

"Hi," she said breathlessly as she approached the table.

"Welcome," the woman said, studying Madeline's face.

"I don't know if you remember me. It's been a long time, but twenty years ago, you helped my baby in the hospital. You gave her a tea that softened her cough."

The woman squinted her eyes, searching for the memory, then her smile grew. "Yes, I remember you. Oh, your baby was so sick. How is she now?"

The words stuck in Madeline's throat, and she glanced away.

"I'm so sorry," the woman said. "Remind me of your name again."

"Madeline." It was the first time since she met Gwen and Ben that Madeline had given a stranger her real name.

"I'm Wanda," the woman said, pressing a hand to her heart.

Madeline took in the booth, which was larger than the rest. One end boasted jars of jam and dried herbal teas labeled Calm, Digestive, Focus, Anti-inflammatory, Joint Pain, and Sleep. A wooden bowl sat in the corner, full of tumbled, shiny stones. Madeline knew without further investigation that this woman was a witch; of what variety, she wasn't sure. Scanning the rest of the table, Madeline's eyes widened at what she saw. Produce. Produce that held the heat of summer. Tomatoes she couldn't hold in one hand, greens, onions, carrots, beets.

"Where did this come from?" she whispered in amazement.

"Well, I'm actually covering another booth today, for a family that lives up yonder on the mountain. Beatrice and Forest."

Madeline's heart stopped at the names. *She's alive.* And Forest. Forest must be the young man.

"She has this huge greenhouse. I've never seen it, but Forest says it's gigantic. If you want those tomatoes, you better grab them. They go quick."

Madeline placed the tomato down, hoping she would see the greenhouse soon enough. Next to the produce were rows of glass bottles of shampoo: rosemary lavender, lemon balm, chamomile. She picked up a bar of soap and inhaled. It smelled like her daughter. Her gaze landed on rows of wood carvings. Small, medium, and large, richly stained wood carvings of beaver, coyote, otter, rabbit, and ...

Madeline's hand reached down to pick up the small eagle.

"He does custom work as well." Wanda bent down and pulled from under the table a carving larger than the rest.

Beatrice.

She stood, dressed in a collared, long-sleeved shirt on which the whittler had etched a plaid pattern, and pants rolled up to the ankles. Madeline's lips curled at the thought of her daughter abandoning the long dresses she and her mother and grandmothers had worn. Beatrice's eyes stared straight ahead, her face both peaceful and fierce. On an outstretched arm sat an impossibly large eagle.

"It's ..." Madeline again couldn't find the words.

"They are quite the mother and son," Wanda said with a chuckle.

Son.

Madeline's heart clenched.

I have to get to them.

"Why aren't they here today?" Her shaky voice revealed her panic.

Wanda glanced briefly from side to side as if to make sure no one else was listening. "Well, Forest is preparing for a little gathering we're having day after tomorrow."

"The solstice?" Madeline kept her voice low.

Wanda nodded and a look of recognition passed over her face. "We have to be careful," she said. "Anyhow, Beatrice went out of town early this morning."

"Do you know when she'll be back?"

Wanda now eyed Madeline suspiciously. "I don't."

Madeline knew she couldn't press too hard. There was no way of knowing what Wanda knew about her family. A stabbing in her palm reminded her of the eagle she was squeezing too tightly. She put it down quickly and picked up a coyote, a bar of soap, a bottle of shampoo and conditioner, and a bottle of lotion. After paying for the purchase, Madeline said goodbye to Wanda, then walked toward the mountain with heavy, leaden legs and eyes on fire.

***

Branches stood stark against the bright morning sky, their leaves shaved off by the wind. A thick blanket of slick oranges and yellows all turning to brown covered fallen branches and rocks, making it difficult for Madeline to see the hazards. Tiredness caused by lack of sleep, lack of yoga, sadness, anger, and grief oozed through her body. The thought of Gwen crept in; a clenching that started in her low abdomen traveled upward and into her chest. She stopped walking.

It was wrong to come.

Without hesitation, Madeline turned, determined to abandon this futile journey and make her way home to Gwen. Her hasty movements brought her to the ground with a grunt, and Madeline squeezed her eyes at the pain in her right ankle. She pulled herself up and rested her forehead against the bark of a tree. A shuffling movement broke branches close by and she opened her eyes. Her body tensed as she repositioned her walking stick in front of her and, holding her breath, moved to look around the tree with such deft agility that no twigs broke underneath her. As she rounded the tree, she came nose to nose with a black bear.

Madeline had faced a bear once before and used speed to get away, but this bear, small and healthy, with a sleek coat and bright eyes, stood on his hind legs six inches away from her face. It bellowed, then bent down to grasp Madeline's right ankle in his jaws, pulling her to the forest floor.

Fuck.

He began to drag her and Madeline held tight to the shoulder straps of her backpack, intent on keeping her belongings with her. After the first bump of rock against her skull, she crossed her arms behind her head to protect herself. The bear's hold wasn't strong enough to puncture Madeline's skin or break her bones, and she realized he wasn't trying to harm her.

"I'll follow you," she screamed. "Stop dragging me, dammit, and I'll follow you."

The bear, whom Madeline decided had to be either Forest or Beatrice's companion, let go of her ankle, opened its mouth in a gigantic roar, then ran, leaving Madeline scrambling behind him. She found herself grateful for yoga as she dashed over roots and rocks, grateful for the strength Gwen had brought to her balance and to the smallest muscles and tendons in her ankles and calves. She tripped once and recovered. The bear hurried, leaving Madeline panting.

Eventually, the animal paused at the edge of something familiar. It stretched out in front of her, wide and flat and terrifying. Images flooded her brain of the night thirty-five years ago when her mother had screamed at the sky and the Rock and begged them not to take her.

Madeline held her breath, then inhaled in a delicate, shaky tremble. She turned around in a circle, trying to find the place where the earth took her mother, but only a footprint of the roots remained. She glanced up at the other trees around the Rock and a memory stirred. She had been to the Rock only twice in her life: once to conceive Beatrice, and once to bear her. Before then, First Mother had been all Madeline knew of the trees, and the walks her mother took to the Peak to plead for the Goddess to change her fate.

So, when eyes began to open slowly, cautiously all around her, Madeline had to clench to keep from wetting herself. A rattling of tree limbs filled the forest, but none of the trees spoke. Regaining composure, Madeline balled her fist by her hips and wailed, "Where is my mother?" The volume of her voice surprised her and caused the bark-lidded eyes around her to widen.

"She left us." The voice came from an amber-eyed tree.

Madeline opened her mouth to ask how her mother left, but the bear returned to her side and tugged at her sleeve, and Madeline followed.

Only when she reached the other side of the Rock did the realization slam into her sternum that she was inside the Hedge. Rage, excitement, and fear entwined through her as she dashed toward home. What would she say to Beatrice? Madeline's mind often played tapes of herself begging Beatrice for forgiveness, even as another part of her wanted an apology for the creation of the Hedge that separated them.

The cold air burned as it entered her lungs, but her pace persisted and eventually, the rear of her old home came into view. When she came to the newly painted red door, Madeline crumpled to the ground, placing one hand against the cold logs. Pain poured down her cheeks in salt water and spilled onto her shirt. Once empty, she stood, ready to face her daughter.

The wooden door opened willingly to her touch, and she stepped across the threshold. A menacing, tail-rattling serpent faced her on the other side. Assuming that the snake was another companion and that she could talk some sense into it, Madeline straightened and raised her chin.

"I am Madeline. Beatrice's mother. Forest's grandmother. This is my home."

Her connections with Beatrice and Forest didn't seem to matter. The snake only lifted itself higher and rattled more fiercely. If talking didn't work, Madeline would have to use her gift.

Stella!

Madeline stood even taller. "And I am friends with Stella."

At Stella's name, the snake stopped shaking its tail, uncoiled, and slithered away. Madeline closed her eyes and released a sigh. When she opened them again, her eyes moved to the evergreen tucked in the corner which stood only partially decorated for the solstice, as though it had been left in a hurry. The wooden trunk where generations of women had tucked their handmade decorations was partially open, and Madeline moved toward it, pulling out years of felt ornaments: stars, the moon, deer, snowflakes, and suns. Beatrice had insisted Madeline create the contradictory figure for the tree, needing the reminder that the light would return. Set aside was a pile of pressed Queen Anne's lace blossoms, firmly dried and preserved. A few of them were already on the tree.

"Beatrice." The name wouldn't leave her lips with any strength, so she cleared her throat and tried again. "Beatrice."

No, Beatrice wouldn't come. Madeline shook her head, remembering her daughter was out of town. Clearing her throat again, Madeline called, "Forest!"

When no one came, she once again fixated on the tree. Her hands took control before she realized what she was doing, and as she adorned the tree, tears came again. Madeline filled up the tree with flowers and ornaments and, once finished, she sat down in a rocker that faced the hearth, ever blazing in the winter, and admired the tree, wondering if her daughter would be home soon.

She became aware of her bones and how much they ached, and moved to the kitchen to make herself some tea, knowing Beatrice would have copious amounts of an anti-inflammatory concoction. Madeline admired the way Beatrice had arranged things. Plants vined along the ceiling and bundles of herbs hung on nails fastened throughout the room. The earthiness of soil married with scents of rosemary, basil, and sage. Madeline could perform miracles, but she struggled to keep plants alive, and what Beatrice accomplished in this space was nothing short of miraculous.

Madeline walked to the herb and spice cabinet and smiled at Beatrice's rearrangement. She found a jar of tea labeled "Calm," with the listed ingredients of lavender, lemon balm, and chamomile. She filled a teapot with water from the ever-flowing faucet, placed the pot on the stove, then sat at the kitchen table waiting for it to boil. It was larger now, the table, with seven chairs instead of two. Perhaps when she was done with her tea, she would survey the smokehouse.

The water boiled, and Madeline poured water into the cup holding leaves, then took the cup in her hands. She wanted to be outside with the land that once belonged to her, the land to whom she once belonged. It wasn't until she settled into one of the front porch rockers that she noticed the large birch tree situated to the left of the house. She stopped rocking, all feeling leaving her body. Her fingers trembled around the mug, so much so that she brought her gaze to her hands and mindfully set the cup down on the floor beside her so as not to drop and break it.

Barely breathing, she descended the stairs and placed her hand on the smooth, gray bark. The bark shifted, and the bluest eyes opened. A mouth opened.

"My Madeline."

Madeline found her mother's voice still young, though thin and tired, and she flinched when a root wrapped around her shoulder.

"Mama," Madeline whispered as she sank to her knees.

"I have missed you. I can't see you. My eyes have gone."

"How did you get here?" Madeline questioned.

"I walked," Beulah responded with a touch of triumph in her voice. "You're finally home. What took you so long, daughter?"

Madeline could feel it. The understanding that she was an outsider crept into her limbs, and her eyes moved to the ground. "Will you tell me where she is?"

A sound like a breath drew in and moved out, a gathering of energy. "She went to find you."

Madeline's eyes jerked upward. "Beatrice went to New York?"

"Yes." The word seemed to groan out of her.

At first, the knowledge that Beatrice had gone looking for her stirred a tenderness within Madeline, but then those tendrils of comfort grew thick and thorny.

"She's gone for Gwen!" Madeline pressed herself up to standing, ready to run for her lover, but both bear and timber rattler positioned themselves in front of her, and their clicking teeth and rattling tail forced her to step back.

"Madeline, listen to me. Trust your daughter." The words

grew scratchier as the tree spoke. "And when I fall, burn the tree."

Madeline moved back to her mother and put her hands on the tree once more. "You can't go anywhere. I need you."

"I need me, too," Beulah whispered as her eyes drifted shut.

"I'm sorry," Madeline said. "I'm sorry I never came to visit. I was so scared of that place."

"You did as you were told."

Eyes closed, and her mother grew silent.

Both bear and snake calmed but stood at attention, readying themselves in case Madeline dared to make a move. She trembled as she recalled the image of Gwen entangled in the vines spilling from Beatrice's hands. Gwen would climb this mountain. Of that she was certain. Madeline could only hope she was stronger than her daughter.

CHAPTER 24

Gwen

Despite her brother's discouragement, Gwen insisted on seeing the studio. Ben had explained that after the attackers assaulted her, they smashed the windows and vandalized the space with homophobic vitriol. To Gwen, the actions weren't just an attack against her, but also against the hundreds of yogis and instructors who called it home every day. She didn't dare reach out, but she worried about the woman, a loyal customer of the studio, who had come out as a lesbian to her husband, the leader of the attack.

Gwen prepared for the worst, but when she arrived, she found love in flowers extending from one end of the storefront to the other. Cards were propped against floral arrangements, and small statues of Buddha and quote books lay here and there. Gwen picked up card after card and token after token of affection and felt her eyes burn.

"The church across the street offered to help clean up," Ben said. "I let them. I hope that's okay."

Gwen nodded as she picked up a book and held it to her heart.

The studio windows were boarded up, but the door was still intact. Gwen opened it gingerly. The front desk still stood upright, but the computer was gone, and the display case that once held books, mats, straps, and blocks was now empty.

"What happened to the merchandise?" Gwen's voice cracked as she asked.

"They destroyed it, in one way or another."

The smell of fresh paint replaced the normal lavender and lemongrass scent of the studio, and Gwen noticed that the cubbies where practitioners placed their shoes, keys, and water bottles were now a sage green instead of white. Hesitantly, she pulled open the French doors that led to the practice room, to find floorboards pulled up and the mirrors that once covered the front wall removed.

I always hated those mirrors.

She sank to her knees.

"I called your insurance. You'll have what you need to fix this." Ben tried to continue speaking, but Gwen stopped him.

"I'm closing the studio."

She felt her brother sit down beside her.

"You don't have to do that, Gwen. It will take a few weeks to get it back into shape, and that will give you time to heal."

Gwen just shook her head and peered at Ben through her left eye, her right still swollen and throbbing. "Can I have a minute, please?"

"I'll be out front," Ben said and placed a warm hand on her back.

Gwen sat on the backs of her heels, remembering. Remembering the way it felt to breathe in and breathe out. Remembering the early days when she taught only three or four people. Practitioners learned under her, grew under her, and as a result, the studio exploded. All of it flashed before her eyes as her dream died. She squeezed her eyes and swallowed deeply when she remembered meeting Madeline for the first time in this room. Another deep breath. Stillness. Underneath paint fumes, she caught the lingering smell of lavender.

Then, the door to the lobby creaked open and her brother asked, "May I help you?"

Women's voices spoke tenderly, and Gwen assumed they were students coming to bid her well wishes. She kept her eyes closed. The voices continued, raising slightly, though Gwen couldn't make out the words. Ben, eventually and with finality, said, "Listen, she cannot see you right now."

But the women were persistent.

"Can *you* help us then? We're looking for Madeline Woodson. She's a psychic and goes by the name Marin."

Gwen's eyes opened wide.

"I definitely cannot help you with that. Please, I must ask you to leave."

Gwen imagined her brother, polite even when frustrated, holding the door open for the women on the way out.

"Please. My name is Stella, and this is Beatrice, Madeline's daughter. She's come a long way to see her mother."

Fear, a frozen ice cube, slid down Gwen's throat. Over the past few days, nightmares of vines had invaded the space between nightmares of the attack. Gwen held her breath and stilled her body even more, as if the stillness would keep her safe.

"Leave now, or I will call the police."

The voices continued to rise as Gwen stood, mindful of the intense pain in her ribs that stabbed as she got to her feet. She moved toward the French doors, positioning herself so that she could see out without being seen. The three were positioned exactly as she predicted; the women stood outside the door that Ben held open. Gwen let her eyes move first to a woman she had met briefly before, the woman that had Madeline stumped. Stella, with her round face and brilliant green eyes. Then, with the cold feeling of death's hands wrapping around her aching ribs, she turned her gaze toward Beatrice. She was tall, like Madeline, but her hair was dark and highlighted by silver strands throughout.

The face.

Gwen knew the face from dozens of pictures Madeline had tucked in a photo album, pictures that were now hooked on the Christmas tree. Beatrice was no longer a fourteen-year-old girl, and Gwen watched her chest move deeply in and out with her breathing, her eyes bewildered, her face pale.

Beatrice's jaw tensed, and the woman stretched out her hands. Vines slithered toward Ben and wrapped themselves around him. Once she held him firm, Beatrice drew Ben closer and turned him upside down by his legs, her face revealing amusement.

"Beatrice," Stella chided.

"Tell me where my mother is." The vines brought Ben so close Gwen knew he could feel the woman's breath, and the thought made her shiver. Those brown eyes seemed determined to memorize every angle of her brother's face.

Gwen closed her eyes briefly, thanked the fear for keeping her safe, and opened the door. "Beatrice." Her mouth made the words and her feet moved forward as if disconnected from her brain. "Put my brother down."

"Gwen, what are you doing?" Ben yelled.

"It's okay," she said, looking into her brother's face. "What will be will be."

"No," Ben insisted as he writhed within the vines. "You know Madeline is never wrong. Divorces. Jobs lost. Miscarriages. Fires." Ben paused. "Death."

"I know," Gwen whispered.

"My mother had a vision about me?" Beatrice asked as she turned Ben upright and drew him closer.

"She saw you kneeling over my sister's dead body. She saw you kill her."

Beatrice's eyes furrowed and, inch by inch, she withdrew her vines. "I'm not here to hurt anyone."

"You just wrapped me in vines and held me upside down."

"Only long enough for you to agree to help me." Beatrice clicked her tongue, cocked an eyebrow, and pressed her body closer to Ben's. Ben did not back down.

"I will *not* help you."

"Can we breathe, just for a moment? Clear our heads," Gwen pleaded, glancing back and forth between Beatrice and Ben, who held each other's gaze.

"I didn't hurt you," Beatrice said, firmly. But then she asked more softly, "Did I?"

"I don't care what you do to me," Ben said through gritted teeth. "I'll take you to your mother. I'll do whatever you want. Just please, don't hurt my sister."

Gwen pored over Beatrice and saw not a ghost, nor demon, nor murderer. She saw temperance, even in the woman's attempted ferocity toward Ben, and though she could have chosen anger or fear, Gwen chose kindness. Pain slashed across her side as she reached for her shoes, forcing her to pause and sit.

Stella kneeled and moved Gwen's shoes closer to her.

"Please don't pity me," she said, but as she tried to put her shoes on again, the pain intensified. Stella, saying nothing, slipped the shoes on her feet. Gwen felt her face grow hot.

This isn't who I am. I'm a warrior.

She couldn't bring herself to say thank you.

"Well," Gwen said as she made eye contact with Beatrice. "Let's get you to your mother."

"One problem with that," Ben interrupted, his voice

returning to gentleness. "Madeline flew to West Virginia this morning."

Gwen's shoulders fell. "You're kidding."

"I'm afraid not."

"That is what you saw while we were eating lunch," Beatrice said to Stella, who nodded then began to nibble at her thumbnail. "Then why am I here?"

Anger undulated across Beatrice's face in ripples, and Gwen watched her cross her arms, and release them, furrow her brows, and clench her jaw.

"I keep seeing a blue orb," Stella explained, releasing the assault on her thumb. "We're supposed to take it home." She turned her attention to Gwen. "A container of some kind. Blue ceramic. Do you know what it is?"

"It's an urn," Gwen explained, the softness of her voice surprising her.

"What's an urn?" Beatrice asked, and Gwen felt jealous that she had never experienced burying the dead.

"An urn is a container where we place the ashes of people who have died and choose to be cremated. In this case, both Eric and Gertrude," Gwen explained, and Beatrice raised both of her eyebrows and took one step closer to Gwen.

"What happened to him?"

Gwen felt the grief in Beatrice's voice.

"I think that's a story your mother should tell you."

"Can we take it?" Stella asked.

It felt strange for Gwen to be the one in charge of Madeline's belongings, but she wanted to help. "You can ... if I can still get into the apartment."

"She didn't change the locks on you, Gwen," Ben said.

Gwen could feel Beatrice's glare, and she looked up at her. She felt naked and dissected, as if Beatrice could see into every space, and yet, behind the hardness of her brow and the tenseness of her jaw, there lived something soft.

"When we get to your apartment," Beatrice said quietly,

"will you let me treat your face? I can't do anything about broken bones, but I can help the inflammation … assuming my mother keeps herbs and spices."

"She has a pantry full."

"I'll go get the car." Ben sighed and left.

Beatrice sat down beside Gwen, who struggled to keep from squirming. "How is she?"

"I haven't talked to her in the past couple of days." Gwen pulled at her right earlobe.

Silence impregnated the room once more, until Ben parked in front of the studio and waved to them. Gwen shut and locked the studio doors, then took a deep breath and placed a palm against the glass chilled by the December air. Once in the car, questions began to gnaw at her insides while the pain in her ribs caused her to shift in the seat.

"What time was her flight?" she asked.

"I think she said 5:30 this morning," Ben said.

"How long would it have taken her?" Beatrice asked from the back seat.

"Well, she most likely had to take a connecting flight. It took me five hours of flying. And then a few hours south by car," Stella explained.

"We have to get to her. It's not safe," Beatrice said.

"She's familiar with the dangers on the mountain. She'll be fine." Gwen did her best to reassure.

"She'll be safe with Forest, Bea," Stella said.

"Who is Forest?" Gwen asked.

"My son."

Gwen nodded and picked at her fingernails. Then she thought of the man in Madeline's visions. Dark green eyes. Dark curly hair.

"Maybe she'll make it through the Hedge this time." Gwen wanted to turn and look at Beatrice as she spoke her next words, but the broken ribs wouldn't allow it, so she flipped down the visor, opened the mirror, and positioned it to where the two could lock eyes. "She's tried to get home to you ever since she left. Every month for the last twenty years."

The reflection of Beatrice's face fell, and the movement of her chest weakened. The woman's eyes fluttered down, then moved toward the window. Gwen thought she saw tears in them. The rest of the drive was quiet, but occasionally, Gwen would look up into the mirror to see Madeline's daughter staring out the window, wiping away teardrops with her fingertips.

***

When they arrived in the parking lot of the apartment building, Ben gestured to the elevator, and Gwen grunted with frustration that in her condition she couldn't handle the stairs. As the machine pulled them upward, she watched Beatrice fumble for the grab bar with widened eyes.

"See," Stella whispered to Beatrice loud enough so they all could hear, "we have magic out here, too."

"I did *not* like how that felt."

"But you'll jump off a twenty-foot cliff into a swimming hole," Stella said.

Beatrice smirked smugly, the closest thing to a smile she'd given since her arrival.

There it is.

No other part of Beatrice resembled Madeline, but this, this was her mother's smile.

The smell of incense wafted out of the apartment when Gwen pushed the door open, and she found the space neat and tidy, the way Madeline always left things. Unable to stand the darkness, she turned on the lamps and plugged the tree in. Nestled in the green branches, she found the picture of Madeline pressing a kiss onto her cheek. She remembered the moment; it was the first time her lover had seen the ocean and dolphins. After moments of watching them, Madeline cried over the dolphins. "If Beatrice were here, she could call them to us," she had said.

If Beatrice were here. How many times had Gwen heard it? And now, Beatrice was here, and her mother was not, and Gwen had to figure out her place in the vines. She turned to Beatrice, who was engaged at the altar, pulling a candle from the cabinet, anointing it with oil, and lighting it with a match. Then she reverently touched the feet of the felt goddess and bowed her head. With a sigh, she rose with the felt sculpture in her hand, and turned toward Gwen.

"Is this supposed to be our Goddess?"

"Yes."

"How does she know what the Goddess looks like?" Beatrice asked as she placed the Goddess back on the table.

"You'll have to ask her."

Beatrice worked her jaw then asked, "Where are her herbs?"

Gwen walked her to the kitchen pantry where rows upon rows of alphabetized herbs sat neatly on a rack.

Beatrice tutted. "It will take me a minute to find everything."

"They're in alphabetical order," Stella pointed out.

"Exactly," Beatrice responded, eyebrow raised. "I made the mistake of rearranging them once. She put them right back like this ..." She wiggled her finger at the jars. "She told me I could organize them however I wanted to when it was my house. When it was obvious that she ..." Beatrice didn't finish the sentence as she pulled the jars toward her and tucked them in her arm.

"How do you arrange them?" Gwen asked quizzically.

"By how they interact with each other. It makes things easier. Anyway, I need boiling water."

Gwen moved to fetch a pot, but pain ripped through her.

SORREL D. RICHMOND

Beatrice placed her hand on her shoulders, which brought tenseness into her belly.

"Please rest," the woman urged.

Ben urged her to lie down with a pat on the couch. Gwen closed her eyes and listened to Beatrice move around the kitchen, as the concoction she was brewing released minty, herbaceous smells. Eventually, Beatrice entered the living room with a pot in one hand and a mug of steaming liquid in the other. Muscles throughout Gwen's body clenched. Madeline had healed her before with just a touch. The flu. A pulled muscle. But the woman towering over her wasn't Madeline. Gwen tightened her eyes and thought of the vision.

It doesn't take place here. It takes place in the woods.

Still, Gwen's hands balled into fists. Eric hadn't appeared when the four of them arrived at the apartment, and Gwen wondered if he'd come if she called him again. Why had she never asked him about Beatrice?

"We'll take care of this inside and out," Beatrice assured, then took a sip of the tea and nodded with satisfaction. "Drink this," she said, and Gwen sat up. The liquid tasted as it smelled, minty and cooling, but a lingering bitterness made it hard to swallow.

"I wish I could knit bones back together, but I can't."

Once Gwen finished the tea, Beatrice encouraged her to lie down, then placed a hand on her shoulder. "I will not hurt you."

Then she draped a cloth soaked in the liquid from the pot across Gwen's eyes. It tingled.

"Wait." Gwen removed the towel from her eyes, then, keeping her voice low so Ben couldn't hear she asked, "Will you please keep your vines off my brother?"

Beatrice glanced over her shoulder, then turned back toward Gwen, brandishing a half smirk. Leaning close, she whispered in Gwen's ear conspiratorially, "I'm not sure I

246

can promise that." Beatrice's face was flushed when she pulled back. "But I promise not to hurt him." She ran her fingers through Gwen's hair and the tenderness brought tears to her eyes. Her body warmed, and the pain subsided, though it did not completely disappear. Beatrice whispered "sleep," and she did.

CHAPTER 25

Beatrice

Beatrice straightened from Gwen's side and turned to the mantel, aware of Ben's eyes fixed on her. Her face flushed as she considered what she had whispered in his sister's ear.

What has gotten into me?

She lifted the urn and pulled it toward her. The weight of it surprised her, though she wasn't sure whether she expected it to be lighter or heavier. She sat on a yellow armchair, embroidered with an assortment of birds in cages, and placed the urn in her lap.

"Papa," Beatrice whispered.

I want to go home, Beatrice. Take me home!

She hadn't heard the voice since she was fourteen, and the sound of it tightened her throat.

"I'll take you home, Papa. Don't worry. Will you tell me what happened?"

Please don't ask me to. Just take me home.

Beatrice closed her eyes and tried so hard to hear them, her grandmothers on the mountain. She had been so preoccupied during her travels that she hadn't paid attention to how much distance it took to lose the connection, but now that it was gone, she felt desperate for it.

Ben cleared his throat, and the sound brought Beatrice back to the room, back to the urn laying heavy in her lap, and back to the face her mother had sketched decades ago.

She scanned that face, which still held skepticism and fear, but also something else. Something captivating that Beatrice couldn't define. In the studio, she had wrapped him tight and held him close, and for the tiniest sliver of time, she hadn't wanted to let him go. She blinked her eyes, trying to shoo away the strange sensations she felt when she looked at him. She swallowed, then cleared her own throat.

"She'll feel at least a little better when she wakes up."

"Thank you. You should fly back this time." Ben brought his gaze to the floor. "I can get you an ID; maybe a fake driver's license."

As much as Beatrice admired planes, she had no desire to get on one.

Stella spoke up. "What line of work are you in?"

"Real estate. But, that one and I," Ben said, pointing to Gwen, "got into all sorts of trouble before she settled down and became a yogi."

"I'll need your picture," he said as he stood. "Stand here." He motioned to one of the few blank walls in Madeline's home.

"Alright," Beatrice said hesitantly. She returned the urn to the mantel and kept her eyes downward until she was at the wall, then her eyes flickered upward and she tucked her hair behind her ears.

When's the last time I had a photo taken?

Papa's camera was so different from the phone Ben held in his hand: bulky and brown with buttons, knobs, and dials. Papa had taught Beatrice how to load it carefully with film, and she spent an entire summer photographing her life. Many of the photos now hung on her mother's tree. Now, Beatrice didn't know if she could smile when asked.

"Say cheese," Stella urged, and Beatrice followed the instruction.

When Ben finished, he surveyed the glowing rectangle, his eyes squinting. "You look nothing like your mother," he said, walking toward her to show her the photo. "It's a lovely picture."

And Beatrice, too, found it lovely. Her dark hair lay in giant curls that hit her body just below her collarbone and it seemed to glitter with the silver tucked here and there.

"This is what I look like." It was both a statement and a question.

"No mirrors on the mountain?"

"Yes, but it's different to see a picture."

"Well, this is what you look like." Ben cleared his throat again, then placed his phone in his pocket.

Stella, who silently eyed the pictures on the tree, punctuated the tense moment. "I think you and Gwen should come with us," she suggested.

Ben didn't hesitate in his response. "Absolutely not."

"Madeline is wrong," Stella said.

"What do you see?" Beatrice asked, turning to her.

"It's not what I see." Stella turned away from the tree. "It's what I know. Her interpretation comes from a place of fear, and I think she's wrong. I know you, Beatrice."

"Please don't ask her," Ben responded, his arms crossed as he took steps toward Stella. "She'll go with you, and death waits for her on that mountain."

Beatrice searched her own heart. She saw herself in Gwen's beaten body and knew she could not possibly hurt the woman. She locked eyes with Ben. "I won't hurt her. I promise you."

"She has four broken ribs, and you think she should climb a mountain?"

"You've seen how strong my vines are." Beatrice forced down the desire to wrap the man up again, draw him close, and ... then what?

Stop it, Beatrice. Just stop it.

"She should decide," Beatrice said.

Ben's throat bobbed as he spoke. "I'll pack a bag and purchase two extra tickets, but so help me ..." He stopped himself, uncrossed his arms, ran his fingers through his hair, then scratched at the base of his neck. "I'll be back in a few hours with dinner."

And with that, he was out the door.

Beatrice felt a wave of exhaustion pass over her as she made her way to the chair to sit, and her eyes glanced toward Gwen. "You don't think I could—"

"Of course not, Beatrice," Stella said.

"He hates me and she is terrified of me."

"He's fighting his attraction toward you," Stella said, smirking.

Beatrice jerked her head toward Stella, shook it, then turned back toward Gwen. "I know what she's going through," Beatrice explained. "I grew the Hedge for a reason." She glanced down at the hardwood floor, investigating the dark knots within the planks.

"Come look at the tree," Stella said.

Beatrice stood and walked toward the tree, which produced the spicy, fragrant aroma of pine. She placed her nose against a tickling branch and inhaled the scent deeply, then pulled down the first picture. Papa stood, thin and tall, with his arm around Beatrice, and together they held an enormous fish. He had taken Beatrice down the mountain and to the river. Mother had been most impressed by the catch. She took it over when they brought it home, scaled it, gutted it, and fried up buttermilk-battered filets for supper.

In another, Mother cradled her ripe belly in her hands, her smile brighter than the full moon, eager to meet her new daughter. Photo after photo brought memories. Beatrice holding Gertrude in her arms, not knowing at the time that the same spirit would tuck her in her wings and shelter her during her darkest times. Papa and Mother dancing in the rain when they thought Beatrice wasn't watching. It was Mother's favorite, and Papa framed it and placed it on their bedside table.

In the middle of the faded sepia memories, a newer, brightly colored photo hung. The faces were so close to the camera that only the sky was visible behind them. Gwen faced forward, eyes closed, and nose crinkled in a grin. Mother, radiating beatific happiness, pressed her lips firmly against Gwen's cheek. Beatrice pulled the photo down and inspected it carefully. A jealousy arose. Her mother told her once that she loved love itself as much as she loved Eric.

"They seem happy," Stella said, and Beatrice agreed, placing the photo back where it belonged. "I'm going to find the guest bedroom and take a nap."

"Rest well," Beatrice replied.

One by one, Beatrice fingered each photo without taking time or care to put them back on the tree. She simply tucked one behind the other as the memories flooded her. Here and there were more pictures of Gwen. Some included her mother, others did not. She meditated on each photo, considering the way Mother had woven her past and present together on this tree. So many words would need to be said. Would her mother hug her? How would it feel? Questions stumbled, at first one by one, through Beatrice's mind. The trickle became a torrent culminating in one question that pressed hard against her chest: what happened to Papa?

A small cough broke the thoughts that clouded Beatrice's

mind, and she turned to find Gwen squirming and pulling on the washcloth that still covered her face. Two long strides and Beatrice was by her side, lifting the washcloth and whispering, "It's alright, be still."

When Gwen opened her eyes, her right eye was no longer swollen. The puffiness was gone, and the bruises were much less vivid. By tomorrow, Beatrice knew, the bruises would be gone altogether.

"Here," she said, smiling over her patient, "Let's go rinse all of this off."

Gwen took a deep inhale, and Beatrice helped her up, noticing the woman's sharp intake of breath. She followed Gwen to the bathroom where she turned on the faucet and brought water to her face with cupped hands, making obvious efforts not to look.

"Feel better?" Beatrice asked, watching Gwen pat her face with a towel. "You should look," she encouraged.

Gwen hesitated but finally lifted her face and curled her lips, seemingly unsurprised by her partially healed face.

"Thank you. My face doesn't hurt anymore, at least." She wiped up water around the sink. "I have to ask. Is Eric talking to you?"

"You can hear him, too?" Beatrice stared into Gwen's reflection, locking eyes in the mirror.

Gwen shook her head but pointed to the area behind Beatrice's left shoulder. "I can't hear him—or any of them—but I can see him. He's right behind you."

"He wants to go home." Beatrice turned her head and blinked away tears. "That's all he'll tell me. Does my mother know that you see him?"

"Yes." Gwen's smile broadened. "It freaks her out, so I don't talk about him much. Eric, what do you think?" she asked the space behind Beatrice. "Do you think she'll kill me?"

Beatrice waited for Papa to answer, but he didn't. "He didn't respond," she confessed.

"Well, he's looking at me like I have two heads," Gwen said. "She'll take you home, Eric. Don't worry."

The idea of Papa's spirit stuck in this apartment in the middle of this formidable city filled Beatrice with both sadness and a renewed purpose.

Take care of Gwen now.

Papa's calmer voice relaxed Beatrice, and she refocused on the woman in front of her. "I wish I could help you more. My mother could help you, if you came with us."

Gwen's countenance shifted from gratitude to fear. "The vision your mother saw of you hurting me happens on the mountain."

"But she can help you," Beatrice argued.

"And you could kill me." The words were like daggers leaving Gwen's mouth, but then the woman's face relaxed. "And ... we didn't end on the best terms," she admitted as she exited the bathroom.

"Your brother is packing a bag and buying two extra tickets," Beatrice said, following Gwen, who kept walking. "He'll go with us if you want to go."

At that, Gwen stopped and turned around. "Does my brother think he can stop you?"

Beatrice's throat constricted. "I can stop me."

She walked around Gwen, and removed the picture centered on the Christmas tree. She turned to find Gwen in the room with her, rubbing her earlobe. Beatrice handed her the photo and watched the woman's face tighten and release as she took the photo in her hands and sat down on the couch with a wince.

"What happened?" Beatrice prodded.

"You know, Madeline asks questions she shouldn't, too."

"I'm sorry." Beatrice's face grew hot; it felt like the time Mother caught her sneaking an extra piece of cake after bedtime and told her there would be no cake the next day. She hadn't been true to her word, and gave her a slice despite her transgression.

"No," Gwen said. "I'm sorry."

A silent pause passed between them, then Gwen released a sigh. "I asked her to marry me, and she said no." Her voice was just above a whisper, and it cracked as she spoke.

"Did she give a reason?"

Gwen's face filled with regret. "You."

Beatrice pressed her hand to her chest and moved to sit on the coffee table so she could face Gwen. "Me? Why me?"

"She didn't want to give up on you, so she kept going up the mountain. She was convinced that one day she would make it to you and the Rock would devour her, leaving me alone."

Beatrice clicked her tongue. "We're past tradition at this point." She couldn't fathom the Rock swallowing her mother up and rearranging her being into a tree.

"More than anything, it was the vision of you and me."

"What exactly did she see?"

Gwen's gaze returned to the picture, and she changed the subject. "I asked her to choose me. To give up. And she couldn't do that." Her locked eyes with Beatrice's. "I hated you at that moment. How terrible is that? I hated a fourteen-year-old girl."

After having Forest, Beatrice hadn't had the time to speculate about what her mother was doing off the mountain. To know that her absence had affected Madeline's day-to-day life so dramatically filled her with so many conflicting feelings. She took Gwen's hand in her own. "I'm not a fourteen-year-old girl anymore."

Gwen smiled. "No. You're really not."

"Come with us."

"I'm not well enough. I can barely breathe. I wouldn't make it."

"I will help you."

A knock on the door alerted them that Ben was back, his arms weighed down with bags of food that smelled wonderful. "I bought Chinese," he said, avoiding Beatrice's eyes. "My bag is in the car already. I bought tickets. I bought one for you, too, Gwen."

"A foregone conclusion?" Gwen asked, and Ben shrugged.

"We fly out at 5:30 a.m."

Within moments, Stella was in the dining room saying, "Something smells good."

The four of them sat around Madeline's table and sorted out who wanted what. Beatrice noted what Gwen put on her plate: a few pieces of mixed vegetables and some rice. Dinner started in silence, but Beatrice felt the truth rising from her belly to her throat. She put her fork down and closed her eyes.

"My mother isn't always right."

She opened her eyes to find Gwen and Ben looking at one another. "She was wrong about Gertrude. She didn't listen to me. She thought I was jealous and making it up. She thought I didn't ..." She closed her eyes again and hung her head. "I don't know what I ever did to make her believe I could ..." A new possibility hit her.

Did Mother think I wanted Gertrude dead?

"Tell me what she saw." Beatrice raised her voice and shifted her gaze between Gwen and her brother.

Ben shook his head at Gwen, but his sister turned to Beatrice. "Vines. She saw vines coming from your hands, wrapping all around me and going down my throat."

Stella placed her hand on Beatrice's shoulder. "Vines. Beulah used her roots to cure you. She can make them thin. Tiny. Microscopic, even. Maybe the image isn't of Beatrice killing you," Stella insisted, turning toward Gwen. "Maybe she's healing you. Beatrice. Remember what First Mother said. 'The mountain will burn if you don't heal.'"

"I don't know that I can do that, Stella."

"Let's try." Stella stood, went to the kitchen, and returned with a knife.

"Stella, no!" Beatrice objected.

"Nothing too deep, I promise."

Beatrice watched, appalled, as Stella glided the blade across her palm. Then the woman nodded to her. Her hands had grown so many things, but never vines thin enough to sew ripped skin back together. She closed her eyes and gathered the feeling inside of her. It started at her toes. A pulling. Pieces of individual cells giving themselves over to be formed into something new.

Her palms opened with a tingle, and Beatrice could feel the vines crawl from her skin. She opened her eyes to find thick vines roping from her hands and coaxed them with her mind into thinner and thinner tendrils, thinner still until they weren't visible.

"Go," she whispered, "and mend."

By this point, blood had pooled into Stella's hand, but the tubes moved over the skin, knitting it back together once more.

"I can do more," Beatrice said, and encouraged her mind's eye to follow the tube into Stella's skin, where she tended to the rips in the tiniest capillaries.

She withdrew.

Stella wiped a paper napkin across her hand and showed the table that not only had the bleeding stopped, but no scar remained.

"You think you can fix my bones that way?" Gwen's face held hope.

"Maybe."

"Doctors don't even do anything but prescribe pain meds for broken ribs," Ben interjected.

"Which I won't take—"

"Because you're stubborn."

"Because our father was an addict," Gwen's voice raised. "The pain, Ben." She rubbed her fingertips across her forehead.

"If you're going to do this, why don't you do this here, in New York?" Ben crossed his arms. "Where we have doctors who can help if something goes wrong."

"That's not a bad idea," Beatrice agreed.

Gwen shook her head. "No. Madeline is supposed to see it."

"First Mother told me that if I didn't heal, the forest would burn." Beatrice faced Ben. "If we're going to do this on the mountain, I need you to trust me. If my mother's hands glow red, stop her."

Dinner continued, and no one spoke. When everyone finished, they cleaned up, and Beatrice said, "I think we should sleep."

She offered an herbal tea to help everyone sleep, which Gwen did not accept. Stella tucked herself into the guest bedroom while Ben lay down on the couch. Beatrice found a blanket for him, and he whispered a short "thank you," and rolled over.

"I'm sorry, again. I didn't know the impact the vines would have on Gwen and you."

Ben rolled over to face Beatrice, and she kneeled so that her eyes lined up with his.

"I often wish Madeline had never walked into her studio. That Gwen had never fallen in love with her."

Beatrice's eyes fluttered downward. Until Stella, Beatrice hadn't worked too hard to make strangers comfortable. She never cared what people thought of her, or what they said behind her back. But these two—Ben and Gwen—didn't feel like strangers at all.

"My mother told me once that you couldn't help who you fall in love with."

Ben sat up. "Your mother struggles to regulate herself,

and if you think that I'm not just as scared of her as I am of you, you're wrong."

Beatrice bit her lip. "I'm sorry," she said and stood.

"I know I can't stop you, but if you or your mother come for my sister, I will give you both hell."

"Please ..." Beatrice whispered. "I don't want you to think that way about me."

"What is it you expect me to feel?"

Beatrice shook her head. She herself didn't know the answer to that question. She forced a polite "goodnight," and headed toward the guest bedroom.

Before she tucked herself in next to Stella, Beatrice knocked quietly on Gwen's door, who opened it and leaned against the door frame in a gesture of avoidance.

"Are you sure I can't help you? Beatrice asked.

"Sleep has been hard."

Beatrice understood. "All the more reason to allow for a little help, right?"

"It's terrifying," Gwen continued. "Nightmare after nightmare. I'd just as soon stay awake until I can't anymore."

"I can make something that will take away dreams and put you into a lighter sleep, where you can at least get some rest."

"Will it take away every dream, or just the nightmares?" Gwen asked as she pulled away from the door frame.

"All of them."

Gwen shook her head. "No, thank you."

"Why?" Beatrice asked.

"Because once in a while, I dream of her. I don't want to risk not seeing her face."

"You'll see her soon."

"Maybe," Gwen responded, and Beatrice slumped away and lay down beside Stella.

Sleep had not held her long when a piercing scream reverberated throughout the apartment. Beatrice jolted in bed, but Stella stayed asleep. Beatrice didn't knock this time. She threw open the door and ran to Gwen, who sat on the edge of the bed with her hands covering her face and her breath coming and going in violent rasps. Beatrice lowered herself to the bed beside the panicking woman, wrapped an arm around her, and pulled her close. Eventually, the tension in Gwen's body relaxed.

"Was that one about me?" Beatrice had to know.

Gwen shook her head.

"I wish I could say that they go away forever," Beatrice said. "They won't. But the time between nightmares will grow. Days. Weeks. I haven't gone a month without one. But a time will come when you remember the person you were before."

Beatrice tucked Gwen back in, then moved a quilt from the rocking chair in the corner, curled into its study frame, and lay her head against the back, where she would sleep on and off, taking care of Gwen between nightmares.

CHAPTER 26

Gwen

When Gwen awoke, Beatrice lay beside her, holding her hand. Nightmares had kept them both awake most of the night. Gwen figured she'd slept an hour or two, but she wasn't sure about Beatrice. She gave the woman's hand a squeeze and whispered, "Hey."

Beatrice jolted like a kernel of popcorn.

"We have to get going."

Beatrice's eyes closed, and she gave a low grunt. "Okay."

A nervous energy electrified the apartment as the four buzzed around, preparing for the trip. No one spoke. Once they had eaten a small breakfast of toast and fruit, they each hoisted their bags and headed for the door.

"I need to speak to my brother for just a second. If you don't mind ..." Gwen gestured to the door.

"Of course," Beatrice said with a nod.

Gwen closed the door behind them, then turned to Ben. "I don't know what's coming, but I trust Beatrice."

Ben drew in a deep breath, then let it go. "Well, she didn't hold you upside down."

Gwen let out a short laugh at the light playfulness of Ben's tone. "Was it scary?"

Ben's brow furrowed, and he took a minute before answering. "For a moment, but then she looked at me like I was a puzzle to figure out, and I saw her humanness. She's as bewildered as we are."

"What do you think of her?" Gwen watched her brother blush, and her brows shot upward. "Oh! She makes you blush."

"I'd be lying if I said I didn't find her attractive. But if she kills you, then—"

"She won't kill me. She may not save me, but she won't kill me." Gwen peered into Ben's concerned eyes. "Do you think she shares the same attraction?"

"I don't know, Gwen." Ben shrugged.

"If things work out, investigate it. You deserve to be happy." Her eyes roved over the Christmas tree. "And so does she. Well, here goes nothing, I guess." Gwen opened the door, and she and Ben took the elevator to the street, where Stella and Beatrice waited for them.

***

Trembling, Gwen stared across the road at the face of the mountain she and Madeline climbed months before. The cold felt impossible and pricked through the layers, gloves, and hat that Gwen wore. These icy fingers pulled at her ribs and brought wave after wave of pain until she felt her stomach churn. Still, she crossed the road and stood with Beatrice, Stella, and Ben at the foot of the mountain.

"I can't climb it," she said, panting. "I can barely breathe as it is."

"You don't have to," Beatrice whispered and opened her palms.

Gwen made eye contact with her brother, who gave a wary nod.

"I won't hurt you. I promise you."

264

Gwen and Stella had sandwiched Beatrice on the plane. Beads of sweat had popped up on the woman's pale face and she repeatedly wiped her hands on her pants. It had been Gwen's turn to be the comforter. During takeoff, Beatrice squeezed pain into Gwen's hand.

Vines began to creep, thick and gray, woody and dead. "Are they dead?"

"If I cover us in summer-green vines, people will be more likely to notice."

Beatrice enveloped the group in a blanket of vines, and, as darkness covered them, Gwen felt living ropes create a cradle for her. Beatrice, Ben, and Stella climbed, using the vines as handholds and footholds, but the cocoon Beatrice made gently lifted Gwen.

Is this what Madeline saw?

Gwen estimated twenty minutes of travel up the mountain before she felt herself land on the ground, and, slowly, the vines unfurled. Sunlight assaulted her eyes, and she squinted for a moment.

"I need to sit," Beatrice said, and sat down on a fallen log, her breath coming out in pants.

"Thank you. I could not have climbed that."

"I know," Beatrice said, and Gwen could hear the exhaustion in her voice.

"Do you think that's what Madeline saw?" she asked.

"No." Beatrice shook her head. "I don't think so. Didn't you say she saw a vine go down your throat?"

Gwen's insides were now colder than her outsides.

"She did," Gwen responded.

How hard had she and Madeline railed against what Beatrice was about to do to her? But when Gwen searched those brown eyes, she saw the fourteen-year-old girl in Madeline's pictures, holding a fish next to her Papa, and she knew Beatrice would not hurt her. She sat down beside the woman and rubbed her back with one hand. Ben sat down beside her, but Stella paced back and forth restlessly.

"You'll get to see her soon enough," Beatrice said with a smile, and Stella gave a hesitant nod in response.

"I know," Stella said, continuing to pace. "I just miss her."

"That's how I feel about Forest."

"No, Beatrice. This is different."

After taking a few sips of water, Beatrice stood. "Let's go," she said, and the four continued walking.

As they moved, the pain from Gwen's broken ribs subsided, only to be replaced by a tight corset of anxiety. Stella took the lead at the front of the group and set a quicker pace. Occasionally, Beatrice and Gwen locked eyes, terrified of what lay ahead.

They came upon the Hedge. It was just as Gwen remembered—thinner and shorter, but still very, very green in the winter freeze. Beatrice gestured for them to follow her, and they moved to a thin opening, each of them turning sideways to slither through. They came to a large slab of stone Gwen could only assume was the Rock, and a gaping hole that Stella ran to, then fell to her knees, palming at the soil.

Beatrice moved beside her and kneeled. "Where is she?"

"I don't know," Stella responded with notes of excitement in her voice.

"Stella ..." Beatrice said.

"We'll see, won't we?" Stella smiled.

Stella stood, Beatrice followed, and they continued walking even more quickly now; Gwen desperately tried to keep up.

The structures were visible. Gwen's eyes found Beatrice's one last time, knowing the woman had the same question: when is this thing going to happen?

The next step brought Gwen down. Her foot caught on a tree root, and she collapsed, a rock wedging itself against her already-broken ribs. A searing rip of tissue stole Gwen's breath. Her wild eyes searched for her brother's face as she felt him roll her onto her back. Her lungs pulled into themselves, sticking together.

Sound faded into a background buzz as Gwen's eyes lolled in her head.

"Beatrice, it's now," Stella said.

"Go get my mother," Beatrice responded.

Before her eyes closed completely, Gwen saw Beatrice's palms upturn, and vines spring forth.

CHAPTER 27

Madeline

A bang on the bedroom door jolted Madeline upright in the bed. She ripped the sheet and quilt off to find Stella standing in the doorway.

"Come." The woman waved, then thrust a coat and a pair of boots in Madeline's direction.

Madeline heard Ben's voice as she followed Stella's lead through the frigid forest.

"She's dying," he cried.

Madeline's body trembled from cold and fear as she gathered all that she needed within her to stop Beatrice from killing her lover. Ben kneeled next to Gwen's body while Beatrice sat on the other side, already at work, her head down, her hair falling over her face.

Madeline felt a fire stir within her, aware that her hands glowed red and her eyes burned. The flames expanded from her hands and moved around her entire body from toes to crown.

Stella turned abruptly and held her hands up toward Madeline. "Trust her!"

"You should move," Madeline snapped at Stella.

Small vines crept from Beatrice's skin and around Gwen; the tendrils tapered into smaller and smaller cylinders that Madeline could not see. Ben sat, holding Gwen's hand. Madeline watched as Beatrice shook her hair out of her face, her eyes closed, and her brows knitted with concern.

Trust her.

"No!" she answered her mother's plea out loud.

The flames pulsed. Madeline lifted her arms into the air. The firestorm threw itself in every direction, a force Madeline couldn't control. But Beatrice was ready. Vines flowed from the woman and wrapped around Madeline's wrists and arms, while increasing their assault on Gwen. The fire brought a spitting sizzle to the plant matter as Madeline pressed heat from her body.

"Madeline, stop screaming!" Ben's voice was close as he shouted. "She's healing her, not hurting her. Let her focus."

Trust her.

No!

Madeline squeezed every muscle inside of her, drawing energy from each individual cell, then released it in an explosion that set the trees around her aflame. She roared into the air as she ran to Gwen, but the only response to her scream was silence.

Silence. Everyone was still except for Beatrice, who breathed loudly as she worked.

Madeline could feel the heat from the trees behind her, but she didn't look back. She fell to her knees and prayed for the Goddess to heal Gwen as she ran her fingers across one cold, graying cheek. The only sounds for minute after endless minute were Beatrice's breathing, Ben's sobs, and Madeline's whispered prayer. She realized her daughter couldn't heal Gwen on her own, so she rubbed her hands together, bringing forth healing energy. She didn't need it.

The moment came with an implosion of breath; Gwen's body arched as the air pushed its way into her lungs, and Beatrice withdrew the vines. Gwen coughed until vomit came to her lips and rolled onto Madeline's leg, relentless until it seemed there was nothing left. Madeline rubbed Gwen's back, pulled her closer, and allowed the tears to flow. Ben sat, holding his sister's feet. Madeline wiped her eyes and rubbed her fingers through Gwen's hair as the woman kept her face close to Madeline's legs for several deep breaths. Gwen attempted to sit, collapsing once again.

"Maddie," Gwen whispered with a raw voice, tilting her head to look at Madeline.

"Hi, Gwenny."

"I threw up all over you." Gwen's eyes grew misty, and Madeline bent down to kiss in between them. Bubbling up in Madeline's throat were cross reprimands. *I asked you to never follow me. How did you think you could climb a mountain with broken ribs?*

"How do you feel?" Madeline asked instead.

"I've been better." Gwen tried to smile. "But I've been worse. I can breathe better than I have since the night I proposed." Gwen looked past Madeline's shoulder and her eyes widened. "Maddie! The trees are on fire!"

Madeline looked up to find her daughter had already moved to the foot of the trees, pressing her palms into the ground around the roots.

"Stella!" Beatrice cried. "Go ask the trees for help."

Stella threw Madeline a sideways glance before she jogged away. Madeline watched as her daughter peeled herself from the ground, stood, turned toward her, and growled, "Do something."

Like what?

She wanted to hurl defenses at the faces gaping at her, but the need to make things right pushed her to turn back to the flames.

"Can you pull it back in like Beatrice can do with her vines?" Ben asked, now standing beside her daughter.

Unable to answer, Madeline closed her eyes, opened her fingers and arms wide, and allowed herself to feel. Adrenaline coursed through her as she connected with the heat, with the hot particles of gas and searing plasma. Drawing in a breath, Madeline pulled the conflagration toward her, feeling her skin broil as she drew it closer and closer, knowing that the flames that licked about her and set her clothes aflame could kill her. As the scalding pain ripped through her, Madeline cried, her tears reduced to salt as they left her eyes. She could hear their voices, all shouting around her.

"Mother, stop!" Beatrice pleaded, but the pain subsided, and Madeline continued drawing the violent element into her muscles and down into the center of her core. A cooling tingle began to flow around her, and she knew if she opened her eyes, she would see the golden energy swirling around her charred flesh. Once she knew her body was whole again, she opened her eyes.

Stella came running back to the group, heading toward Beatrice.

"The trees started arguing about what to do," she panted, and Beatrice tutted. "But it looks like it's under control now?"

Beatrice gave one nod, then turned to Gwen. "I'll take your bag to the bathhouse. You can clean up there."

The deep voice brought a lump to Madeline's throat, but she mustered the courage to face her daughter. Her tearful brown eyes locked on Gwen's. Beatrice's face, dewy with perspiration, conveyed exhaustion.

"Beatrice," Madeline said, and her daughter's gaze moved in her direction. Beatrice's lips pressed into a thin line just as they did when she was a child swallowing her feelings, unable or unwilling to voice them.

"Mother." The words cracked through Beatrice's throat, staticky and weak.

Madeline opened her arms out by her side and took a step toward her daughter, only to be met with an eyebrow raise and a quick glance down at her shirt. The sour reek of vomit wafted to Madeline's eyebrows.

"I'll grab you a change of clothes, too, Maddie," Ben said. "You're pretty gross yourself."

"Thanks, Ben."

Ben squeezed Madeline's arm, then rejoined Beatrice. Gwen cleared her throat.

"Here, let me help you up." Madeline pulled Gwen to her feet and reached for her hand.

Gwen's eyes followed her brother and Beatrice as they took steps toward the house then stopped at the silent birch tree. Beatrice fell to her knees and placed her hands on the trunk, first stroking it, then slamming her fists on it with a "Where are you?"

Ben placed his hand on Beatrice's shoulder and walked her into the house.

"You were wrong about her, Maddie." Madeline side-eyed Gwen. "She and I have a lot in common. There's a reason she grew the Hedge. She didn't tell me what, but it wasn't to keep you out."

With a sigh, Madeline encouraged Gwen to keep walking. "I could reprimand you as well, you know," she admonished.

"I'm not reprimanding you." Gwen turned toward Madeline. "I feel protective of her. And you set her home on fire."

"I know. It's well within her right to ask us to leave."

"She won't," Gwen replied. "She likes me. And I think she *really* likes my brother."

"Really?" Madeline asked.

"Didn't you see?"

Madeline stopped them at the tree that stood in front of the home, placing her hand on the bark. "This is my mother,

273

Gwen. She talked with me last night, but stopped. It's like she was tired." She kneeled at the roots. "Mama," she whispered, but there was no movement. Madeline stood and held Gwen's hand as she led her to the bathhouse.

"Hey!" Ben called. He stood at the door, holding a jar. "Beatrice prescribed a bath, a nap, and lunch ... in that order."

He handed Gwen the herbs and she rolled the jar around in her hand, a small smile forming on her face. "Put it in your bath water. She asked if you ..." Ben gestured toward Madeline. " ...well, demanded that you make a pan of biscuits after you get Gwen settled. And told me to tell you to thank Martha for the water, and Edith for the fire."

"Where is she?" Madeline asked.

"Resting in her room. She needs a minute. Don't worry. I'll check on her."

Madeline drew in a long inhale, paused at the top, sighed it out, and turned toward Gwen. "Let's get you cleaned up."

Steaming water and the glow of oil sconces warmed the bath house. "Thank you, Edith," Madeline said and touched the metal sconce. The words felt strange in her mouth, but she dipped her fingers in the water and whispered, "Thank you, Martha."

"You're so welcome, Madeline." A voice Madeline had never heard before spoke the words aloud.

Gwen's eyes widened, and she smiled. "Welcome home, Maddie."

"See if it's too hot," Madeline urged, and Gwen dipped her fingertips in and shook her head. She undressed Gwen, noting the goosebumps that popped up on her skin and the thinness of her body. "Have you been eating?"

"Not really."

"You're cold." Madeline broke Gwen's gaze. "Let's get you in."

She supported Gwen as she stepped into the tub, then unscrewed the jar of herbs and sprinkled the contents into the bath, swirling it around with her fingers.

"May you be well, Gwen."

"Maddie," Gwen breathed, "get in with me."

Emotions imploded, and the anger Madeline had swallowed spewed out. "Gwen, what were you thinking?"

"That I missed you. And ..." Gwen paused. "The moment with Beatrice was going to happen no matter what." Gwen brought her hand up to Madeline's face. "Get in with me. You're covered in puke."

The warm wetness of Gwen's hand and the gentle fragrance of chamomile and lavender softened Madeline. She pulled off her soiled coat, nightgown, and panties, and joined Gwen in the water. She laid her head against the edge and felt her legs lengthen against her lover's.

"Did I ever tell you that it stays this warm? And clean?"

"You did, but you never told me how."

"I didn't really know how. A charm, I guess. Edith and Martha."

Gwen moved around in the water and Madeline felt her lover take her foot and massage it gently, applying pressure to various spots on various toes. Madeline moved her body toward Gwen and brought her lips down to hers, but Gwen pressed a finger to her lips.

"I never should have said those things. I'm sorry I was so cruel."

"I should have said yes to you. I choose you. If you want to get out of this tub and climb down the mountain and take off for home, we'll go."

"Why would I do that?" Gwen reached up and ran her fingers through the long ponytail Madeline wore. "You have to face your daughters."

Daughters.

The word landed in Madeline's womb.

"Have you seen Gertrude?" Gwen asked.

Madeline's chest seized. "How could I have seen ..." Her voice trailed off.

"Have you been to the Rock?" Gwen asked.

"For a moment. It was terrifying. Especially when I realized my mother was gone."

"How did she get here?"

"She told me she walked." Madeline smiled and whispered, "She's more powerful than she realized."

Gwen's eyes grew wider. "The three of you are intimidating."

Madeline jerked her head in surprise.

Using her fingers to tick off Madeline's supernatural skills, Gwen explained herself. "You're a telepathic, telekinetic, fire-wielding healer who can tell the future. Your mother is a tree, and Beatrice ..."

Madeline's eyes furrowed. "Was she kind to you?"

Gwen closed her eyes. "I've had so many nightmares, Maddie. She kept me company all night. And healed as many wounds as she could."

Madeline placed her forehead against Gwen's and kissed her, first on the lips, then on the neck. She lifted her lover out of the water and kissed her between her breasts, and Gwen sighed.

"I need a nap," Gwen confessed, breathless.

Madeline nodded, lifted herself out of the tub, and offered to help Gwen. They slipped into clean clothes, stepped out of the bathhouse, and walked toward Madeline's mother. She placed her hand once more against the cold bark.

"Your mother is a tree, Madeline," Gwen whispered as the two of them climbed up the front porch.

"Did you not believe me?" Madeline asked with playful incredulity, but Gwen turned to her with a serious countenance.

"It's one thing to believe something, Maddie. It's another to see it."

"I know, Gwen. I know."

"No," Gwen rebutted, "you don't."

Madeline guided Gwen down the hall to the bedroom she had claimed for herself. She pulled the covers down and neatened them for Gwen to crawl in.

"I'm going to tuck you in," Madeline said, then yawned. "Then I'm going to go make my daughter her favorite biscuits."

"The man with curly hair … it's her son, isn't it?"

"Yeah." Madeline nodded. "I'm pretty sure."

"Are you going to tell her?"

"I don't know. Any advice?"

"I'm not sure there's a right or a wrong way to go on this one. Will you hold me?" Gwen asked and turned to her side. Madeline curled in beside her and, against her own will, fell asleep.

CHAPTER 28

Beatrice

Beatrice slid onto the floor of her bedroom, the same gutted depletion she felt after the hunter left her for dead leaving her heavy and numb. With the exhaustion came relief that the fated entanglement with Gwen had ended well, despite the singed trees. The moment had opened Beatrice to a further understanding of her capabilities. She had, in fact, created something stronger than her mother, and this knowledge stirred within her both remorse and empowerment.

Beatrice felt it would be right to cry, so why couldn't she? Perhaps she was dry from pouring so much green life into Gwen. She didn't know what it would mean to talk about the man; she had never done so. Not with Stella, and not with Gwen, who she knew would understand more than most. Not even with Grandmother. But she had to explain it to the woman who had birthed her.

Her mother.

As images and smells and tactile sensations flooded her, Beatrice realized that once again her mother had not chosen her. The woman would have burned the forest down to save Gwen, and Beatrice with it.

Now the tears began to spark, painful in the backs of her eyes, and her body started to shake. She clenched her teeth and pulled at the hair on each side of her head, rocking forward and backward. Though she tried to hold back her anguished screams, roars rumbled from just under her rib cage and tore through her throat, turning into sobs that shook her until her stomach roiled.

"Hey." A warm hand on each of Beatrice's arms followed the sound of Ben's voice. "Shh-shh-shh. Can I sit next to you?"

Embarrassment encircled Beatrice's chest with violent heat. She wanted nothing more than to push the man away with both hands or wrap him in vines and tack him to the ceiling where she could deal with him when she was able. But the fatigue left her motionless, and she felt Ben nestle beside her and place a hand against her back.

"I don't have the right words for this situation, so I won't say much, but I want you to know that you're not alone."

Saying nothing, Beatrice leaned into the offering, allowing her head to rest against his chest. Ben wrapped his other arm around her, and she found enough calm to relax her jaw and breathe a little more deeply.

"You were amazing out there," Ben whispered into her hair.

"She would have killed me." The words came out squeaky, and Beatrice felt herself shrivel up again.

"No. She would not have." Ben's hand stroked Beatrice's hair, and her eyelids grew heavy. "What about a nap?"

"I'll have nightmares. Just sit with me like this a few more minutes, then we'll go to the greenhouse and gather things for lunch."

"You got it," Ben said as he pulled her closer.

Beatrice allowed her eyes to flutter closed as she relaxed into his embrace.

When she'd rested enough, Beatrice led Ben through the kitchen and to the porch, grateful that Gwen and her mother were nowhere to be found. Stella was sitting at Grandmother's roots, fear etched on her face.

"Stella, it's cold. Go warm up."

Stella shook her head.

"Here, let me look." Beatrice kneeled beside the tree and searched for her power, but she was empty. "I can't. I guess I exhausted myself. If you see Mother and Gwen, let them know we went to the greenhouse?"

Stella took her eyes from the tree for one moment, glanced up at Beatrice, and gave one nod of her head. Beatrice walked steadily beside Ben, confused by her feelings toward him. She had read novels about romance, but none of those initial feelings of love at first sight matched what stirred within her. Ben brought feelings of comfort and home. She felt at ease with him in a way she had never felt with anyone. Soothed, somehow.

"Thank you for helping Gwen," Ben said as he walked beside her. "You could have resented her the way she did you, before she met you. You have a different heart than others, Beatrice."

Beatrice's eyes widened like a child's. Ben just smiled at her.

"Can I talk to you about your mother?"

The words brought ice to Beatrice's bowels and heart. She swallowed but couldn't bring herself to speak.

Grandmother, where did you go?

Beatrice closed her eyes and listened for her voice. Silence.

Ben stopped walking, forcing Beatrice to acknowledge the question. "I think we should give her a chance."

"We?"

Ben sighed out a long breath. "Madeline's anger and paranoia have kept me from trusting her. But Gwen sees something in her I just haven't had a chance to see yet. I owe it to my sister."

Beatrice continued walking. This stranger had no right to tell how she should handle things with her mother.

"I want Gwen to have some options for lunch," she said, changing the subject. "Does she eat cheese?"

"Yes, she does. So, you grow vegetables all year long?"

"And fruit. Berries. Cherries. Apples. Pears."

"Fruit trees? How big is this greenhouse?"

"Big enough." Ben's smile returned. "Are you not exhausted, too? I don't sleep well, so I'm used to feeling tired most of the time."

"Well, that we have in common," Ben responded. "I ruminate at night."

"What over?"

"What I'm doing with my life. What happened with my marriage. I enjoy my work, of course, but sometimes I get this ache, knowing there's more out there. I feel guilty even thinking that. I'm lucky in a lot of ways."

"What did happen to your marriage?" Beatrice flushed, and she wanted to take back the question. "If you don't mind my asking."

"I don't mind." His face revealed regret as he spoke. "She didn't want children. I knew it going in, but I thought maybe marriage would be enough for me. Maybe I would change. My heart would shift."

"But it didn't."

Ben just shook his head.

"I'm sorry."

He shrugged. "It is what it is."

The two walked in silence for a moment.

"I have no idea what I want," Beatrice confessed. "Forest and I have lived our quiet little lives for so long. We've always had what we needed. There's not much I've *wanted*." Her eyes met Ben's. "But that seems to be changing ... and I don't like it."

As they walked farther into the woods, Beatrice felt the urge to reach out and take Ben's hand. Resisting the pull would be dishonest to herself and to him. The man showed no surprise when she laced her fingers through his. Instead, he gave it a squeeze and brought it to his lips.

"Have you ever been with someone ... romantically, I mean?" he asked.

"No. There have been people who have wanted to," Beatrice responded. "Sam, the baker, for one."

Ben's face questioned her.

"We met him at the farmers' market where Forest and I have a booth. The best bread Forest ever tasted. He said I'm the most beautiful woman he's ever seen." Beatrice shook her head. "Ridiculous."

"You are beautiful, Beatrice."

She grinned. "Thank you."

"And what about the baker? Is he not handsome? Not charming?"

"Oh, he's attractive. And kind enough. But I don't feel anything for him."

"Why me, then?" Ben lifted their entwined hands to eye level. Beatrice felt her face flush now, the heat of embarrassment mixed with shock. He was bold. He seemed to notice her countenance change. "You reached for my hand, Beatrice. Am I mistaken?"

"I don't know exactly what I'm feeling." Beatrice considered pulling away. She hesitated a moment before taking a deep inhale and an even longer exhale. "I feel at ease with you."

Ben squeezed her hand again, and she squeezed back.

"We're here." Beatrice drew her hand from his and opened the door to her greenhouse.

"Beatrice! This is enormous! How did you build it?"

"I had help from my grandmothers. I started the project myself when Forest was a baby. Even though I can grow things straight from my palms, it gets tiring after a while, so I decided a greenhouse would help me. I started going into town here and there, collecting old windows or whatever glass and frames I could find. My grandmothers must have grown tired of my whining, so they offered to help me."

"Where do we even start?"

"This way." Beatrice pointed toward patches of greens and lettuces.

Neither of them brought up the phenomenon happening between them as they picked vegetables for stew and salad. Instead, Ben asked question after endless question about Beatrice's family, and she answered him. Once they filled their baskets and headed for the greenhouse door, Ben brought up Beatrice's mother once again.

"How are you feeling about your mother?"

"Not very brave."

Ben simply nodded and gestured for the door. "Let's go."

Chapter 29

Madeline

Madeline cursed herself for falling asleep. She pulled on fleece-lined jeans, a sweater, and a pair of wool socks and made her way to the kitchen. Beatrice and Ben stood at the wooden countertop, cutting onions and carrots. The urn holding Eric's and Gertrude's ashes sat on the table where the tea had been.

"He wants out," Beatrice said without looking up from her cutting. Ben gave Madeline a thin smile, then returned to his work.

Madeline's throat tightened. "What about what she wants? Does she want out, too?" She knew the words were grenades, but she launched them at her daughter anyway.

Beatrice stopped stirring, covered the pot, wiped her hands on her apron, and then removed it. Madeline took a long look at her. She was every bit as tall as herself, but her hair hung in large, loose curls of roasted chestnut, just reaching the tops of her shoulders. Her brown eyes were narrow and accusing.

"I've learned a few things over the past two days,"

Beatrice grumbled through gritted teeth. "When I was fourteen, you believed the worst possible story you could tell yourself about me. Then you had the vision of me and Gwen and the vines, and you chose to believe the worst again."

Madeline's skin burned as Beatrice moved her face within an inch of hers. "I also learned that I am stronger than you. You haven't lived here for the past twenty years. This is my home. We will deal with Papa. Now. You will face Gertrude, and—"

Madeline cut her off with a raised voice. "I don't want to see her."

Beatrice's face softened. She glanced down at the table, shook her head, then her eyes, almost smirking, turned back toward Madeline. "Yes, you do," she said as she put on her coat and scooped up the urn in her arms.

Madeline had no choice but to follow. When the two found Stella sitting cross-legged on the ground in front of Mother, they exchanged glances.

"Stella," Beatrice said with a warm but firm voice. "I need time out here with my mother. Can you give us a few moments?"

Stella stood and trudged into the house without looking up at either woman. Before she continued speaking, she placed her palm on the tree. "Please come back, Grandmother. I can't do this without you."

Madeline swallowed deeply. Beatrice sat down on a rocking chair, trembling.

"I heard you that night," she said, rocking, her eyes fixated on the tree. "I heard you calling for me."

Madeline gripped the arm of the rocking chair, steeling herself.

"Why didn't you stay with me and send Gertrude with Papa?" Beatrice asked and stopped rocking.

"If Forest was sick, wouldn't you need to be with him?" Madeline responded.

Beatrice's eyes widened as she stood. "You chose her! Even though she didn't choose you back."

Madeline would rather Beatrice had slapped her across the face. She lowered her eyes and scrunched her eyebrows, considering.

"Yes, I did," she confessed. "We came up with a plan that Eric would come back once he got Gertrude and me to the hospital. But things happened so quickly ..." Madeline could have rattled off a long list of defenses, but she stopped herself. "You're right to be angry with me. I didn't keep you safe, and that is a mother's first job."

She searched her daughter's face, hoping to find compassion, but instead, Beatrice balled her fists. "That's not all I'm angry about," she continued with flaring nostrils. "You kept the truth from me, Mother. And I know Grandmother gave you strict orders, but you are your own woman. If you had left me with the trees ..." Beatrice paced. "I didn't have to be alone."

"Beatrice, until I saw their eyes and heard them talk, I didn't know the trees were still ... themselves. Look, I had a dying child. I didn't have time to—"

Beatrice just shook her head and jutted her finger at Madeline. "You chose me to be the one to die!" Then she picked up the urn and stomped off the porch.

Madeline watched Beatrice roll the urn slowly in her hands. "Would you have killed me today?" she asked.

"I'm not good at controlling my anger, Beatrice, but I would not have killed you." Madeline's stomach burned. "I would have made you stop, then healed whatever damage I caused."

Beatrice glared at her through slitted eyes. "I suppose that's why you're here now."

"I suppose." Madeline pointed at the urn holding the

ashes of her daughter and husband. "I had to put their bodies together in the same urn."

"It's beautiful." Beatrice held the urn in front of her with reluctant admiration, then her gaze traveled to the sky. A moment or two passed, and an eagle, larger than was possible, filled the sky with her immense wings and perched with a cry on one of Mother's branches.

"Hello, Gertrude." Beatrice wore an honest smile as she spoke to the bird.

Madeline took a deep breath and locked eyes with her daughter.

"Are you ready?" Beatrice asked.

"No." Madeline grasped the urn and pulled it toward her. At first, Beatrice would not release her hold, but relented after a series of back-and-forth tugs.

"Tell me what cruel reason I could possibly have for doing this," Beatrice growled.

Madeline had no answer.

"Papa wants to be free from the darkness. And he wants to give you and Gwen privacy. He can *hear* you."

Guilt mixed with embarrassment in Madeline's stomach. The eagle launched into the air, and cavernous wings surrounded mother and daughter in circles as its cries became more and more irritated.

"Gertrude couldn't care less about the ashes in that thing."

"Make her stop circling!" Madeline cried.

"I can't force Gertrude to do anything." Beatrice gaffed and successfully pulled the urn from Madeline's hands.

She watched Beatrice hold the urn over her head. The bird moved swiftly, snatching the urn greedily in her talons. Wide-eyed, she watched the eagle, her Gertrude, fly high above their heads. The magnificent bird tossed the urn into the air, only to dive for it, claim it, and then toss it up again.

"What is she doing? Why is she toying with him like that?"

"She's not," Beatrice objected. "They're playing. Don't you remember when she was a baby? The only time she would stop crying was when Papa tossed her up in the air or flew her in his arms."

Madeline nodded and returned her gaze to the sky. Gertrude made one final, high ascent, and Beatrice said, "It's time."

The eagle plunged through the air toward the smokehouse. The sound of the urn shattering reminded Madeline of the time she had pulled a ceramic bowl of perfectly cooked beans off the kitchen table, destroying both contents and container.

Mother and daughter watched the ashes settle on the roof. Beatrice smiled and whispered, "Bye, Papa."

"Can you see his soul like you did Gertrude's?"

Beatrice turned toward Madeline and stared into her eyes for a long time.

"Yes. He's moving on to whatever's next."

Beatrice strode back to the porch, opened a chest, and withdrew two pairs of leather gloves, handing one set to Madeline. She watched her daughter wrap her arms in the gloves and followed suit, then she looked up into her mother's branches. Gertrude perched so big and so strong that the branch appeared tiny underneath her talons.

Beatrice raised her arm and gestured for the bird to come down with the beckon of her index finger. The eagle hesitated and piped a few notes in response.

"Come on, Gertie," Beatrice said, eyebrow cocked. "You owe it to her."

The eagle glided down and landed on Beatrice's arm, causing her to jerk backward. Beatrice stroked the smooth feathers, and the bird pressed her solid, glossy beak against her sister's face. She brought the bird closer to Madeline, and her chest heaved.

"You can say what you need to say now," Beatrice said.

Madeline swallowed and locked eyes with the eagle. "Why did you not want to be with me? Wasn't I a good mother?"

The bird piped again.

"It had nothing to do with you," Beatrice said. "She never wanted to hurt you, but she was tired of suffering." Gertrude continued to make soft sounds. "She hated the way she felt in a human body and wanted to fly."

"Did it hurt?" Madeline whispered to the bird, and reached out to stroke the feathers, which she found smooth and soft.

"Yes," Beatrice translated.

"That's it? Yes?"

Beatrice nodded. "She doesn't want to go into details. She thought we would always be a family, and she missed you very much."

"Does she understand why I left?"

Gertrude responded with a coo.

"She says you should have listened to me."

Madeline turned square to Beatrice. "I am sorry, Beatrice. Do you think you'll be able to forgive me?"

Beatrice was slow to respond, but sighed and said, "I don't know. I'm angrier than I realized. I can't talk about it anymore right now." Beatrice returned her attention to Gertrude. "Now, she wants you to hold her."

Madeline stretched out her gloved hand. Gertrude was gentle as she stepped from Beatrice's arm to hers and stroked her beak along her cheek.

"It's cold," Beatrice said, and rubbed Gertrude on her other side. "Come inside with us, Gertrude. Mother's making biscuits."

Mother.

After all this time, Madeline was still a mother.

"Beatrice." Beatrice stopped walking but didn't turn around. Madeline continued. "Remember, when you accuse me of thinking the worst of you, you did the same."

"True. But I was a child. You were the mother."

CHAPTER 30

Beatrice

"Stew's going," Ben said as Beatrice and her mother entered the kitchen. He had a dish towel draped across one shoulder and a wooden spoon in his hand, which brought a broad smile to Beatrice's face.

Beatrice surveyed the scene and narrowed her eyes playfully. "What if I had specific plans for this stew?"

"I'm a good cook," Ben assured her.

"He is," Gwen said. She sat at the table drinking a glass of water.

"Feeling better?" Beatrice asked, moving toward the stove and giving the stew a mindful stirring.

Gwen nodded, gave Beatrice a smile, then asked, "What about you?"

Beatrice paused as a wave of lightheadedness poured over her crown. "I'll be alright." She looked down at her avian sister, then up at her mostly human mother. "I need another minute, I think." Her eyelids fluttered, heavy enough she could fall asleep standing up.

"Why don't you let Madeline and I finish lunch and you rest?"

Beatrice nodded at Ben's suggestion.

"Will you come with me, Gertie?" she asked the eagle, who piped an affirmation and waddled behind Beatrice. Safe in her bedroom, Beatrice patted the bed, encouraging Gertrude to hop up.

"I need a nap." Beatrice reached out and stroked the bird's feathers. Gertrude moved her body close enough that Beatrice could feel her warmth. She let her eyes close, knowing full well she risked waking up screaming. "What do you think, Gertie ..." Beatrice whispered as sleep began to take her. "Should we give her another chance?"

Gertrude cooed.

"Okay."

***

It wasn't her own screams that woke Beatrice, but the ravenous grumble of her stomach, a throbbing headache, and the panicked voices of her grandmothers. She squeezed her eyes tight.

"Haven't I asked you all not to talk all at once?"

You must bring her. First Mother is coming to the Rock.

Beatrice groaned. She needed food, water, spearmint tea, and some kind of touch from Ben.

"After lunch," she said.

She stood, wobbly with hunger, and moved toward the kitchen where the smell of buttermilk biscuits waved her in. Gwen and Ben sat at the table sipping tea, and Mother stood at the sink washing the bowl in which she had worked magic.

"Madeline couldn't find the biscuit cutter," Ben said. "She said you moved the kitchen around."

Beatrice surveyed her mother's face, which seemed calmer and warmer.

The woman shrugged. "They're going to be square."

Beatrice held her gaze for a moment, then tucked her dark curls behind her ears and moved to pull bowls from cabinets. Just then, the kitchen door opened, and Forest entered without Stella behind him. Beatrice embraced Forest with a tight squeeze.

"I missed you," she said with a catch in her throat.

"You were only gone a day," Forest responded. "You must be Grandmother." He embraced Madeline in a hug. Beatrice watched her mother's eyes squeeze together tightly, tears escaping. When the two pulled apart, Mother placed her hands on Forest's cheeks. "You look just like your mother."

"She found you!" Forest beamed.

Forest glanced at Beatrice who shook her head. "She came on her own. We passed one another. This is Gwen, Mother's partner, and her brother Ben."

"Nice to meet you both." Forest's face lost the excitement and turned away. "The Hedge is down completely. You should put it back up."

Beatrice snorted a laugh. "I don't think I can. I'll try later." She narrowed her eyes at Forest's anxiety. "What's got you worried?"

"Things going on in town. I want to bring Wanda and Dani here today instead of tomorrow. They're not safe."

As if dealing with my mother isn't enough.

Beatrice squeezed her eyes shut and nodded. "Alright."

"Wanda? From the market?" Madeline asked.

"You've met her?"

Madeline nodded. "I met Wanda years ago. She was a nurse who took care of Gertrude. But I also went to the market before I came up the mountain."

"Can you at least take a minute to eat with us?" Beatrice asked her son, who nodded. "Where's Stella?" Forest motioned toward the door and Beatrice clicked her tongue.

Small snowflakes fluttered from the sky to the ground,

but Stella kneeled on the cold earth next to Grandmother. Beatrice watched the woman for a moment. Tears fell down Stella's face, and there was a palpable feeling that her friend knew more than she was letting on. Something odd colored the closeness the woman had formed with the tree.

Without words, Beatrice encouraged Stella to stand and come into the house, but before she opened the door, Stella stopped her.

"I love her, Beatrice," Stella said.

"I know you do. I love her, too." Beatrice cupped Stella's elbow in her hand. "Let's eat, take Mother to the Rock—the trees won't stop chattering—then we figure out what's going on with Grandmother. We won't forget her, Stella."

"I hoped a seat at the table was for her."

Beatrice, brows furrowed, squared her shoulders toward Stella to see her more clearly. "How could you hope for that?"

Stella spoke no more as she made her way into the kitchen. Shuffling of coats, removing of shoes, and the dishing of food eventually culminated in six souls standing around the table prepared for the blessing.

"Has this table ever been so full?" Mother asked, and Beatrice shook her head.

She positioned herself at the head of the table. Tradition held that the mother would say the blessing before every meal, never the daughter, but Beatrice stood in her power and spoke, thanking the goddess, asking for blessings, and giving gratitude to every woman before her. She opened her eyes, sat down, and the others followed.

"I love what you added to the prayer, Beatrice."

"I didn't add it," Beatrice said, pulling a biscuit toward her. "Grandmother took it out."

"My mother?"

Beatrice nodded.

"There are things she didn't tell you." Beatrice slathered

each side of the biscuit with butter. She would explain, but first, a bite. For a moment, she was a tiny little girl sitting on her mother's lap, receiving the smallest bites of salty bread.

"We were never supposed to be mother and daughter in isolation. We were supposed to learn from the trees. Commune with them. Grow, in new and miraculous ways." Beatrice stirred the stew in her bowl. "Before Grandmother, each mother took their daughter to First Mother when her gifts appeared, and the trees celebrated. Imogene brought Ida to her mother. Ida brought Thelma. Thelma brought Martha, and so on."

A bite of stew. A bite of biscuit.

Mother's home.

Beatrice surveyed the furrowed brows and narrowed eyes on the matured face of the woman across from her and continued her story.

"The women worked together to improve the house with their gifts. Martha and Edith keep the tub full of hot water. I've learned a lot from Ida. Anyway, Ola didn't bring Grandmother, because she has no gift."

Madeline laid down her spoon and steepled her fingers. "She told me to trust you." She closed her eyes. "She was so tired she could barely get the words out. She told me she walked from the Rock."

"Is that all that she said?" Stella asked.

Madeline's throat bobbed as she swallowed hard. "She told me, when she falls, to burn the tree."

The image of Grandmother falling and her mother setting the tree aflame flashed into Beatrice's mind with a realness that gripped her chest. She took a sip of water, restored herself, and said, "Well, we've seen that images can be confusing."

They ate in silence for a few moments.

"You can't burn her," Stella insisted, her voice raised. "I don't care what she said."

"We'll cross that bridge when we come to it, Stella." Mother's stolid response caused Beatrice to shift in her seat. "I wish she had told me why. She never explained things to me."

"She didn't know what to do with you, Mother. She felt like a fraud raising a prodigy. You were the strongest daughter yet."

"Until you." A marriage of pride and unease mixed on her mother's face, then her eyebrows twitched upward. "Are the trees talking to you now?"

Beatrice chuckled. "They haven't stopped since I made it home."

"What are they saying? I want to know."

Beatrice pulled open another biscuit. "And I want to enjoy my biscuit. I've missed them."

"You've been making them since you were ten."

"Not like these." Beatrice smirked.

"Beatrice." Her mother's voice became pointed, and Beatrice sighed in response.

"First Mother will meet you at the Rock."

"First Mother. And the rest of them? What do they want with me?"

"They don't know you. They haven't seen you since the day you gave birth to me. You're a hole in our story." Beatrice dusted the crumbs from her hands. "Some are ready to flog you. A few are jealous. You resisted becoming a tree. You found love. Twice." Beatrice smiled at Gwen, who smiled back. "A few are angry that you've broken the lineage."

"Have I?"

"I don't know. I had a son. Things won't continue exactly as they have. Forest gets to start his own line."

Beatrice glanced at Forest, who turned away quickly.

"Will they try to turn me into a tree?" Mother asked, her face pale.

"There is no *they*. The Goddess does the work. And I find it unlikely."

"Ben and I can clean up," Gwen said when the meal was over, then she gestured to Beatrice and her mother. "Give you two time."

"I'm going to go get Wanda and Dani." Forest gave Beatrice a peck on the forehead, wrapped himself in his coat, and was out the door.

Beatrice felt her eyes close, but she nodded and both she and Madeline stood, pulled their coats from the hooks beside the door, and entered the wintered mountain forest.

***

Madeline shivered, her breath releasing in a puff. "It's cold."

"It's winter," Beatrice responded.

"Where are we going?"

"You'll see."

For a time, they walked in silence. Beatrice felt the stew and biscuits churn in her belly.

"There are so many things to say. I don't know how it will all come out."

"What happened, Bea?"

"Let's get there first."

So much anger still crashed within her. Nerves wouldn't allow Beatrice to rehearse the words she would say to her mother, so she focused on the cold air and the sound of their footsteps in the forest.

They finally reached the spot where her family celebrated the changes in the sun and the moon, syncing their lives with the very beating of Earth's heart. The ring of quartz that had once held in the bonfire flames was overgrown and had sunk into the forest floor due to lack of upkeep. The charred remnants of Mother's burned things littered the ground.

299

"You really were angry with me."

"Don't take it personally. It's tradition. There's not enough space to store every woman's belongings, no matter how few there are. Every daughter has done it. I put my own things in the trunk a few months ago."

Beatrice sat down on the large rock where they used to watch the flames dance into the night air, and thought back to the burning sketches flapping crisp wings into the air. She thought about the profile of the handsome man. Ben.

"You drew Ben once. Do you remember?"

Mother frowned, then shook her head. "No, I rarely connected with the drawings when I was that young. I wish you had kept that one."

Beatrice peered into the ash. "Me too."

Without warning, sweat broke out. The fourteen-year-old girl shivering on top of an icy West Virginia mountain surfaced. Beatrice balled her fists and clenched her teeth until she felt pain.

"You don't have to tell me, Beatrice. I know you didn't build the Hedge because of me."

"I think I have to tell it for myself. I just can't make the words come."

Mother sat down next to her and rubbed her back.

"Try this," Mother said, and she pressed her palms into Beatrice's lower back, arched her chest forward, raising her gaze toward the sky, and exposing her throat.

Beatrice tried to follow instructions, but when she tilted her head back, her lunch moved to her lips, and she jolted up to deposit vomit at the base of a tree.

"Oh, honey. I'm sorry. I didn't know that would happen."

"I didn't like that feeling." Beatrice swallowed and felt the tears come as she walked back.

"Did that position hurt?"

"Not physically."

Beatrice sat down again and felt her breath continue to shallow. If she didn't, the memories would choke her.

"It was April after you'd left. I was doing well." Beatrice made eye contact with her mother as she spoke. "Eating well. I had a little garden in the corner of my room." She wiggled her fingers as if to paint a picture. "It was cold. You know how April can be. One night, Willow and I came to this spot, and I built us a fire."

Tears were hot as they fell down her cheek. Her mother had never seen her cry; even when Beatrice was a baby, she had other ways of communicating when she was hungry, wet, or tired.

"I knew the sound. It was the same sound Papa's gun made. I felt it in my own body as it went through Willow."

Beatrice's chin trembled.

"I ran to her, but it was too late. I heard footsteps crunching through the forest and this huge man came. He was at least three times Papa's size." Beatrice paused and looked into her mother's eyes. They glowed a fierce red, her nostrils flared, and Beatrice could feel heat emanating from her.

"Please don't set the forest on fire again."

She turned away and remained quiet until she felt the temperature lower.

"I stood between him and Willow. I didn't want him to take her."

Beatrice described how she fought the man. How she bit him. Kicked him in the groin. Pulled his beard and hair.

"He was so much stronger than me. He just laughed."

"Can I hold you?"

Beatrice couldn't speak, but leaned toward her mother, who pulled her in and stroked her hair. Fluids poured from her eyes and nose onto her mother's chest.

"He took what he wanted."

She felt herself collapse entirely into her mother's

embrace. Her body was limp and numb from crown to toe, her eyes closed, and she drifted back into her fourteen-year-old body, where nothing mattered.

Her mother rocked her back and forth and hummed the song that she sang to put Beatrice to sleep, the song Beatrice sang to Forest when he was a baby. She thought of Forest, then inhaled as though taking her first breath and straightened her body again.

"I'm not done. When he was done, he stabbed me over and over again. That's the last thing I remember. I woke up on the Rock. It was the first time I met Grandmother. She saved my life." Beatrice stared at the forest floor. "Why didn't you tell me about her?" she asked.

Madeline didn't answer.

"I know it was terrifying, but how did you go so long without seeing her?"

"I did exactly what she asked of me."

Locking eyes with her, Beatrice saw the pain and shame her mother felt.

"She was so tender with me," Beatrice continued. "I remember how soft and velvety her roots were. She told me I'd been out for days and that she'd asked the trees for help, but they didn't respond. She assured me I wasn't pregnant. She told me to go home and take care of things and wait for you, but I couldn't make myself move.

"After another day and another night, Gertrude came and picked me up with her talons and took me to her eyrie. She told me she carried the man off the mountain and threw him into the river. She's the one who picked up my broken body and took me to Grandmother. I couldn't eat or sleep. When I did sleep, I'd wake up in a cold sweat, screaming. She started force feeding me raw fish, half digested."

Beatrice felt her stomach turn again.

"She held my lips shut with her beak until I swallowed.

She kept me alive that way for a year. Then, I asked to see Grandmother again. I wanted it all to stop. *I* wanted to stop. That's when Grandmother told me the stories of the Rock, and the Goddess, and where we came from. I begged her to ask the Goddess if I could have my child early. She told me that if I wanted that, I needed to go to First Mother. So that's what I did. Forest changed everything." Beatrice sighed. "It never crossed my mind that the Hedge would be too strong for you."

"I did come back," her mother responded.

"I know. I found the letters when the Hedge started weakening. I would have searched for you sooner, if I had known where to start. I needed Stella."

Madeline's eyes squinted with a question. "Stella. Is she … I mean, the way she speaks of my mother, it's almost like she's—"

"Yes." Beatrice interrupted before her mother could finish. "I think so."

"How?"

"I don't know." Beatrice inhaled and stood. "Neither of them has confided in me, and it's really none of our business."

"Do you think she's going to be okay?"

Beatrice knew she was asking about Grandmother.

"I don't know. I can't hear her. I tried to send roots down, but …" Beatrice held her palms out, fingers splayed wide. "I'm empty."

"I don't know how to help her."

Beatrice shook her head. "Neither do I."

"Gwen told me you helped her through nightmares last night. I cannot thank you enough."

"Well, she helped me on the plane." Beatrice smiled. "I like her a lot."

"Me too."

"Mother." Beatrice squeezed her mother's hand tightly. "Please don't ever think the worst of me again."

"I promise I won't."

Beatrice began walking back toward the house as the snowflakes increased in size.

"What did you think of New York?" Mother asked.

Beatrice chuckled. "I don't know how you stand it." She watched her mother's face fall. "I'm not saying I'd never come visit." Beatrice allowed playfulness into her voice, and her mother smiled.

"I guess I have made a home in New York."

"Mmmhmm, but you always have a home here, too."

CHAPTER 31

Stella

Snow fell at a steady pace. The air smelled of wood smoke drifting from the house and the cinnamon scent of dry, fallen leaves. Though she had wrapped herself in layers, a frigidness invaded Stella, not from the air or the frozen ground, but from the deep-seated knowledge that Beulah was gone. It chilled her blood, gut, and spine.

Sasha had curled up in her shirt, stealing Stella's body heat. For over an hour, Stella talked to Beulah, stroking the space in the bark where her face would reveal itself to her every day. She felt the bark beneath her hand, craving a warm heartbeat. The magic—all those hours of life and drops of blood seeped into Beulah—hadn't worked.

While Madeline and Beatrice were distracted with Gertrude, and Gwen and Ben rested, Stella had sneaked into Beatrice's room, shifted the dresser, and pulled the missing pages of Beulah's book from underneath a loose floorboard. After reading Beulah's words, visions popped back into Stella's brain. All was quiet. Then Beulah fell,

305

with a creak loud enough to deafen the world, and a crack against the ground split Stella in two.

Stella found rising to her feet difficult. She felt aged, her joints and muscles stiff and cold. She would have given Beulah her own body. A new type of vessel, a new home for an old soul. She would have given her last breath a million times over for the continuation of Beulah's consciousness in this world.

Beatrice and Madeline walked toward her from their time together in the woods and Stella saw the puffy redness around Beatrice's face. Beatrice clicked her tongue and took Stella by the arm, helping her up.

"Let me try again." Beatrice kneeled where Stella had been and pressed her palms to the ground. Stella's heart sped up as she waited for Beatrice to share what she saw, but Beatrice only sighed and pressed herself to stand. "I haven't rested enough. My gift isn't back yet."

"There's something I need to show you," Stella said, looking into Beatrice's eyes.

"Later? We need to get Mother to the Rock."

"I know. We need to take them with us."

Stella moved to her bedroom and withdrew Beulah's words from underneath her pillow. Beatrice, Madeline, Gwen, and Ben gathered in the living room; Stella sat down at the hearth, feeling the heat from the fire press into her back. The wax paper felt thin and delicate as she unwrapped the pages and traced Beulah's beautiful, curled writing. She reread Beulah's words, and when she reached the end of the page, she handed it to Beatrice.

More than fear keeps me from appreciating eternal life as a tree. She sleeps peacefully beside me in her crib. My Madeline. She doesn't know what will happen when she turns eighteen and the Goddess gives her a child to raise.

She doesn't know that my body will separate, and I won't be able to braid her hair or hold her or help her raise her child.

I know that there are people out there who live differently. I've read First Mother's book and the tales in the books Imogene kept. People are born, raise children, and die. I would travel down the mountain myself if it weren't for my baby.

The pages passed from Stella to Madeline to Beatrice to Gwen to Ben.

I will raise her differently than my mother raised me. I will give her smiles and hugs and tenderness. I will not question her magic as my mother did mine. I'll make offerings to the Goddess and climb to the Peak to plead with First Mother. But if that doesn't work, and Madeline grows old enough to bear a child and I'm eaten by the earth, my energy will be my own to play with.

Beatrice finished the first page and asked her mother, "Did you go to the Peak every week?"

"She took me until I was three," Madeline said, peering down into the page before her. "After that, she would leave me home with Pepper when she went. We always took a path that went away from the Rock."

"And away from the trees," Beatrice added.

Each person in the room had a different reaction to the pages that passed before them. Stella trembled. Madeline cried. Beatrice raised one eyebrow, then the other. Gwen and Ben were wide-eyed and glanced at each other occasionally, speechless.

Beulah had so much to say.

None of the books mention blood. Perhaps my grandmothers never felt it course through their veins the way I do. Or perhaps the women knew full well the power in blood and that's why they never dared to work with it. Before my mother stopped taking me to the trees, I watched First Mother draw her roots out of the earth and stretch them out thin to soak up the tea I brought her. The same process could soak up blood. Blood has the power to change.

For a moment, Stella stopped breathing, thinking of the droplets that moved through capillary action into Beulah's system. How, knowing what she knew of science, could Stella believe this could work? But then again, she had witnessed miracles. A tear fell down her cheek as she passed the page to Madeline.

Blood. Selfless sacrifice along with prayer to the Goddess with intention and sheer will have the power to work. It must work.
From hardened wood,
return to flesh, my arms and legs,
from leaves upon a branch
restore pinkness to my cheeks
and breath into my chest
withdraw the moss
and let long again grow the hair upon my head
retract my roots into toes
limbs into fingers.
Yes! Those will be my words. But where will I get the blood? I can't take it from my daughter who will be nursing and raising her own child. I won't give her hope that I can stay in physical form. I must pray for someone to bear this burden with me.

Stella's heartbeat faster in her chest as she realized there wasn't any hiding now. They would all know her role in this. They would know she spent hours giving gallons of blood to Beulah. Sometimes, she had felt weak, and Beulah had returned some of the life liquid back to her. Other times, she left with more energy than she came, and she would smile as she walked through the woods, and place her hand on the barks of different trees as she made her way back to the homestead.

I know this person will come. She will love me, and I will love her. She will put her trust in me, and I will put my trust in her. There will be a bond like no other, for I will become part of her, and she will become part of me.

If you are reading these pages, thank you. Regardless of what happens, know that I have an unconditional love for you. You spent time with me and gave me friendship, something I don't have on this mountain. Much love to you forever and always.

Tears fell like a light spring rain down Stella's cheek and dripped off her chin and down her chest as she passed this last page to Madeline, whose eyes met hers as she took the final paper. When Beulah's daughter finished reading the page, she locked eyes with Stella.

"You went to her every day?"

Stella nodded, unable to speak.

Madeline stood, passed the page to Beatrice, and paced around in front of the fire. Once Beatrice finished reading, she stood and moved toward the bookshelf.

"We'll figure this out," Beatrice said, pulling her book from the shelves. "Maybe there's something in my book that could help us."

"I don't have a book, really." Madeline sighed, walking beside Beatrice and tracing her fingertips down the spines of journals. "I kept diaries for a while. Where did these come from?"

"I assumed you boarded them up," Beatrice said, but Madeline shook her head. "I suppose Grandmother did.

Anyway, grab First Mother's." Beatrice gestured to Madeline. "Stella, grab Ida's."

Gratitude eased the tension in Stella's shoulders some as she realized that, finally, Beatrice and Madeline had focused on Beulah.

The three read and read in silence until, finally, Madeline read from First Mother's book.

There shall be no undoing this bond I make for me and for mine. The cycles shall run generation upon generation with no end. We will rise, a family of the forest, the women of the woods. Should any descendent lose faith and act discordant to the will of the Goddess, she will be trimmed quickly, neatly, and permanently, from the very heart of the Goddess, never to know love nor completion nor joy nor grace nor comfort again. There will be an agonizing evisceration of the soul.

Beatrice closed and released her book down on the hearth. Gwen stood and moved behind Madeline and rubbed her shoulders.

"Let's go," Beatrice said, wiping a tear from her face. "They will all be at the Rock. We'll bring these pages with us."

"What if they refuse to talk about Beulah?" Stella rejected the thought that any of these women would help. "Especially First Mother. Her words are so … they sound like the words the evangelicals use against Wanda."

"We'll bring them offerings," Beatrice said. "Extra oranges," she added with a side glance to Stella.

"I'll make the coffee," Stella said and moved toward the kitchen. She would continue offering to Beulah.

Around her, busyness overtook the kitchen, but she focused, pouring her love into a cup of coffee for Beulah, which she took and poured along the tree's roots. Movement in Stella's periphery alerted her to Madeline's presence.

"Was it returned, or unrequited?"

"I honestly don't know," Stella admitted vulnerably. "I don't think she had any understanding of that kind of love, and I don't really understand how I allowed it to happen. She's a tree."

"You saw through the bark and into her soul. Into her heart. That's nothing to be ashamed of."

"Do you understand how lonely she was and how cold she got in the winter?"

A flash of defensiveness passed across Madeline's face, then softened. "I regret that."

Stella's lip quivered.

"Thank you for loving her," Madeline said.

Sobs moved through Stella's chest and out through her throat, and she allowed herself to be taken into Madeline's arms and held until she caught her breath once more, then she pressed Madeline away from her.

"If she falls, don't catch her on fire. Please."

"Stella … I need to tell you about another vision I've had."

Madeline grew quiet and looked over Stella's shoulder as if to see whether anyone else could hear.

"I don't care about your visions right now. Don't turn your back on her again." Stella shouldered her basket and led the group as they walked the path to the Rock.

CHAPTER 32

Madeline

Madeline loaded a basket with apples, pears, chocolate, and cheese. Though Stella's words cut her, she knew she would follow her mother's orders and set fire to the tree when it fell. Except for the day she had gone to the Rock to conceive Beatrice, she always did what her mother asked.

Glancing sideways at Gwen, Madeline's stomach dropped. The idea of losing her now, after they had faced Beatrice's vines, was excruciating. Gwen didn't seem to notice her gaze and continued packing her own baskets.

Beatrice sighed. "Tomorrow is the Solstice. I hope we have time to prepare."

"How can we celebrate without her?" Stella asked.

"First Mother told us to, remember?" Beatrice turned to her mother. "There are things I haven't told you yet. First Mother predicted blood on the solstice. She couldn't—or wouldn't—tell me whose."

Madeline kept eye contact with Beatrice, struggling to keep a neutral face. She couldn't bring herself to share the image of Forest lying on a blanket of red snow.

"I'm here now, and I'll help you."

Madeline felt pressure build in her chest as Gwen eyed her.

"I'm scared for you, Maddie," she said, pulling Madeline into an embrace.

"I know. I'm scared, too." Madeline breathed the words into Gwen's hair.

"How are you going to protect her?" Gwen asked as she pulled from the hug and turned toward Beatrice.

"I don't know," Beatrice answered, putting her coat on.

"Madeline ..." Gwen's voice caught, and Madeline placed her hands on her cheeks and kissed her until she was breathless. Then she poked her head out of the door and yelled, "Walk slowly! We'll catch up!"

Gwen kissed Madeline's jaw and collarbones as they moved to the bedroom. "Let me have you, Maddie," Gwen said. "In case they turn you into a tree."

"They will not turn me into a tree," Madeline rebutted.

They unclothed each other, and Gwen pressed Madeline down onto the bed. Madeline gazed at her lover, who now straddled her with a pleading countenance. Foreplay turned Madeline into melting liquid, but her mind wandered the last time the two of them had sex and how much it had hurt in all possible ways.

"Not that again, Gwen," Madeline whispered. "It's too much."

"I'm sorry, love," Gwen bent down to give attention with her tongue. Madeline felt her muscles undulate and squeeze. Blissfully exhausted, she peered up at Gwen with unfocused eyes.

"That should have relaxed you some," Gwen said, placing a kiss on Madeline's cheek.

***

Madeline and Gwen dressed, then scurried through the forest to catch up. But as they approached the Rock, their pace slowed. The slab of limestone remained dry, though snow bunched all around it. The others turned toward Gwen and Madeline as they crunched through the snow. Silence held the forest only for a moment, then the woods filled with whispers.

"She looks like Beulah."

"Look at those eyes."

"She's as tall as Beatrice."

"Who are the other two?"

Face after face with eyes of different colors appeared within tree bark.

"This is what my head sounds like most of the time," Beatrice said, then turned back toward the trees. "We brought you gifts." She began moving from tree to tree, placing fresh fruits, biscuits, splashes of milk and juices, and other offerings at the trees' feet.

"Thank you!"

"Oh, how lovely!"

Beatrice came at last to Grandmother Ola, who kept her eyes closed and remained silent.

"I made you spiced tea, Great-grandmother."

Madeline watched her daughter pour the steaming liquid onto the roots.

"You remembered me," Ola said, and slowly, eyes so brown they were almost black opened.

"I always do," Beatrice whispered.

"Madeline," the tree spoke. "You look like your mother."

Madeline nodded and felt her eyes burn.

"Let's get a better look at you," the tree said, and roots pulled from the ground and slithered toward Madeline. They wrapped around her ankle, causing her to fall to her back as the tree dragged her closer, until she dangled in the air.

"Maddie!" Gwen cried.

'A shift in perspective is good for the brain,' Gwen had

said once, after assisting Madeline into a headstand, but in this moment, Madeline resisted. Fire stirred within her and a flicker sparked in her palms as the inferno rose to her skin the way it had when the vines consumed Gwen.

"Ahh," Ola said, swinging her back and forth as if she could put out the flames. "Be careful. You don't want to burn down the forest. Your daughter loves us."

Madeline swallowed the heat and closed her eyes. She was the Hanged Man. A forced surrender.

"Did Beatrice tell you what happened when you left? Sliced open like a fish. Left for dead."

"That is not your story to tell!" Beatrice's cried.

Madeline felt it again, the shame of leaving Beatrice. "Put me down," she asked the tree, her voice even.

"She deserved better," Ola said, and Madeline thought she heard a crack in the voice.

"I know," Madeline whispered. She felt lightheaded as the blood continued to rush from her toes to her head.

"That is enough," a new voice boomed. "Put her down."

The vines released Madeline with a suddenness that brought her down hard, and Madeline felt bones within her forearms crack sickeningly. A golden glow mended them.

"Hello, Madeline," First Mother said. The tree's eyes were dark like Ola's.

Madeline dusted herself off and stood. Beatrice was kneeling at First Mother's feet, and Madeline joined her.

"I haven't seen you since you were a toddler. I'm sure you don't remember me."

"Not well, no."

"What gifts do you have?"

Madeline set her gaze on First Mother's roots. A new heat enflamed her face, a sheepishness at knowing that she had more gifts than the rest.

"Fire. Healing. I can read the future. Telekinesis."

The trees chattered around her, and Madeline found

herself dizzy again. First Mother remained quiet and waited for the noise to stop.

"Tell us stories, Madeline. All the stories. We don't even know about your childhood; Beulah doesn't speak to us."

Madeline turned back to Beatrice, who smiled and nodded with reassurance.

"She is our treasure, Madeline."

Madeline noticed a faint flush come over Beatrice's cheeks as she bowed her head once more.

"I think you may need more comfortable seats," one tree voiced. A rumble in the forest brought fallen logs to function as benches for the group.

"Thank you, Ida," Beatrice said and made her way to a seat. Madeline followed. She peered into First Mother's eyes, then around at the other expectant faces. She told her story in vivid detail. As much as she could remember. Much more than she had told Beatrice on their walk. About her mother and her rabbit companion. Pepper, the coyote cub who became her friend and protector. Falling in love with Eric. The feeling of her baby's dead body in her arms and the way Eric's feet hung two feet from the ground when she found him. Beatrice stood at this and paced, with fists balled tight.

"Don't be angry at him." Madeline choked on her words.

"He still had me." Beatrice patted her chest with her hand. "He could have stayed alive for me."

"He could have stayed alive for me, too, Bea."

Madeline moved on, outlining the days after their deaths when she lay in the bed of the hospital house, unmoving, terrified of navigating the world without him. Not sleeping. Not eating. Not bathing. The trees cried for her, drips of sap crawling down their bark.

Madeline unraveled her life in years and months and days and hours and minutes and seconds and breaths in and breaths out. Madeline revealed secrets she'd only ever shared with Gwen. Hitchhiking from one set of mountains in Virginia to another in North Carolina. Witches she met who taught her to read cards and tea leaves and palms. Madeline took the trees with her from village to town to city, all the way to New York, where she squirreled up enough money to take trips to West Virginia. She walked the mountain in heavy rain and snow and high temperatures always to come to the Hedge, never able to cross.

Finally, she came to Gwen, and once again spoke of love at first sight.

"Perhaps that is your greatest gift, Madeline. Falling in love." First Mother smiled. "You've gone so far and seen so much. Thank you for sharing your journey."

"First Mother," Madeline said as she stood to take her mother's pages from Stella. "My mother ..."

The tree seemed to sigh, and Grandmother's branches rattled.

"Yes ... Beulah."

"She's done something," Madeline said. "She's used blood magic ... and now ..."

"Blood magic?" First Mother asked.

Madeline summarized the words in Beulah's writing, glancing occasionally at Stella's red face.

"You cursed her." Madeline's voice was accusing. "You said in your book that anyone who dared go against the will of the Goddess would be severed from Her forever."

Ola spoke up. "Beulah is far from cursed."

"Madeline," First Mother interjected, "I was young when I wrote those words. Even though the Goddess made me Her companion, I was still so angry at the people in town who had locked me up. They're just words. I have no power to separate the Goddess from anyone."

"Words are power." Madeline's words came out more pointed than she intended.

318

"Do you think there is anything we can do?" Beatrice asked.

A dark chuckle rattled out of Ola. "I advise you not to discount my daughter's strength."

"She thinks she's going to fall," Madeline continued. "And she told me to burn the tree."

The trees released gasps into the air.

"I don't know this magic. I don't know what coals she's heaped upon her head. The best thing we can do is come with you."

"Since when can you walk?" Beatrice asked incredulously.

"Since Beulah showed us how," First Mother replied. "We will see if we can help her, and perhaps protect you from whatever threatens blood."

Roots lifted underneath the tree, and she swept paths in the snow as she walked. The other trees marveled at their newfound movement as they joined in, creating a long line as they creaked and moaned on their way home. Madeline's eyes were wide as she found Beatrice smiling on the other side of the line of trees. The two came together at the end of the procession.

Beatrice peeked back over her shoulder at Ola, who hadn't joined. "I'm going to encourage her to come."

Madeline shook her head. "Think of all the energy it took for Mother to get away from her."

"Forgiveness." Beatrice placed a hand on Madeline's shoulder, and then turned back. "You can come with us, you know."

"I'll stay right here for now. I can see the homestead from here. If you need me, I'll come right away."

"Alright," Beatrice said, then rejoined Madeline.

"This—" Madeline gestured in front of her.

"This is our family," Beatrice said.

Gwen came up on Madeline's right side and grabbed her hand.

"Now we just have to get through the Solstice," Gwen said, and the vision of Forest flashed into Madeline's mind.

"I know," she whispered.

CHAPTER 33

Beatrice

The trees walked noisily through the forest and, when they arrived at the homestead, their voices crescendoed into raucous chatter. Some admired the new buildings, others critiqued Beatrice's placement of this or that. They all wished they could see inside and wanted to know if there would be a bonfire for the Solstice.

Beatrice smiled at her mother, who stared at her bewilderedly.

With the grandmother trees encircling the homestead, it felt cozier and safer. The talking among the trees ceased as they turned their attention toward Beulah.

"Oh, my," Ida whispered. "Here, let me look." She closed her eyes and sent roots into the ground. "The tree is dead." A collective gasp echoed through the woods. "There's only darkness, and the smell of blood. It would take the Goddess to bring her back."

Beatrice watched Stella crumple at Beulah's roots; instead of encouraging her to stand, she joined the crying woman. Then she pulled her close and pressed their foreheads together.

"I don't care what they say," Beatrice whispered. "I've seen too many miracles to give up hope."

But Henry's talk of hexes and curses crept into Beatrice's mind. *Did someone curse Grandmother?* Beatrice swallowed down the thought.

A flapping of wings overhead alerted Beatrice to Gertrude's presence, and she raised her head to see the eagle light upon Grandmother's tallest branches.

"Do you have any words of advice?" she asked her sister.

Gertrude swooped down and landed at Beatrice's feet. *Trust her.*

Beatrice's gaze swept around the group until locking in on Stella. "She said to trust her."

"I promised Beulah I'd make her cranberry sauce," Stella said.

"Then that's what you need to do."

"I need to spend time with her first."

"Well," Imogene tutted, "I expected more decorating."

"Imogene ..." First Mother reprimanded.

"That's next on the list ..." Beatrice said, the weight of exhaustion making her movements heavy. "Will you keep watch for us?"

"Of course we will," First Mother said, and the rest of the trees agreed.

Beatrice moved to the living room and sat down in a rocking chair, feeling the heat from the fire move along the front of her body. She closed her eyes.

"We can rest today," Madeline said. "I can prepare for the Solstice in the morning."

"I know you can, but it's my favorite day." Beatrice kept her eyes closed. "And I'm anxious. If I keep busy, I'll sleep better this evening. Forest will be back soon. Maybe the two of you can take care of the boar."

"I'm good with decorations. I make nice bows," Gwen said.

"Let's make wreaths together," Beatrice replied, opening her eyes. "Thank you for finishing the tree, Mother."

"You're welcome."

"Now that I think of it ..." Beatrice furrowed her brow. "I took yours apart."

"My tree? Why?"

"I couldn't stop looking through the pictures, and I didn't take the time to put them back."

The door opened and Wanda and Dani entered her home, with Forest behind them carrying a backpack and a brown paper bag. Beatrice stood and opened her arms to Wanda, who moved in for the hug.

"I was going to bake a pie, but—"

"You're safe now," Beatrice interjected, then scanned the woman from head to toe. "There's an empty bedroom down the hall and to the left."

"Hi, Wanda," Madeline said, and embraced Wanda as well, and followed with introductions to Ben and Gwen.

Beatrice's attention turned to Dani, who gave a quick wave. Beatrice opened her arms, but Dani raised a hand and said, "I don't hug."

"Ahh. Understood." Beatrice gave a short bow.

Wanda grabbed her backpack from Forest and moved to deposit her things in her room, while Dani moved next to him.

"The trees moved!" Forest exclaimed in a breathless whisper.

"They did." Beatrice smiled at him then moved her gaze to Dani. "I assume you know everything."

"Well ..." Dani raised their eyebrows. "I'll believe it when I see it." They smirked and Beatrice knew the two of them would get along.

"I saw Stella with Great Grandmother. What happened?"

Beatrice held up a palm and shook her head. "Not right now."

"Well, put me to use," Wanda said, interrupting the conversation.

"Want to see the greenhouse?" Beatrice asked.

Wanda beamed.

"Hey! I haven't seen the greenhouse yet!" Mother chimed in.

"How about you two gather vegetables? Gertrude will lead you."

Forest gave Ben a pat on the back. "I guess that leaves us in charge of the boar."

Ben and Dani's eyes widened.

"The boar didn't suffer," Beatrice promised. "If it bothers you too much, I'll help him instead."

"I can do it," Ben said, and Beatrice smiled at his confidence.

"Help us with the decorations?" Beatrice asked Dani.

"I'm not very good with my hands. I can be your hype person."

Beatrice frowned, and Gwen giggled at her. Devoid of the energy necessary to ask what a 'hype person' was, Beatrice went back to the box of decorations she'd left in disarray and took it to the kitchen.

"I'll make the wreaths. You make the bows," Beatrice said. She twisted her wrists and filled the table with greenery. "Aha! Well, I suppose I have just enough energy for Solstice decorations." But creating took much more effort than usual, and when she finished, Beatrice rubbed her wrists and hands, wincing at the ache.

"I'm exhausted," Gwen confessed.

"Me too," Beatrice said, then chuckled. "So much has happened today."

"Spill the tea," Dani said, then sipped their own tea from a mug.

"They want you to tell them what happened," Gwen explained before Beatrice could ask, and the two of them launched into a summary of the day.

"I'm exhausted just listening to all of that." Dani stood and took their drink to the sink. "Can you point me to Forest's room?"

"Oh. I mean, yes, of course. Come with me." Beatrice led Dani down the short hallway to Forest's room and gestured for them to enter. "Dani, can I ask you about something?"

"Sure."

"I haven't had a chance to do my own research. On the Equinox, Henry talked about baneful magic. Do you think my grandmother is cursed?"

"Your family is unlike anything I've ever seen. I don't know."

"Have you ever used baneful magic?"

Dani squared themself to Beatrice and locked eyes with her. "I've used bindings before, but not hexes, curses, or jinxes. Forest has strong opinions about it all." They turned away from Beatrice now, then settled their suitcase on Forest's bed and unzipped it.

"What's a binding?" Heat rose to Beatrice's face as Dani tucked their things into Forest's dresser. *Get a hold of yourself. They're both grown.*

"They can tie two people together. Or they can tie someone's hands so they can't cause harm."

"The bindings you've done ..."

"The second kind."

Beatrice wanted to know so much more, but Dani had moved to the bed and removed their shoes and socks.

"I'll leave you to rest."

"Thanks," Dani said, then they rolled over.

Beatrice returned to the kitchen where Gwen folded thick red ribbon into fat loops. They stayed silent for a long time.

"No one should have to go through it," Gwen said after a while, her voice shaking.

"No," Beatrice whispered. "That's beautiful," she said when Gwen finished her first bow.

"My mother taught me," Gwen said, handing the bow to Beatrice. "She made them every year and gave them to friends."

"Is your mother living?"

Gwen shook her head and grabbed another piece of ribbon, which she weaved between her fingers. "She passed a few months ago. Not unexpectedly, really." Gwen didn't look up, but the muscles in her face grew tense. "She had a heart attack that she couldn't recover from. Maddie was there and offered to help her." Her eyes misted over, and a rueful smile formed on her lips. "For a moment, she was completely lucid. She told us she was ready to go. It was beautiful. It really was."

Beatrice looked down at the table full of greenery and pulled twine from the box.

"What do you think happens when someone—"

"Dies?" Gwen stopped working with the ribbon. "I think the soul, life force, energy, whatever you want to call it, moves onto a new form. A new body."

Beatrice began twining the pine into wreaths and handed them to Gwen, who affixed the beautiful red bows with twine.

"One for each window, and one for the door," Beatrice said.

At that moment, Wanda and Mother entered with baskets full of produce, and Ben and Forest returned with the boar, all seasoned and ready to be roasted.

"You survived," Beatrice said to Ben, who smirked.

Stella came in, too cold to stay outside any longer, and she began deseeding the pomegranates she'd brought from New York. Beatrice tasted the juicy rubies and squinted at the tart sweetness, and Stella smiled for the first time since they had been back on the mountain.

As they prepared for the Solstice, the group nibbled bites here and there of cheese and nuts and sliced apples. They opened jars of Wanda's jam and slathered it on leftover biscuits, their snacks becoming dinner. When they were finished, they secured the wreaths to the windows and the door and nestled in around the fire.

"Will we build a bonfire?" Madeline asked, staring across the room at Beatrice.

"I hope. Can you imagine? With all the trees around?"

"She used to love it, too," Madeline said, and Beatrice knew she was talking about Grandmother.

Silence wrapped around them as they sipped on mugs of tea, then gradually, each member retired to bed until Ben and Beatrice were the only two left. Beatrice asked him about having a twin sibling and about his job and life in New York. Ben asked about herbs and magic and what it was like to raise a child. Eventually, the conversation dwindled, as did the tea in their cups, and Beatrice took them to the kitchen. When Beatrice returned to the living room, Ben peered at her questioningly.

"You never told me where to put my things. I don't mind sleeping here." He gestured to the floor in front of the fire. "But maybe there's a better place for my pack."

"Well, the floor won't do. I'd offer to take that spot, but I need to sleep. We all do. My bed isn't huge, but we can fit."

"We've known each other for a little over twenty-four hours. I'm not sure ..."

"Look, I'll wake Stella or Wanda if I crawl into bed with them. We'll be fine."

Beatrice held out her hand. Ben took it and followed behind her. Secured within the confines of her room, Beatrice placed her hand on the man's face and traced his hairline behind his temple, then she pulled him close and kissed him. She'd once read about kissing and rolled her eyes at the stories of fireworks and internal explosions that came with physical touch, but when she touched Ben, all the walls that she had built, melted. Something new replaced the cynicism, fear, and shame that left her body.

When she pulled back to see Ben's face, his eyes were warm and soft.

"Beatrice," he whispered. "I could fall in love with you."

Beatrice's face flushed. She apologized, took a step back, and offered to sleep on the floor.

"No, don't sleep on the floor. I just haven't felt this way for a long time. I've forgotten how scary it is."

"I've never felt this way before, so ..." Beatrice took a deep breath. "I won't do that again. We'll share the bed for tonight and make different arrangements tomorrow."

Ben nodded, his eyes revealing regret.

The two turned their backs toward one another as they slipped into pajamas. Beatrice felt heat rise to her face again as she tucked herself in next to Ben.

"Goodnight," she whispered.

"Goodnight, Bea."

CHAPTER 34

Madeline

By the time morning came, the snow had stopped, and the white blanket shone with a brilliant brightness that hurt Madeline's eyes as she stepped down from the front porch. Her body ached from lack of sleep. Sometime after midnight, she had ventured outside to check on her mother, who remained silent. Much of the night, she paced in front of the fire, reliving her visions. One minute she cuddled with Gwen, the next she checked on members of the household. First Forest and Dani, then Wanda. When she found Beatrice curled up in Ben's arms, she pulled away from the door and paused in the living room. How had she not noticed this thing happening between them? Had Gwen noticed? What would she say?

The night before, Madeline had sat down on the floor beside Gwen and practiced breathwork with her. The juxtaposition of her two worlds left her spiritually confused for a moment. Pranayama seemed so strange in the space back on her land, with the Goddess of the Trees watching.

But her bones settled, the rhythm of her heart changed as her breath lengthened, and she let the confusion go.

The wink of the sun as it moved up the mountain petrified Madeline. The day was starting.

"It's the solstice!" Gwen smiled as she entered the room and kissed Madeline on the cheek. "Do some salutations with me. They'll make you feel better."

Madeline relented and found a space on the floor where she tucked into child's pose beside her lover. Gwen cued the movements only with her breath, and the two of them moved their bodies in meditation, saluting the sun.

"I can't do one hundred and eight of these, Gwenny," Madeline huffed.

"How about eight?"

"Okay. Eight is good."

Forest entered the room next.

"Happy Solstice, Forest!" Madeline said, her body in downward-facing dog.

"Happy Solstice," he replied and moved to a chair beside the fire.

Madeline returned to child's pose for a moment, and Gwen moved behind her and pressed down on her hips.

"Mmm," Madeline said with a sigh. "Thank you."

"I'm going to wash up some before the day starts. Join me?"

Madeline stood up from the pose then sat on the rocking chair next to Forest.

"You go ahead."

"Alright."

"How did you sleep, Grandmother?" Forest asked.

"I didn't."

"Not at all?"

She shook her head.

Stella was up now, and rushed out to visit Beulah without speaking.

"I'm worried about today," Forest said.

"I know," Madeline said. "I am, too."

Madeline stood and began boiling water for coffee. She could hear Wanda enter the living room, talking with Forest. As the coffee steeped, she peeked outside to see Stella pleading with the dead tree trunk.

Wanda scurried through the kitchen and headed for the restroom, while Forest began breakfast.

"Biscuits?" Madeline asked.

"I'm sure my mother would appreciate that."

Just as Madeline started cutting the biscuits into circles, Gwen reentered with a freshly washed face, her hair brushed and neatly tucked behind her ears.

"My brother isn't up yet?" she asked, wrapping her arms around Madeline from behind.

"No." Madeline couldn't bring herself to say more.

Gwen pulled away slightly so she could see into Madeline's face. "Where did he sleep? Things were so hectic that I don't even remember him getting a bedroom."

Beatrice entered the room, gaining Gwen's attention.

"Happy Solstice!" Gwen said and embraced Beatrice in a hug, seeming to forget the question.

"Happy Solstice, Mother. You look tired," Beatrice said, appearing rested and unbothered.

"I didn't sleep. Couldn't quiet my thoughts."

"The trees have given me hope. Stella's outside?" Beatrice asked, glancing toward the door.

"Afraid so."

"Have you seen my brother?" Gwen asked.

Madeline watched a pink hue warm her daughter's face. Beatrice shifted her feet. "He's still asleep."

Gwen took a moment to make sense of the information, then nodded with a knowing smile.

Once the biscuits were ready, Beatrice drew Stella in, and the eight sat around the table eating amidst the hovering nervousness. Solstice preparations began once breakfast was over. Beatrice checked on the boar and arranged carrots, potatoes, and onions around it and stuffed the mouth with an apple.

Wanda, Dani, and Forest created a perimeter of salt around the floorboards and whispered incantations of protection under their breath. Madeline spent time in meditation, wrapping a cloth around her eyes to help her withdraw into herself. Desperate to clarify her visions, she drew cards with Wanda and read the leaves of each cup of tea consumed. But nothing new appeared. Only blood seeping into snow. The tree that was her mother falling to the ground. Forest, gray-skinned on the ground.

She muttered prayers to herself that all would be merry. The aromas within the house began to meld, the spices of the cranberries and the herbs and vegetables and roasting boar. Madeline, weary, acquiesced when Gwen pulled her into the living room to snuggle on the couch. Beatrice sat down on the hearth, close to Ben's feet, and Wanda took her place in the rocking chair. Stella came in and sat next to Forest and Dani.

Madeline drew in a deep breath. "I think it's time to put the Hedge back up, Beatrice." The words felt as thorny as the vines and bushes that had once encircled the place.

"I've already tried," Beatrice replied. "I can't."

Madeline closed her eyes and rubbed them with her fingertips, then she tried to conjure fire as the group watched on. When that didn't work, she tried healing. "Me either." She sighed.

"We have the trees surrounding us," Beatrice said. "They will help us."

"Do they know how to heal using vines, the way you and my mother do?"

"I don't know." Beatrice shrugged.

A rattling that didn't start small, but rather as a fierce,

aggressive reaction to a threat, interrupted the conversation. Sasha raced to the front door, uncoiling the length of her body until she stood upon her tail, hissing, her rattler fully engaged. Beatrice was the first to grab her coat, and the others followed. Madeline felt the pit of her stomach drop and a chilly liquid took the place of her blood.

Outside, the snake noisily circled the perimeter. Forest, Dani, and Wanda held tight to their wands. Beatrice tried to regrow the Hedge but couldn't. Madeline begged the Goddess for heat or healing, but neither came. Figures materialized in the woods. Madeline counted six men, each of them with guns holstered. The town police had made it up the mountain.

"May we help you?" Madeline asked, her voice firm.

"Sam?" Madeline watched Beatrice make eye contact and step toward a man with curly hair. "Why are you here with them?" The hurt in Beatrice's voice was unmistakable.

The man's throat bobbed, and he slipped his hands into his pockets.

One officer gestured to the buildings. "Do you have a deed to this land? Cause you're smack dab in the middle of a federally protected national forest."

Beatrice furrowed her brow and crossed her arms. "Actually, this isn't part of the national forest, and yes, we do have a deed. I'll get it." She turned back to the house and returned with folded documents in hand. "Surely you checked the register of deeds before you hiked all the way up the mountain."

"Are you Beatrice?" the officer asked.

"I am."

The man handed the papers back to Beatrice.

"You're the gentleman that makes all of those fine carvings, aren't ya?" the man asked Forest, who nodded with a "yes, sir."

"I see you carve other things as well." The man chuckled and pointed to the wand.

Except for the man with curly hair, the man Beatrice called Sam, the rest of the men joined in robust laughter.

"Plan on casting a spell on us?" another muttered.

"Now that you've seen the deed, is there anything else you need?" Madeline questioned.

"Actually, there is. We're looking for that woman right there." A finger jutted toward Wanda. "You're under arrest, ma'am." The police officer withdrew handcuffs and walked toward Wanda with a swagger that made Madeline sick.

"For what, sir?"

"You're charged with operating a fraudulent school."

"It is not fraudulent. I went through —"

"Ma'am, I'm going to read you your rights now."

Though Madeline wished the woman no harm, she would allow this injustice, knowing it could be made right later if it meant keeping Forest safe.

"She has done nothing wrong," Forest demanded, moving toward the group of men. "Sam, tell them."

"Forest, stop," Madeline insisted, and Forest listened.

"Sorry to interrupt your séance, or whatever the hell y'all are doing up here."

As the men turned to leave, pressing a crying Wanda forward, a rustling in the trees drew the crowd's attention. Arcas. He came bounding toward the group, his black fur resplendent with a bright sheen in the morning winter sun. When he was within a few feet of the police officers, he stood on his hind legs and bellowed a tremendous roar. Without pause, the men drew their guns. They aimed. Forest ran. Beatrice ran. The men fired.

Madeline watched as a bullet entered Arcas's skull and his head whipped back on his neck. There was a crack, a thud, and a moaning exhale as Arcas breathed his last breath. A scream tore through Forest's lungs. He, too, had fallen, and a circle of red broadened on his shirt and another on his upper thigh. He fell inches away from his companion. Madeline's eyes moved toward Beatrice, who lay limp, blood seeping into the snow.

A new sound that made the ground tremble tore from the earth. Her mother. The roots of the tree ripped from the ground and, with a groan, the birch tree fell upon all six men at once. They lay moaning underneath the weight that no doubt crushed bones.

Madeline wanted to run to Beatrice. She wanted to run to Forest. But when she rubbed her hands together and begged them to glow, all that came was fire.

Burn the tree.

The flames leaped into Madeline's palms, and she walked closer. She hurled fire at the bark, and the wood erupted without hesitation. The men screamed. Stella screamed louder. One man shouted, "Thou shalt not suffer a witch to live!" as he clawed the earth with his hands.

The heat began to devour the men's clothes, and as their flesh and the smell of putrid roasting wafted in smoke upon the air, Madeline realized what her mother had done. She had cleaned up their mess for them.

Madeline ran to Beatrice, while Wanda inched toward Forest.

"Can one of y'all get the key and get me out of here?" Wanda asked.

Ben and Gwen both moved toward the flames, grabbed long branches, and poked around for the key. Eventually, Gwen drew it toward her and unlocked Wanda, who began working her magic on Forest. Ben pulled his belt from his waist and formed a tourniquet around Forest's leg.

Madeline rubbed and rubbed, but healing wouldn't come, so she cried. "Can any of you help?" she shouted to the trees.

"We don't know how to heal with our roots!"

335

"My mother didn't know until she did. Try. Please."

Roots pulled from the ground and writhed their way toward Forest and Beatrice. Another sound echoed. A crunching through the woods.

Ola.

Madeline watched as the tall oak swept her roots across the whitened forest floor and landed beside her.

"Move," the tree instructed, and Madeline did.

Roots, glowing this time, moved over Beatrice's body. Madeline chose trust and ran to Forest, rubbing and rubbing and rubbing, her body refusing to give.

"Please, please, please," Madeline pleaded.

"We need to get him to the hospital," Ben said.

"There's no time for that."

Madeline glanced over her shoulder to see Ola continuing to work on Beatrice. The tears came, and Madeline choked on her sobs.

"Can you help him, too? Please!"

The tree responded by stretching out her roots, grunting with strain, until they reached Forest's body and wove around him. Madeline sank into the snow and closed her eyes; she felt Gwen move near her and wrap her arm around her body. Madeline and Wanda whispered prayers, Gwen and Ben held space, and Stella wailed in the snow beside the burning birch tree.

CHAPTER 35

Beatrice

Smoke carrying putrid, vile smells burned Beatrice's nose and forced her eyes open. Roots, glittering with healing energy, pulled away from her body.

"Grandmother," Beatrice whispered, but when she looked up, it was into deep brown eyes, not blue.

"You're alright." The voice wasn't Grandmother's, but Great-grandmother Ola's.

"Forest!" Beatrice shouted and pressed her palms into the frigid, red-stained snow. Blood. Her blood.

She made her way to seated, then to standing. She took in the sight of her grandmother's tree body cracking and hissing underneath leaping flames. Stella jogged the length of the tree, back and forth, screaming at the sky. Gertrude swooped in circles overhead, piping panicked utterances about Forest. Beatrice swiveled her head to the right and saw Wanda, her mother, Gwen, and Ben surrounding him. Near to him, Arcas lay on a blanket of crimson snow. Revived by an ample dose of adrenaline, Beatrice ran to her son and willed tendrils from her palms.

337

"It's too late, Beatrice," her great grandmother said. "We did all that we could."

"No." Vines sprouted forth from Beatrice's hands and tapered thinner and thinner until small enough to slip into Forest's skin. Beatrice focused all her attention on her son, forcing out any discernible words the group around her spoke. Someone placed a hand on her shoulder to jostle her from her efforts, but she shrugged them off and summoned all the force within her to cocoon her and Forest with vines.

"Please, Forest, don't leave me. This isn't the way it's supposed to be for you."

Beatrice had learned when she was five years old how long she could hold her breath. She had convinced her mother to allow her to forage in the forest by herself. Following the trails through the woods had led Beatrice to the edge of a pond. She tiptoed to the edge, her basket around one arm and her favorite doll tucked in the other. Misjudging the angle of the bank, Beatrice tipped headfirst into the water. Panic took her, and she flailed, trying to make her way to the surface. She didn't know what creature had pulled her from the water, but she'd never forget her mother's face when Beatrice stood waterlogged on the front porch. Mother's face held the same panic now, and Beatrice's heart clenched shut.

Blood that should flow within capillaries and arteries and veins seeped all around, soaking the tissues of Forest's heart.

How do I do this?

Forest's breathing grew thinner, his heartbeat slower and slower.

I have to try.

She thought about Gwen and her punctured lung, and what it took to start her heart again, but she couldn't start there. Lack of blood prevented Forest's heart from beating.

Beatrice realized in that moment that two things had

to happen simultaneously. She sent a net of vines around Forest's heart and encouraged them to squeeze in rhythm with her own heartbeat. She slithered a strong vine down his throat and into his lungs and urged them to give him air. Then she found the blood vessels torn by the bullets and began their reconstruction. Time meant nothing and everything all at once. Beatrice worked and worked, repairing the veins.

How do I get the blood back in?

Grandmother.

Thin capillary tendrils siphoned the blood that had oozed in all directions and injected it back into the vessels. Her vines weaved and knitted muscle fibers back together. Still within Forest's body, she surveyed her work. He seemed alive again, under her gentle contractions of his heart and the oxygen she provided his lungs.

"Please, Forest. You're not like Gertrude. You're not like Grandmother. You want to stay. Don't you?"

Beatrice opened her eyes and explored her son's face. In the shimmering green glow, she couldn't tell if his cheeks were pink again. Gwen's return to life had been an explosive one with gasps of air and an emptying of her stomach, but Forest was so still; so very, very still. The world was quiet and somehow Beatrice wasn't cold, though she kneeled in snow half a foot deep. She breathed deeply, knowing that her energy kept him alive.

A new shimmer slipped through a small crack in the cocoon Beatrice knew she had made impenetrable. A soft, gray, luminous ribbon drifted down. That was when Beatrice understood that, for moments, Forest had been gone, his soul untethered from his body. The ribbon hovered in the air just over Forest's forehead. Faith and reluctance entwined as Beatrice withdrew hesitantly.

As soon as the vines released Forest's body, the ribbon eased down through Forest's mouth, and he drew in a breath. Only then did Beatrice allow herself to cry. She pressed her forehead against his chest and sobbed in a way she never had before. Guttural, primal sobs, the sobs of a mother who had almost lost her child, filled the space now completely darkened without the shimmer of Beatrice's healing.

"Forest," she breathed into his chest. He said nothing, but his chest moved up and down, and his heart thumped below Beatrice's ear. How long she kneeled by his side, Beatrice wasn't sure, but eventually, she noticed the cold and wetness that penetrated her clothes. She pulled her vines into her palms and allowed her eyes to adjust to the bright light.

The crackle of wood and the smell of burning flesh flooded her senses. She couldn't bring herself to turn around to see the men melting and her grandmother reduced to ash. She kept her eyes on Forest, touching a hand to his cheek, noticing the flush of life on his skin. Convinced again that he was alive, she allowed herself to acknowledge those around her.

Dani kneeled close to Forest's body, their eyes puffy and red, their face streaked with tears and snot. Her mother and Gwen stood holding one another, crying silent tears. Ben leaned against a tree, arms crossed, eyes furrowed with concern, and when Beatrice made eye contact with him, he was the first to move toward her. He kneeled beside her, unconcerned about the snow wetting the knees of his jeans, and placed a hand on her back. When he smiled, Beatrice released tears again, which he caught with his fingers.

"He's breathing," he whispered to her, and she nodded quietly. "We need to get him inside, Beatrice. It's freezing."

But her body couldn't move. Ben helped her to her feet, but she stumbled back down to the ground.

"I can help," Ida said. "Don't worry. I won't forget Forest."

Vines formed a cradle that Beatrice rested in, and carried her through the front door, through the kitchen, the living room, and into her bedroom where Ida gently laid her on her bed.

"Rest now, Beatrice."

***

Beatrice woke, thirsty and ravenous after her long, dreamless nap. Ben's arm wrapped tightly around her, but when she rolled over, she found he wasn't sleeping. Pulling his arm away, he stroked her face with his hand.

"You slept a long time."

"Did I?"

He nodded his head and kissed her.

"Forest?" Beatrice asked.

"Still asleep. The others rotated between sitting with him and napping and preparing for the Solstice, except for—"

"Stella."

"We can't get her to come in. The tree is ash now. All the men ..." Ben's voice trailed off. Beatrice didn't need him to continue.

"I am so hungry and thirsty," Beatrice said as she stood. Though it needed nourishment, her body felt revived.

Ben stood and moved close to her and wrapped his arms around her waist. "I have feelings for you, Beatrice," he said.

Perhaps she felt it, too, but couldn't say it back. It wouldn't matter if she reciprocated the feelings. Ben's home existed in the tall buildings of New York, with his job and with his sister, and hers existed in the tall trees with her son and Stella.

Beatrice unwrapped herself from Ben and turned to make her way from her bedroom. She did not stop to speak to Gwen and Wanda, who sat at the kitchen table, but ran toward Forest's room. With each step, the space between her gut and her ribs turned and squeezed. His door was partially open. Beatrice pressed through and dropped to her knees. Forest lay curled on the bed in a fetal position, his breath slow but sturdy. A laugh in Beatrice's throat gave way to a choked sob as she ran her fingers through his hair.

"He's going to be alright."

Beatrice looked over her shoulder to find her mother in the rocking chair, hair loose and wild, a tired smile on her face. Beatrice continued to cry. "I'm so glad you're here," she whispered.

"Me too," Madeline responded. "I'm going to give the two of you a moment. Dani, will you come with me?"

Beatrice hadn't noticed Dani standing in the corner, arms tightly crossed.

"No," they responded with a hoarse voice.

"It's okay. You don't have to." Beatrice stroked Forest's cheek and felt the warmth of it under her hand.

"The binding didn't work." Dani kneeled beside Beatrice. "I tried to keep Wanda safe from the people harassing her."

"Well, Wanda is safe." Beatrice rubbed Dani's back. They responded with a choked sob.

With a groan, Forest rolled onto his back and cracked his eyes open.

"There you are," Beatrice whispered.

"Arcas?" Forest croaked.

Beatrice shook her head in response to Forest's question, which caused him to bring his hands to his face.

"I'm so sorry, Forest."

"Are the men gone? What about everyone else?"

"The men are dead."

"How? Did you—?"

"Grandmother, she ..." Beatrice paused and closed her eyes tightly to squeeze out the memory of the burning tree. "She fell on them, then Mother set the tree on fire."

Forest's eyes were wide as he glanced away from Beatrice and toward the ceiling.

"Is she?"

"Grandmother's gone."

Tears formed in Forest's eyes, and he wiped them away with his fingertips. "What happened to her, Mother?" he asked, his voice thick with sadness. "You left for New York, and I went to town for one night, and now ..."

"I'll let you read the pages of her book. She was working on a ..." Beatrice paused and swallowed. "A spell, I suppose. A spell to make her human again."

"What?" Forest pressed himself up. "Why?"

"She hated being a tree. She used Stella's blood."

Forest's eyes went wide. "And now she's gone?"

"Yes, Forest." Beatrice bristled at the impatience in her voice, and she averted her eyes.

Forest's stomach gave a low groan. "I think I'm hungry."

"The meal is almost ready. At least that's what I'm told."

Forest frowned, searching her face for answers.

"I was out for a while myself."

"Did they shoot you, too?" Forest gripped Beatrice's hands.

"Yes, but I'm alright."

"It felt like fire." Forest stood up from the bed, and Beatrice watched with relief and gratitude.

"I'm wearing different clothes." He stretched out his arms.

"So am I," Beatrice said. "They took good care of us."

He ran his fingers through his hair and straightened his clothes, then they made their way to the kitchen. Gwen, Ben, and Mother spoke in whispers as they arranged plates and utensils around the table. Dani brooded in a darkened corner of the living room. In the middle of the table sat the boar, apple in mouth, nestled within mounds of carrots, onions, and potatoes. Wanda sat butter on the table along with jars of her jam. They all looked up at Beatrice and Forest.

Wanda moved the fastest toward him, and Beatrice took a step back as she watched her son bend and give his mentor a big embrace.

"Dinner smells good," he said, then moved to Dani who moved into his arms, their head resting just under his chin.

Relieved laughs passed around the table like piping hot bread.

"I'm going to get Stella." Beatrice wrapped herself in her coat, pulled on her boots, and stepped out into the dark. Smoking embers provided the only light, and Stella's outline stood out against the orange glow.

"Stella," Beatrice said, trudging her boots through at least half a foot of snow. Stella didn't respond, so Beatrice moved closer until she placed her hand on the woman's shoulder. Goddess, she was tired of crying, but the tears came as she wrapped her arm around Stella's waist.

"Do you think there's a chance?" Stella's voice scratched through her throat as though she had screamed and screamed and screamed.

"I don't know." Beatrice glanced back at the embers.

"Ida tried," Stella said. "She's almost all ash now. How can we eat and have a—?"

"We don't have to have a fire," Beatrice replied, "but we need to eat. And you're soaking. Let me take care of you."

Beatrice guided Stella through the kitchen, past concerned eyes, and to her bedroom, where she pulled out warm clothes. Beatrice stripped Stella of her wet clothes one layer at a time until she stood naked and shivering, then helped slip on dry pants and a sweater. The two moved back into the kitchen. Candles lit the table and the counters, and Beatrice closed her eyes and took in all the smells. She opened them and regarded her mother.

"Will you do it tonight?" she asked, and her mother nodded.

Mother blessed the meal and gave thanks for the energy that flowed through the meat, vegetables, and fruits. She gave thanks for those around the table, and for Forest's life. She praised the Goddess for the sun's return, and opened her eyes with, "Let's eat."

Beatrice served everyone a bit of everything, and when she sat down, she tasted the cranberry sauce Stella had made first.

"This is delicious, Stella," Beatrice said, but there was no response. "I don't know that a fire is a good idea," she added as she looked around the table.

"We have to have a fire, Mother. It's your favorite part."

Beatrice glanced at Forest, pulled pieces from a hot biscuit, then to Stella, whose eyes stared into a place past the table.

"Why don't we eat and decide later?" Madeline responded. "There's more snow now. It would take a lot of effort to shovel it."

"You're a flame wielder, Maddie," Gwen countered. "You could melt it."

"Ooh," Mother said. "I don't know. It comes out of anger and fear."

"Well." Gwen's voice was silky now. "There are other ways to heat you up."

Beatrice watched as her mother turned to Gwen and they shared a short kiss. Silence wove around the table, interrupted occasionally by whispers and longing glances between Mother and Gwen that made Beatrice uncomfortable, though she wasn't sure why. From time to time, it made her blush, and she wished she were sitting beside Ben so she could steal small moments with him.

"Wanda, thank you for helping with the meal," Beatrice said as if talking could take the edge of the awkward grief.

"It was my pleasure, Beatrice. You know it was."

Beatrice smiled, but as the woman's face twisted with sadness, she felt her own face fall.

"What's the matter?"

"This was all my fault, Beatrice," Wanda choked.

Beatrice searched her heart and found a small nugget of resentment and blame toward Wanda for the men coming to the mountain, for Forest's injury, for Arcas's death, for Grandmother ...

No. That one was not on Wanda. None of them were.

Beatrice reached across the table and took the older woman's hand. "None of this was your fault." Her eyes moved to Dani, who poked at the food on their plate. "Are you alright?"

"Today was ..." Dani's throat bobbed, and they remained silent for a moment. "It was a lot, and all the adrenaline is gone. I'm just tired."

"Is your food alright?"

"It's delicious." They smiled and put a spoonful of mashed potatoes in their mouth.

"We should save room for dessert," Mother said and took her plate to the sink. "I can clean up. It won't take long."

"Madeline," Gwen said, wrapping her arms around her lover and pressing her cheek to her back. "We need to make sure you can conjure fire."

Madeline closed her eyes for a moment, then squinted apologetically toward Beatrice.

"We'll be right back," she whispered, and the two scurried out of the kitchen.

Beatrice went to the sink, and Ben made his way beside her and offered to dry the dishes as she washed them. Stella left the room in silence. Wanda moved around, collecting food, wrapping parchment around bowls, preparing them to go to the dairy shed. Forest and Dani helped her carry the leftovers out, leaving Ben and Beatrice alone.

"Do they ever actually come 'right back?'" Beatrice asked.

Ben responded with a laugh. "Sometimes. Once, when we went on vacation together, they locked themselves in their room for five hours in the middle of the day. We had lunch reservations ..." He rolled his eyes.

Beatrice stopped drying. "Five hours?"

Ben nodded and chuckled again. "They very much enjoy one another's company." He moved closer to Beatrice and wrapped his arms around her. "I thought you were gone," he said.

Beatrice let him tuck her body into his arms, with her head against his chest so she could hear the thud of his heart.

"I know it's too early to fall in love," he said.

The front door opened, and Wanda, Forest, and Dani came back into the kitchen. Perhaps it crossed Beatrice's mind to pull away, but the comfort in Ben's arms was too great, and his heartbeat kept her still. She closed her eyes and breathed him in, waiting to be alone in the room with him once more.

"What if I don't feel the same way yet?" she asked.

"That's okay," Ben said and rubbed his hand up and down her back.

"We've got fire!" Gwen said with excitement, and Beatrice pulled away from Ben reluctantly. Gwen and Madeline, with the family drum in hand, flew into the kitchen. Madeline set the drum on the table and grabbed her coat off the rack along with Gwen's.

"I still have no rhythm," Beatrice confessed.

"Neither do I." Madeline chuckled. "But she does." She pointed to Gwen.

Beatrice remembered her mother this exact way, with a wide smile and her hair down instead of tied into braids, her eyes bright with love. She observed Forest, who had his arm around Dani. "Are you up for this?" she asked.

"Definitely."

"Let me check on Stella," Beatrice said and walked down the hall toward her room. "Stella," she whispered as she knocked quietly and opened the door.

Stella was curled into a ball on her bed, Sasha draped around her shoulders. Beatrice moved closer, but the snake raised its head and thrashed its tail ferociously.

"I love you, Stella," she whispered. "You're not alone in this."

Beatrice turned and made her way back to the kitchen where the rest of the group waited. She put on her own winter warmth, then opened the door, motioned to the thick layers of snow, and said, "Alright, Mother. Do something."

CHAPTER 36

Gwen

After spending half an hour stoking Madeline's fire, Gwen watched the yellow glow in her lover's palms turn to orange and then to flames that flowed from her. Madeline directed the heat toward the snow, melting a path in front of her, then traced a circle around the spot where Beulah's burning charred the earth. Her brow beaded with sweat. She moved until the ground was clear and dry enough for fire, then she asked the others to gather wood.

"I can get it," Ben said.

Beatrice moved to help him, but Gwen stopped her. "No, Bea. I'll help," she insisted.

As Gwen stood, a rumbling startled her.

"You'll need places to sit," Ida said, and logs rolled from the darkened forest and formed a circle.

Gwen caught her brother's gaze and smirked at his wide, disbelieving eyes. They hauled over large pieces of firewood as well as smaller sticks for kindling. As the human-bodied arranged the firewood into a pyramid, the surrounding trees shared memories of previous Solstices and singing with their daughters. When all was ready, Madeline started the bonfire with ease.

Gwen sat on a log, drum in hand, and began the beat for the song that Madeline hummed all year long, regardless of the season. She started singing and the rest of the group joined, including the trees. Madeline stood and danced around the fire, pulling on Beatrice's hand as she passed, encouraging her to join. A lightness greater than the heaviness of losing Arcas and Beulah and, years ago, her innocence, brought buoyancy to Beatrice's steps.

Forest joined while Dani grinned and sang from their seat, and Beatrice latched onto Ben with a laugh. They swirled round the fire, hand in hand. The trees added the percussion of rattling branches, and voices rose in a harmonic timber of earth and grass and river and the very heart of the forest, the very heart of the Goddess.

Gwen watched Madeline and Beatrice stop and lock eyes. For a moment, like the moment just before a raindrop turns to ice, it was just the two of them. Mother and daughter, before Forest and Stella and Gwen and Ben, before Gertrude or Eric. Gwen continued to sing, but only heard Madeline and her daughter laughing. After a few more rounds of dancing, Madeline strode toward her. She stopped singing when Madeline eased herself down onto both knees, then reached into her pocket and withdrew a small box.

Sound ceased as trees and humans held their breath. Gwen felt all eyes on the two of them as she peered down into Madeline's face.

"Gwen," Madeline said, opening the box to reveal a ring of white gold, the center of which folded into a rose, with a small amethyst resting in the center. "It's my turn to offer myself to you. Will you marry me?"

Gwen nodded, eyes burning, and felt her smile grow

into a grin as she stretched out her hand and shivered as Madeline slid the ring onto her finger. Celebration erupted as the whole family cheered.

Gwen held Madeline's face in her hands. "I love you so much."

"I love you, Gwenny." Madeline's eyes sparkled as she stood. "I'm ready for apple pie and cocoa. You?" She reached her hands out. Gwen grabbed them and let herself be pulled up.

"I'll help you," Gwen said but lingered behind to chat with her brother.

"Are you okay?" she asked, wondering if it was difficult for him to see her so happy.

Ben's face dropped. "I am in over my head, Gwen."

"I know how you feel," she whispered, as they climbed the stairs into the kitchen.

Madeline worked at warming milk, shaving in baking chocolate, and adding heaps of sugar into a pot. Wanda brought out the apple pie, and Madeline took a break from stirring to warm it in her hands. When the spiced aroma filled the air, Wanda carved equal slices and slid them onto plates. They made a plate and a mug for Stella, and Gwen took it back to her room, shaking her head as she came back into the kitchen.

"She's not even moving. And the snake won't let me get close to her." Gwen squared her body to Madeline's and ran her fingers through her hair. "Do you remember what it was like? That feeling that you've lost the only one you'll ever love."

"I do," Madeline said.

They each took a mug and a slice of pie outside; Wanda and Ben doubled back after handing pieces to Beatrice and Forest. They all resettled on the log, and each began their attack on the dessert.

"Oh, this is so good." Madeline closed her eyes. "My mother made such an unbelievable pie. And she loved it."

"There's one piece left. Give it to her," Wanda suggested.

"She loves hot chocolate, too," Beatrice added.

Setting her own food and drink down, Madeline made her way back inside and returned with a steaming piece of pie and mug of cocoa. She melted the snow and warmed the earth where her mother's roots once held firm, then urged the pie off the plate and poured the drink over it. Silence filled the circle and the trees.

"Do we have any sort of rites?" Madeline asked, turning to the trees. "Any way to honor her?"

First Mother spoke. "We've never needed them. I know some church hymns we could sing."

Madeline shook her head. "No, that won't work."

"Why not?" Wanda challenged Madeline with a shrug. "There are beautiful ones."

"I'm not sure Grandmother would relate to them." Beatrice replied. "We could tell stories. Let's wait until tomorrow and see if Stella will join us."

Madeline insisted on using her gifts to clean the kitchen. Gwen gave hugs all around and stopped by Stella's room on the way to her own.

"Stella," she whispered and moved toward the bed. The thick-bodied snake raised its triangular head, and Gwen moved no further. "I just wanted to say goodnight."

Gwen stepped back, not knowing how to help. Not knowing if it was even her place to help. She nestled into bed and closed her eyes, exhaustion waving over her. A gentle knock at the door brought her back to seated.

"Come in," she responded.

Beatrice, clad in flannel pajamas, hopped next to her. "I wanted to check in on you."

Gwen smiled. "I'm alright."

"Congratulations."

Gwen held out her hand for Beatrice to survey the ring. "It's beautiful."

Gwen held Beatrice's gaze for a long time. "Can we celebrate the Solstice together every year?"

Beatrice nodded. "Absolutely."

Madeline came into the room, smiling broadly at what she saw, and threw her own body onto the bed. "My two favorite women. Are you okay, Bea?" Madeline asked.

"I'm sad. I think we're all sad. And I'm worried about Stella. But I'm okay."

Beatrice pressed herself up, said goodnight, and left the room.

"Has Ben said anything to you?" Madeline whispered.

"Just that he's in over his head. You're an overwhelming family to come into, Madeline. He's catching feelings for her, and he watched her almost die." Gwen pulled Madeline closer and wrapped her arms around her waist. "Has she said anything?"

Madeline shook her head. "I don't know what to make of it."

"Let it be. They'll figure out what they need from one another."

Gwen held out her hand again and moved the ring around. "Beatrice likes the ring. She congratulated me."

"She really likes you, Gwen."

"And I her," Gwen said.

"I need time with her," Madeline said, scooping Gwen's hands into her own. "We can't leave until the snow melts, anyway."

"I don't know when Ben will want to leave, but I won't leave without you. You don't think Beatrice would come to New York, do you?"

"No, no. She may visit, but ..."

"I know, I know. She is home among the trees." Gwen

353

smiled, but the smile dissipated. "Did you have time with your mother before she stopped talking?"

"Only a few minutes." Madeline let her body fall onto the bed. "The fact that she's gone hasn't sunk in yet. And I'm so exhausted."

"Me too, Maddie."

Gently, the two of them found sleep.

CHAPTER 37

Madeline

The day after the solstice, Madeline encouraged Stella to come out from her room and help consecrate Beulah's final resting space. The snake reared its triangular head and exposed its fangs when she entered; Madeline responded with flames.

"I mean her no harm."

The snake coiled at the edge of the bed.

"Stella, we have to say goodbye to her. You knew her better than the rest of us."

Stella didn't move. Madeline sat down on the bed, placing a hand on Stella's shoulder. The woman wasn't asleep, but she wasn't awake either, her eyes locked in an unfocused stare.

"Stella," Madeline urged. "Stella, please come. We gave her apple pie and hot chocolate last night."

Madeline shook the woman's shoulders, and Stella ripped herself up, nostrils flaring. "I don't owe you anything." Stella rolled back over, and the snake slid by her side.

Madeline returned to the chatter around the fire.

Beatrice cleared her throat. "I guess I'll start."

She began with the story of Forest's birth and moved on to the lessons Beulah taught her. When she finished, Madeline took over, sharing stories about Willa the rabbit, and Beatrice's birth. The stories went on and on until everyone tired. Afterward, no one spoke of Stella, but they brought her plates of food and glasses of water and mugs of coffee. She consumed just enough to keep her alive. Every day, Madeline checked in on her, and every day, Stella rejected her.

For three days, the air was so dry and bitter cold, and the sun so sheepish behind the clouds, that not one flake melted. Then, on the fourth day, Christmas Day, the sun came out and made the snow glisten.

"We should get out of the house," Beatrice said at the breakfast table. "Let's go sledding!"

"Where?" Gwen asked incredulously. "Down the face of the mountain?"

Beatrice laughed. Sparks of Beatrice's playfulness revealed themselves in small moments like this, allowing Madeline to relax more into the role of mother to a grown daughter.

"There's a clearing that isn't very steep. I doubt you've seen it, Mother. We have to hike a bit."

"Glad I brought my snow boots," Ben replied with a grin.

"I'm tired of sitting, myself," Wanda chimed in.

"I have to sit this one out," Dani said.

"I'll carry you on my shoulders if you'd like." Forest flashed Dani the mischievous smirk that he'd inherited from his mother.

"Go have fun. Could I read the books while you're out?"

Madeline opened her mouth to reply, then realized the question was directed at Beatrice, who took a few steps toward them.

"Will you see if we've missed something that could help Grandmother?"

"Of course."

Madeline narrowed her eyes at Dani. She'd never seen someone move so little. She had mentioned her observation to Gwen, who'd chastised her for judging.

Forest checked on Stella before they left. When he returned to the kitchen where the others were putting on boots and scarves and coats, he just shook his head and sighed.

"Grief takes a long time," Gwen said. "We're doing the right thing. Showing her love, then giving her space."

Once bundled, everyone followed Beatrice past the buildings and up the side of the mountain. Forest and Ben each carried a sled. The group invested their energy in climbing instead of talking. When they reached the top, they took sips of water from jars they packed. Madeline evaluated the slope, just steep enough for a good ride.

"Who wants to go first?" Beatrice smiled, and Ben positioned the sled at the top of the hill.

"Come on, sis. Let's race," he said to Gwen, who smirked and situated the other sled about six feet away from her brother's.

"We're going to need a push." Gwen glanced at Madeline, who moved behind her while Beatrice positioned herself behind Ben, competition sparkling in her eyes.

"On your mark, get set, go!" Wanda shouted.

Madeline pressed firmly into Gwen's back until gravity took her, then she watched as her lover sped down the hill, giggling the entire way.

"I wish Stella were here," Beatrice said. "She'd love this."

"You and me next?" Forest asked, and Beatrice nodded.

Each person raced down the hill at least three or four times. Hunger grew within their bellies and muscles ached at both the chill and the effort of climbing up and down the hill. The crew took turns washing up and putting on clean clothes before settling down for a lunch of vegetable stew. The sun continued to warm the snow, and the snow continued to melt.

"Merry Christmas," Gwen exclaimed with a laugh at the end of the meal. Madeline knew she was laughing at the absurdity. Gwen, the lighthearted, cheerful soul that she was, hated the overspending and the greed that the season whipped up in people.

Beatrice gave a small smile, shook her head, then checked on Stella, only to come back disappointed.

***

On the evening of the seventh day, while Madeline sat stabbing at wool with a felting needle, Ben pulled Gwen aside. Instead of watching them, Madeline examined the rabbit taking form in her hands. Beatrice sat at the kitchen table, working various herbs into small glass jars and labeling them. When the twins broke their huddle, Ben asked to speak to Beatrice alone for a moment, and the two made their way into her bedroom.

"He wants to leave, doesn't he?" Madeline asked, unable to hide her disappointment.

Gwen nodded. "But I'm sure we could negotiate. Or he can go, and we can stay longer."

"Can I talk with her about it?"

"Of course. I don't want to rush you. I don't want to do anything that will hurt—"

Madeline grabbed Gwen's hand to stop her. "Gwen, what do *you* want to do?"

Gwen swallowed before answering. "I want to go home."

Beatrice came out of her bedroom and went straight back to working with her herbs. Gwen took a deep breath and let it out with a sigh. Ben came out a few minutes later with red-rimmed eyes.

Madeline stood and sat down across the table from her daughter. "Want to take a walk?"

"Not really," Beatrice responded, continuing to fill bottles aggressively until one slipped from her hand, scattering dried chamomile blossoms across the table. "Okay," she said. "Maybe we should."

They bundled up and made their way into the winter air. The sun had done its job, and only traces of snow lay here and there around the bases of trees.

"I knew you'd leave at some point."

"We'll come back, Bea."

"I know you will. You and I will write to each other. And I'll come to town twice a week to call you."

Beatrice's words spilled rapidly from her mouth until Madeline grabbed her daughter's hand and stopped walking.

"Beatrice, take a deep breath and tell me."

"I don't know what will happen with him."

"Do you love him?"

Beatrice withdrew her hand and continued walking. "I thought it was a bunch of hogwash," she said and waved her hands. "The tingling and fireworks and ... anyway. I wish I'd never met him."

"I don't believe that."

"He asked me to go with him, and I can't. This is my home. Forest and Stella need me, I can't just ..." Beatrice screwed up her face and began to cry.

"Beatrice." Madeline squared her body with her daughter's and wrapped her in a hug. "Sweetheart, don't assume it's over." She pulled away and aligned her eyes with Beatrice's. "You can write him letters, too. And come to town and call him. Maybe *you* could visit *us*."

"I wouldn't mind it. But I don't know if Stella will ...

Beatrice shook her head at the ground. "I'm frustrated with her. We all lost Grandmother."

"Oh, but Beatrice, losing your love is another thing altogether."

Beatrice's throat bobbed.

"Is he mad you aren't going?" Madeline asked, turning the conversation back to Ben.

"Disappointed. But understanding. He told me he'd wait for me. Is it fair to ask that of him?"

"Not forever, but for a bit, while the two of you sort things out. So, was it good?" Madeline asked with a broad smile, and a blush blossomed on Beatrice's face.

"We haven't done that, Mother." She huffed.

Madeline nodded, reached for Beatrice's hand, and held it the rest of the way home.

The rest of the day passed with silence as Madeline, Ben, and Gwen gathered their things. Beatrice helped Ben off the mountain so he could buy plane tickets, and the two returned in better spirits than when they'd left. That night, they gathered around a fire, sang together, and told stories until exhaustion took them.

***

Morning came too soon. Madeline jolted out of bed with a sense of urgency, leaving Gwen to doze for a few more minutes. She promised her daughter one last pan of biscuits. She stood at the counter mixing flour with buttermilk and butter, allowing the tears to mix with the dough.

How can I leave her?

Madeline cut out perfect circles with the biscuit cutter, then balled the remaining dough together, rolled it out again, and created two more.

Wanda was the next one to rise. She bundled up and went to the dairy shed to retrieve jam and juice for breakfast.

Forest entered the kitchen and gave his grandmother

a long hug. "I can't wait to visit New York," he said cheerfully, but when he pulled away, there were tears in his eyes.

Gwen came in and sat down at the table. "I wish we had booked a later flight," she said, rolling a jar of jam around in her hands.

With dark circles under red-rimmed eyes, Beatrice and Ben entered together. Beatrice sat down across from Gwen and laid a bag on the table, pulling out a variety of lotions, shampoos, and teas she'd gathered for her.

Gwen beamed. "Thank you, Beatrice."

"Write to me, and answer the phone when I call," Beatrice urged.

Gwen's eyes misted over. "I'm going to miss you."

When breakfast was over, Madeline tiptoed toward Stella's room. Sasha didn't hiss, so Madeline made her way to the edge of the bed and sat.

"Stella." She stroked the woman's hair. "We're leaving today. Will you come say goodbye?"

Stella said nothing for a long time, but when Madeline stood and turned toward the door, she whispered, "Beulah loved you so much."

Madeline closed her eyes, then looked back at Stella, who sat now on the edge of the bed. She took in the sight of her face, gaunt from under-eating, eyes sunken from lack of sleep. "I loved her, too, Stella. Do you know how sad she'd be if she knew—"

"But she doesn't know, and she'll never know."

"Come on," Madeline said, reaching her hand out. "There are three leftover biscuits."

The whole group made a fuss when Stella came into the kitchen and sat at the table. Forest poured her coffee, Wanda slathered a biscuit with butter and jam, and Beatrice fried a scrambled egg. Stella said little, and the group didn't press her. Eventually, a little color returned to her cheeks.

Then, the time came. Madeline, Gwen, and Ben strapped their backpacks to their backs, and the rest followed them outside. Forest and Wanda made the first round of hugs, followed by Stella who only offered a goodbye.

"She loved you. In case you ever question it, reread her words," Madeline told her, then watched as she turned and walked back toward the house.

When it was Beatrice's turn, she started with Gwen. Madeline's body, mind, and heart seized up with resistance.

How can I leave her?

"I'm so glad Mother found you," Beatrice said to Gwen, and the two embraced.

Beatrice turned toward her mother, tucked her chin, and glanced up with a side eye. "This isn't like before."

"I know," Madeline said, but she didn't know. For a moment, Beatrice was that fourteen-year-old girl staring up at her.

"We have so much to look forward to," Beatrice said, taking her mother's hand. "A wedding, for one thing. Don't pay for flowers," she whispered, drawing closer. "I'll do them for you."

Madeline couldn't stand it anymore. She drew her daughter into her and broke into sobs. "I don't know how to walk away from you."

Beatrice pulled away, wiped the tears from her eyes, and dabbled a handkerchief at her nose. "You're a city girl now, Mother. Face it."

Madeline chuckled, then watched as Beatrice turned her attention toward Ben. Ben pulled the backpack from his back and threw it on the ground. He wrapped his arms around her and kissed her as though it were only the two of them in the forest. Gwen whooped. Forest laughed. The trees whispered and giggled.

When Ben let go, he grabbed his bag and strode to the

front of the group. The trees spoke to Madeline as she walked through them.

Take care, dear.

Be careful in the city.

It was so good to see your face.

After every few breaths, Madeline glanced behind her to see how much distance stretched between her and Beatrice, until eventually she was no longer in view. When they got to the foot of the mountain, Madeline stared up. No more Hedge. No more wondering if her daughter was dead. Beatrice was alive and well, and more powerful than Madeline ever could have imagined.

Madeline pressed her palm against the cold, flat rock and closed her eyes. She was once again a child of the woods.

CHAPTER 38

Stella

Lips dry and head pounding, Stella opened her eyes to the bright sunlight slipping through the curtains. She thought the days would pass a little easier now that Madeline was gone and she didn't have to lay eyes on the woman who had turned her love to ash, but no. An unceasing pain gnawed at her, relentless teeth thrashing at the edges of her heart, a sharp tugging deep inside her muscles as though her blood vessels would rip themselves out of her body just to get to Beulah.

Perhaps once a day, a toxically positive thought would pass through Stella's mind. Something her therapist would say, something so bitterly saccharine like, "you can do hard things, Stella," would bring her to the brink, and she'd walk outside and scream at whatever celestial body was lighting the world at that moment. Unfailingly, Beatrice would run to her, wrap her in vines, and squeeze her tight.

At other times, Stella would stare at the ground and swear she saw movement. Small shifts here and there. A tumbling of the tiniest piece of gravel. She'd run and get

Beatrice, who'd thread vines into the ground, her face as hopeful as Stella's, only to slump with disappointment.

But mostly, Stella existed in a state of agony as physical as it was mental. None of her systems seemed to work anymore. Beatrice and Forest kept telling her to eat and drink, but Stella knew her body was suffering from more than a lack of nutrition. Beulah had taken a part of Stella, a part she could never get back. And this hollow anguish whispered new thoughts in Stella's ear, thoughts that she'd never considered, even in her darkest hour. Maybe if she ended it, she would find Beulah on the other side. The other side of what, Stella didn't know, nor fucking care.

Forest always found her when those feelings threatened to drown her. Like now. A light rap on the door, and there he was, sitting on the edge of her bed.

"Hey," he said.

Stella rolled toward him and cleared her throat.

"I brought you something to eat."

Forest offered a plate that held a pancake with a bacon smiley face, a pat of butter, and a drizzle of syrup. Sasha pressed her body through the covers, slithered onto Forest's knee, around his back, and finally perched on his shoulder, where she began to rattle. The snake had taken to tough love, threatening Stella with tail and teeth until she'd eaten.

Forest used one arm to help Stella up, then handed her the plate. "Want to stay in here, or eat with us in the kitchen?"

"Here."

At her response, Sasha began her tantrum again.

"Shhh-shhh-shhh. It's okay, Sasha." Forest was the only one other than Stella who could calm Sasha with his voice. "Stella, I know you're hurting. We all are."

Stella's eyes moved to the ground. She gritted her teeth and shook her head.

"Hey, look at me."

Though it took almost all her energy, Stella lifted her head.

"Mother and I know that what you're experiencing is ... unique. We see it. We see you. Grief is destroying you in every single way."

Forest's eyes conveyed something Stella needed to see, something more than empathy or compassion. Forest *believed* her when she said her body wasn't hers anymore.

"And I'm sorry. We're both so sorry. And if I'm honest, Stella, we don't know how to help you. Neither do the trees. But maybe ..." Forest took Stella's hand and gave it a gentle squeeze. " ...if you turn toward us instead of away from us, we can figure it out together."

Stella couldn't bring herself to say thank you, but she gave one nod and pressed to stand.

Beatrice was sitting at the table, elbows propped atop it, her face held in her fingertips. She turned at the sound of Stella entering and attempted a weak smile.

"Hi," Beatrice whispered as she patted the table, urging Stella to sit.

Stella sat and took in the sight of her friend. Her eyes were red and watery, her skin pale, and dark circles rimmed puffy eyelids. Beatrice swallowed hard and locked eyes with Stella before she spoke.

"I want you to stay, Stella." Tears spilled down Beatrice's face. "But if it's too hard to be here, if it's too much ..."

Beatrice didn't finish.

The mere thought of returning to New York sent a stabbing pain into Stella's chest. She couldn't breathe. Her eyes widened and her head shook back and forth, back and forth in a pleading no.

"Stella!" Beatrice's vines poured from her hands and wrapped around her, tighter and tighter, until she found her breath again.

"I can't leave this mountain, Beatrice. Please don't ask me to."

"You didn't hear me right. I want you ..." Beatrice glanced up at Forest " ...we want you to stay. But you know yourself better than anyone else. Will you be alright here?"

Stella closed her eyes and searched for something, anything, that could bring a smile to her lips so that Beatrice wouldn't worry and wouldn't ask her to leave. Those blue eyes. Those two warm hands framing her face. Those words, so soft and sweet.

I love you, Stella.

Stella's face muscles pulled on the corners of her mouth and turned her lips as much as she could stand.

"I'll be alright, Beatrice," she assured her friend.

Then she focused on her plate and forced the first bite of pancake into her mouth.

Chapter 39

Beatrice

Beatrice existed to soothe Stella and Forest through their grief. Eating continued to be a struggle for Stella, and Forest grew more and more disinterested in activities he'd once loved. Wanda and Dani left the day after Christmas, and Beatrice felt more alone than ever. A few nights, she spent a little longer in the bath, curled into a tight ball, arms around her shins, forehead to her knees, and wept for the losses. Then she'd tuck herself in bed and miss the man she'd once slept next to.

Beatrice had given more of her body to Ben the night before he left. He'd kissed her skin, every inch of it, each toe, fingertip, the nape of her neck, in between her thighs. She had lost control under his touch three times that night, but she couldn't bring her guard down enough to allow him entry to her most sacred space. By the end of their intimacy, Beatrice had also given the man a piece of her heart, but not the words that went with it.

Now, she walked toward Great-grandmother Ola with

a steaming cup of tea in her hand. Kneeling, she placed one hand against the bark.

"Great-grandmother, thank you for helping us."

Beatrice tipped the spicy liquid onto the tree's roots and looked up again to see deep brown eyes staring into hers. What she saw there shocked her. Instead of the cranky woman who had hung her mother upside down, she found a compassionate face within the bark.

"I don't know how to do this without my grandmother," Beatrice said to her.

The tree sighed. "My dear, there is so much you don't know about Beulah."

A heat that arose from loyalty flushed Beatrice's chest; she stood and took a step back.

"Well, she certainly told me a lot about you."

"I'm sure she did. I'm sure some of it's true. But you knew a different Beulah than the one I knew."

Great-grandmother's use of past tense stung the space behind Beatrice's eyes.

"Before you go storming off, I just want you to think about this: how did she know she would fall? Maybe ..." Great-grandmother's voice remained calm as she spoke. "...maybe she needed that fire for what she was trying to do."

Beatrice's eyes widened, and her eyes searched the forest floor as she tried to make sense of what the tree was suggesting. "You think it was part of the spell?"

"I don't know, but I know this ..." Ola's voice firmed and deepened. "Beulah is by far the most powerful of us all. I can't tell you any more than that."

"Why the hell not?" Beatrice balled her hands into fists.

"Because I love my child so, so much. And if she comes back, I don't want you to fear her." Roots loosened themselves from the ground and traveled up to embrace Beatrice's shoulders. "Beatrice, you have all of us."

One set at a time, the eyes of each grandmother-tree popped open, and more roots extended until Beatrice felt the energy of each woman coursing around her.

"You're good at taking care of Stella and your son, but you have to take care of yourself as well."

Beatrice's throat thickened. "I don't know how to do that."

"Let us help you, dear," Ida chimed in.

"Have courage. Get through this day. Tomorrow could be one of the good ones," Great-grandmother said.

Tomorrow, Beatrice would take a trip to town, call the man she promised herself she wouldn't love, the mother she missed more than she'd expected, and her new best friend. Perhaps she'd run Ola's theory past her mother. But today, she allowed her grandmothers to cradle her within a woven fabric of love, allowed them to rock her and sing to her, and, just for today, Beatrice allowed herself to rest.

ACKNOWLEDGMENTS

Producing a novel is a more complicated process than I ever imagined, and I could not have done it all on my own.

Thank you to my wife for your patience, support, delicious meals, affection, and being one of my first readers.

My children for providing fun and beautiful distractions.

Friends and colleagues for your knowledge and cheerleading. Your brilliance still intimidates me.

Lucy, Truffle, and Tamari for your sweet snuggles.

My publishing team including beta readers, my editors Megan Harris and Hilary Doda, and my cover designer My Lan Khuc.

And to all the amazing content creators across social media platforms for sharing your knowledge and expertise..

ABOUT THE AUTHOR

Sorrel D. Richmond is a West Virginia transplant now living in a small town in central North Carolina with their wife, two kids, two sneaky cats, and willful beagle. Sorrel teaches English and Creative Writing on the high school level and is an avid backyard gardener with a love of okra and a hatred for squash bugs. Their characters often have a passion for nature and a love of love itself.

CHAPTER 1

Beulah

The urgent resurrection that bore Beulah up into a tall birch tree had been too quick to be painful the first time. Now, the cold dirt pressed against her from all directions. Downward against her skull. Upward against her feet. Down her throat. Unable to breathe, she questioned if she was alive or in a frigid hell. Signs of life gave Beulah evidence that the world she left still thrummed around her, and somehow, she was still part of it. Some days, Beulah could focus enough attention on the sense of hearing that the voices of her family singing rang through, and when she brought all her attention to her skin, she could feel earthworms slither across her hands. Gentle drips of rain slipping down. The taste of beets in her mouth. She warred with the desire to thrash against the pressure encasing her, but over time, she understood that stillness, patience, and time were necessary if she wanted to reach the surface.

Milton Keynes UK
Ingram Content Group UK Ltd.
UKHW042109151024
449742UK00012B/133/J

9 798990 983403